THEATER: THEORY/TEXT/PERFORMANCE
Series Editors: David Krasner and Rebecca Schneider
Founding Editor: Enoch Brater

Recent Titles:

No Safe Spaces

Re-casting
Race, Ethnicity,
and Nationality
in American Theater

ANGELA C. PAO

The University of Michigan Press • *Ann Arbor*

2013   2012   2011   2010   4   3   2   1

Library of Congress Cataloging-in-Publication Data

Pao, Angela Chia-yi.
   No safe spaces : re-casting race, ethnicity, and nationality in
American theater / Angela C. Pao.
      p.   cm. — (Theater: theory/text/performanc)
   Includes bibliographical references and index.
   ISBN 978-0-472-07121-0 (cloth : alk. paper) — ISBN 978-0-472-
05121-2 (pbk. : alk. paper)   1. Theater—Casting—United States.
2. Race in the theater.   3. Ethnicity in the theater.   4. Theater and
society—United States.   I. Title.
PN2293.C38P36   2010
792.02'8089—dc22   2010022083

Some of the material in this book appeared in previous publications:
parts of Chapter 2 appeared as "Recasting Race: Casting Practices and
Racial Theories," *Theatre Survey* 41, no. 2 (November 2000), 1–22; parts
of Chapter 3 appeared in "Ocular Revisions: Re-casting *Othello* in Text
and Performance," in *Colorblind Shakespeare: New Perspectives on Race and
Performance,* ed. Ayanna Thompson (Routledge, September 2006),
27–45; and parts of Chapter 4 appeared in "Changing Face: Recasting
National Identity in All-Asian American Dramas," *Theatre Journal* 53, no. 3
(October 2001), 389–409. Grateful acknowledgment is given for permission to use this previously published material.

ISBN13: 978-0-472-02797-2 (electronic)

Illustration: East West Players' production of Equus (2005),
featuring Trieu D. Tran and Wesley John. Photo by Michael Lamont.

For Pete
THEN, NOW AND ALWAYS

Acknowledgments

There should have been, if not a tenth Muse, at least a minor deity for the art of expressing appreciation to individuals and organizations that provide the information, materials, support, and inspiration that make a research project possible. Without the aid of such a being, I can only offer inadequately expressed but sincerely felt gratitude to the following people and groups (organized, like the rest of this book, according to genre):

Theater companies, archives, and organizations (listed in order of first visitation): The librarians and experienced copy staff of the Performing Arts Collection of the New York Public Library. The Non-Traditional Casting Project / Alliance for Inclusion in the Arts, particularly director Sharon Jensen for giving me a clearer picture of the organization's history and mission. Kirstin Franko of the Arena Stage and the curators of the company's archives at George Mason University. The National Asian American Theatre Company and its founding director Mia Katigbak, the company's heart and soul, who has been generous with her time and company resources. At the Oregon Shakespeare Festival, Timothy Bond and Libby Appel for taking the time to discuss the work of the OSF as well as their views on nontraditional casting. Very special thanks to the OSF's Kit Leary, exemplary archivist and knowledgeable oral historian. Moving down the west coast, the San Francisco Public Library for keeping track of Bay Area theater companies. At the Cornerstone Theater Company, Lynn Jeffries, Bill Rauch, and Shishir Kurup shared artistic perspectives; Lee Lawlor was a very helpful host and guide through the company's archives. Beth Downing made my visit to the La Jolla Playhouse an enjoyable and profitable one. For their help in getting the all-important and sometimes hard-to-unearth illustrations: Lauren Beyea and Amy Scott-Douglas (Shakespeare Theatre Company of Washington, DC), Amy Richard (Oregon Shakespeare Festival), Romy Eletreby (Cornerstone Theater Company), Jeremy Megraw (New York Public Library for the Performing Arts).

Institutional funding and support: a fellowship from the National Endowment for the Humanities funded a year of research, during which I was able to travel around the country to visit various library collections and theater companies. Additional support was provided by an Indiana University supplemental grant, and an IU emergency grant-in-aid subsidized the cost of obtaining photographic reproductions and rights.

The University of Michigan Press: LeAnn Fields, whose early and sustained interest in the project and whose sound advice at the various stages of development have put these words in print. Scott Ham, for his expert attention to all the essential details. The Readers, whose positive comments offered encouragement and whose constructive critiques greatly improved the final product

At home: Guinevere—for her willing service over the past five years, even as her battery faded and power supply became increasingly erratic, until this project could be completed. Pete for all his technical, emotional, and practical support (valued not necessarily in that order). Gloria and Ginny for sharing the best of times and the worst of times. My family and friends who have been theatergoing companions over the decades and provided hospitality during research expeditions.

Contents

Introduction

Non-Traditional Casting is the casting of ethnic, female or disabled actors in roles where race, ethnicity, gender or physical capability are not necessary to the characters' or play's development.

—BEYOND TRADITION: FIRST NATIONAL SYMPOSIUM
ON NON-TRADITIONAL CASTING

I hate that term non-traditional casting. I believe that the kind of casting we are talking about is traditional casting. Casting that comes out of the great traditions of this country. I would propose a change of terms. I would prefer to isolate what 90 percent of our theatres are doing as non-traditional casting since it does not represent what America is—the American people.

—ANNA DEAVERE SMITH

Over the past several years, there has been a sustained and productive convergence of concepts and concerns in the fields of theater and performance studies, American ethnic studies, and national and transnational studies. Scholars working in these areas have conducted complex investigations into the nature and forms of racial, ethnic, and national identity and difference, moving away from traditional conceptual and geographical boundaries. At the same time, theater practitioners, particularly artists from internal racial or ethnic minority groups, have explored and deconstructed conventional notions of identity through new approaches to playwriting, intercultural performance, and performance art. Performance artists, in particular, have taken advantage of the properties of embodiment to revise concepts of human identity.[1]

One strategy for reforming visions of identity, however, often has been highly controversial in practice but remains relatively lightly explored from a theoretical perspective. This strategy (or more accurately, these strategies) is the rich array of casting practices—designated as multiracial, multiethnic, multicultural, color-blind, diverse, innovative, experimental, or nontraditional—that have burgeoned in the United States since the 1960s.[2] Unlike forms of performance that rely on the creation of new cultural institutions and original works to engage with long-standing notions of and attitudes toward race and ethnicity, these (re)visionary casting practices, developed more or less systematically during the second half of the twentieth century, issue their challenge to Eurocentric conceptions of American society and culture from inside the very institutions dedicated to preserving a European-American dramatic heritage. This interior positioning is the source of both the potency of casting against tradition and the acrimonious controversies that have often surrounded these practices.

The most enthusiastic supporters of what has commonly been called *nontraditional casting* see these practices as a form both of social action and of artistic exploration. Such advocates are committed to a larger social mission of inclusion and stimulated by the interpretive possibilities opened up when the bodies, minds, and experiences of a new set of actors are brought together with roles that have been performed hundreds or thousands of times since they were originally written. Such innovations in casting solicit original acts of imagination not only on the part of the directors and actors engaged in creating the productions but of the audience members who see them as well. Those ardently opposed to revising established practices are dismayed, even outraged, by the disregard for theatrical tradition and historical "authenticity." In general, opponents regard nontraditional casting as attempts "to graft a social agenda onto the face of artistic enterprise."[3] Resistant spectators are unsettled rather than stimulated by the violations of expectations that innovative casting entails. They are distracted by racially mixed casts, finding the results implausible if not outright offensive. Others just don't see the point.

Given the fact that these new forms of casting were designed to dislodge established modes of perceiving and patterns of thinking, it is not surprising that their initiation has been accompanied by disagreement, both acrimonious and productive. Since the 1960s, these differences have been played out on a daily basis in theaters around the country as productions are planned, directors chosen, casting decisions made, and performances staged, seen, and reviewed. On several occasions, landmark cases or decisions created highly publicized controversies that brought national attention to casting issues. These include Samuel Beckett's opposition to Joanne Akalaitis's 1984 staging of *Endgame* for the American Repertory Theater, the 1990 *Miss Saigon* controversy over the casting of a Caucasian actor in a Eurasian role, an attempt made in 1992 by Samuel French publishers to prohibit gender-switching in plays they represented by attaching a rider to their standard licensing agreement, and finally the exchanges between August Wilson and Robert Brustein that took place over several months in 1996. In these instances, which will be discussed in more detail in this introduction and in subsequent chapters, the rights of playwrights and their estates have been opposed to those of directors, the principle of artistic freedom weighed against larger moral and social considerations, and the value of culturally specific theaters measured against the benefits of greater diversity in regional and commercial theaters.

History and Terminology

Many of these issues crystallized during discussions over the very terminology used to describe the casting practices and their evolution over the past forty to fifty years. The efforts to change the complexion of American theater institutions and make a lasting impact on the way plays were cast emerged as a concerted endeavor in the 1950s and 1960s. The primary impetus for changing not just casting but hiring practices in regional and commercial theaters was the desire to achieve racial integration in all social, political, educational, and cultural institutions in the United States. The New York Shakespeare Festival under the leadership of Joseph Papp, Washington, DC's Arena Stage, headed by Zelda Fichandler, and the Los Angeles Inner City Cultural Center were among the first theater companies to make integrated casting central to their artistic policies. While different race-conscious and race-neutral methods were tried, the most common and readily accepted approach was one that did not call attention to the race of the actors. By the 1970s, the term *color-blind* was being applied to this approach, but in popular usage it was also often being used rather indiscriminately to include various color-conscious strategies that were being devised.

The expression *nontraditional casting* gained currency in the 1980s, largely because of the work of the Non-Traditional Casting Project

(NTCP), an advocacy group formed in 1986 under the leadership of Harry Newman and Clinton Turner Davis to promote the inclusion of racial and ethnic minorities, women, and the disabled in all areas of theatrical activity—performing, directing, designing, managing, producing. The NTCP worked to accomplish its objectives through national and regional conferences, forums, seminars, and roundtables on casting and diversity; publications such as a national newsletter, *New Traditions,* and a resource guide for employers of actors with disabilities; and a national talent bank of Artist Files, which contains the résumés and pictures of actors, directors, writers, designers, choreographers, and stage managers of color or with disabilities. The organization recently changed its name to the Alliance for Inclusion in the Arts.[4] As the original name suggests, however, the initial incentive for the founding of the NTCP and its most prominent achievements have been in the domain of casting practices. In addition to the umbrella term for the new philosophy of casting quoted at the beginning of this introduction, four subcategories were put forward to make finer distinctions among the strategies being employed:

COLOR-BLIND CASTING. Actors are cast without regard to their race or ethnicity; the best actor is cast in the role.

SOCIETAL CASTING. Ethnic, female, or disabled actors are cast in roles they perform in society as a whole.

CONCEPTUAL CASTING. An ethnic, female, or disabled actor is cast in a role to give the play greater resonance.

CROSS-CULTURAL CASTING. The entire world of a play is translated to a different cultural setting.

Harry Newman, the first executive director of the NTCP, stipulated that "the concepts and definitions of non-traditional casting . . . are in no way meant to become new formulas to replace existing ones. These definitions and ideas are presented solely to stimulate creative decision-makers to begin thinking in the broadest terms."[5] In actual practice, the approaches frequently overlap and new variations are constantly being developed.

During the 1980s and 1990s, the term *nontraditional casting* was widely adopted among theater professionals and the mass media. At the same time, as Anna Deavere Smith's words in the epigraph indicate, dissatisfaction with this designation surfaced along with questions as to whether it is always clear when race, ethnicity, or gender is central to the development of a particular character or play. The qualification *nontraditional,* however, does have certain advantages. It is inclusive in terms of both the people affected and the approaches developed. Perhaps even more importantly, it foregrounds the fact that what American audiences were accustomed to seeing on the stage before the era of multiracial casting was not a truthful correspondence to reality, as one might think from hearing many of the objections, but the application of historical conventions. In the Anglo-American theater tradition, biologically appropriate casting dates back only to the Restoration in the case of gender, and it is a twentieth-century phenomenon in the case of race. In professional theaters in the United States, up through the early decades of the twentieth century, it was still possible to have black characters played by white actors in blackface without disrupting audience reception. Caucasian actors commonly played Asian and Asian American characters through the 1970s until a landmark decision by the New York State Human Rights Division in 1973 (see chapter 5) and the 1990 battle over *Miss Saigon* made that practice untenable in professional theaters. Until very recently, non-Hispanic actors were regularly being cast in major Latin American and Latino roles in theater and film. Cases that provoked protests by Latino actors include the Broadway production of *Death and the Maiden* (1992), in which the characters Paulina Salas, Gerardo Escobar, and Roberto Miranda were played by Glenn Close, Richard Dreyfuss, and Gene Hackman respectively. Luis Valdez's plans for a film biography of Frida Kahlo in the early 1990s also had to be abandoned after Latino actors vigorously protested the announced casting of an Italian-American actor as the iconic Mexican artist.[6] The 2009 bilingual Broadway production of *West Side Story* represents a breakthrough with the casting of Latino and Latin American actors as the Puerto Rican characters, who speak and sing in Spanish or a mixture of English and Spanish when they are interacting with each other.

Perhaps the most desirable attribute of the qualification *nontraditional* is its foreshadowing of its own obsolescence. As racially diverse casting becomes the established practice in theaters across the country, a new tradition is being forged. Even now, following the turn of the century, use of the expression has declined noticeably. Theater companies who have adopted racially diverse casting as a regular practice now are most likely to describe their practices as *multicultural* casting. Paralleling the ascendancy of the term in general usage, this move may be interpreted to serve both progressive and conservative inclinations. From a progressive point of view, multicultural casting is one manifestation of the greater "multiculturalist project," which "calls for decisive changes, changes in the way we write history, the way we teach literature, the way we make art, the way we program films, the way we organize conferences, and the way we distribute cultural resources."[7] The premises and goals of multicultural casting are the same as those of a national diversity project. In Stam's words the task is "at once one of deconstructing Eurocentric and racist norms and of constructing and promoting multicultural alternatives."[8] In a specifically theatrical context, this means not just superficially using the visible racial characteristics of actors, often in ways that inadvertently promote stereotypes or essentializing models of difference, but having artists of different racial, ethnic, and cultural backgrounds actively and assertively contribute to the creative process.

At the same time, speaking of different "cultures" rather than different "races," and emphasizing culture rather than color can be seen as a concession to the sensibilities of residential theaters' traditional subscription audiences, who have been and remain predominantly, in some communities even exclusively, white and middle class. The rhetoric of "multiculturalism" has proven to be highly compatible with traditional American narratives of cultural pluralism, which include groups of European origin, and consequently has been employed to reassure potentially resistant audience members that diverse casting is "not political."

Art, Politics, and Employment

In actuality, it is difficult, even impossible, to separate the history of casting practices and the discourses surrounding them from contemporaneous political and social developments. Initially, with the moral and political convictions of theater professionals providing the driving energy for artistic activity as a form of social engagement, casting policies formed part of a national discourse on social justice. A generation later, the pervasive structural transformations brought about by the civil rights movement and the attendant salutary changes in the manner and extent to which racial and ethnic minorities were represented in visual, dramatic, and narrative mediums (textbooks, television, movies, print media, etc.) created conditions that brought an influx of young black, Latino, and Asian actors into the acting profession. Increasingly, arguments for casting actors of color in "white roles" (a tellingly ambiguous term in itself) were advanced in the name of equal employment opportunities, understandably the primary concern of most of the actors involved. In response to this growing constituency, the Actors' Equity Association began to play a more prominent role in bringing collective pressure to bear on institutions and decision makers who continued to have artistically or economically motivated reservations regarding nontraditional casting. As Morris Kaplan, lawyer and labor negotiator for the League of Resident Theatres, stated, "We cannot defer to a social objective, however desirable, at the expense of the art."[9] Currently, Equity contracts negotiated with major regional, Broadway, Off-Broadway, and other commercial and not-for-profit theaters and producers include both a nondiscrimination clause and an advisory clause that specifically encourages racial diversity in casting.

Such initiatives were readily accepted, but in 1990, the governing board of Equity ventured beyond the safe territory of attaching recommendations to documents that regulated salaries, benefits, and working conditions. The board took a proactive role in blocking the casting of a Caucasian actor in a starring Eurasian role in the Broadway production of *Miss Saigon*. The organization quickly found itself embroiled in a transcontinental and transatlantic controversy over the boundaries between legitimately protecting the professional interests of the union's ethnic minority members and upholding moral principles on the one hand and interfering with artistic decisions on the other. Highly publicized and often highly emotional positions were taken by theater practitioners, critics, public figures not professionally involved in the arts, and ordinary theatergoers. In the end, Equity's actions did not affect the original Broadway casting of the musical, but the case demonstrated the impact that centrally organized and authoritative bodies could make. (See chapter 2 for further discussion of the *Miss Saigon* casting controversy.)

At the same time that union activities responded to the frustrations of talented actors of color who faced limited opportunities, the importance of placing these interests in a broader perspective was recognized. As Zelda Fichandler has stated, "Nontraditional casting in the end becomes a matter not of employment, but of politics and of art."[10] There was a clear need for an organization equally devoted to promoting awareness of the interpretive possibilities of casting against tradition; facilitating contacts between ethnic minority actors and those responsible for casting productions in theater, film, and television; and securing the support of the most influential and authoritative bodies of theater professionals and institutions. The language of the Non-Traditional Casting Project's mission statement reflects the general contemporary trend to portray American race relations in terms that are at once more inclusive and more benign than the discourses of the 1960s:[11]

> NTCP works to increase the participation in theater, film and television of artists of color—African American, Asian American, Latino, and Native American; female artists; Deaf and hard-of-hearing artists; and artists with disabilities—ambulatory disabled, blind and low vision. Our principal concerns are that ethnic, female and disabled artists are denied equitable professional opportunities; that this lack of participation is not only patently discriminatory, but a serious loss to the cultural life of the nation and has resulted in a theater that does not reflect the diversity of our society.[12]

The founding of the NTCP was prompted by the state of affairs revealed by a Theatre Communications Group survey of American professional theaters in the mid-1980s. The study revealed that more than twenty years after integrated casting had been established as a practice in key urban theaters, approximately 90 percent of theater productions were continuing to feature all-white casts, only 10 percent of roles on Broadway were cast with black actors, and nonwhites were being hired in regional theaters for 9 percent of available roles.[13] In the leading American Shakespeare festivals, the ratio of racial majority to minority actors was nine to one.[14] Apparently, artistic directors and producers who were personally committed to artistically innovative and culturally inclusive casting were already actively engaged in the process. In an effort to encourage more institutions to follow suit, in November 1986, the NTCP organized the First National Symposium on Non-Traditional Casting at the Broadway Shubert Theatre, bringing together almost one thousand producers, artistic directors, directors, playwrights, actors, casting directors, agents, critics, and educators. A smaller Second National Symposium, held in January 1990 at New York University, was organized to focus on nonprofit professional theaters, which were seen as being in a stronger position to implement culturally diverse hiring policies because of their institutional base. In addition to these national conferences, the NTCP cosponsored or served as advisors for regional conferences held in Los Angeles, San Francisco, Washington, DC, Boston, Philadelphia, Rochester, Toronto, Hartford, and Dallas, and also helped organize over ninety local forums on the topic for theater organizations, community groups, colleges and universities, and student organizations. At the national symposiums and regional conferences, influential figures from the national, regional, or local theater worlds participated in panels with titles such as "Non-traditional Casting: What Tradition?" "Realizing the Play, or Playing with Reality?" "Re-viewing the Audience," and "The Next Tradition." The program included the staging of scenes from the classical tragedies and comedies and the modern and contemporary dramatic repertoire with ethnic, female, and disabled actors in principal roles.

During the 1990s, the NTCP worked with organizations such as Actors' Equity, the Casting Society of America, the League of American Theatres and Producers, the Dramatists Guild, the Society of Stage Directors and Choreographers (SSDC), the League of Resident Theatres (LORT), the American Federation of Television and Radio Artists, and the Screen Actors Guild to promote culturally inclusive practices. In 1996, representatives of the governing bodies of the first four of these organizations ratified a joint "Document of Principle" in support of greater diversity in the theater. The statement endorsed "the goals of diversity, inclusion, and the principles of equal opportunity for all who work in the theater industry" and condemned "racism, prejudice, discrimination and exclusion in the theater."[15] These goals were to be attained through a two-pronged approach: providing employment and production opportunities and challenging stereotypical representations.[16] The text of the document was disseminated to members of the League and to the unions and guilds through their membership publications.

Many people in the theater world celebrated these developments and the noticeable increase in racially diverse productions and staffs they helped bring about. But at almost the same time that the Document of Principle advocating diversity in American theaters was being drafted and ratified, a high-profile attack on the participation of racial minorities in "mainstream" theaters was being launched from a new direction. In his keynote address at the June 1996 National Conference of the Theatre Communications Group, August Wilson denounced racially mixed theaters in general and color-blind casting in particular as renewed expressions of white dominance through assimilationist cultural policies. He called instead for support for black theaters and playwrights, and in the process criticized Robert Brustein for his disparaging comments about the artistic merit of culturally specific theaters. Brustein replied by denouncing institutional separatism along racial lines as a throwback to the pre–civil rights era and by decrying the politicization of arts funding. The debate was carried out on the pages of *American Theatre* magazine through the fall of that year and concluded in January 1997 with a face-to-face confrontation on the stage of New York City's Town Hall. By then, the battle had been joined by theater practitioners, critics, and scholars, whose views appeared in articles, editorials, and letters in major newspapers and trade publications including the *New York Times, Village Voice, Variety,* and *Back Stage.* (See chapter 2 for an analysis of the debates and their aftermath.) The words exchanged orally and in print demonstrated yet again theater's deep engagement with the racial formations of the country.

Race, Ethnicity, or Culture?

Whatever the context in which casting practices of the latter half of the twentieth century and the opening decade of the twenty-first century are being discussed, the ways in which the key terms *race, ethnicity,* and *culture* (whether with or without the ubiquitous prefix *multi-*) have been used are, as one might expect, highly inconsistent, varying from one situation to another and from one speaker or writer to another. These variations underscore the need to treat these terms not as abstract categories but as material signifiers that acquire meaning through specific instances of usage, which are far from consistent. The meanings may shift even in the course of a single sentence, as the NTCP's very definition of nontraditional casting demonstrates: "the casting of ethnic, female or disabled actors in roles where race, ethnicity, gender or physical capability are not necessary to the characters' or play's development."[17] The first adjectival "ethnic" serving to qualify the type of actor would seem to subsume race. (This would be contrary to popular American usage, which sees ethnicity as a subcategory of race.) The brief enumeration of pertinent aspects of the role, however, separates race and ethnicity as distinct characteristics. In an open letter to the members of the American theater community, Clinton Turner Davis addressed the failure of theater companies to invite and employ "black and ethnic" artists, asking:

> Why is it certain theater companies can only identify one or two ethnic directors and designers to work in their theaters? . . . Why does the hiring of one ethnic director often preclude the hiring of others? Why is s/he hired to direct or design only the ethnically specific

work? Is it a question of willful ignorance of the talent pool, or of find-ing one's level of comfort with an ethnic artist? Is it a belief that eth-nic artists are not capable of creating beyond their own ethnicity? Is the black artist, the ethnic artist, still perceived monolithically—un-der the assumption that the one who is hired can speak of and for the entire race? Or are we being blacklisted because we continue to ask difficult, uncomfortable questions, to name names.[18]

The flexibility of the terminology in these examples is typical of the lan-guage used to talk about casting practices and the inclusion of artists, ad-ministrators, and audiences who cannot be identified as "white." At times *race* and *ethnicity* are used interchangeably; at times *race* designates a black-white distinction with *ethnicity* reserved for Asians and Latinos, sometimes ethnicity is seen as a subcategory of race, and sometimes the opposite is suggested.

This slippage is not just a matter of linguistic carelessness. It derives from the complex and varied histories of colonization and immigration that shaped the nation. As far as the fundamental distinction between race and ethnicity goes, theatrical practice has on the whole been con-sistent with current general usage in English-speaking societies, where "a physical feature is taken to indicate that an individual is to be assigned to a racial category while a cultural feature is taken as a sign that the indi-vidual is a member of an ethnic group."[19] But in the United States, the term *ethnicity* has been used in a particular way that reflects the compos-ite nature of American cultural identity. Popular and official usage alike have supported the transformation of the former nationality of first-gen-eration Americans into their "ethnicity"; for the second generation and after, ethnic identity is defined by the national origins of the ancestors who emigrated to the United States. This model is readily applicable when the point of origin is in Europe, Asia, Latin America, or the Middle East. Large-scale immigration from these regions took place after na-tional borders had been drawn and under circumstances that permitted ongoing contact with the country of origin. In the case of African Amer-icans, however, the forced mass migration of West Africans took place long before the continent was divided into postcolonial national entities and under conditions that severed ties with homelands—ties that would have allowed a sense of specific ethnic origin to be retained through sub-sequent generations. Race therefore superseded ethnic or tribal origin for black Americans. As tribal and ethnic distinctions became increasingly blurred, "cultural features" became attached to the racial group as a whole. In the past couple of decades, however, renewed voluntary emigration from Africa and the Caribbean has begun to modify this situation as patterns of cultural identification among newer African Americans come to more closely resemble those of other twentieth- and twenty-first-century immigrants.

While race and ethnicity are consequently equally active cultural categories both in contemporary American society and in the language of nontraditional casting, this is not true where actual *practices* of nontraditional casting are concerned. Experience has demonstrated that the functional category is very much race rather than ethnicity or nationality, although the constructed nature of racial and ethnic classifications quickly becomes evident.[20] Harry Newman has described how the guiding principles of the Non-Traditional Casting Project were put into practice with the original arrangement of the organization's Artist Files. Initially, the actors' résumés and photographs were placed in two parallel files. One was organized according to four categories commonly used to classify U.S. "ethnic minorities": African American, Asian / Pacific Islander, Latino, and Native American. The second was organized by character type (e.g., leading man or woman, older character actor, etc.) with actors of all races and ethnic origins mixed together. This file remained unused and was eventually discontinued.[21] This state of affairs has been corroborated by the testimony of many actors who found themselves rejected for parts for *looking* too Asian or black or Hispanic, for instance, or not Asian, black, or Hispanic enough.[22] Rarely, if ever, has an actor been rejected for looking or not looking (much less being or not being) Chinese, Japanese, or Korean, or Mexican, Chilean, or Puerto Rican. It becomes clear that in the vast majority of cases, what is involved and being reinforced are visually identifiable characteristics associated with broad racial categories rather than more specific ethnic identities. The erasure of cultural, ethnic, or national specificity has taken on new inflections with the growing presence of Middle Eastern Americans and South Asian Americans in the theater, film, and television industries, and a rising number of Middle Eastern characters appearing in movies and on television. In response to these developments, the Alliance for Inclusion in the Arts updated its Artists Files categories to include both Arab Americans and Persian Americans. In practice, however, any actor with an ancestor originating from anywhere along the geographical band extending from North Africa to South Asia would be considered an "authentic" casting choice for an Egyptian, Saudi Arabian, or Iraqi character.

If questions of ethnicity do come into play, it is most likely to be in culturally specific theaters.[23] At the NTCP's First National Symposium, an audience member who identified himself as an unemployed Puerto Rican actor observed:

> We have a lot of so-called ethnic companies that do not hire too dark Hispanic [actors] or too light Hispanics or too dark blacks or too light blacks within our own realm. I find it hypocritical, because I hear all the time from my Japanese actor friends and my Chinese friends that they couldn't get the part because they were not Japanese, in an "Asian play," or because they were Japanese and the part called for a Chinese, even though there was not a Chinese actor to fill the part.[24]

The degree to which culturally specific companies will take ethnic, or in the case of Native Americans, tribal origin, into consideration varies considerably. As their mission statements reveal and the cast lists of productions confirm, Asian American companies that perform dramatic works are predominantly pan-ethnic both by necessity and by choice.[25] In order to form a company or cast of the most talented and experienced performers, artistic and production directors prefer to sacrifice ethnic distinctions. Latino or Hispanic companies—most notably those formed by Puerto Ricans, Cubans, or Chicanos—on the other hand, have historically been far more conscious of national origins.[26] It is relatively recently that, in order to achieve critical mass and influence "mainstream" casting practices, Latino actors and other theater artists have increasingly acted as a united group. The pan-ethnic nature of a company or a cast for a particular production reflects the larger social and political situation in the United States that has predominated up until the present: national origin and ethnic descent are eventually used in conjunction with, if not replaced by, identification according to racial categories.

The practices of both major regional and culturally specific companies further reveal the simultaneous resilience and arbitrariness of ethnic and racial categories. When a company requires a particular racial background, very often the criterion reverts to a genetic definition. One of the most vivid examples of this was offered by the National Asian American Theatre Company's all–Asian American production of *Othello*. In appearance, the actor playing Othello was white, while all the other actors were visibly of East Asian descent; the production thereby preserved the critical factor of Othello's difference in relation to the other characters. The actor's website at the time described him as being of "British, Filipino, Spanish, Russian and Turkish descent."[27] The Filipino fraction, although neither a noticeable factor in his physical appearance or a formative element in his lived cultural experience, enabled the National Asian American Theatre Company to remain faithful to its founding mission to promote and support Asian American actors, directors, designers, and technicians.

When I and those I quote use the terms *Chinese, Japanese, Mexican, Spanish,* and so on, the issue has never been an individual's nationality—that is, his or her citizenship. The process of immigration to the United States, supported by academic and official discourses and common usage over the nineteenth and twentieth centuries, has effected the transformation of national identity into ethnic identity. In the discourses and practices associated with nontraditional casting, while the concepts of race and ethnicity have received considerable attention, the terms *nation, nationality,* and *nationalism,* although often implicit, rarely surface. When they have been used, it has most often been to describe culturally specific theaters as institutions promoting cultural nationalism, most notably black nationalism. The absence of any constituency for "multinational" casting as a practice or a term is telling—a constant reminder of the need to consider casting practices not just in terms of discursive categories and ideological interests but also as an employment policy subject to many of the same pressures and policies as other forms of work and commerce. At the same time, as Anna Deavere Smith reminds us, while national identity in itself may not be a criterion when matching an actor with a role, it is very often at the heart of the debates over nontraditional casting.

Scope and Structure

As the proponents of nontraditional casting have contended, when casting is approached with an open mind, the possibilities are boundless. Any attempt to study the field of accomplishments and possibilities in this area, however, cannot share the same latitude. As its subtitle indicates, the purpose of this book is to study multiracial casting in live theater in the United States. This restricted purview ensues from the foundational premise that in order to be profitably examined, casting practices must be understood in terms of both the semiotic properties specific to a particular medium and the context of social and political conditions that affected designated groups in the history of a given nation. This means that I will not be systematically considering nontraditional practices that focus on cross-gender casting or the casting of differently abled actors. Like members of racial and ethnic minorities, women and people with sensory impairments and physical disabilities have been subject to prejudicial attitudes and discriminatory practices; the biologically defined characteristics of their bodies have been invested with social significance through the combined action of discursive practices, institutional regulation, and everyday experiences. But racial markers, sex-linked traits, and alterations to and limitations of sight, hearing, and mobility all inflect the human body in ways that are radically different from one another. While often intersecting, the histories of semiotization and regulation of the bodies of women, of racial and ethnic minorities, and of people with disabilities have each had their own trajectory. The interconnected yet ultimately distinct nature of the three trajectories is evidenced in the modifications to the mission statement of the Non-Traditional Casting Project / Alliance for Inclusion in the Arts and shifts in the focus of the organization's activities over the past two decades. The original mission statement of the 1980s, previously quoted, named "artists of color—African American, Asian American, Latino, and Native American; female artists; Deaf and hard-of-hearing artists; and artists with disabilities—ambulatory disabled, blind and low vision" as the focus of NTCP initiatives. Women as a category no longer figure in the Alliance's revised mission statement, which now reads:

> The only organization of its kind in the country, the Alliance's principal concerns are that artists who are African American, Asian Pacific American, Caribbean Black, South Asian, Latino, Arab American, Persian American, Native American, Deaf and hard of hearing, blind and low vision, artists who have mobility, physical, developmental or intellectual disabilities are denied equitable professional opportunities; and that this exclusion represents a serious loss to the cultural life of the nation.[28]

The Alliance's website (http://www.inclusioninthearts.org/mission frame1.htm) clearly reflects the Alliance's increased attention on projects that promote awareness and inclusion of artists with disabilities. The homepage features links to three resources: DEAL (Disabilities in Entertainment and the Arts Link), a project of the Alliance that is described as "a collective of arts and entertainment professionals dedicated to the full inclusion of people with disabilities—physical, developmental, intellectual, and sensory—in all sectors of American arts and entertainment";[29] "Written on the Body: A Conversation about Disability"—a 2006 panel discussion for writers, directors, actors, and filmmakers about "what distinguished authentic portrayals from clichéd, symbolic, or token representations of disability" and the "natural connections between disability and other social issues (poverty, race, sexuality, family)";[30] and "Listening With an Open Eye," the first in a series of resource guides intended "to provide employers background and practical information with respect to working with Deaf and hard of hearing actors in auditions, rehearsal and performance."[31]

The time period I will be covering begins with the 1960s and continues to the present. While, as I have already indicated, there has been a history of cross-racial casting and adaptations of European classics in African American culture since the nineteenth century and isolated examples of companies or productions with black casts that would play to mixed-race audiences (the African Company of the early 1820s, the Astor Place Company of Colored Tragedians of the 1880s, and performances by the Negro units of the Federal Theatre Project in the 1930s provide notable examples), it was not until the civil rights era that concerted and sustained efforts to institutionalize multiracial casting in regional and commercial theaters across the country were initiated.

This was a period of highly creative and often controversial variations in casting, which closely reflected the radical shifts in institutionalized race relations that began with the passage of civil rights legislation in the 1960s and has continued to the Supreme Court's reaffirmation of the constitutionality of affirmative action policies in 2003. The convergence of these currents with the various forms and modes of dramatic representation would result in new artistic conceptions and sociopolitical implications of cross-racial casting that differed significantly from earlier manifestations. The mid-twentieth-century drive to stage classic dramas, from ancient Greek tragedy to contemporary American domestic drama, with racially mixed casts would participate in the restructuring of the racialized sociopolitical order that had prevailed since the first Africans were brought to the American colonies as slaves. No longer were cross-racial or mixed-race stagings just isolated opportunities for black actors to perform in plays recognized to be among the most complex and important works of the English-language repertory. For many African American artists, such performances had been viewed both as marks of professional achievement and as contributions to the advancement of the black race, particularly when these performances took place before white audience members.

When exercised in the context of the radical structural changes initiated by the civil rights movement, cross-racial and particularly mixed-race casting became highly, even aggressively, politicized acts. Racially mixed companies and productions became instances of the integration of the workplace, schools, and residential neighborhoods that was being legislated and celebrated on one side and often very violently opposed on the other. As a result, new tensions and new energy surrounded the presence of actors of color and racially mixed casts. For directors and administrators of theaters that attracted predominantly if not exclusively white audiences, even before the civil rights era, the decision to cast actors of color in canonical Euroamerican plays was an acknowledgment of the abilities of black and other racial minority Americans and of their rightful claim to all aspects of the national cultural heritage. It was also an implicit or explicit expression of support for their struggles against racial discrimination and for equal rights and opportunities. In the climate of the 1960s and 1970s, the stakes were raised as nontraditional casting choices were intended and received as strong statements of a broader political position. A new element of risk was introduced when resentment against government-mandated integration in other areas of life and anxiety over racial activism carried over into the theater. Whereas in the past, watching black actors playing white characters could be regarded as an entertaining novelty with no wider ramifications, this was no longer the case. With the disruption to and the reconfiguration of all areas of public life, the symbolic force of cultural institutions and works that had been designated as bearers of the nation's prestige was intensified. The power and privilege to define dominant social and cultural values that had been assumed and protected as the exclusive privilege of white Americans of European (preferably northern or western) origins was very visibly challenged by cross-racial and interracial casting, as black bodies both literally and metaphorically were placed in roles previously assumed only by whites.

The elevated levels of both positive energy and antagonism extended well beyond the most turbulent years of the 1960s as a result of both vol-

untary projects and coercive measures. Many leaders in the world of theater—governing boards, producers, administrative and artistic directors—actively built multiracial companies and casts, developed and produced plays by writers of color, and sponsored outreach programs to
diversify audiences. At the same time, federal, state, and local government funding policies increasingly required theater organizations to
demonstrate that they had made concerted efforts to promote racial and
ethnic diversity in order to be eligible for public support. Adopting the
tactic, common in the civil rights era, of organizing protest demonstrations to call attention to the exclusion of minorities or the perpetuation
of racial and ethnic stereotypes, activists—some of whom were professionally involved in the theater, film, and television industries and many
of whom were not—continued to exert high-visibility pressure when they
felt it was called for. For fifty years now, even with all the changes that
have taken place in the theater and in society, these three driving forces
have retained the potential to generate enthusiasm and to provoke alienation among theater practitioners, audiences, and, on occasion, the general public. Although originally motivated primarily by social and political rather than artistic concerns, these initiatives, incentives, and
disincentives have had the cumulative effect of irreversibly altering many
of the core conventions of modern dramatic representation.

For the most part, I have proceeded on the assumption that the most
telling material would be located at the sites of greatest resistance—social, cultural, institutional, and literary resistance. This meant focusing
on productions staged for major residential and commercial theaters
with long traditions of staging canonical European and Euroamerican
plays for aesthetically conservative and predominantly white audiences. I
have not analyzed the productions of smaller companies and venues that
cultivate directors, actors, and audiences with a shared interest in push-
ing the boundaries of performance and challenging social norms. Such
institutions have certainly produced fascinating treatments of dramatic
works by manipulating race as a category and a sign. In these instances,
however, the primary insights are revelations regarding the play itself
rather than the milieu in which it is produced. When the commentary
on social or racial issues is a shared discourse between the artists and the
audience, the stagings do not put pressure on the audience's sensibilities, nor is the audience pressured in a way that exposes sociocultural
fissures and ideological differences.

Similarly, community-based theaters like the Classical Theatre of

Harlem, the African American Shakespeare Company in San Francisco, or the Latino Shakespeare Company may present radically altered adaptations of canonical works, but the company's mission authorizes departures from established traditions of performance and even textual fidelity. It is ironic that when community companies acquire sufficient funding to employ more experienced professional actors and mount more elaborate productions, they become subject to the evaluation of spectators (e.g., professional drama critics) who often apply protocols and standards of reception that do not match the performance context. When such encounters have involved the staging of the particular plays I have chosen as points of concentration, I have included nonresident theater productions in the discussion. I have also given considerable attention to productions of one culturally specific theater group—the National Asian American Theatre Company. Unlike other culturally specific companies, which promote new work by minority playwrights and adaptations of European and Euroamerican classics in settings that justify their performance by minority actors, NAATCO's founding mission was to stage "European and American classics as written" with all Asian American casts. The initial funding statement emphasized that the plays were to be presented without any transposition to an Asian milieu. More recently, NAATCO has expanded the scope of its activities to include adaptations of these classics by Asian American playwrights (but with "no forced Asian cultural associations"), and the staging of "new plays—preferably world premieres—written by non–Asian Americans, not for or about Asian Americans, but realized by an all Asian American cast."[32] In making the casting rather than the writing the key to bring new meanings to a play, NAATCO's philosophy more closely resembles that of "mainstream" companies and so provides a different and often illuminating perspective on many of the same theoretical issues.

While I have attempted to achieve some degree of geographical representation, my purpose has not been to be comprehensive. The sheer volume of productions using different forms of racially significant casting over the past forty to sixty years makes such an enterprise impossible, even undesirable since the critical issues would risk being buried under the weight of examples. Instead, I have focused on a number of exemplary high-profile cases where the intersection of generic properties and nontraditional casting practices has introduced new ways of producing meaning that enlighten us on the functioning of particular dramatic works, dramatic genres, theatrical institutions, and social communities.

Since my aim was to contribute to an understanding of nontraditional casting as a sociocultural practice, I concentrated on source materials that constituted the public discourses, whether supportive or resistant, surrounding and constituting the development and promotion of cross-racial casting. These materials included articles, interviews, letters, and critical reviews published in mass circulation newspapers and magazines; programs and publicity material produced by the theater companies (photographs; newsletters and other publications produced for season subscribers or members; archival material made available on company websites); and critical essays and performance reviews in publications intended primarily for theater and academic professionals. The body of published reviews generated by specific productions generally contained the most revealing evidence of gaps or frictions that reflected conflicting social values or aesthetic standards.

In her introduction to *Colorblind Shakespeare: New Perspectives on Race and Performance,* Ayanna Thompson addresses the problem of attempting to theorize color-blind casting practices. She observes: "In some ways, it is difficult to write about color-blind casting because its theoretical underpinnings are so unstable that they make the practice itself not one practice but a set of practices that not only are in competition with one another but also are deconstructing one another."[33] This problem is magnified when not just color-blind but all varieties of nontraditional casting are the subject of study. The structure as well as the content of this book reflects my solution to this problem, offering an overarching account of the ways in which nontraditional casting practices function as meaning-making theatrical and social practices while at the same time respecting the vast and unruly variety of insights that particular productions provide into the relationship of theater and society, of race and performance, and of bodies and identities. The first two chapters of this study lay the theoretical and historical foundations for the following four chapters, which are devoted to four principal categories of text-based American theater: classical forms of tragedy and comedy (e.g., ancient Greek and Roman, neoclassical, English Renaissance and Restoration, seventeenth- to nineteenth-century comedy of manners), modern domestic drama, antirealistic drama, and the Broadway musical. These forms share common venues of performance; are created by the same pool of actors, directors, and writers formed by the same traditions of training; and are evaluated by a common corps of professional critics. The first chapter, "Bearing the Weight of Reality: The Theatricality of

Cross-Racial Corporeal Encounters," examines nontraditional casting as an eminently theatrical practice, one that is enabled by the unique semiotic and phenomenal properties of live theater at the same time that it illuminates those qualities. I analyze properties, notably those associated with the paradoxes of the actor, that enable cross-racial casting in live performance. A central premise here is that the complexly produced "reality effect" central to text-based theater in the European tradition depends on genre-specific contracts between actors and spectators, which must be renegotiated in particular ideologically informed ways when the various forms of nontraditional casting are deployed. The second chapter, "Re-casting Race: Nontraditional Casting Practices and Racial Formation," demonstrates the homologous relationship that exists between the main paradigms of nontraditional casting that emerged between the 1960s and 1980s and the paradigms that dominated contemporaneous American racial theories.

I have made dramatic genres the central organizing principle for the chapters that focus on specific productions with the understanding that generic classifications, however arbitrary, identify significant patterns of textual features and sets of spectatorial conventions. For each form, I consider how the generic conventions (notably the underlying assumptions regarding the relationship between the theatrical representation and reality) frame the very intimate encounter between a character of one race and an actor of another. The individual works I focus on are all considered "classics" of their genre, meeting one or more of the following criteria: they are widely regarded as having historical significance in the development of the genre; they are considered outstanding examples of the dramatic or theatrical form; they possess some kind of enduring moral or social value; they have been accorded canonical status in the repertories of American theater companies. Chapter 3, "Bodies Like Gardens: Classical Tragedy and Comedy in Color," begins with a brief overview of the casting actors of color in classical tragedies and comedies in the twentieth century, and then contrasts the course of multiracial casting in urban centers with diverse populations with the history of racially mixed casts and casting in a regional theater, the Oregon Shakespeare Festival, located far away from large cities. The second part of the chapter focuses on three productions of Shakespeare's *Othello* in which racial permutations were used to underscore traditional interpretations of the work or to introduce new inflections. In chapter 4, "Beyond Type: Re-casting Modern Drama and National Identity," I begin by probing the semiotic bases for the continued reluctance on the part of many theater artists, audience members, and critics to accept multiracial casting in modern domestic drama long after such casting in classical tragedy or comedy and historical dramas has been widely accepted. This resistance is then linked to the higher stakes involved, namely the fashioning of a national identity, when dramas by writers like Arthur Miller, Eugene O'Neill, and Tennessee Williams are cast interracially. If the strong reservations about unconventional casting in modern realistic drama are readily explained by the defining characteristics of the genre, it follows that nontraditional casting of modern antirealistic plays should arouse the fewest objections. It was therefore rather surprising to find that some of the most controversial instances of nontraditional casting involved works that rejected a mimetic relationship to reality. In chapter 5, "The Theater, Not the City: Genre and Politics in Antirealistic Drama," I consider the controversies surrounding the casting of nonwhite actors in plays by Samuel Beckett, Bertolt Brecht, and Thornton Wilder. These cases effectively demonstrate how, by disregarding or misconstruing the conventions of representation, individuals or groups were able to use works defined by their "scorn of verisimilitude" to reinforce or undermine the structure of actual social relations. The final chapter looks at racial and ethnic transformations in four Broadway musicals from the 1960s to the present: *Hello, Dolly!*, *Guys and Dolls*, *Falsettoland*, and *Fiddler on the Roof.* Productions of these works provide unusual insights into the ways "ethnicity" operates as a category distinct from "race" as nontraditional performances of Jewishness are staged.

An afterword assesses the status and lasting impact of multiracial and cross-racial casting practices in the early part of the twenty-first century, when such practices have become a well-established tradition and proven their ability to act as a powerful revitalizing force in American dramatic theater.

CHAPTER ONE

Bearing the Weight of Reality

The Theatricality of Cross-Racial Corporeal Encounters

In the theatre, one can say, "this is just an act," and de-realize the act, make acting into something quite distinct from what is real. . . . The various conventions which announce that "this is only a play" allow strict lines to be drawn between the performance and life. . . . On the street or in the bus, the act [of transvestism] becomes dangerous . . . precisely because there are no theatrical conventions to delimit the purely imaginary character of the act, indeed, on the street or in the bus, there is no presumption that the act is distinct from a reality; the disquieting effect of the act is that there are no conventions that facilitate making this separation.

—JUDITH BUTLER

The potency of nontraditional casting as a form of social activism, a forum for cultural criticism, and a source of artistic innovation derives from a peculiar situation created by modern realistic and naturalistic acting traditions whereby two more or less fully constituted identities—that of the actor and that of the character—inhabit the same body. In Western dramatic theater, this relationship has been variously construed from the time of the ancient Greeks to the present, but by the turn of the nineteenth century, the tradition of mimetic representation had evolved into a full-fledged commitment to creating the illusion that the actor was no longer simply playing a character but actually becoming that other personage. Konstantin Stanislavsky designated the "embodiment of the role" as one of the key phases in its creation. The first part of the process of embodiment began with "the intellectual creation of an outer image, with the aid of the imagination, the inner eye, ear and so forth."[1] From there the actor went on to transfer the design or "typical lines" of the character's external appearance to his own face and body:

> He tries all kinds of ways of dressing his hair, of using his eyebrows; he contracts various muscles of his face and body, tries out various ways of using his eyes, of walking, gesticulating, bowing, shaking hands, moving about. This experiment is carried further with make-up. He will put on a whole series of wigs, paste on all sorts of beards, mustaches, use colored creams to try to find the exact shade of complexion, lines of wrinkles, shadows, highlights, until he stumbles on the thing he is looking for.[2]

If, however, actors trained and working in the realistic tradition are to be judged according to their ability to successfully inscribe another being's history as well as their appearance onto their own bodies, what happens when the racial identity of the actor does not match that of the character as originally conceived? This is a complex question that can only be answered by considering casting as part of the greater semiotic system of theatrical activity—activity that is an artistic, sociocultural, and historic process of creation and communication.

Paradoxes of the Body

> The actor is everything in the theatre. We can do without everything in a performance except him. He is the flesh of the show, the spectator's pleasure. He is, irrefutably, presence itself. But capturing him as a function of the signs he produces is not an easy task. . . . He is the site of all paradoxes.[3]
> —ANNE UBERSFELD

Traditionally, in the more or less realistic modes of dramatic performance that dominated the Western stage after the Renaissance, the theatrical or performant aspects of the staged production were subordinated to and finally even dissolved into the fictional or diegetic elements. Increasingly, the imaginary universe of the play came to take precedence over the real time and place shared by actors and audience. The conventions of realism and naturalism require that all the elements on stage work with the cooperation of the audience to sustain the mimetic illusion, in which iconic signs refer directly to reality. A comfortable distance must be set up between the performer and the observer as the time and space of the stage is differentiated from that of the auditorium.

As far as the actor-character relationship is concerned, the conventions of realism demand that in the dialogue between the real presence of the actor and the imaginary figure of the character, the voice of the former must be submerged beneath the voice of the latter. In a situation where both actor and character lay claim to the same body, the dramatic actor must appear to cede ownership for the duration of a performance. In modern Western theater, the dramatic actor's methods of preparation and style of performing and the audience's mode of reception always cooperated, until relatively recently, to endorse the ascendancy of the character over the actor. In twentieth- and early twenty-first-century American theater, these are the conventions that have prevailed whether the play is a classical tragedy or comedy, a modern domestic drama, or an American musical. In contrast, antirealistic forms of theater, usually viewed as standing in stark opposition to realistic or naturalistic theater, rely on "the sort of reproduction that declares itself as artificial, fictive and theatrical." There is a deliberate break with mimesis so that instead of referring to a "real" world, signs in antirealistic theater refer to themselves. This is how Fernando de Toro makes the distinction:

> One only has to think of Artaud or Brecht. Brechtian theatre is based on theatricality and the reflexive nature of the sign that actually creates itself. The distance effect caused by the characters (imitating but not incarnating, speaking in quotes), by other components of the production (lighting, film projections, etc.), and even by the story structure (fragmented, autonomous scenes) . . . inform[s] us that "we are in the theatre." In non-illusionist theatre, what is most real and fundamental is the message and playfulness, and not the referential illusion.[4]

Although actors may still impersonate characters, the success of the performance does not rely on the seamless simulation of a living human being.

Like all artistic innovations, the array of race-conscious approaches to casting promoted since the 1960s necessarily developed within the framework of these preexisting forms and conventions. But taking shape at a moment of historical rupture, they also broke with past practices to introduce a new register of meaning and new enunciative possibilities for all forms of dramatic theater. Nontraditional casting represented a shift in theatrical signification of an order that had last occurred in Anglo-American theater three hundred years earlier, when female parts began being played by female actors. Indeed, the innovations of the mid-twentieth century were even more radical in terms of both the representational and the sociocultural dimensions of performance. As far as the relationship of the fictional or diegetic world to the real world was concerned, the casting of women to play women diminished the distance between representation and reality, thus reinforcing what has been the dominant impulse in Western dramatic theater. In contrast, most forms of nontraditional casting serve to widen those gaps. In the process, in ways that I will discuss below, the actor's corporeality acquired a new significance, and the semiotization of the actor's body advanced in unprecedented ways.

As a sociocultural institution, the theater has always been closely linked to the political aspects of civic, state, and national life, and casting has been a visibly, even notoriously, politicized process. Prior to the inception of nontraditional casting, however, as far as the *selection* of actors was concerned, ideological forces operated through the patronage of particular companies or the hiring, as opposed to the casting, of individual actors. By the same token, negative pressure was applied through the banishment or proscription of entire troupes and the imprisonment or, in more enlightened times, the firing of individual thespians whose allegiances or opinions offended those in authority. The distribution of roles in individual productions, however, was not in itself instrumental in relaying social values or challenging political positions until nontraditional casting emerged as a concept and a practice. The very idea of a casting schema as a semantic field or an interpretive register for a dramatic text emerged only when the race or ethnicity of the actor became a relevant factor. The casting of dramatic roles, heretofore relegated to the semiotic cellars of theatrical convention or mimetic correspondence, became elevated to the status of an expressive language of the stage.

Nontraditional casting added new codes to the elaborate repertoire of signs produced by the actor's body. Ubersfeld has described the actor as "a human being, whose role, in his own practice, is to create signs, to be transformed (to transform himself into a system of signs)."[5] She goes on to note: "but this transformation cannot be complete," for "there is an unsemanticized remainder."[6] As long as acting companies and casts were composed exclusively of white or Caucasian actors and played to predominantly or entirely white audiences, natural skin color and facial features (as opposed to facial expressions or features altered by makeup or dye) that marked an actor as belonging to a particular race remained among these unsemanticized elements. This situation mirrored the social privilege of white neutrality or invisibility. In continental European theaters, color-blind, cross-cultural, or race-based conceptual casting remained so marginal or foreign that none of the impressive studies of theater semiotics published in Europe in the 1970s and early 1980s even mentions an actor's racial or ethnic characteristics as a source of potential signifiers.[7] Racially diverse casting practices effected the transformation of the formerly transparent physical features commonly used to identify an individual's race into a rich variety of theatrical signs—signs produced conjointly by the director and the actor. This process of transformation was not confined to actors of color but extended to white actors as well. Once endowed with semantic force, the physical and visual racial markers did not just function as discrete signifiers; they instigated a new dialectical relationship with the other signifiers generated by the actor's body and with other signifying systems of the stage—sets, costumes, lighting. Most importantly, nontraditional casting revises the most critical relationship in dramatic traditions—that which exists between the actor and the character—prompting the spectator to exercise new modes of perception and learn new protocols of reception.

Adjustments to the standard actor-character relationship, such as those imposed by nontraditional casting, have a critical impact beyond the way one experiences the actor's performance, because that performance is not just one element among others in the meaning-making system of the realistic or naturalistic stage. More than any other single element, the actor's physical presence on stage controls the production of meaning as his or her body becomes the most arresting point of intersection for visual, auditory, sociocultural, and ideological codes. The full implications of the animating effect of the human presence on stage are vividly summarized by Gay McAuley in her study of theatrical space:

> The stage, even when set and lit ready for the performance, will keep the spectators' attention for a very short time if no actors are present, for in the theatre it is the presence of the actors that makes the space meaningful. It is through the body and the person of the actor that all

the contributing systems of meaning (visual, vocal, spatial, fictional) are activated, and the actor/performer is without doubt the most important agent in all the signifying processes involved in the performance event.[8]

Without the performer, there can be no theatrical semiosis. Consequently, as Ubersfeld notes, the audience's observation of the actor is its most difficult and most exciting task.[9] Much of the pleasure and fascination of watching a performance comes from seeing how actors resolve the fundamental paradox of the dramatic actor performing in a realistic or naturalistic mode—the contradiction between the presence of the flesh-and-blood performer and the absence of the imaginary character. This live balancing act also maintains the relationship between the real time of the performance and the diegetic time of the dramatic action, the actual space of the auditorium and stage and the fictional location of the play's setting. Forcing spectators to become aware of the concrete materiality of the actor's body rather than leaving them free to focus on the illusion of the character's physical and psychological qualities therefore does not merely require a re-encoding of the signifying functions assigned directly to the actor; any such shift instigates a realignment that traverses the entire semiotic system of a production. This is what happens when nontraditional casting magnifies the effects of the paradoxical relationship between actor and character.

The precise nature and degree of realignment varies according to the textual form of the play (classical forms of tragedy and comedy, realistic domestic drama, antirealistic drama) and the mode of performance associated with each (conventionalized, analogic, deconstructive), variations that will be illustrated in greater detail in chapters 3–6. Equally important are the variations that arise from the specific type of nontraditional casting used. Although all forms of nontraditional casting are commonly spoken of as if they belonged to the same order of theatrical representation, this is not the case. For example, if we consider the four approaches to race and casting originally identified—color-blind, conceptual, cross-cultural, and societal—we find that each type assumes and generates a different relationship between representation and reality.

The ideal of color-blind casting asserts a radical split between the theatrical and the actual, claiming a high degree of autonomy for the representational space of the stage. The audience is asked to accept situations and relationships that generally run counter to actual experience and that contradict or disregard both history and biology. Although few directors actually expect audiences to be truly unaware of an actor's race, we are meant to remain unperturbed by the knowledge that England's kings and queens have all been white when we see black actors playing a Henry or a Richard or an Anne. Similarly, a racially mixed nuclear family in medieval Britain or nineteenth-century Scandinavia should not raise questions or objections of a scientific or sociological nature. What is believed or hoped is that race or ethnicity can in fact be neutralized as a signifying element. An actor's race will undoubtedly be noticed upon her or his entrance as the spectator takes an inventory of the character's or actor's physical attributes; but if the play subsequently fails to draw the audience's attention to the actor's difference, either directly or through allusion, this characteristic blends into the visual landscape of the scenic space. To put it another way, the actors' bodies become "unmarked" in terms of race or ethnicity. This dissolution of markers relies on the audience's capacity to separate the fictional world of the stage from the world of lived experience and to give it precedence over a received body of historical knowledge.

But as we are constantly reminded, the racialized body or the markers of race cannot be made to disappear so readily in all circumstances and in all locations. Indeed, racially conscious or "conceptual" casting taps the awareness of differences to critique contemporary racial divisions and hierarchies while at the same time offering new insights into a particular dramatic work. When the casting scheme is integral to the directorial concept, when it functions as a key component in realizing the interpretation of the text, the phenomenon of embodiment engages with, rather than being parasitical upon, the world of lived experience. Spectators are positioned to incorporate their knowledge of racial histories and relations into their experience and interpretation of the performance. For instance, in the fall of 1992, the Shakespeare Theatre staged a production of *Troilus and Cressida* that was designed to suggest parallels with Operation Desert Storm. In a casting distribution that reproduced the racial hierarchy of the American armed forces, the middle-aged Grecian generals—Ulysses, Agamemnon, Menelaus, and Nestor—were played by European American actors; while the warrior heroes Achilles and Ajax, the ones sent into actual combat, were played by African Americans.[10] In this case, for the play to succeed as an act of communication, a continuous sociocultural space extending from the stage to the audience to the world of actuality had to be established. When their full potential for producing meaning is realized, conceptual approaches to casting belong to a different order of signification: they move a production from the field of artistic representation to that of cultural criticism.

Cross-cultural casting differs from other forms of innovative casting in that the transposition of the "world" of a play to another cultural context can take place only in partnership with other theater artists: for example, a writer to adapt the script and designers to create the sets, costumes, and props. Technically, the first type of transposition is not a matter of casting but of playwriting. In works like Mustapha Matura's *Playboy of the West Indies* and *Trinidad Sisters,* the translations of the situations and dialogue of J. M. Synge's *Playboy of the Western World* and Anton Chekhov's *Three Sisters* have all taken place on the page. The casting process then proceeds in a traditional manner with the race of the actors matched to that of the characters as rewritten. Many culturally transposed productions, however, use the same texts and translations as conventional productions of the play. The race of the actors combined with sets, costumes, and props tells us that we're in a different cultural setting. Between the poles of productions that employ a new playwright and those that look to designers to reset a play, are countless permutations that involve different degrees of rewriting and of shifting of time and place. Depending on the genre of the work and the director's approach, the change in cultural context may function as a mere decorative novelty, or it may bring new resonance to the author's work. In the latter case, cross-cultural casting is essentially conceptual casting on a collective and comprehensive scale.

Societal or sociological casting, in choosing an actor to play a character who historically could have been of the same race as the actor, preserves the traditional mimetic relationship between the world of social realities and the realm of dramatic representation. As an audience member at the First National Symposium on Non-Traditional Casting (1987) pointed out: "If you look at a casting description in the script, it may say, for example 'a factory worker.' Not a *white* factory worker. It's the convention that writes white in there."[11] It is therefore not surprising that this is the only form of "nontraditional" casting—which is in fact entirely traditional in its fundamental principles—that has had a significant impact on casting for commercial film and television. It is a simple and uncontroversial matter to cast black, Latino, or Asian actors as teachers, lawyers, police officers, or store owners in a movie or television series episode. In works set in the past several decades, it is implicit that the increasing inclusion of actors of color will simply be a corollary and a reflection of sociopolitical activity and changes in hiring practices that alter the public complexion of American and European societies. The illusion of an unproblematic one-to-one correspondence between the fictional and the actual is in no way upset.

A societal casting approach becomes more interesting from an artistic point of view when the play in question is from an earlier era. Directors applying this approach to the casting of historical plays will use historical or ethnographic research to open up the casting possibilities, as Harold Scott did for his Shakespeare Theatre production of *Othello,* in which he cast black actors in the roles of Iago and Emilia as well as Othello. His conception was grounded in the history not just of Renaissance Venice, but the western Mediterranean of the time, which saw a dispersion of Moors along the northern as well as the southern shore following their expulsion from Spain in 1492. He also used research on the Tuareg tribe of Mauritania to create a backstory for Othello, Iago, and Emilia that would explain many of the more puzzling aspects of their dynamics. (See chapter 3 for a detailed discussion.)

In each of the above cases, indeed in all instances where race on stage has been an issue, the effects produced by the performer's racial identity depend not just on the intellectual processes that read and imagine across the semiotic boundary established between the actors' space and the spectators' space. For while these two spaces are semiotically distinct, from a phenomenological standpoint they are continuous. This continuity is inherent in the "homo-materiality" of theatrical signs and the things they represent.[12] In other representational arts—such as drawing, painting, sculpture, fiction, or film—the objects, beings, and actions being imitated are almost always rendered in another medium: charcoal and paper, paint and canvas, stone or metal, ink or celluloid. In theater, as Bert O. States points out, there is no ontological difference between the object and the image—things actually *are* what they seem to be to an unusual degree; objects are represented by themselves, and human action is imitated in the medium of human action.[13] Whenever an actor imitates a human action, he or she must perform that action in a mundane as well as a theatrical sense. Under these conditions, the "body represents a rootedness in the biological present that always to some extent escapes transformation into the virtual realm."[14]

The serious consequences of this physiological grounding when race is a factor have been evident since American theater institutions emerged. It has mattered little whether the particular theatrical form was strictly presentational, strictly representational, or somewhere in between. In *Racine et Shakespeare*, Stendhal cites an incident that was alleged to have taken place on a nineteenth-century Baltimore stage during a performance of Shakespeare's *Othello:*

> Last year (August of 1822), the soldier standing guard at the interior of the theatre in Baltimore, seeing Othello who, in the fifth act of the tragedy of that name, was going to kill Desdemona, cried out "It will never be said that in my presence a damned black would kill a white woman." At that moment the soldier fired his gun, and broke the arm of the actor who played Othello. Not a year goes by without newspapers reporting similar facts.[15]

This account may very well be apocryphal,[16] but such racist sentiments were expressed throughout the course of nineteenth- to mid-twentieth-century American theater history. If more such incidents did not actually take place, it was largely due to the preemptive precautions of producers and performers themselves. Such measures were sometimes deemed advisable even in nonrepresentational forms of theater. In his study of blackface minstrelsy, Eric Lott cites the problems P. T. Barnum faced when he wanted to feature an exceptional dancer who was "a genuine Negro," at a time when "there was not an audience in America that would not have resented, in a very energetic fashion, the insult of being asked to look at the dancing of a real Negro."[17] The solution was to have the performer appear in blackface, which would serve as a protective shield by having the ironic effect of disguising his black body as white by implication. To nineteenth-century audiences like the one described by Barnum, it would have been irrelevant that the black dancer was separated from them by the edges of the stage—the common air they were breathing provided the only meaningful spatial context.

Up through the middle of the twentieth century, although the presence of black performers was increasingly accepted, even the pronounced mimetic mode of a Shakespearean tragedy would not have protected the actors if the audience's tolerance for the enactment of sexual contact between a black man and a white woman had been exceeded. In 1942, Paul Robeson became the first African American actor to play

Othello with a white professional cast in the United States. This production came twelve years after Robeson had performed the role in London. That production had not crossed the Atlantic because of the strong resistance to interracial casting that prevailed in the United States. The American production starring Robeson, Mel Ferrer, and Uta Hagen first played in more liberal university towns like Cambridge, Princeton, and New Haven to test the waters before a New York opening was attempted. Theater critic Elliot Norton's eyewitness account of opening night in Cambridge evokes the uncertainties and risks surrounding the event: "Only two American managers had had the courage in that year to put on this production with Robeson. The rest were scared to death. The whole Broadway community was hiding in closets when the subject was brought up. Nobody knew what would happen."[18] While the play proved to be a great success on Broadway, where it ran for 296 performances, this enthusiastic reception was no guarantee of a similar response on all stops of the national tour that followed. The company refused to play to segregated houses, which generally served to restrict the tour to more hospitable locations and audiences. In St. Clair Bourne's 1999 documentary *Paul Robeson: Here I Stand,* Robeson recalls the tensions that surrounded the performance in Cincinnati, Ohio, which had attracted many people from Louisville, Kentucky: "For half the performance nobody knew what was going to happen; everything was very tense; and I was very careful how close I'd get to Desdemona. I didn't get too close there. There was real tension."[19]

This testimony contradicts the assumptions concerning the protection afforded by conventions of theatrical performance such as those expressed by Judith Butler in the passage cited as the first epigraph of this chapter. Evidently, as far as theater is concerned, there are no safe spaces—only safe times and safe places. It is precisely when issues of race are involved that "the theater" is revealed as a site, or more accurately as multiple sites, for the contestation of cultural power and as a potential location for restructuring the social and symbolic orders. Nontraditional casting practices exercise their capacity for intervention by capitalizing on a quality of theatrical performance that is absent from film or television. In the words of Herbert Blau, "The critical thing . . . in the institution of theatre is not so much that an actor is there, but that an actor is so vulnerably there. Whatever he represents in the play, in the order of time he is representing nobody but himself. How could he? That's his body, doing time."[20]

The Limits of Genre

> Understanding itself is genre-bound. The generic conception
> serves both a heuristic and a constitutive function.[21]
>
> —E. D. HIRSCH, *Validity in Interpretation*

> Since a "single" genre is only recognizable as difference, as a fore-
> grounding against the background of its neighboring genres,
> every work involves more than one genre, even if only implicitly.[22]
>
> —THOMAS O. BEEBEE, *The Ideology of Genre*

While it would be going too far to say that the actor's body is doing time
in any sort of prison-house—whether linguistic, theatrical, or social—the
actor's presence and gestures are always framed and constrained by various conventions. Chief among these are the conventions of genre that
outline vital parameters for the director's and the actor's interpretations
of the dramatic text and the conditions for the spectator's interpretation
of the performance text. While, as Beebee observes, genres are in many
ways arbitrary and mutable classifications, generic categories, much like
racial categories, remain both inescapable and meaningful. The relationship between representation and reality associated with a particular
genre is instrumental in determining how readily and productively the
conventions of realistic illusionism can be breached by nontraditional
casting. The remaining chapters of this book will be devoted to considering this problem in greater detail through the analysis of individual
productions. These productions illustrate the extraordinarily rich variety
of ways in which different permutations and combinations of generic
frames and race-based casting concepts have manipulated the relationship between representation and reality, between actor and character,
and between text and performance to serve both artistic and social interests. In the current chapter, I will discuss how generic properties in
general function to set the stage for the intimate encounter between a
character of one race and an actor of another.

The more prescriptive dimensions of genre as they relate specifically
to theatrical communication have been concisely set out by Marco De
Marinis, who states: "the identification of genre . . . is a cognitive operation indispensable to the comprehension of a given performance text,
or to its full semantic and communicative actualization. Only after having recognized the occurrence in question as theatrical and having assigned it to a given subclass of performance text can the spectator coop-

erate in the way(s) 'foreseen' by the text."[23] He goes on to summarize the main areas of cooperation: (*a*) activating pertinent systems of expectation, (*b*) correctly choosing the possible world of reference, (*c*) selecting the appropriate (common and intertextual) frames, (*d*) assuming adequate cognitive dispositions, and (*e*) making grounded judgments of acceptability and appropriateness. By focusing on the performance rather than the literary or dramatic text, this model embraces avant-garde or innovative productions where the director seeks to extend or overturn prevailing conventions and expectations. Such productions afford audiences the exciting opportunity to get involved in renegotiating familiar generic boundaries. These renegotiations are not anomalies in the interpretive process, but as E. D. Hirsch points out, an integral and normal part of the process of reception:

> [W]hile it is not accurate to say that an interpretation is helplessly dependent on the generic conception with which an interpreter happens to start, it is nonetheless true that his interpretation is dependent on the last, unrevised generic conception with which he starts. All understanding of verbal meaning is necessarily genre-bound.[24]

The possibility that spectators may well choose to be uncooperative participants in such ventures is of necessity implicit in this model. The existing comprehensive models of theater semiosis envision the uncooperative or unreceptive spectator as being resistant to radically altered staging conventions solely on aesthetic grounds. When traditional generic limits are stretched or tested by race-based casting, however, we are reminded of the often-overlooked ideological properties that are integral parts of generic systems. At the most fundamental level, these properties derive from the "reality effect" (*l'effet de réel*)[25]—the impression and belief central to Western dramatic theater since the Renaissance that what is evoked on the stage should correspond to some sociohistorical reality. The strength and pervasiveness of the reality effect varies from era to era and from genre to genre, and its relative potency is a defining characteristic of generic categories. From the standpoint of the twentieth and twenty-first centuries, the connections between what is presented on stage and what is presumed to have existed in the historical world being depicted have become distinctly attenuated in classical forms of tragedy and comedy—ancient Greek and Roman, Shakespearean, neo-classical, Restoration, eighteenth century, and Romantic.

Temporal and geographical distance from the author's society or the fictional world reinforces the theatricalizing effects of elements such as archaic language, verse dialogue, and artificial plot devices, diminishing expectations or assumptions regarding mimetic fidelity. At the other end of the spectrum, the conventions associated with modern domestic drama invite, even require, the misprision of representation for reality. The scenic conventions of the fourth wall, which are both prescriptions for staging and a set of protocols for reception, summon the spectator to confuse drama and life utterly and gladly. The way is paved by dialogue purporting to reproduce everyday speech acts, structured scenes disguised as spontaneously unfolding events, costumes cut from the same patterns as clothing worn on the streets, and furnishings and props that are actual objects playing themselves. In the case of the classical Broadway musical, the joyous surrender of critical and emotional distance is enhanced by the tantalizing suspensions of dramatic action brought about by the interpolation of songs and dance numbers. Rather than canceling the impression of reality, these interruptions embellish the mimetic illusion. Of the dominant dramatic genres that remain viable in American theaters, only antirealistic dramas are not characterized by or dependent on the generation of a reality effect to communicate with spectators.

The conviction that dramatic performances must refer to a lived or once-lived reality is perhaps the most cherished illusion of many modern audiences. In truth, as Ubersfeld points out, "theatrical manifestations never refer to something real, but to a discourse on the real."[26] Consequently,

> The reality effect in theatrical referentialization always corresponds to an ideological function; the stage always tells us not what the world is like, but what the world it is showing us is like. It is for the spectator to construct—and no one will do this for him—the relationship with what is real in his own experience.[27]

It has always been precisely when a spectator has not been able to relate the world being shown on the stage to his or her own experiences of, or more accurately, his or her own perceptions of, a lived reality and to familiar conceptions of a historical reality that nontraditional casting is rejected as a viable or desirable practice.

This knowledge carries important implications for more fully understanding negative or ambivalent responses to nontraditionally cast productions. While raw racism and racist attitudes undeniably have been at the root of the earliest and the most deeply entrenched hostile responses to the abandonment of all-white casting, more moderate but long-lived resistance has been sustained by a reluctance to relinquish the illusion of verisimilitude. A significant (but seemingly ever-decreasing) number of spectators have proved unable or unwilling to establish any connections between the world on stage and any real world, past or present, when a play is cast against tradition. But exactly which world or whose world has been rendered unrecognizable and therefore unacceptable? All more-or-less traditional dramatic theater productions refer to between one and three frames of reference: (1) the era of the author, (2) the era of the director/actor/spectator, and (3) the era of the fictional world of the play. These frames may all coincide (e.g., a 1950s American production of *Death of a Salesman* or *A Raisin in the Sun*); the first and second may be the same (e.g., a production of Racine's *Andromaque* at the court of Louis XIV); the first and third may be the same (e.g., a Molière comedy being performed in the twentieth century); or all three may be different (e.g., a nineteenth-century production of Shakespeare's *Julius Caesar*). During the twentieth century, many directors began adding a fourth frame by using sets and costumes, and sometimes revised dialogue, to create references to yet another era (e.g., Roger Planchon's production of Shakespeare's *Antony and Cleopatra* set in 1930s Hollywood).[28] Accordingly, audience members who find the presence of actors of color unrealistic and therefore unacceptable, may in fact be formulating their objections on any one of these levels or some combination of them. A black Romeo or Juliet can be disturbing or disorienting because this does not square with what is commonly known about Renaissance Italy, Elizabethan England, or a spectator's own twentieth-century American world. While it is important to keep in mind that there are ideological dimensions to all historical and cultural narratives or representations, the controversies generated by race-sensitive casting make it clear that the present time and place stand apart from other domains as a field of contested representation. Disputations over historical accuracy or authenticity have generally excited little interest beyond professional and academic circles. When arguments over casting practices themselves or the conditions under which they are employed have become heated and acrimonious, it has been whenever fundamental conceptions of twentieth- and twenty-first-century American society and culture are at stake. For nontraditional racial casting exposes and destabilizes not just the normativity of all-white casting practices, but, more significantly, the normativity of white social and cultural dominance, both of which could be taken for granted until the 1960s.

The linked resistance to the disruption of theatrical and societal norms has frequently surfaced in the form of trenchant objections against the color-blind or color-conscious casting of family members when there is no textual or historical basis for a mixed-race configuration. The creation of an "interracial" family on the stage where none existed on the page has the potential to generate controversy whether the script in question is a historical drama or period piece, a modern realistic drama, or a Broadway musical. The most unequivocal objections are similar to those provoked by René Buchs's 1996 staging of *Romeo and Juliet* for the Oregon Shakespeare Festival. These excerpts are from letters that were printed in the *Ashland Daily Tidings:*

> To really stretch credibility, a white Romeo had a black mother and a white Juliet had a black father! How unreal can you get? . . . I believe that OSF ought to decide to put on the best Shakespeare it can, and not sacrifice quality to promote affirmative action.
>
> Our final comment has to do with (what else?) political correctness. We found it particularly distracting to find Romeo and Juliet with one black parent apiece.[29]

Joanne Akalaitis's production of *Cymbeline,* in which she cast a white actor as the Queen and a black actor as her son Cloten, generated a more high-profile and less straightforward debate. In his review for *New York* magazine, John Simon wrote:

> Watching Akalaitis' staging of "Cymbeline," you wondered whether the production was suggesting that the queen had a black son as the result of an adulterous affair. Eventually you figured out it was just nontraditional casting . . . but why should the mind be sent off by ways that are counterproductive for the understanding and enjoyment of the play rather than be allowed to concentrate on the issues at hand?[30]

New York Times critic Frank Rich offered an even more scathing denunciation of the casting choices, even as he advocated a more sweeping approach to multiracial casting:

The casting is bizarre. . . . While one can applaud Ms. Akalaitis for casting a black actor as Cloten, doesn't credibility (and coherence for a hard-pressed audience) demand that his mother also be black? . . . We are also supposed to believe . . . that Imogen would mistake Cloten's decapitated torso for her husband's, yet the scene and Imogen are rendered ridiculous here by the conflicting races of the confused corpses. It's productions like this, which practice arbitrary tokenism rather than complete and consistent integration, that mock the dignified demands of the nontraditional casting movement.[31]

Typifying the paradoxical nature of protests against multiracial casting, these responses suggest that spectators may be unsettled because they feel that what they are witnessing is either too real or else it is not real enough. These paradoxes derive from and expose the fundamentally paradoxical nature of realistic or naturalistic dramatic performance. If we break down the negative reactions provoked by seeing some combination of parents, children, and siblings who are of markedly different races, we find that responses fall into three broad classes: audience members may be offended at the sight of actors of different races in intimate situations, disturbed by the implication of interracial sexual relations, or profoundly annoyed at the disruption of the mimetic illusion. In the first case, the audience members are relating to the actors as flesh-and-blood human beings occupying the same time and place as themselves; in the second, we have spectators who are taking the characters and their actions as seriously as if they were real people and actual occurrences; and in the third we have thwarted accomplices, whose suspension of disbelief has been pushed beyond the limits of goodwill. In the last case, to the authority of sociohistorical knowledge, has been added the weight of scientific principles concerning heredity and genetics. This type of reaction is illustrated by another letter protesting the mixed-race families created in Oregon Shakespeare Festival productions, this time in *The Winter's Tale* and *Coriolanus:*

> Why do you try to shove race at us by mixing family relationships which directly contradict genetic laws? Very disconcerting and we're not racist.[32]

Actor, director, critic, and scholar Richard Hornby carries to an extreme the genetically informed logic that a realistic mode of production and reception would seem to demand, but only in order to dismantle the foundations of that logic. He begins:

> Yet white women can have black children. She is his mother by a marriage previous to her current one with King Cymbeline; we do not know who Cloten's father was, nor anything about the Queen's own ancestry. In the same vein, Arviragus' brother Guiderius was played by a white actor, Jesse Borrego, but we do not know what race the characters' mother was, nor anything about the ancestry of their father Belarius. If this seems like a tedious lesson in genetics, it was meant to be.[33]

He then goes on to discount the legitimacy of the genetic argument by pointing out that the sight of a blond-haired couple with a brown-haired child on stage causes no objection, even though this is genetically impossible, whereas the sight of a light-skinned parent with a dark-skinned child would seem to excite controversy, even though this is a biological possibility:

> It is not *realism* that causes us to concentrate on the racial mixture, but rather the cultural codes by which we live, which condition our way of perceiving and thinking. Of course the distinction is *there*, on the stage, but we "read" that distinction as something important, in the same way that we read what is on this page as words rather than just black markings, because of what we have learned and then internalized.[34]

His concluding observation reinforces Ubersfeld's essential point that dramatic performances acquire meaning not from references to lived realities but from references to culturally encoded and ideologically framed discourses on the real.

It is a testament to the active engagement between theater and society—and a reminder of the dialectical relationship between the two—that the various paradoxes discussed in this chapter have not resulted in an impasse but have led to productive changes not just in theater practices but social relations. The shifts in casting policies, practices, and paradigms have had a reciprocal effect on paradigms of thought that shape the ways that race and ethnicity are understood and performed both on stage and in everyday life. As the examination of particular productions in subsequent chapters will reveal, the forms and outcomes of interaction between the theatrical and social are myriad—as varied and numerous as the permutations of text, staging, spectator, venue, and moment. Before we proceed to these case studies, which are both generic and specific in nature, the relationship between nontraditional casting practices and broader social processes must be analyzed in greater detail. The current chapter examined nontraditional casting as part of a system for producing meaning in the theater; the next will consider casting as a subfield of cultural production.

CHAPTER TWO

Re-casting Race

Nontraditional Casting and Racial Formation

Eyes are bold as lions,—roving, running, leaping, here and there, far and near. They speak all languages. . . . The eyes of men converse as much as their tongues, with the advantage, that the ocular dialect needs no dictionary, but is understood all the world over.

—RALPH WALDO EMERSON, "BEHAVIOR"

Nontraditional casting was a practice born of a moment. It was not just a product of, but also a participant in, the radical social changes of the middle decades of the twentieth century. Like all sociocultural practices, the new approaches to casting were as much a new way of thinking as a different way of doing things. They were at once ideologically motivated and artistically inspired. Up to the present moment, every production of a European American play in which actors of color play white characters has participated in the profound shifts in social formations, specifically racial formations, that have been taking place over the past fifty years. The history of nontraditional casting practices provides a lucid illustration of how cultural, social, and political factors provide a contextual frame for interpreting the content of a play, yet also affect the structural possibilities of cultural practices. In the previous chapter, I discussed the ways in which different approaches to nontraditional casting reflected varying assumptions regarding the relationship between representations and reality. In this chapter, I will demonstrate how racially aware casting practices have corresponded to the broader racial formations of society as a whole. To focus the discussion, I will use the two most highly publicized controversies over contemporary casting practices: the August Wilson–Robert Brustein debates of 1996 and the *Miss Saigon* protests of 1990. The course and terms of these debates provide an exemplary field for understanding the complex relationship between casting paradigms and race relations in the United States.

The Wilson-Brustein Debates

In June 1996, August Wilson delivered a passionate keynote address at the Eleventh Biennial National Conference of the Theatre Communications Group in which he denounced color-blind casting. The positions articulated during the conference, in the pages of *American Theatre* magazine through the fall of that year, and finally during a live confrontation between August Wilson and Robert Brustein in January 1997 reflect a wide range of assumptions regarding the nature of racial and cultural identities and the role of theater in defining and redefining those identities. The rekindled debates also offer critical insights into the ways conceptions of race, ethnicity, and culture are constantly being created, perpetuated, and transformed. The larger significance of the discussions that have been taking place in the world of theater becomes evident when casting practices and policies from the 1960s to the present are examined in relation to the major contemporary theories of how racial meanings are constructed and altered.

Given the wide-ranging nature of the subsequent discussions, it would be useful to recall the core of the original argument as it related to casting practices. In calling for a renewed commitment to the support of black theaters, August Wilson denounced what has come to be called color-blind casting not only for deflecting funding from these institutions, but for perpetuating an assimilationist ideology that denied the existence and worth of a unique black worldview, values, style, linguistics, religion, and aesthetics. Wilson stated unequivocally, "Colorblind casting is an aberrant idea that has never had any validity other than as a tool of the Cultural Imperialists who view American culture, rooted in the icons of European culture, as beyond reproach in its perfection."[1] In his view,

> To mount an all-black production of a *Death of a Salesman* or any other play conceived for white actors as an investigation of the human condition through the specifics of white culture is to deny us our own hu-

manity, our own history, and the need to make our own investigations from the cultural ground on which we stand as black Americans. It is an assault on our presence, our difficult but honorable history in America; it is an insult to our intelligence, our playwrights, and our many and varied contributions to the society and the world at large.[2]

In effect, an actor of color performing a role written for a white character is seen to be engaging in a form of passing on stage, which entails all the associated psychological damage of attempting to pass in society. As far as Wilson is concerned, an African American actor who plays the role of a Shakespearean English king allows his body to be used in "the celebration of a culture which has oppressed [black people]."[3] His conclusion is, "We do not need colorblind casting; we need some theatres to develop our playwrights."[4]

In replying to Wilson's criticism of opinions he had expressed in an article titled "Unity from Diversity" (*New Republic,* July 19–26, 1993), Robert Brustein sustained a diametrically opposed viewpoint. He characterized Wilson's "appeal for subsidized separatism" as "a reverse form of the old politics of division, an appeal for socially approved and foundation-funded separatism,"[5] and contended that racially mixed companies and casts represented a major step forward in American political and cultural history. Taking exception to Wilson's statement that separate black theaters are necessary because black and white Americans "cannot meet on the common ground of experience,"[6] Brustein argues instead for a transcendent unifying theater that will recognize that "the greatest art embraces a common humanity."[7]

These opinions and approaches are largely rearticulations of views first advanced twenty to thirty years ago. These views were not formulated in isolation from nontheatrical events, discourses, and practices. Equivalent or parallel positions have been articulated in relation to society as a whole. These positions can be identified with the dominant currents of American racial theory of the past fifty years. In their study *Racial Formation in the United States from the 1960s to the 1990s* (1986 and 1994), Michael Omi and Howard Winant have outlined the main paradigms of racial theory that have come to prominence since World War II. They point out that both "mainstream" and "radical" theories have generally treated race as a subordinate and derivative category, a "mere manifestation of other supposedly more fundamental social and political relationships" such as ethnicity, class, or nation.[8] It is well recognized that such views have directly influenced areas such as political action, public policy, and social services. What has not been as widely acknowledged is the impact these paradigms have had on theater activity, notably on nontraditional casting practices and culturally specific theaters.

"Color-Blind" Casting and the Ethnicity Paradigm

Among the various types of nontraditional casting, color-blind casting—like the model of a color-blind society it is supposed to exemplify—has been seen at once as the most idealistic and the most pernicious form. In its evolution, the notion of color-blind casting has displayed key characteristics of what Omi and Winant have designated as the "ethnicity paradigm." According to racial theories that follow this model, race is "but one of a number of determinants of ethnic group identity or ethnicity. Ethnicity itself [is] understood as the result of a group formation process based on culture and descent."[9] Consequently, it is believed that members of different racial groups, like members of any European ethnic groups that have immigrated to the United States, can eventually be fully incorporated into American life, sharing in all the rights and opportunities the country has to offer. These were the conclusions of a landmark collaborative study of the race situation in the United States funded by the Carnegie Commission and headed by Gunnar Myrdal. The findings and recommendations of the study were published in 1944 under the title *An American Dilemma*. The work discredited essentialist theories of race based on biology and saw as increasingly untenable the fact that American ideals of "democracy, equality and justice had entered into conflict with black inequality, segregation, and racial prejudice in general." In the face of this dilemma, assimilation was considered "the most logical and 'natural' response."[10]

Within the ethnic group paradigm, Omi and Winant have identified two major subgroups: assimilationists and cultural pluralists. In their words, the main point of disagreement between the two groups concerns "the possibility of maintaining ethnic group identities over time, and consequently the viability of ethnicity in a society characterized by what [has been] labeled 'Anglo-conformity.'"[11] The assimilationist view supported the granting of full rights to various ethnic groups and saw their complete absorption into the mainstream of American life as desirable and inevitable. Cultural pluralists, on the other hand, see immigrants and their descendants preserving group identity characteristics distinct from those of the country of origin but also different from those associated with other American communities.

In their evolution since the 1960s, casting policies that have professed indifference to an actor's race and ethnicity have shared key assumptions with racial theories modeled on the ethnicity paradigm. All such policies are predicated on the assumption that actors of different races, like actors of different European ethnic groups, can be brought together to create a unified and coherent whole. They differ, however, in regard to the degree to which racial difference can or should be elided. The cultural pluralist view is replicated in productions such as those of the New York Shakespeare Festival, particularly in the 1960s and 1970s, while the color-blind casting practices of the 1980s and 1990s most closely approximate assimilationist views. Before entering into a discussion of the parallels between social theories and theatrical practices, it should be recalled that the earliest instances of matching an actor with a role without considering race or ethnicity could not properly be called "color-blind." While race might not have been a factor in matching a particular actor with a particular role, it was important that audiences be very much aware of the racial diversity being presented on stage. As Joseph Papp put it, "I was thinking of ways to eliminate color as a factor in casting, but be on the other hand . . . very aware of color on the stage."[12] In fact, given the historical events that provided the context for the earliest innovations in casting, it would have been extremely difficult not to be aware of race.

Although Actors' Equity, the Dramatists' Guild, and local groups had begun to address the problem of desegregating theaters as early as the 1940s, such efforts did not meet with much recognition or success until the middle to late 1950s and 1960s. Of these ventures, Joseph Papp's New York Shakespeare Festival gained the widest recognition and lasting success. Closely tied to political and social movements of the time, the company's policies were described in terms of integration and desegregation, never in terms of color-blindness. Documents from that period emphasize that the NYSF was committed to integration at all levels: within the organization itself (both on stage and behind the scenes) and in its audiences. The September 13, 1965, semiannual report of the organization's Department of Education lists two of the main objectives:

- The desegregation of career opportunities for Negro and Puerto Rican minorities in the City of New York.

• More appropriate representation of minority groups at the administrative level of the Festival operation and on its Board of Trustees.[13]

The company's Mobile Theater performed plays by Shakespeare in public parks in all five boroughs of the city. The chosen sites included parks in predominantly black, Hispanic, and working-class neighborhoods. Photographs in the company's 1964 annual report reflected the racial, ethnic, and generational diversity of the audiences. Large families, groups of teenagers, and elderly couples were shown sitting side by side, watching white, black, and Hispanic actors performing on stage.

The range of reactions to these theatrical experiments paralleled the range of reactions to integration in other public institutions. The racially mixed casts did not seem to disturb either critics and reporters writing for New York City newspapers or audiences who watched the free performances. Reporters and critics rarely mentioned an actor's race in their reviews or feature articles. Most commonly, only when there was an accompanying photograph would this aspect of the performer's identity become evident. The casting policies of the NYSF were mentioned merely in passing. For instance, a critic reviewing the August 1963 production of *The Winter's Tale* simply noted: "The supporting cast is an integrated company with Negro players assuming the roles of Sicilian courtiers."[14] A 1965 study of audience reactions to the Mobile Theater's interracial production of *A Midsummer Night's Dream* revealed a similar response among spectators. When asked what they had liked best about the show (interviewees were never directly asked about their reaction to the casting), most respondents who spoke of the acting did not emphasize the casting. Rather they praised the acting in general terms or commented on the actors' ability to concentrate in the distracting conditions of an outdoor theater or on the way they "threw themselves into their parts."[15] Respondents who were most likely to focus on the racially mixed casting were middle-class African Americans. One black woman who was active in community affairs noted:

> I think for one thing a lot of people didn't expect the cast to be interracial, and I thought that was very nice. In fact, it was very helpful for the area, being that this is a predominantly Negro neighborhood. I think everybody thought it would just be an entirely white cast. You don't know that there are many colored—many Negro people—affiliated with Shakespeare. I told them [her neighbors] that there are.

They don't come to this neighborhood, and you just don't see it. . . .
It made the people realize that this was not only for white people, but
it was general for everybody. At first it was a shock [the integrated
cast] because nobody expected it.[16]

If popular audiences and those writing for mass circulation publications did not find the casting objectionable, this was not the case with
some critics affiliated with publications intended for a more education-
ally and culturally elite readership. John Simon, writing for the *Hudson
Review* and *Commonweal* at the time, deplored the very notion of popu-
larizing Shakespeare. In a 1965 piece entitled "Mugging the Bard in
Central Park," Simon said of the NYSF's casting practices: "Out of a laud-
able integrationist zeal, Mr. Papp has seen fit to populate his Shakespeare with a high percentage of Negro performers. But the sad fact is
that, through no fault of their own, Negro actors often lack even the
rudiments of Standard American speech. . . . It is not only aurally that
Negro actors present a problem; they do not look right in parts that historically demand white performers."[17]
The production that made it eminently clear that the NYSF productions of the 1960s were about color-awareness rather than color-blindness was an integrated *Antony and Cleopatra* that was to go on a six-week
tour of twenty southern cities in 1964. The tour was seen by Papp as "the
most appropriate way to commemorate the 400th anniversary of Shakespeare's birth." On April 11, 1963, the *New York Times* headline read, "Integrated Cast Will Act in South" and the project was described as "a
graphic illustration of racial harmony."[18] The company was to include
ten black actors (about half the company) and this time, they would not
just appear in supporting roles: a black actress, Diana Sands, was to play
the part of Cleopatra opposite Michael Higgins, who was white. It was
stressed that in any theater where the production was to be performed,
the seating would also have to be integrated. The significance of the
project was to be emphasized by having the production unveiled at a special performance in Washington, DC, for members of the cabinet and
other high government officials before it opened to the public in the
Howard University auditorium. It was noted that the project had the
"best wishes" of President and Mrs. Kennedy. Although Papp didn't expect "too much opposition," others apparently found the project ill-ad-
vised and he was able to raise only $11,250 of the $50,000 needed to

finance the tour. Its cancellation was announced on August 23, just five days before the Civil Rights March on Washington.

In a 1979 interview, Papp clarified his position: "I believe in integration, but not assimilation . . . I love the differences."[19] Differences were not only to be visual but aural as well. Although speech coaches might work with actors to change pronunciations that would make it hard for audiences to comprehend what was being said, no attempt was made to erase accents or alter speech patterns. Speaking about a Hispanic actor, Papp said, "The beat doesn't fall where you expect—but it's not incorrect—it's a way of grabbing the words, and it makes you listen to a familiar line in a new way."[20] When the NYSF formed a company to perform in the city's schools, he announced, "Our company will include black, Hispanic and Asian actors, and they will articulate Shakespeare in good American speech with their own particular cultural sounds."[21] Visible and audible differences were significant not only for their own sake, but because they were associated with deeper cultural differences. Papp believed that the way actors felt about the circumstances in a play, based on their own backgrounds and experiences in life, would inevitably show in their performances and prompt shifts of view among audience members. These differences clearly did not preclude inclusion in "mainstream American culture," here represented by the repertory of European classics.

In their rejection of assimilation and their joining of a desire to preserve difference within the context of a functioning unified whole, these statements emphasize the rapport between casting practices such as those of the NYSF and central assumptions of the ethnicity paradigm in its cultural pluralist incarnation. It is perhaps not entirely coincidental that the work to first articulate this position—Nathan Glazer and Daniel Patrick Moynihan's *Beyond the Melting Pot*—was published in 1963 and so was contemporaneous with the formative years of the NYSF. The authors moreover based their study on the social and political situation in New York, making their conclusions highly compatible with Papp's own perceptions. Glazer and Moynihan argued that immigrant groups formed "communities distinct not only from each other and their pre-existing sociocultural milieux, but also from their communities of origin"[22] and that these ethnic groupings and distinctions persisted even as the original immigrants established permanent residency, acquired citizenship, and produced native-born Americans.

As the work of desegregation proceeded, it eventually became possible to carry the conceptual implications of assimilationist theory to their full extent. In 1944, Myrdal had declared that if "America in actual practice could show the world a progressive trend by which the Negro finally became integrated into modern democracy, all mankind would be given faith again—it would have reason to believe that peace, progress, and order are feasible."[23] By the mid-1980s, the ideal of not merely an integrated but a color-blind society was being proposed. The vision offered was one of "the contemporary U.S. as an egalitarian society" whose recent history represented "a period of enlightened progress—an unfolding drama of the social, political, and economic incorporation of minorities which will not be thwarted or reversed. The 'color-blind' society . . . [was to] be the end result of this process."[24]

Concurrently, the notion of color-blind casting as it is understood and practiced today gained in popularity. It became generally accepted that one of the ultimate aims of color-blind casting should be to produce color-blind audiences who would retain this perceptual incapacity when they left the theater. The optimistic and visionary spirit of advocates of integration and color-blindness resonate in the words of Harry Newman, cofounder of the Non-Traditional Casting Project (now the Alliance for Inclusion in the Arts):

> We speak of actors and then of ethnic actors, as though they were of different kinds. We speak of writers and then black writers or Hispanic writers or Asian writers. If someone said, "I saw a terrific white play last night," it would sound ludicrous. Why is it acceptable the other way around? It is time to recognize all artists as individual artists first, apart from categories that only serve to limit our imaginations.[25]

Newman answered those who objected to nontraditional casting in general and color-blind casting in particular by reassuring them that

> Non-traditional casting does not of necessity imply tokenism or loss of identity. It's about having all artists considered as individuals with individual qualities, apart from belonging to groups based on often arbitrary distinctions such as skin color or ethnic origin. To be judged on individual ability is not "playing white" either. It is allowing each artist to bring whatever she is to her work.[26]

His comments bring to the surface the underlying conceptual frame-work of color-blind casting, which is aligned with theories that see racial structures and dynamics as approximating those of white European eth-nicity. Both are characterized as being similarly arbitrary distinctions and both are seen as elective features, which, ideally, can be made relevant or irrelevant, significant or insignificant, at will. As Newman puts it, "if a person is very involved with his ethnic or cultural background and it influences his choices, there is nothing wrong with that."[27] At the same time, all artists should be free to be recognized purely as artists without any racial or ethnic identification. Race and ethnicity are defined from the perspective of the individual rather than the group. It is to be hoped that individuals will have the option of assuming or shedding group identities in order for their unique personal qualities and abilities to be best appreciated.

In actual experience, however, an actor's racial characteristics con-tinued to be a significant factor. As I noted in the introduction, the Non-Traditional Casting Project organized actors' résumés and photographs into two parallel files—one arranged according to four categories of race or ethnicity (African American, Asian / Pacific Islander, Latino, Native American)[28] and the other according to character type (e.g., leading man or woman, older character actor, etc.) with actors of all races and ethnicities mixed together. Newman noted that this was "how we ulti-mately wanted people to think."[29] Meanwhile, actors themselves contin-ued to find that they were rejected for parts for looking too black or too ethnic, or not black or ethnic enough. Ellen Holly, an early member of the New York Shakespeare Festival, recalled that she was viewed as "in-appropriate for white roles because [she] was black and inappropriate for black roles because [she] was light."[30] Apparently, a few decades did not ameliorate the situation significantly. In 1992, an actor of a younger generation who self-identified as "inter-racial" noted that "because I'm perceived as a relatively light-skinned black actor, I just don't get cast in black roles. (In other words, if they want someone 'black'—why cast me?) The industry wants its identifiable types."[31] These experiences reflect both the persistence and the arbitrariness of racial categories. At the same time, they offer a telling illustration of the shortcomings of so-cial theories that seek to understand nonwhite race in terms of Euro-pean ethnicity. Far from race being subsumed under ethnic categories, ethnicity is subordinated, indeed is dissolved into what can only be described as race, in its reliance on biologically based physical characteristics. As Oakland-based director Benny Sato Ambush has noted, "The term 'color-blind' casting is a problem. Acting has to do with being seen."[32]

Culturally Specific Theaters and Cultural Nationalism

Unlike the connections between variations on the ethnicity paradigm of racial theory and the different stages of "color-blind" casting, which have been implicit rather than explicit, the links between calls for culturally specific American theaters and nation-based theories of race have always been overt. Nowhere is this more evident than in Wilson's keynote address, where he firmly identifies himself with the Black Nationalist movement of the mid-1960s—"the kiln in which I was fired"—and its antecedents extending back to the nineteenth century. Not only does he invoke the names of Martin Delaney and Marcus Garvey, leading thinkers of mid-nineteenth- and early twentieth-century Pan-Africanist movements, but the very line of his argument parallels those of nation-based analyses of race.

The common link discerned by Omi and Winant between approaches as diverse as Pan-Africanism, cultural nationalism, internal colonialism, and Marxist-influenced theories of race is the grounding of these movements in the dynamics of colonialism. In their words, "In the nation-based paradigm, racial dynamics are understood as products of colonialism and, therefore, as outcomes of relationships which are global and epochal in character."[33] Consequently, these approaches are multifaceted (i.e., they consider different elements of racial oppression such as social inequality, political disenfranchisement, territorial and institutional segregation, and cultural domination) and rely on a historical rather than a taxonomic conception of race. Present-day racial oppression is seen as a continuation of the national oppression that prevailed during the era of European colonialism, beginning with the expeditions of the fifteenth century and culminating in the colonial empires of the late nineteenth and early twentieth centuries. According to this model, the situation can only be remedied by the formation of "organizations and movements uniformly composed of the 'colonized' (i.e., victims of racial oppression)" and the promotion of "'cultural autonomy' to permit the development of those unique characteristics which the colonized group has developed or preserved through the ordeal of subjugation."[34]

Of the often divergent nation-based perspectives, cultural nationalist theories like those of Harold Cruse are particularly relevant for discussions of theater. Cruse saw cultural programs as an essential complement of economic, social, and political programs working to radically alter American society and to dislodge permanently the centuries-old racial order. In his view, the object of a cultural program would be to recognize "both the unique characteristics of black cultural traditions, and the essential part that these cultural elements—for example in music, art, or language—played in the cultural life of the U.S."[35] This cultural program along with its counterparts in other arenas would put an end to conditions associated with what has been characterized as "internal colonialism." The elements of internal colonialism pertinent to the situation in theater include

- A dynamic of *cultural domination and resistance,* in which racial categories are utilized to distinguish between antagonistic colonizing and colonized groups, and conversely, to emphasize the essential cultural unity and autonomy of each;
- Institutionalization of *externally based control,* such that the racially identified colonized group is organized in essential political and administrative aspects by the colonizers or their agents.[36]

The general correspondence between such views and the call for all-black or other culturally specific theaters is self-evident. Wilson's speech is exemplary in its application of these ideas to the debates over casting. His repeated characterization of color-blind casting as a form of cultural imperialism immediately situates it within the dynamics of colonialism, and his extended justification for independent cultural institutions deepens the correlation between sociological theory and theater practice. After establishing his theoretical affiliations, Wilson goes on to recall:

Growing up in my mother's house . . . I learned the language, the eating habits, the religious beliefs, the gestures, the notions of common sense, attitudes towards sex, concepts of beauty and justice, and the responses to pleasure and pain, that my mother had learned from her mother, and which you could trace back to the first African who set foot on the continent. It is this culture that stands solidly on these shores today as a testament to the resiliency of the African-American spirit.[37]

He specifies that the "term black or African-American not only denotes race, it denotes condition, and carries with it the vestige of slavery and the social segregation and abuse of opportunity so vivid in our memory."[38] The origins of black theater are traced to the cultural activity of the slave quarters where the African sought "to invest his spirit with the strength of his ancestors by conceiving in his art . . . a world in which he was the spiritual center" and to "create art that was functional and furnished him with a spiritual temperament necessary for his survival as property and the dehumanizing status that was attendant to that."[39] Wilson decries the constant failure to recognize the deep impact black art has had on American culture as a whole and ends with a summons to African Americans not to "allow others to have authority over our cultural and spiritual products" and instead "to become the cultural custodians of our art, our literature and our lives."[40]

In all forms of performance, particularly the dramatic, conceived according to cultural nationalist principles, racialized physical appearance functions as a powerful signifier of cultural integrity and authority. As Josephine Lee has written: "Cultural nationalism's reinvention of race sought to stress what it felt to be an indelible and inescapable racial difference, both biological and cultural. In direct opposition to integrationism, cultural nationalism reiterated, even insisted upon, the racial body as a reminder—not just a declarative statement, but an imperative—of difference."[41]

Casting Practices in the Era of Multiculturalism

The antipodes of complete color-blindness and total separation of the races have proved to be impossible extremes, as unrealizable as they are undesirable in society and in the theater. Apart from doubts about the very possibility of achieving color-blindness and getting beyond race, the desirability of these goals has been challenged with renewed energy as outside the theater the ideal of "color-blindness" and an attendant belief in universal themes and values have been appropriated to serve both conservative and liberal political interests in the 1980s and 1990s. Beginning under the Reagan administration, the principle of color-blindness has increasingly been invoked to contest legislation and institutional practices that were put in place to counter past and to prevent continued discrimination. Neoconservative arguments maintain that affirmative action and other programs designed to insure equal opportunity perpetuate racial divisions and institute reverse discrimination against whites. To counter this backlash, the neoliberal theme of "racial universalism" was introduced during the 1992 Clinton campaign as part of a strategy to acknowledge minority group constituents of the campaign while at the same time avoiding racially specific issues that risked alienating white voters. As Josephine Lee points out, liberal integrationism as a social policy and the parallel notion of blindness to color on stage carried with it certain paradoxes:

> Thus the paradox of colorblind casting is also the paradox of the ideology of liberal integrationism. On the one hand, since integrationism honed its racial philosophy in response to open demonstrations of racial inequality, it had to acknowledge and disprove the significance of existing differences and group affinities. On the other hand, integrationism saw these traits simply as exterior "masks" over an integral self, which must ultimately be rejected or at least relegated to secondary importance in order to achieve its ideal of color-blindness. Any emphasis on racial identity that would complicate the individual's entry into an unqualified "American" identity had to be discarded. Race thus became the actor's false mask over a more "universal" humanness; nonetheless it was a mask that maintained its stubborn presence no matter how hard one worked to eradicate it.[42]

Both neoconservative and neoliberal ideologies would surface in connection with controversies concerning casting decisions and practices during the 1980s and 1990s. The events that incited demonstrations, heated professional debates and press coverage unprecedented for a casting decision centered around the Broadway production of the musical *Miss Saigon*.[43] In the summer of 1990, British producer Cameron Mackintosh announced that Jonathan Pryce, who had been starring in the role of the Engineer in the London production, would play the part when the musical opened on Broadway. Asian American theater artists led by playwright David Henry Hwang and actor B. D. Wong protested against this decision; they sought the support of Actors' Equity in condemning the casting of a Caucasian actor in a part described as "Eurasian." Equity was asked to exercise its authority to deny foreign actors permission to perform in the United States. At a meeting attended by approximately half of the Equity council's sixty-nine members, the majority voted by a narrow margin to oppose the casting of Pryce. In his statement to the press, Alan Eisenberg, the union's executive secretary, said:

After a long and emotional debate, the Council has decided it cannot appear to condone the casting of a Caucasian actor in the role of a Eurasian. The casting of a Caucasian actor made up to appear Asian is an affront to the Asian community. The casting choice is especially disturbing when the casting of an Asian actor, in this role, would be an important and significant opportunity to break the usual pattern of casting Asians in minor roles.[44]

Eisenberg characterized the decision as a moral one.

Cameron's response was to announce the cancellation of the show, commenting that "Racial prejudice does seem to have triumphed over creative freedom."[45] He noted: "Equity has rejected our application solely on the grounds that Mr. Pryce is Caucasian. . . . By choosing to discriminate against Mr. Pryce on the basis of his race, Equity has further violated fundamental principles of Federal and state human rights laws, as well as of Federal labor laws."[46] In addition to being charged with reverse racism, Equity was accused of contradicting its own policy of promoting nontraditional casting practices.[47] Mackintosh compared the casting of Pryce as the Engineer to the casting of Morgan Freeman as Petruchio in the New York Shakespeare Festival's Central Park production of *The Taming of the Shrew*. Arthur Rubin, vice president and general manager of the Nederlander Organization, maintained, "The issue of an Asian role being played by a white man is an incorrect issue in this day and age, when we want blacks to be able to play whites and Asians to be able to play whites. . . . We are trying to establish the fact that anybody should be able to play anything."[48] *New York Times* theater critic Frank Rich wrote:

> By refusing to permit a white actor to play a Eurasian role, Equity makes a mockery of the hard-won principles of non-traditional casting and practices a hypocritical reverse racism. This is a policy that if applied with an even hand would bar Laurence Olivier's Othello, Pearl Bailey's Dolly Levi, and the appearances of Morgan Freeman in "The Taming of the Shrew" and Denzel Washington in "Richard III" in Central Park this summer.[49]

In response to such arguments, the Equity statement stressed that its decision was "aimed at creating equal casting opportunities for its minority members" and pointed out that "nontraditional casting was never intended to be used to diminish opportunities for ethnic actors to play ethnic roles."[50] For leaders in the Asian American theater community, those who sought to defend the casting of Pryce in the name of equal-opportunity recognition of artistic talent were passing all too quickly from the era when Asian roles, particularly leading ones, were invariably played by Caucasians to a phase where racial correspondence between character and actor was deemed irrelevant to the casting process. Dom Magwili, then director of the Asian American Theatre Project at the Los Angeles Theatre Center, noted that in an ideal world color-blind casting would be practicable and just. But, he said, "That's not the way of the world. Asian Americans have not been able to function in non-ethnic specific roles, but at least we had Asian roles. Now that door is closed. It becomes unacceptable and immoral for a white to dress in yellowface."[51] The Non-Traditional Casting Project, after considerable debate among the members of their board, came out in support of the casting of Pryce. Their decision, however, was based primarily on Mackintosh's assurances that Asian American actors would be hired to understudy Pryce and prepared to assume the role after he left the production. They felt the principle of respecting ethnicity when it was germane to the role was not being violated in this case since the character was described as a "one-half French, one-half Vietnamese wheeler-dealer."[52] Some Asian American artists were dismayed both by the loss of opportunities to showcase their talent as well as by the precedent being set by the actors' union's curtailment of artistic freedom. In a letter to the *Los Angeles Times,* producer and director Jon Lawrence Rivera recalled how proud he felt when he watched the London production of *Miss Saigon* in which more than half the actors were of Asian (particularly Filipino) descent. He wrote:

> I am not particularly proud right now, however, for all the commotion that my Asian peers have started, especially when 34 Asian actors (including Salonga's bravura portrayal of Kim) are being sacrificed due to the pigeonholing decision that Actors' Equity has taken. I believe in the principle that Equity is backing, but the signals it has sent are poisonous.[53]

Links between the views being expressed in the *Miss Saigon* casting controversy and contemporary political positions and events in American society at large were not merely implicit. Columnists, theater critics, and theatergoers almost immediately placed the events in the context of the "culture wars" that had erupted in the 1980s. George F. Will began his *Washington Post* column with the following assertions:

No matter how low your expectations for contemporary liberalism start, or how fast and far you lower them, there is no keeping up with the degradation of that dogma, as in the scandal of "Miss Saigon." The infrequency and inadequacy of liberal thinking is now threatening to take a new toll by darkening the Broadway theater in which "Miss Saigon" was to open next March.

That musical has thrilled audiences in London's West End. But in an act of real moral heroism, the producer has announced cancellation of the Broadway run rather than tolerate the liberal racism of an American union, Actors' Equity, which wants to dictate the racial composition of the cast in one crucial particular.[54]

Will designated Equity's actions and statements as instances of "dressing up reverse discrimination as 'affirmative action'"; he categorized the *Miss Saigon* controversy as part of Justice Brennan's legacy, which in Will's mind involved "giving a constitutional imprimatur to the poison of 'progressive'" racism seeping through the American system.

Such attacks were countered on the same terrain by people like Gordon Davidson, artistic director and producer at the Mark Taper Forum, who stated:

> The major threat to our artistic freedom today is coming from an atmosphere created by attacks on the National Endowment for the Arts from members of Congress, the government bureaucracy and right-wing groups across the country. The actors union (along with artists and arts supporters) has been a steadfast supporter in this struggle to counteract this suppression.
>
> [The] major challenge concerning artists of color is not fighting off demands from too-powerful minority groups (a real oxymoron) but continuing to empower people of color in our still far too insufficiently integrated society.[55]

Michael Omi has identified these developments in the realm of theater as "a classic example of racial politics in the post-civil rights era" when segments of the white population are expressing a "dissatisfaction, even hostility, towards the liberal racial reforms of the civil rights movement."[56] Nontraditional casting, like equal opportunity and affirmative action legislation, was intended to create professional opportunities that would counteract the historical prejudice against minority actors. In Omi's view, "At the heart of the 'Miss Saigon' controversy is a neoconservative backlash to the legitimate claims of racial minority artists." The arguments made in connection with the *Miss Saigon* debates, Omi noted, closely paralleled the backlash against the racial reforms of the 1960s in intellectual circles. In particular, he cited Harvard scholar Nathan Glazer's contention that affirmative action had subverted the very principles of the civil rights vision by making the United States a more rather than less color-conscious society. His summation of the neoconservative conviction that "attempts to remedy the plight of racial minorities are themselves discriminatory" and that "supporters of affirmative action are the new racists" could be used to describe the body of objections raised against the protest of Asian Americans and Equity's initial decision to bar Pryce. According to Omi, "Jonathan Pryce is not a victim of Actors' Equity or militant Asian American artist organizations; he is a victim of a long and sad history of racism in the organization and production of films, plays and television."[57] Omi suggested that Pryce, like a long line of actors before him, benefited from a particular kind of affirmative action that allowed white actors to play anybody while actors of color could not even be sure they would have the opportunity to "play themselves."

As the debates continued, the binary terms of the discussion became complicated by additional perspectives. The biracial identity of the Engineer was seen not just as an all-too-common subterfuge to justify the casting of a Caucasian actor in an Asian role, but as a defining characteristic that was not to be overlooked or dismissed. As playwright Velina Hasu Houston, who was president of the Amerasian League at the time, pointed out, if it was a gross distortion of the principles and practices of nontraditional casting to classify the casting of Pryce or any other Caucasian actor in a nonwhite role as "nontraditional," it was also questionable to claim that it was more appropriate for an Asian, rather than a Caucasian, actor to play Eurasians or Amerasians:

> "Miss Saigon" among other things, is about the Amerasian experience. Amerasians are neither American nor Asian. We are painfully, inseparably, blessedly and cursedly both. This conflict emphasizes that few understand Amerasian identity. It's sadly ironic that such a musical has led to a public battle about race—a battle where both sides ignore the fact that the character in question is biracial.[58]

As Houston (whose father is African American and whose mother is Japanese American) put it, it was hard "to listen to arguments about something being red or blue, when that something is actually violet. The role of the Engineer is neither Caucasian nor Asian; it is Eurasian—half Caucasian and half Asian. If the issue were simply about whether the role should be cast appropriately regarding race, then we should be lobbying for a Eurasian." Because of the complexity of the racial situation in the case of the Engineer, Houston felt that it was not the best battleground on which to take a stand on racially specific casting. She cautioned, "Minority artists must choose their battles carefully. If a battle is fought with blurred vision, the cause is set back." In her view, keeping Pryce from performing did little to solve three crimes: "misunderstanding race (an American affliction), the legacy of racism in American theatre, and the manipulation of the true spirit of non-traditional casting."[59] She further invited Asian Americans involved in the arts and literature to examine how their own policies had discriminated against multiracial Asians. By thus complicating the issues of racial identity and identity politics raised by *Miss Saigon,* which otherwise opposed minority to majority and Asian to white, Houston called for an expansion of the horizons of thinking about race in theatrical terms.

With the inclusion of complicating views like Houston's, the terms of the debates in the theater world further paralleled the evolution of conceptions and policies surrounding racial and ethnic identity. A call for recognizing the full complexity of cultural identity was introduced into the discussion. In 2007, David Henry Hwang himself would explore these complexities and ambiguities in a seriocomic play titled *Yellow Face,* which took his part in the *Miss Saigon* protests as a point of departure. In this new play, which mixes autobiographical experiences with fictional events, Hwang's alter ego inadvertently ends up casting a Caucasian actor as an Asian in one of his own plays. The attempts to cover up this mistake, along with the miscast actor's subsequent successful search for his nonexistent Asian roots, test the reliability of biological, sociocultural, and performative bases for constructing racial and ethnic identities. In an interview, Hwang explained that ever since the *Miss Saigon* controversy, "I've been trying to figure out how we can talk about some of these issues in a more nuanced way, and also more expansive. Not just about what it means to play Asian on stage, but what does it mean to play Asian in real life? How do we play race off the stage? Is it possible for an Asian person to be in 'Yellow Face.'"[60]

While it may be true that the positions taken on both sides in the *Miss*

Saigon debates either oversimplified or misrepresented key issues, *Miss Saigon* proved to be the right field on which to stage a confrontation because of the very prominence of the production. Since then, the presence of Asian American actors on stage and screen has increased noticeably—a change that has taken place in tandem with increased Asian American visibility in highly public fields such as politics and journalism. After Pryce left the role and in various touring productions, Asian American actors were always cast as the Engineer. The theater, film, and television industries have finally abandoned the practice of "yellowface" casting as well as what could be called "the Eurasian stratagem." In the *Miss Saigon* casting debates, most participants lost sight of the fact that the critical manipulation of racial categories to accommodate commercial interests and an audience's ability, or inability, to relate to characters across racial lines was not so much in the casting of Pryce as the Engineer, but in the writing of the Engineer as a biracial character. This stratagem in itself threatened to become something of a tradition ever since the protagonist in the 1970s television series *Kung Fu,* Kwai Chang Caine, was identified as biracial in order to make it possible to cast a Caucasian actor as the central figure. Caine was described as the orphaned son of an American father and a Chinese mother, raised in a Shaolin monastery. In contrast, in the post–*Miss Saigon* martial arts television series *Raven,* aired in 1992, the main character is also an orphan who has become an Asian martial arts master; but now there is no attempt to establish an Asian, in this case Japanese, genealogy for him. Jonathon Raven's links to Japanese culture are not biologically inherited, but skills acquired through choice and training. While this new scenario reflects the strong impact the *Miss Saigon* debates had on entertainment industry practices, it also reveals the ways in which institutions have the power to renegotiate racial and cultural categories in order to maintain the ascendancy of the dominant cultural group. For once the character was diegetically disengaged from an Asian or half-Asian body, producers were once again free to cast a white actor. Moreover, the background plot of *Raven* replicated the *Madama Butterfly / Miss Saigon* paradigm in that the eponymous character has a liaison with a Japanese woman who then dies after giving birth to their son. If the *Miss Saigon* protests had succeeded in establishing a stronger presence and voice for Asian American artists, there were distinct limits to the progress that had been achieved.

Casting and Racial Formation

The New York Shakespeare Festival's commitment to integration, August Wilson's advocacy for a black theater, the (mis)appropriation of the term *nontraditional casting,* and Velina Hasu Houston's breaking down of clear-cut racial identities and alignments, whether considered individually or *en masse,* affirm an understanding of race as "an unstable and 'decentered' complex of social meanings."[61] Rather than seeking to understand race in terms of the dynamics of other categories or concepts, we must posit race as a fundamental structuring and representational element of society. Instead of approaching race as a "problem" that should eventually and ideally be done away with, it should be seen as "an element of social structure rather than as an irregularity within it . . . as a dimension of human representation rather than an illusion."[62] Omi and Winant's account is particularly apt for understanding the manipulations of race unique to theatrical institutions in the context of social conditions and historical events because of their concept of racial formation. As they describe it,

> Racial formation . . . is a kind of synthesis, an outcome, of the interaction of racial projects on a society-wide level. These projects are, of course vastly different in scope and effect. They include large-scale public action, state activities, and interpretations of racial conditions in artistic, journalistic, or academic fora, as well as the seemingly infinite number of racial judgments and practices we carry out at the level of individual experience.[63]

Theater, then, is one of the many institutions taking part in the generation of racial meanings at the same time that they draw on conceptions already in circulation.

At the heart of Omi and Winant's model is a definition of race that restores the human body as a critical factor in understanding how social meanings become attached to race. Their definition states that "race is a concept which signifies and symbolizes social conflicts and interests by referring to different types of human bodies."[64] At the same time, they stress that "although the concept of race invokes biologically based human characteristics (so-called 'phenotypes'), selection of these particular human features for purposes of racial signification is always and necessarily a social and historical process . . . [T]here is no biological basis for distinguishing among human groups along the lines of race." They also remark that "the categories employed to differentiate among human groups along racial lines reveal themselves . . . to be imprecise, and at worst completely arbitrary."[65] It must be recognized that nowhere have these precepts been more visibly and provocatively demonstrated than in the innovations in casting that have been introduced since the 1960s.

CHAPTER THREE

Bodies Like Gardens

Classical Tragedy and Comedy in Color

'Tis in ourselves that we are thus or thus. Our bodies are our gardens, to the which our wills are gardeners.

—IAGO, *Othello*, 1.3

He used to come to the house and ask me to hear him recite. Each time he handed me a volume of *The Complete Works of William Shakespeare*. . . . He wanted me to sit in front of him, open the book, and follow him as he recited his lines. I did willingly. . . . And as his love for Shakespeare's plays grew with the years he did not want anything else in the world but to be a Shakespearean actor.

—TOSHIO MORI, "JAPANESE HAMLET"

They All Want to Play Hamlet

Toshio Mori's fictional account of a young man's growing ambition to become a Shakespearean actor would be unremarkable were it not for the fact that the character in question is named Tom Fukunaga, a Japanese American born and raised in California in the 1920s and 1930s. As things turn out in this particular story, years go by without any visible progress being made toward his goal of becoming a classical actor, until finally the now not-so-young man's family and friends urge him to grow up, forget his dream, and get a real job. Interestingly, however, it is never openly suggested or even indirectly implied that Tom's ambitions are futile because of his race or ethnicity. Earle Hyman did hear such admonitions in his real-life version of this story with its far more successful outcome. In an interview that appeared as he was about to open on Broadway in the role of Colonel Pickering in Shaw's *Pygmalion,* Hyman recalled how as a young actor he adored Shakespeare and walked around with a volume of his work under his arm. An older actress who saw this asked why somebody hadn't "told that boy that he's colored?" But, Hyman said, "I couldn't help it; I loved the plays that weren't written for me."[1] Carl Sandburg's poem "They All Want to Play Hamlet" could have been written for people like the young Earle Hyman and Tom Fukunaga:

> They all want to play Hamlet.
> They have not exactly seen their fathers killed
> Nor their mothers in a frame-up to kill,
> Nor an Ophelia dying with a dust gagging the heart,
> Not exactly the spinning circles of singing golden spiders,
> Not exactly this have they got at nor the meaning of
>   flowers—O flowers, flowers slung by a dancing
>   girl—in the saddest play the inkfish, Shakespeare,
>   ever wrote;
> Yet they all want to play Hamlet because it is sad
>   like all actors are sad and to stand by an open
>   grave with a joker's skull in the hand and then
>   to say over slow and say over slow wise, keen,
>   beautiful words masking a heart that's breaking,
>   breaking,
> This is something that calls and calls to their blood.
> They are acting when they talk about it and they know
>   it is acting to be particular about it and yet: They
>   all want to play Hamlet.[2]

Sandburg's tribute to Hamlet and the actors who long to play him regards author, play and players alike with the same mixture of admiration and familiar affection. The solemn and the humorous are juxtaposed, as the most melancholy of the inkfish's ill-fated creations is coveted by aspirants even though they cannot really relate to the characters or fully comprehend all aspects of the drama. They are irresistibly drawn by the power of the "wise, keen, beautiful words," the striking images, and rending emotions; but just as influential, Sandburg reminds us, are the popular mystique and the professional prestige that envelope the role. The role's iconic status carries with it a host of clichéd attitudes and expressions, the repetition of which constitutes a performance in itself. Until relatively recently, however, not every person and not every actor could aspire to the onstage and offstage performances described in the poem; to do so has been a sign of cultural privilege.

The racial dimensions of this privilege become apparent when a turn-of-the-century popular song titled "I Want to Play Hamlet" is considered alongside Sandburg's poem. The lyrics of the song were written by Paul West and the music composed by John W. Bratton.[3] Published around 1903, the sheet music's cover depicts gross caricatures of two black men in Elizabethan costume, both speaking mangled lines from Shakespeare. The figure in the foreground holds a black skull in one hand and declaims, "Impureious Caesar! At last, poor Yorick, now get thee to Melindy's Henroost." The one in the background has a stranglehold on a chicken and wonders, "Two bee, or not two bee," as two bees with dancing feet hover around his head. In the lower left corner, the two gravediggers are gambling, with one calling out "Roll dem bones" as he throws the dice. The three stanzas and chorus tell the story of Bill Johnson, "an actor coon" who was a star as a dancer, but decided he was qualified "to elevate de stage" and perform Shakespeare because his uncle used to shine Edwin Booth's shoes and he had inherited his talent. He chooses to play *Hamlet,* "the melancholy swede," for his dramatic debut. On opening night, the house is packed with people wild to see the "Ethiopian Hamlet." But Bill is seized by stage fright and his company fails him. Ophelia gives in to the audience's demands for a cakewalk and then, "Dat fixed de play; de whole black troupe jes dropped de Shakespeare game, / An' busted into ragtime, till poor Johnson wept in shame."[4] But still, "His voice could still be heard as he exclaimed with bitter tears:

> (*Chorus*)
> I want to play Hamlet, An' do de straight legit . . .
> "To be or not to be" Mah voice will fit.
> Ah got a plenty talent, Ah'm an artist bred,
> Ah'm a gwine to play Hamlet, And kill 'em dead, dead, dead, dead
>   dead![5]

The point made by the song—that while black performers could provide excellent entertainment with popular forms of African American culture, it was presumptuous and ludicrous to think they could be serious actors in classical roles—was visually expressed by the sheet music's cover. A small black-and-white photograph inset amid the flagrantly racist caricatures depicts an elegant black couple in full evening dress— Charles and Dora Dean Johnson, the first African American dance team to perform on Broadway in 1897. The Johnsons were known for their elegant and expensive costumes and for their stylization of the cakewalk that turned it into a high-stepping show dance.[6] The contrast between the flattering portrait of the dancing Johnsons and the raw denigration of the fictional acting Johnson indicates what was at stake ideologically when it came to recognizing the right and ability of African Americans to perform Hamlet and other Shakespearean roles. As Ania Loomba points out in her foreword to *Colorblind Shakespeare,* the cultural prestige of Shakespeare gave his plays the symbolic power of a double-edged sword in confrontations between dominant and subordinate cultures:

> Because of the global cultural capital of Shakespeare, people disenfranchised on varied grounds have felt empowered by laying claim to his plays. At the same time, of course, such claims reinforce the authority of dominant culture in all sorts of ways, suggesting that Shakespeare and other Western works are indeed of universal relevance or value and making difficult a critique of their ideologies and prejudices.[7]

Nontraditional casting practices, when applied to Shakespeare's work as well as to other canonical tragedies, comedies, dramas, and musicals have the potential to cut either way: they can have the effect of reinstating the social and cultural norms that were dislodged by the civil rights movement and its aftermath, or they can continue to deconstruct normative practices and assumptions that sustain a monocultural society reliant upon the assimilation or the suppression of difference. In the best-case scenarios, multiracial casting approached as a process rather than a product leads to explorations on the part of both artists and audiences of how race and ethnicity function as material constructions and imaginary conceptions. Given the indisputable cultural prominence, ideological force, and exceptional variety of Shakespeare's plays, it seems logical to begin by focusing our attention here.

By the time previously all-white theater institutions presenting European classical tragedy and comedy were prepared to integrate in the 1960s, there were many African American actors with extensive professional experience in theater and film. Historically black colleges and universities along with community, semiprofessional, and professional groups were maintaining an African American tradition of performing European and North American classics begun in the previous century. Shakespeare's plays, which dominated the repertory, were presented both with and without adaptation.[8] Many were performed with a racially neutral approach, minimizing the impact of the actors' race on the interpretation of the text. Those that were adapted constituted the first examples of "cross-cultural" casting, incorporating African Americans' cultural heritage, contemporary experiences, and artistic forms, particularly music. During the 1930s, the Federal Theatre Negro Units of New York and Los Angeles performed cross-cultural versions of *Macbeth* (the 1936 "voodoo" and the 1937 African adaptations respectively). In 1936, the Chicago unit staged an updated *Romeo and Juliet, Romey and Julie,* set in Harlem. The feuding groups were native Afro-Americans (Romey's family) and recent immigrants from the West Indies (Juliet's family), who considered themselves socially and culturally superior to the longtime Harlem residents.[9] Also staged during this period were notable musical versions of *A Midsummer Night's Dream* (*Swingin' the Dream,* 1939) and *The Taming of the Shrew* (Seattle Negro Repertory Company, 1939). These adapted productions by all-black or predominantly black companies established a performance tradition that has been continued in the present by the work of the African American Shakespeare Company in San Francisco and the Classical Theatre of Harlem.

By the time Paul Robeson performed his Othello on Broadway with an otherwise white cast in 1943, there was therefore an African American tradition of performing Shakespeare both as canonical drama and as popular theater that was more accessible to a mass audience. By World War II, black actors had also performed works by Sophocles, Euripides, Molière, and Oscar Wilde outside of academic settings. In 1955, Earle Hyman became the first African American actor to be invited to join a professional company with a classical repertory—the American Shakespeare Festival Theatre in Stratford, Connecticut. He played two of the roles most often associated with black actors—Othello and Caliban, but was also cast without regard to race in *King John* (the French lord Melun), *The Winter's Tale* (the rogue and thief Autolycus), *Hamlet* (Horatio), and *Antony and Cleopatra* (Cleopatra's attendant Alexas). Nevertheless, Robeson and Hyman, along with William Marshall, who played Othello with the New York Shakespeare Festival in 1958, proved to be exceptions, and through the 1950s black actors were generally not considered for classical roles in professional theater productions. In 1959, Actors' Equity Association organized what could be seen as the original nontraditional casting showcase. The playbill for the "Integration Showcase" at the Majestic Theatre in New York called upon "all responsible creative elements of the theatre arts to grant freedom of choice, to cast aside preconceptions regarding the casting of Negro artists, to extend their scope and participation in all types of roles in all forms of American entertainment."[10] The New York Shakespeare Festival under the direction of Joseph Papp had already begun to apply this policy, as discussed in chapter 2, integrating the casts and bringing the productions to the racially and ethnically diverse audiences of New York City. Casting truly was without regard to race, and black actors played English kings and queens, members of the European nobility, Roman patricians, comic figures, and fairies. One of the first performances by an African American actress was in the role of Desdemona in a 1958 production of *Othello*. The innovation may have been more significant from the actor's perspective than the audience's, however, since Ellen Holly was so light skinned that the visual contrast with William Marshall's Othello remained.

As companies presenting European and American classics began to diversify their casts, certain patterns emerged. Shakespeare's plays, which dominated classical repertories especially outside of major cities, were considered the most hospitable sites for interracial casting. This can be attributed to the fact that they were at the same time very familiar and very unfamiliar to audiences. The author and plays themselves were familiar because of their inclusion in school curriculums and the film versions of Shakespeare's works that reached a wide public. For willing spectators, any alterations or modifications instigated by changing casting traditions could be absorbed or comprehended more readily and more effectively since reception was already grounded in prior experiences and familiarity with the dramatic works. At the same time, the fictional worlds were distanced in time by anywhere from about four hundred to three thousand years (as in the case of *Troilus and Cressida*) and in place. This distance was reinforced by the language of the plays, so that there was no familiar lived reality against which to match the staged representations, only prior productions and other print or media representations of those eras. Classical Greek tragedy has proved similarly hospitable, but, because of the sheer volume of the Shakespearean canon, the vast host of characters it contains, and the greater appeal of the Bard's work in Anglo-American cultures, it is through an examination of Shakespeare's plays that the history and politics of nontraditional casting in the United States can most comprehensively be traced.

Under the leadership of artistic directors committed to integration and making classical theater accessible to all members of their community, companies located in large cities with racially and ethnically diverse populations took the same approach as the New York Shakespeare Festival. In such theaters—which included the Inner City Cultural Center (Los Angeles), the Milwaukee Repertory Company, and Los Angeles Theatre Center—actors of color played a full range of roles. In areas where the population was predominantly or almost exclusively white or where a theater's artistic or administrative leadership was more conservative or cautious, black actors (it is rare even now to find Latino and Asian American professional actors performing in classical theater companies except on the West Coast and in cosmopolitan cities in other parts of the country) were and still are often cast in a manner that would be least likely to provoke controversy. Avoiding controversy generally means achieving the closely linked objectives of minimizing alterations to the text ("tampering") and not offending the social sensibilities of almost exclusively white middle-class audiences. Although the casting strategies that seemed best able to achieve these ends were first used when federally enforced integration and equal employment legislation had just been introduced in the 1960s, companies located away from major urban areas would still have to follow such practices decades later to introduce nontraditional casting to their audiences. Controversy was most easily avoided by having black actors play characters who are non-European and, if not black, at least brown. For male actors, the category comprised Othello, Caliban, Aaron the Moor in *Titus Andronicus,* and the Prince of Morocco in *The Merchant of Venice.* For women, options were far more limited, with only Cleopatra fitting into this category. A similar logic led to the common nontraditional casting choice of having black actors play supernatural or mythical characters such as Oberon, Titania, Ariel, and Hippolyta, Queen of the Amazons. The actors' physical differences served to accentuate the fact that they are beings of an order totally different from that of the ordinary mortals who peopled the stage.

A more enterprising conceptual approach involves using racial differences in the casting to underscore opposing sides in any form of conflict. Plays involving military conflict lend themselves particularly well to this type of race-conscious casting because of the clear binary oppositions incorporated into the structure of such dramas. In the 1988 production of *Coriolanus* at the Old Globe Theatre (San Diego), white actors were cast in the roles of the Romans while the Volscians were actors of color. Tullus Aufidius, General of the Volscians, and his two main guards were played by African Americans and his Lieutenant was an Asian American. *Romeo and Juliet* has been one of the most obvious and popular choices for this approach. Productions on stage and screen have cast one family as black and the other white[11] or one as Anglo-American and the other Latino.[12] Interracial casting in *Romeo and Juliet* often involves updating and geographical transposition through the set and costume design, but the lines themselves have proved exceptionally accommodating to such shifts. The principle of visible differences made it possible for the National Asian American Theatre Company to stage a production of *Othello* (2000) without deviating from its policies of performing works "as written, with no forced cultural association" while exclusively casting actors of Asian heritage. In this production Othello was played by an actor whose multiethnic heritage included Turkish and Filipino ancestors as well as Europeans. His physical appearance, however, would commonly be characterized as white or Caucasian, so that he stood out in isolation against a cast of visibly Asian American actors—Filipino, Japanese, and Chinese Americans.[13]

In the above instances, few or no adjustments to the text are necessary and interpretations can follow established critical traditions. This general approach to race-conscious casting minimizes the possible objections of those opposed to radical revisions of canonical texts, those who were resistant to integration in the 1950s and 1960s, and those who continue to feel that having actors of color in classical plays is an inappropriate intrusion of the social and political into the realm of art. Even here, however, acceptance depends on spectators' tolerance for innovation and change, whether theatrical or social.

The history of the Oregon Shakespeare Festival in Ashland typifies in many respects the trajectory of multiracial casting in resident theater companies outside of the most racially and ethnically diverse cities. The company was founded in 1935 in a county where the black population grew from twelve in 1950 to fifty-one in 1970.[14] Information on the development of diversity at the OSF from 1950 to 1997, compiled by Judy Kennedy, shows that the 1950s and 1960s saw one African American actor per decade.[15] On both occasions, the actors were cast in *The Comedy of Errors*—Patricia Norman played the courtesan in 1950 and Adolph

Joshua Spafford (Othello) and Tina Horii (Desdemona) in the 2000 National Asian American Theatre Company production of *Othello,* directed by Jonathan Bank. (Photo by Carol Rosegg.)

Caesar an officer in 1962. It was not until the early 1970s that black actors began to appear more regularly as the company expanded and increased the number of productions offered each season. Mostly, actors were hired to play "black" roles—Tituba in *The Crucible* (1972), Othello (1973), Aaron the Moor (1974), Cal and Addie in *The Little Foxes* (1976), or Crooks, the Negro stable hand in *Of Mice and Men* (1980)— and then also performed smaller parts in the season's rotating repertory of historical and modern plays. Keith Grant, for instance, performed the role of the Duke of Suffolk in *Henry VI, Part 1* in addition to Cal. As Alan

Tina Horii (Desdemona) and Tess Lina (Emilia) in the 2000 National Asian American Theatre Company production of *Othello*, directed by Jonathan Bank. (Photo by Stephen Petrilli.)

Armstrong points out in his study of multicultural casting at the OSF, it was the need for "theatrical economy" rather than a commitment to a color-blind approach that first introduced race-neutral casting as a practice at the OSF.[16]

During the 1980s, there were years when no black actors worked with the company and others when three or four would be in the company. The years when larger numbers of black actors were on the roster were years when the plays co-created by Athol Fugard, John Kani, and Winston Ntshona—*Sizwe Bansi Is Dead* (1980) and *The Island* (1981)—and Fugard's "*Master Harold" and the Boys* (1987) were being presented. In addition to the types of roles already mentioned, what Armstrong describes as the "exotic" or "alien" roles like Oberon and Hippolyta were also given to black actors:

> During this period, then, one of great ferment for urban theaters actively embracing the possibilities of multicultural casting, the Oregon Shakespeare Festival was moving much more slowly towards diversity, with a fluctuating, tiny minority of actors of color . . . but, at least nominally, a policy of color-blind casting. Locally, to predominantly white audiences and OSF leadership, these changes seemed momentous and sufficient.[17]

In a 2003 interview, Derrick Lee Weeden (whose first season at the OSF in 1987 included roles as Oberon, a murderer in *Macbeth,* and Dodger in *The Shoemaker's Holiday*) recalled how limited the opportunities for classically trained African American actors were at that time: "At the time I came to the Festival there were maybe only two or three theaters in the country that were interested in diversity. New York Public Theatre and Milwaukee Rep had reputations for being interested in a diverse outlook. . . . [O]ut of 30 auditions I would have had maybe 3 or 4 offers for other than traditional black roles."[18]

Beginning in 1992, the situation at the OSF moved in a direction that sets it apart from many other similarly situated companies. In the 1990s, the Festival had two new artistic directors—first, Henry Woronicz (1991–95) and then Libby Appel (1995–2007)—who actively sought to build a company of actors, directors, and designers that would reflect the cultural diversity of the country. Beginning in 1993, for the first time actors who self-identified and presented as Latino, Asian American, and Native American began to appear regularly in dramatic roles.[19] In 1997 Timothy Bond was appointed associate artistic director and developed the OSF's diversity program, which includes diversity forums for all company members and a career development program to attract young professionals of different cultural backgrounds. By the close of the decade, of the company's seventy-three actors, sixteen were African American. Beginning with the 2000 season, the OSF adopted the following mission statement:

> The mission of the Oregon Shakespeare Festival is to create fresh and bold interpretations of classic and contemporary plays in repertory, shaped by the diversity of our American culture, using Shakespeare as our standard and inspiration.

By 2002, with some thirty actors of color performing in featured roles, the OSF could claim to have "the most diverse theatre company in the West."[20] During the 1990s, these actors played roles in works by Shakespeare, Molière, Sheridan, Wilder, and Lorca, as well as in contemporary plays. The critical mass of black actors who wanted more opportunities to perform works that reflected their cultural heritage and experiences also led to plays by African American, African, and African diaspora playwrights in the repertory every year. Works by Latino writers also started appearing on OSF stages: Octavio Solis's *El Paso Blue* (1999) and Nilo Cruz's *Two Sisters and a Piano* (2001). Both productions were directed by African Americans, Timothy Bond and Andrea Frye respectively. Interestingly, however, although the OSF had started including modern European and American drama in its repertoire in the 1970s (prior to this it was primarily works by Renaissance and Jacobean playwrights that had supplemented the Shakespearean productions), it was not until 1998 that actors of color began to be cast in works by authors such as Chekhov, Brecht, or Tennessee Williams (a phenomenon that will be discussed in greater detail in the following two chapters).

Initially, a color-blind approach to nontraditional casting was taken at the OSF. In a 1996 letter to the town newspaper, the *Ashland Daily Tidings,* associate artistic director Fontaine Syer, who coordinated the OSF's diversity efforts before Bond joined the company, stated, "Unless a play is about race or gender, the Festival casts without regard to race or gender."[21] As always, this move was appreciated by some viewers and deplored by others, with the latter being more vocal about their feelings. The *Ashland Daily Tidings* became a forum for expressing different reactions. The positive reactions are represented by a letter one woman wrote in June 1996:

> I hope the day will come when we can see beyond skin color to the essence of a person. I commend the OSF for its color-blind casting honoring talent as the means for selection.

Writers who protested against racially mixed casting were primarily disturbed by this approach when it involved characters who were members of the same family. Reactions to productions of *The Winter's Tale* (1996), *Coriolanus* (1996), *Romeo and Juliet* (1996), and *Cymbeline* (1998) included the following comments:

> You should understand that some of us can see that black is not white and become overly upset when you try to con us.
>
> Casting—when characters are related in plays please make some attempt to match the race. One brother as played by a black actor while the other brother is played by a white actor does not work.
>
> I could not reconcile a white-skinned King and a white-skinned Queen and their offspring was a young black woman. She was gorgeous; but that did not work out for me.
>
> Klotten [*sic*] could not stay in character. His movements were too ethnic. The interracial couples did not work. This casting distracted from the authenticity of the play. It appeared that diversity was given top priority over acting skills and suitability for the role.[22]

Racially mixed casting was often described as an inappropriate application of the principles of "affirmative action" and therefore characterized as instances of "political correctness" (as seen in the examples of letters already quoted in chapter 1). This last position was most succinctly articulated by a letter writer when Libby Appel cast a black Ophelia as the daughter of a white Polonius in her 2000 staging of *Hamlet:* "Diversity is a political, not an artistic cause. Whatever happened to art for art's sake."[23] Appel's response to such objections also brings an important clarification to the way in which multiracial casting was expected to make a significant impact on the artistic process: "It has nothing to do with political correctness. It's the enrichment as a result of people of various backgrounds coming together to explore the play. I don't expect people to not see the difference, I expect them to take it in."[24]

The objections of the audience members who had indeed taken in the differences but didn't like what they saw expose the anomalies that characterize discussions of nontraditional casting and race in a multiracial and multiethnic society. While all the writers framed their objections in terms of "black" and "white," no one mentioned that several actors in leading roles were Hispanic or Latino—Juliet was played by Vilma Silva, Romeo by Mikael Salazar, Benvolio by Triney Sandoval, and Balthazar by

Lorenzo González. Silva and González have worked with one of the most politically active Chicano theaters, El Teatro Campesino, and Silva would play the part of Maria Celia in OSF's *Two Sisters and a Piano* in the 2001 season. Those who complained that an "affirmative action" or "politically correct" approach was being applied to casting did not comment on the substantial presence of actors who belong to the second major group that benefits from affirmative action legislation. Evidently, they were simply considered "white" and their presence was therefore untroubling to spectators. Furthermore, while letter writers noticed that Lord Montague and Lady Capulet were black, they identified Lady Montague as white, when in fact the actress who played her, Demetra Pittman, is both African and Asian American. Her acting résumé includes the Lady in Blue in Ntozade Shange's *For Colored Girls Who Have Considered Suicide When the Rainbow is Enuf*, Lena in Fugard's *Boesman and Lena*, and Luna C in Regina Taylor's *Oo-Bla-Dee*. So that while objections may have been made on the grounds of genetic plausibility, DNA actually had little to do with it. As long as actors looked and acted "white" on the stage, their genetic makeup, status under federal government legislation, and racial, ethnic, or cultural heritage was considered irrelevant.

Such resistance to nontraditional casting can be seen as symptomatic of what Gina Marchetti has characterized as "that fundamental contradiction within the American psyche between the liberal ideology of the 'melting pot' and the conservative insistence on a homogeneous, white, Anglo-Saxon, American identity." She further notes that "this division is usually a false one since the liberal call to 'melt' presupposes a white, English-speaking 'pot.' "[25] When Latino or biracial actors are light-skinned and speak English with standard American accents, they blend in. Negative attention focuses on African Americans who do not blend in, particularly when interracial sexual relations are depicted or implied. Armstrong suggests that "a possible explanation for the different responses is that anxiety about racial miscegenation, rather than offense to the logic of theatrical realism, actually fuels these impassioned denunciations of color-blind casting."[26] While not all the negative reactions to racially mixed casting can be attributed to antimiscegenist sentiments, the well-documented history of *Othello* certainly demonstrates that deep-seated racism is most likely to surface in the theater when interracial sexual relations are represented. The case of the La Habra Community Theatre's 1990 production of *Romeo and Juliet* reveals the extent to which such feelings may continue to exert pressure on theater companies, particularly those that depend on homogeneous local support. The community theater had scheduled a production of *Romeo and Juliet* for fall 1990, with Marla Gam-Hudson as director. An emergency meeting of the theater's board of directors was called after Gam-Hudson placed ads seeking a black Romeo in the Los Angeles theatrical trade publication *Dramalogue.* Her intention had been "to make the main relationship interracial as a commentary on bigotry."[27] According to the director, some board members were concerned that "La Habra's 'predominantly older' audience 'would not easily accept a mixed racial relationship' in the play," and told her that "casting a *Romeo and Juliet* of different races was 'an exciting idea but just not appropriate for this community theater at this time.' "[28] One member of the board of directors told the press that their decision to stop the director from casting Romeo and Juliet as an interracial couple did not preclude a multiracial cast; the board just did not want the play to be cast "in a way that emphasized racial differences between the families or the lovers." He added that "the board's concern was less with casting than with changing the focus of the play. . . . They did not want some sort of racial message one way or another placed on 'Romeo and Juliet.' "[29] The city's representative on the board, Gregory Kind, said the decision was not racial in nature, pointing out that the theater had staged several multiracial productions in the past, and explained that the board wanted a "traditional version" of Shakespeare's play to provide the audiences with "a point of comparison" for *West Side Story*, which would be the next play of the season. The *Los Angeles Times* reporter who covered the story closed his article by noting, "Non-traditional casting in theater is not a new concept but has become an increasingly controversial issue."[30] As examples, he cited two other productions of Shakespeare's plays, both of which involved interracial couples in which the man was black and the woman white: *Romeo and Juliet* at the Cornerstone Theater in Port Gibson, Mississippi, and a 1987 La Jolla Playhouse production of *The Tempest*, in which Ferdinand was played by a black actor and Miranda by a white one. In the end, the board rejected Gam-Hudson's casting plan. Although no interracial couple appeared on the stage, outside the theater, a group of actors protesting the decision performed a skit featuring a black Romeo and a transvestite Juliet.[31]

Sometimes, as much as the vocal protests that have greeted multiracial productions, the silence of those who accept and even favor nontraditional casting offers pertinent insights into the politics and principles of nontraditional casting. Since the early days of integrated casting in the late 1950s and 1960s, it has been a tacit understanding that if the director casts a production without regard to race, an actor's race is not to be mentioned in professional critical reviews. A company's general policy to use a color-blind approach to casting and the absence of any indication in press releases, interviews, program notes, or the production itself that the visible cultural identity of the performers is central to the directorial conception will be taken as a signal concerning the appropriate mode of reception. As a result, there have been occasions when a production has been race-coded, but this was not brought to the attention of the general public or press and never figured in the reviews.

An exemplary case is the *Coriolanus* directed by Tony Taccone for the Oregon Shakespeare Festival's 1996 season. Coriolanus, his mother Volumnia, and his young son Martius were played by African American actors (Derrick Lee Weeden, Debra Lynne Wicks, and D'Marion Joseph). Coriolanus's wife, Virgilia, was played as a blonde white woman by Cindy Basco. None of the other principal characters were black. Dramaturg Barry Kraft's program notes stress the political content and politicized production history of the work in Nazi Germany and Stalinist Russia, its adaptation by Brecht, and its role in inspiring Gunter Grass's *The Plebeians Rehearse the Uprising.* The director's note that appeared in the souvenir program elucidated his interpretation of *Coriolanus* as a play about class warfare that corresponds to the situation of the United States at the close of the twentieth century:

> There is a war currently being waged in the United States: a war between those benefiting from profit-taking and those who do not have the means to do so; a war between those championing the ethos of "survival of the fittest" and those seeking to preserve the economic and social contract of Roosevelt's New Deal and Johnson's Great Society; a war over who has the right to lead and the rights of those who do not, over who has the right to citizenship and the very definition of freedom.[32]

Taccone concludes by endorsing an approach to Shakespeare that draws out a play's "pressing questions for the society in which we live," since "This is, after all, what Shakespeare's legacy is all about: a way to imagine the past, to examine the present, to reinvent the future."[33] Taccone's statement speaks of economic disparities and inequalities in access to power, but the word *race* is never uttered. In his interview with Alan Arm-

Coriolanus (1996). Oregon Shakespeare Festival. Directed by Tony Taccone. Debra Lynne Wicks (Volumnia), Derrick Lee Weeden (Coriolanus), D'Marion Joseph (Martius), Cindy Basco (Virgilia). (Photo by Christopher Briscoe.)

strong, however, Derrick Lee Weeden confirmed that the director "explicitly used casting to make the play speak to the multicultural society of the United States in 1996, impelled by the discovery of a thematic resemblance between the family of Coriolanus and inner-city African-American families, in the tangled threads of social alienation, matriarchal family structure and masculinity expressed through acts of violence." Reinforced by the contemporary aspects of the costume design (a mixture of contemporary and ancient Roman clothing and props) and frequent references to American popular culture, "this distinction of color invited a different take on the Coriolanus family, as relative outsiders in the patrician ranks (excluding Virgilia, presented as a blond trophy wife), and changed the valence of Coriolanus' fierce pride."[34] While reviewers did refer to the parallels Taccone drew between Rome in the early fifth century BC and America in the late nineteenth century, no one suggested that the racial distribution of roles made the actors a material bridge between Shakespeare's representation of the emerging Roman republic and our own era.

The inhibitions that seem to apply where race is concerned (except for people who are most offended by having their attention drawn to it) do not carry over to nontraditional casting where gender is concerned. In 2001, Penny Metropulos directed a production of *The Tempest* in which Prospero was played by a woman, Demetra Pittman.[35] Pittman, a leading member of the company since 1986, self-identifies as nonwhite. While she is actually of both African and Asian descent this is not evident from her physical appearance. Prospero was now the Duchess of Milan and the usurper was her sister Antonia. Prospero's retreat to the island became an opportunity for self-reflection with inflections of Asian spirituality. Ariel was played by Asian American actor Cristofer Jean, draped in saffron in a manner reminiscent of Buddhist monks. Both he and Prospero used hand gestures that seem inspired by Hindu mudras. In her program note, Metropulos stated: "Gender is not the issue of this production. Casting Prospero as a woman has only helped us explore the themes in a new light."[36] A woman in the role of Prospero made it easier to make the play more about forgiveness than revenge and to transform Prospero's studies in isolation from a quest for knowledge and power into a search for self-reconciliation. Caliban, incidentally, was played by a white actor, which helped remove the focus from the colonialist aspects of the drama, which have been emphasized in many recent productions.

Whether because of the authorization conferred by the director's direct address of the gender issue, or because gender was not a socially and politically contested issue in the 1990s as it was, for instance, during the era of the women's liberation movement of the 1960s, critics also felt free to take up the subject. The reviewer for the *Ashland Daily Tidings* said: "the woman Prospero seems to be trying to regain those very worlds of emotion and the senses that she put aside when seduced by the power of the intellect, of knowledge, of magic."[37] Ron Cowan from the *Salem* (Oregon) *Statesman's Journal* commented, "Part of the freshness of this conception is the new dynamics of mother-daughter, sister-sister and a woman acting with maternal rather than paternal passion."[38] In an article in the *Jefferson Monthly,* Molly Tinsley, speculated, "If *The Tempest* teases us into surrendering our preconceptions about what is real and what imagined, if as Prospero concedes at the end of the play such concrete structures as towers, palaces, and temples are as insubstantial as dreams, what does that make our propositions about gender?"[39]

The Tempest (2001). Oregon Shakespeare Festival. Directed by Penny Metropulos. Demetra Pittman (Prospero) and Christofer Jean (Ariel). (Photo by David Cooper.)

The volubility, articulateness, and comfort level so apparent in discussions of gender present a striking contrast with the silence surrounding race, both in the printed materials produced by the OSF and in the published reviews. Taken together, the professional silence and the public objections point to a lasting legacy of tension that has adhered to American race relations since the colonial era. While there may be ob-

jections to cross-gender casting, they have rarely displayed the same ve-
hemence and accusations of "political correctness" that objections to
cross-racial casting have shown. After all, everyone in the audience is either a woman or else has a woman as a mother, sister, wife, or daughter.
Casting a woman as Prospero or Hamlet or Lear brings a radically different perspective to the play that may be disputed, but this new interpretation does not take the drama or the theatergoing experience out of the
realm of a familiar cultural context—the system of white middle-class values and experiences shared by almost everyone in regular audiences of
theaters with classical repertories. If, however, the gender switching were
also to challenge heterosexual norms, reactions could be expected to be
much more openly hostile almost anywhere outside of places like New
York City, San Francisco, or Los Angeles. Casting members of nonwhite
racial and ethnic groups, particularly when this is done in a way that reminds audiences of historical and ongoing competition for social, political, economic, and cultural power and resources, forces spectators out
of the comfort zone conferred by sociocultural dominance.

Even when theaters and directors are interested in exploring the possibilities for new interpretations and stagings through nontraditional
casting, experiences of the past forty years have shown how important it
is for artists of color to be in decision-making positions and for actors of
color to achieve critical mass within a company. In the absence of these
conditions, multiracial casting may be used in ways that subtly or not so
subtly draw on cultural stereotypes and contribute to reifying them.[40]
For instance from the 1960s to the present, African American women
have often been cast in the roles of strong and domineering women like
Lady Macbeth, Goneril, Regan, Volumnia, and the Queen in *Cymbeline*.[41]
Rarely, if ever, has an Asian American woman performed these roles in a
racially mixed company. On the other hand, Asian women have been
found playing Juliet, Cordelia, and Agnes in Molière's *School for Wives*.[42]
Questions about stereotyping in casting and directing choices were
raised in 1977 in relation to the La Mama Experimental Theatre production of *Macbeth* directed by Jonas Jurasas, a Lithuanian exile. Ellen
Foreman, reviewing the production for the *Black American*, questioned
the racial perceptions that may have led to having Barbara Montgomery
be Lady Macbeth in a cast that was otherwise white, except for one Asian
actor. Foreman asked: "Was it intentional to link sexuality and evil with
blackness? For what other purpose is the interracial aspect stressed?"[43]
One might also wonder about the casting of the only other nonwhite cast

member—the Asian actor played a doctor. Armstrong notes that the pre-1990s history of the Oregon Shakespeare Festival raised questions along these lines: "Why assign African-American actor Susan Champion the role of courtesan in *The Comedy of Errors;* put onstage a black Jane Shore, the mistress of King Edward merely mentioned in *Richard III;* or invent a scene for *Othello* in which a black Bianca (Champion again) is groped by a crowd of Venetian officers and soldiers?"[44]

African American men have been readily cast in the parts of men of power and action, both mature and young: Lear, Macbeth, Coriolanus, Tullus Aufidius, Brutus, Achilles, Ajax. *Coriolanus* and *Julius Caesar* were the first two plays chosen for the NYSF's Third World Company in 1979. The Achilles (Timothy Stickney) in the Washington Shakespeare Theatre's 1992–93 *Troilus* and the Tullus Aufidius (Keith Hamilton Cobb) in their 1999–2000 *Coriolanus* are young African American men with long braids or dreadlocks and impressive physiques, which audiences are given opportunities to admire without the impediment of shirts.[45] But in the forty years since multiracial casting first became an established practice, certain roles still do not come as readily to actors of color. The most notable of these is perhaps Hamlet.

Although African American actors have played Hamlet since the nineteenth century, it has either been in Europe or in all-black American productions. Earle Hyman for one, made his debut in the role in 1951 in a production directed by black playwright, poet, director, and professor Owen Dodson for the Howard University Theatre. Hyman was twenty-five at the time. Errol Hill summarizes Dodson's assessment of Hyman's performance, as he described it for the Hatch-Billops oral history collection:

> [H]e played the prince "as a tortured youth. It had a quality of such beauty . . . that all Washington came out to see it. We turned away 500 people from our little theatre on the last night." In his view, Earle Hyman's Hamlet was equal to or better than all the professional Hamlets of the age. It was meditative and of deep understanding. The feeling of inner torment was conveyed by the actor's speaking of the soliloquies almost in a whisper. This gave a mystical quality to the performance and had a strong effect on the audience.[46]

Although Hyman played Horatio to Fritz Weaver's Hamlet for the American Shakespeare Festival Theatre, he would never reprise the title role of the play in a racially mixed professional production. On the occasion when a black actor, Cleavon Little, did perform the role of Hamlet in a New York Shakespeare Festival production, it was in a drastically truncated ninety-minute "pop" version of the tragedy created for a four-week touring program in the city's parks. In this adaptation, Little's Hamlet was plotting to overthrow his white stepfather, who apparently was made up to resemble Fidel Castro. Gertrude was described by the *New York Times* critic as "an aging red-haired beauty who probably once hustled in a Havana bar." The review concluded: "Unfortunately, however, Shakespeare was not writing about either Caribbean politics or a biracial societies, nor did he write the outline for an absurdist comedy, which is the way this *Hamlet* winds up."[47] The only high-profile instance of a black actor playing Hamlet in the United States was the American tour of Peter Brook's 2000 production with Adrian Lester in the title role.

The Ocular Proof: Re-casting the Tragedy of Othello

More than any other classical play, Shakespeare's *Othello* has demonstrated that human bodies are gardens not only for the human will but for the social and historical processes that define racial identities. *Othello* offers particularly fertile ground for semiotic analyses of race in performance because of the exceptionally rich variety of casting configurations it has invited. First of all, it provides the most common example of cross-racial casting in the Western tradition: white actors playing the parts of nonwhite characters. Well into the twentieth century, more than one professional critic has been known to argue that black actors should not perform the role of Othello because "Shakespeare wrote this part for a white man to play."[48] Overviews of the production history of Othello from 1604 through the 1990s demonstrate convincingly that racial sensibilities, varying according to time and place, influenced the manner in which the figure of Othello was imagined by critic, performed by actors, and cast by directors.[49]

It is indisputable that Othello's cultural identity as a "Moor" was always considered one of his most important attributes as a dramatic character. It is also apparent from the earliest recorded reactions that a reader's or spectator's attitudes toward peoples of different races and cultures, especially those distinguished by their skin color, affected their response to the character and therefore to the play as a whole. It is well known that in his 1693 essay, the earliest known criticism of the play,

Thomas Rymer derides the notion of a Negro being appointed to an elevated station in Venice and being allowed to wed an aristocratic lady:

> The Character of that State is to employ strangers in their Wars; But shall a Poet thence fancy that they will set a Negro to be their General; or trust a *Moor* to defend them against the *Turk*? With us a Blackamoor might rise to be a Trumpeter; but *Shakespear* would not have him less than a Lieutenant-General. With us a *Moor* might marry some little drab, or Small-coal Wench; *Shakes-spear,* would provide him the Daughter and Heir of some great Lord, or Privy-Councellor: And all the Town should reckon it a very suitable match: Yet the English are not bred up with that hatred and aversion to the *Moors,* as are the Venetians, who suffer by a perpetual Hostility from them.[50]

It is less well known that this sardonic critique was answered by Charles Gildon, one of Rymer's contemporaries, who defended Shakespeare's choice of a black protagonist with an indictment of racist attitudes that used skin color as the basis for condemnation and subjugation. (Apparently, Gildon considered distinctions based on class to have a more legitimate foundation than those based on race.) His recommendation that poets be lauded rather than condemned for presenting an ideal situation rather than the unfortunate reality where cross-cultural or interracial relations are concerned could serve to answer modern criticism of nontraditionally cast productions:

> 'Tis granted, a *Negro* here does seldom rise above a Trumpeter, nor often perhaps higher at *Venice.* But then that proceeds from the Vice of Mankind, which is the Poet's Duty, as he informs us, to correct, and to represent things as they should be, not as they are. Now 'tis certain, there is no reason in the nature of things why a *Negro* of equal Birth and Merit should not be on a equal bottom with a *German, Hollander, French-man,* &c. The Poet, therefore, ought to show Justice to Nations as well as Persons, and set them to rights, which the common course of things confounds. . . . The Poet has therefore well chosen a polite People to cast off this customary Barbarity of confining Nations, without regard to their Virtue and Merits, to slavery and contempt for the meer Accident of their Complexion.[51]

While literary critics may have debated the issue of Othello's racial identity and the implications it may have held for the meaning of the play as early as the seventeenth century, actors and audiences from the Renaissance through the eighteenth century do not seem to have been greatly troubled by the question. Marvin Rosenberg's examination reveals that Othello's cultural origins do not enter discussions of actors' interpretations until the nineteenth century, when it was used as an additional justification for Edmund Kean or Tommaso Salvini's unusually passionate, even violent, impersonations. Nor was it ever suggested by the many white actors who played the two principal male roles through the nineteenth century, that racial hatred was partly to blame for Iago's concerted efforts to destroy Othello. Othello's racial and cultural difference provided a convenient tool or vulnerable point to be exploited, but was not in itself considered a motivating element.[52] By the 1990s, as we shall see, this idea would become so widely accepted that any apparent elimination of racial prejudice as a contributing factor to Iago's actions would draw protests.

Virginia Mason Vaughan's historical and sociocultural research corroborates Rosenberg's evidence that until the nineteenth century, the circuits of theatrical production and reception functioned in the same manner for *Othello* as they did for Shakespeare's other tragedies.[53] Except for the use of blackface makeup to alter an actor's complexion, no divergences from rhetorical, costuming, or movement practices were employed. Seventeenth- and eighteenth-century depictions of Othello based on performances always show him dressed as an upper-class English gentleman or military officer in contemporary clothing, sometimes even including a powdered wig. Vaughan concludes that "for actors and audience alike, race seems not to have been a controversial issue in public performance. Blackface might have hidden the actor's facial expressions, but it did not necessarily signify Otherness. Othello was conceived as an officer and a gentleman, not a representative of an alien culture. Beset by a villainous hypocrite, he is tempted from without, not from within."[54]

This situation would change significantly in the nineteenth century. While many of the changes reflected general shifts in performance practice that were initiated in the previous century (notably the greater concern with historical and cultural authenticity), Edward Pechter discerns a new "nervous kind of excitement" surrounding theatrical productions of *Othello,* which he connects with the increased racial self-consciousness of nineteenth-century thought.[55] He relates the concern with racial issues in Shakespeare's *Othello,* as expressed in the writings of literary critics such as Lamb and Coleridge and the performances of actors like Edmund Kean, to a broader racial anxiety, an anxiety that must be placed in the context of European colonial encounters with Africa and the Near East and the destabilization of black-white relations in the United States. Under these conditions, the question of whether Othello was imagined or should be played as a black sub-Saharan African or a tawny North African Moor emerged as a literary, historical, ideological, and pragmatic problem. Vaughan argues that beginning in the nineteenth century, audience response no longer depended on relating to Othello as "one of us," as had been the case through the mid-eighteenth century. Henceforth, both an actor's portrayal of the Moor and an audience's response were complicated by the need to balance dual demands: the compulsion to conceive of Othello as being essentially different while at the same time remaining able to empathize with him as a tragic figure.

Apparently, for audiences in Great Britain and on the European continent, where African American actors Ira Aldridge, Morgan Smith, and Paul Molyneaux performed the role many times, having a black actor in the role did not necessarily disrupt audiences' ability to relate to the character and action in the accustomed manner. While their appearances were met with hostility or derision by some, most reviews and descriptions of their performances show that viewers were able to apply the same criteria as they would in judging a white actor.[56] In the United States, however, it would seem that in the face of Othello's essential difference, the quality of essential sameness had to be secured by having the Moor played by a white actor. This practice was assured by the systematic repression of black performers and companies that sought to enter the domain of classical drama.[57] With black actors barred from the American stage, audiences had to deal with the question of race only on the diegetic plane. As any spectator with minimal theatrical competency would understand, whatever they were witnessing was in actuality taking place between a white male and a white female and therefore not an appropriate trigger for racist outrage.

Valuable testimony regarding the strategic separation of the race of the actor and the race of the character is offered by Charles B. Lower in his study "Othello as Black on Southern Stages, Then and Now." His arguments are based on evidence from regions that historically have exhibited the most hostile attitudes toward interracial sexual relationships, particularly between a black man and a white woman. Lower refutes the common impression that the popularity of *Othello* in the antebellum South, equal to that in other parts of the country, must be attributed to local perceptions of the work as an antimiscegenation play.[58] Citing the evidence of numerous reviews and other eyewitness accounts, he maintains that just like northern audiences, most southerners watching the tragedy "recognized Iago as its villain and not as the scourge of abhorrent miscegenation, and sympathized with a tragic *blackamoor* Othello."[59] The knowledge that beneath the black or brown makeup was a white-skinned actor allowed spectators to empathize with the racial "other" who was routinely denigrated in discourse and subjugated in practice. Lower further demonstrates that this empathy did not rely on having Othello made up as a tawny Moor rather than a darker-skinned African, basing his conclusion on both established theater practices and verbal accounts of actual performances in southern theaters. He suggests that the frequently cited examples of negative reactions to a black Othello, invariably attributed to southern racial prejudice, can just as well be ascribed to a lack of theatrical sophistication. He argues that for southern audiences Shakespeare functioned as the ultimate theatrical signifier of the cultural sophistication of a city. To confuse the fictional and the real would be a mark of provincialism. As a representative of "consummate Art," the action and characters of *Othello* were removed from the realm of everyday attitudes toward race. At the same time, Lower acknowledges that the screen between art and life lowered by Shakespeare's elevated status would never have withstood the reality of a black actor in the title role until desegregation had effected profound changes in southern life and institutions. He writes, "Theater as Art kept Othello from being 'the negro part' on the stages in the slaveholding South. *Othello* thus could and did flourish on antebellum southern stages, could and did move those audiences." But, he continues, "No antebellum southern audience would have been prepared for the 'untheatrical' experience of a black actor as Othello."[60]

This said, it must also be recognized that beginning in the nineteenth century, the process of reception as I have outlined it would not apply to all segments of the audiences. For if Othello was no longer easily identified as "one of us" by his traditional audiences—white spectators, particularly those formed by Anglo-Saxon cultural values—new readers, performers, and audiences for Shakespeare were emerging who could now claim Othello as one of them. This new audience was brought into existence by three hundred years of slave trading between Africa and the Anglophone territories of the Western Hemisphere and by the nineteenth-century British colonial incursions into Africa, the Middle East, and Asia. Despite the thwarted attempts of all-black professional companies to perform Shakespeare in the 1820s and again in the 1880s, an African American tradition of performing Shakespeare was developed by individual performers, small amateur or semiprofessional groups, and all-black colleges and universities. Once classical works could finally be included in the repertories of professional black companies and previously all-white theater companies were integrated in the twentieth century, a new tradition for casting Othello was forged in theater institutions on both sides of the Atlantic.[61] In the United States, Paul Robeson's historic 1942–43 performances introduced the practice of casting black actors as Othello in otherwise white companies. While it would still be possible for a white actor to play Othello in a professional production through the 1960s, and even into the 1970s in some parts of the country, Robeson's performance marked the beginning of an irreversible trend toward having the role reserved for black actors. Occasionally, exceptions may be made for actors of color with star status (for example, Raul Julia, who performed Othello as recently as 1991 in the New York Shakespeare Festival's outdoor production), but by and large it is now the casting of a nonblack actor as Othello that has become "nontraditional." Unless color-conscious casting is part of the production concept, it has become untenable for white actors to play the role in the United States or United Kingdom.

Since 1990, *Othello* has indeed provided fertile ground for some of the most innovative experiments with race-conscious casting. Because of the exceptionally tight concentration of the action, which each principal character performs a vital role in constructing, casting against tradition in any one role has profound repercussions for all the characters and their interrelationships. Three productions took particularly provocative approaches to race-switching: in the first variation, Iago and Emilia as well as Othello were cast as black; in the second, Iago and Othello were played by black actors; and in the third Othello was white, while Desdemona, Iago, Emilia, and all the other characters with speaking roles, except Bianca, were played by black actors. These casting permutations radically revised or subtly complemented standard interpretations of the text of *Othello* and at the same time transformed theories of race into practice.

Iago and Emilia, the Moors of Venice

The Shakespeare Theatre Company

Over the past two centuries, directors, actors, critics, and scholars have constantly returned to two central questions: what were Iago's motives for destroying Othello, and how could a man of Othello's stature and achievements be so easily manipulated?[62] Satisfactory answers to these complementary questions form the foundation on which interpretations not just of the two roles but of the play as a whole rest. Director Harold Scott, a former Othello himself, says he always had trouble believing Iago—not because of the way the part was acted but because of the way it was written. He points out that even George Bernard Shaw "found it impossible to believe that a man as brilliant as Othello could be this stupid."[63] In his 1990 production of *Othello* for the Shakespeare Theatre Company (then known as the Shakespeare Theatre at the Folger), Scott solved the double problem of Iago's motives and Othello's trust through a radical application of nontraditional casting: he cast African American actors in the roles of Iago and Emilia.[64] For Scott, the common racial identity of the principal actors made it possible to construct a shared past history that would have forged strong cultural and personal bonds between Othello (Avery Brooks) and Iago (Andre Braugher). Scott imagined Othello and Iago as having come to Venice together. Their common cultural origins and past experiences, combined with their shared status as partially assimilated outsiders, would place Iago in a special close relationship to Othello that could explain the latter's willingness to believe his innuendoes concerning Desdemona and Cassio. These same factors would magnify Iago's sense of betrayal and rejection when Othello promoted Cassio. His resentment would be compounded as he watched Othello solidify his position in Venetian society by marrying a highborn Venetian lady, but fail to use his power and influence to make sure that Iago advanced with him.

Scott saw his casting decisions as "filling a void" by adding "a sociological rationale that makes what Shakespeare wrote more credible for a contemporary audience."[65] When asked if the casting of Othello, Iago, and Emilia as black would diminish Othello's isolation, thereby altering the dynamics of the play, Scott replied: "No, rather it heightens [his isolation] because three people can be isolated as one. If a culture locks you out, it doesn't lock you out just individually."[66] The new dynamics cre-

Andre Braugher as Iago and Franchelle Stewart Dorn as Emilia in Shakespeare Theatre Company's production of *Othello,* directed by Harold Scott. (Photo by Joan Marcus.)

ated by the casting were to be understood in cultural rather than racial terms. When asked if Iago's betrayal of Othello intensifies because it becomes a racial betrayal, he responded:

> No—I've had critics ask me if it's Black on Black crime. Well, yes, I suppose that's there, but what I meant was more of a cultural than a racial betrayal. If you and I come from similar circumstances, such as

the same home town, I would think there are grounds for trusting you beyond the people of the culture we're both alien to. Iago's racist remarks then become simply anything he can grab at to dig Othello to Roderigo, the "white boy."[67]

The conception and casting of Iago were unconventional in another sense as well. It has been the custom to cast actors who seem equally matched as adversaries in the roles of Othello and Iago; in age, they are almost always contemporaries. Scott, however, was struck by the line that gives Iago's age as twenty-eight ("four times seven years" 1.3.313), making him significantly younger than the Moor. Envisioning Othello's relationship to Iago as that of a mentor provided an even more powerful explanation for the intensity of Iago's desire to destroy Othello's happiness—enormous love has turned to hate. When Scott restaged the production for the 1993 Great Lakes Theater Festival in Cleveland, in an interview with the *Plain Dealer* he proposed a specific scenario in which Othello had rescued Iago when he was a boy, raised him as a son, and saw him married to Emilia before they all came to Venice. We could say that according to this version, events are sent along their tragic course not because Othello failed to believe in Desdemona's love but because Iago lost faith in Othello's love. Scott explains: "Othello's choice of Cassio is purely political. I see Cassio as the epitome of a West Point cadet, unsophisticated about the workings of politics, untried in battle. Othello promotes him but not with any intent of overlooking Iago. He has better plans for Iago later, but being a very private man, he never tells Iago about them." Iago's "devotion and dependency on Othello are such that he can't do without him. When that connection is taken from him, he snaps completely."[68]

All the modifications to the fabric of the play were to be conveyed without any alteration of the original text. The impact of the nontraditional casting was to be conveyed solely by visual impressions and the effects created when unfamiliar images were juxtaposed with the familiar text. In her review of the production for the *Shakespeare Quarterly*, Miranda Johnson-Haddad captures the powerful transformative effect the altered visual configurations could have on an audience's perceptions of the individual characters and their interpersonal dynamics:

[B]y far the most significant and provocative visual impressions resulted from the fact that the actors playing Iago and Emilia were both African-Americans. . . . Frequently one of the most obvious visual fea-

tures of a traditionally cast *Othello* is that Othello himself stands out as
a solitary figure among the white Venetians; his difference is palpable,
and in many productions this difference is further emphasized by
Othello's native African or specifically Moorish garb. In this production, however, it was Othello and Iago who stood out together. In
scenes involving Othello, Iago, Emilia, and Desdemona, it was Desdemona who stood out. In Cyprus, Desdemona became the outsider,
and as the play progressed, we had an increasing sense that she had
fallen into a situation where the customs were not her own and she
did not know the rules of the game. Emilia's "Is not this man jealous?"
was thus more than the commonsense observation of someone with a
more objective perspective on Othello's behavior than Desdemona
possessed; it was the recognition of someone more familiar with Othello's background and cultural context than Desdemona could perhaps ever hope to be.[69]

The casting of black actors in the leading roles of Iago and Emilia, as
well as in various nonspeaking parts, was reinforced by the costume design and musical score. Daniel Lawson's costume designs were
influenced by North African textiles and clothing. Othello makes his entrance wearing an African robe (specifically a form inspired by the dress
of the nomadic North African Tuareg tribe, which includes a headdress
that covers the head and all of the face except the eyes) over which he
dons a Venetian gown for his meeting with the Senate. The links between Othello and Iago are stated visually by having both wear blouses of
brightly colored African cloth that show beneath their black doublets.
Both also appear wearing Tuareg turbans and necklaces with crosses, indicating that Iago has also converted to Christianity. Lawson intended
the layering of fabrics to reflect cultural layering. He says of Othello, "He
has adopted the Venetian conventions, mostly for the sake of appearances, but the fabric closest to his body is always African."[70] Iago, on the
other hand, never appears in full African dress, although Emilia wears
bright African gowns and jewelry.

The historical and ethnographic details were meant to work with
rather than displace the other layers of characterization or serve as a sub-
stitute for other dimensions of the action. Scott actually found the au-
tumnal nature of the play to be even more significant than the racial issues. Brooks was interested in exploring the ties between racism and
sexism and the hierarchy of relationships, noting that "it's too convenient

to talk about it simply in terms of color."[71] Braugher was in harmony with the more senior members of the cast, stating, "I don't think it's a play about race, but about pride and love gone bad." His primary concern was to make the character of Iago "a real human being"—"a very proud and loving man" who was reacting to severe emotional pressures.[72]

For Scott and the actors, it was important that all elements of this "Afrocentric" production be compatible with the dialogue and situations of Shakespeare's text. Scott points out that the rich multicultural nature of the Mediterranean—particularly in cosmopolitan Venice and on Cyprus, an island located at the eastern end of the sea—would have made the presence of Moors along the European shores a common occurrence, especially following their expulsion from Spain in 1492. Consequently, Othello need not have been an isolated figure or unique in becoming partially assimilated into the social and political structures of the state of Venice. The association of Othello, Iago, and Emilia with the Tuareg tribe of Mauritania (Avery Brooks's contribution) not only respected the text but strengthened or enriched its logic. From his study of African cultures, Brooks learned that Tuareg society was matrilineal and women were able to choose their husbands—hence Othello's delight rather than alarm when Desdemona took the initiative to indicate her interest in him as a spouse. But Tuareg culture also authorized the sacrifice of an unfaithful wife, so that in Othello's mind, Desdemona's death would not have been a passionate murder born of jealousy, but a resolution required by social and religious custom.

Culture rather than race may have been the primary concern of the artists involved in producing the Shakespeare Theatre *Othello,* but once the play had opened, discussions were framed primarily in terms of race—or the absence of race as an issue. The *Washington Post* drama critic, Lloyd Rose, gave the production a very positive review, affirming that the risks taken by the director and cast had resulted in a vital and memorable performance of the play. His enthusiasm, however, was built on a rather questionable foundation, reflected in the bold opening assertion: "With one stroke of nontraditional casting, the director Hal Scott cuts 'Othello' loose from racial melodrama and reestablishes it as pure tragedy." For Rose, "Iago's racial hostility toward his general and victim, inevitable with a white actor in the role, is removed as a motive, and we get to see his villainy in its sheer malignant egotism."[73] The implicit assumption that racialized attitudes are only a relevant factor when members of different races are placed in direct opposition overlooks the structural and systemic nature of racism and its durable and pervasive effects, which are not suddenly called into being at moments of interracial contact. When asked about Rose's remark, Brooks replied, "On the contrary, a black Iago deepens the issue of race."[74] When he met with black high school students from northeast Washington who had seen the production, Brooks encouraged them to heed the lessons that nontraditional casting had added to Shakespeare's play. He told them, "The lesson of a black Iago is profound for black people. When you betray your brother, you plot your own death, the death of your people and the death of your culture. We must never forget that we need each other. We must learn to value life again." Apparently, this was a point readily understood by his listeners. According to one sixteen-year-old, *Othello* was about "one black man undercutting another. . . . A black Iago allowed me to update what was happening in Shakespeare's day with what is happening today on the streets."[75]

When the production was restaged for the Great Lakes with Delroy Lindo and LeLand Gantt playing Othello and Iago respectively, the play itself was contextualized by well-publicized events that would foster links with black American history and culture. A daylong symposium titled "Othello the Moor: Approaching Shakespeare's Majestic Tragedy from African-American Perspectives" was cosponsored by the theater festival and Cleveland State University's Black Studies Program. In a move contrary to Rose's impulse to cut Shakespeare loose from social concerns such as race relations, the conference sought to examine "the links that unite literature, the performing arts and society's conscience."[76] Free performances of Lonne Elder's *Splendid Mummer,* a one-man play about the life and career of Ira Aldridge, were offered during the month preceding *Othello*'s run. In the first of several articles reporting on the production, the *Plain Dealer*'s theater critic Marianne Evett characterized the play as "a story of jealousy and betrayed trust that also examines racial divisiveness" and told readers: "Director Scott, who staged the Great Lakes production of 'Paul Robeson' in which Brooks starred last season, intends to focus on the racial issues by casting black actors in the roles of Iago, Othello's nemesis, and Emilia, Iago's wife. The casting will add another dimension to Iago's betrayal of Othello's trust."[77] While this may not have been a completely accurate statement of Scott's intentions, judging by the material released for the Shakespeare Theatre production, Cleveland audiences were nevertheless being prepared to watch this version of *Othello* in a manner that foregrounded black-white relations. The production concept may have been the same as in Washington, but a different frame had been placed around it.

After noting the innovative casting of Scott's production, almost in passing, the reviewers for the New Jersey, Washington, and Cleveland versions inevitably fell back on traditional criteria for discussing the production. Rose, as we have seen, felt the casting eliminated the question of race. In his discussion of the original Rutgers Art Center production, the *New York Times'* Alvin Klein said only, "Much publicity has attended the casting of a black Iago. Although Shakespeare's setting—Venice and Cyprus—remains unchanged, presumably they are members of a North African tribe."[78] In her review for the *Plain Dealer,* Evett wrote: "This 'Othello' is different from others because Scott has cast black actors as Iago and his wife Emilia, as well as a few ensemble members. But the idea does not seem revolutionary—it seems perfectly natural here."[79]

With the changes in casting, the most problematical moments are obviously those where the now-black characters utter racially derogatory lines or hear them spoken by others. Where previously Othello was the only target, Iago and Emilia are now implicated, even when the words fall from their own mouths. Act 1 presents the first challenges with racial slurs being vindictively and manipulatively cast about by Brabantio, Roderigo and Iago himself in scene 1. Shortly thereafter, in 1.3, Iago appears to be reacting angrily when Brabantio utters racist slurs and is calmed by Othello's gestures. Before the Venetian Senate, Iago's "solidarity" with Othello is conveyed mimetically through facial expressions and gestures and phenomenally through the material presence of his black body. The contrast between Iago's words and behavior in act 1, scene 3 and act 1, scene 1 provide evidence of his duplicity and malice no matter how the role is cast, but a black actor is confronted with new choices in deciding how to play the opening scene, which now inevitably adds new dimensions to the betrayal. We have already seen Scott's explanation of the exacerbated perfidy, and another common suggestion would be that Iago, tainted by a racial self-hatred fostered by living in a society that considered him inferior, was trying to prove to himself and to others that he had more in common with the white Venetians than the black Othello. As with all complex plays and roles, Braugher's performance could have accommodated more than one interpretation without disrupting the coherence of the production. Whichever answer makes the most sense to a spectator, the important fact is that suddenly, after decades, even centuries of a circumscribed range of possible characterizations, an entirely new set of interpretive possibilities was opened up by the casting.

The same is true with a black Emilia. The unfamiliar casting serves to focus much-needed attention on a role that is too often considered of secondary importance. In fact, little or no attention was paid to the effects of switching Emilia's cultural and racial identity in the public discussions of this production. Neither Franchelle Stewart Dorn, who played Emilia, nor Jordan Baker (Desdemona), was interviewed for the issue of *Asides* that focused on the winter 1990 season. Dorn's performance drew one sentence in Lloyd's lengthy review of the production (Desdemona got three), which merely said, "Franchelle Stewart Dorn turns in her usual strong work as Emilia."[80] Allying Emilia with Iago and Othello culturally and racially was in fact a key move, serving to define the dynamics between the four major characters as much as the decision to have a black actor play her husband. If Emilia were still to have been played by a white actress and therefore identified as Venetian, Iago's status in relation to Othello's would change radically and the entire balance of the play would be drastically altered. Certainly the shock value of Othello's marriage to Desdemona would be significantly reduced if Iago had managed to marry a Venetian woman, even if one of appropriately lower social status, before him. The impression of Othello's exceptional stature as an outsider accepted only because of his extraordinary military skills would be dulled if interracial or intercultural marriage were to be perceived as a more common, although not readily welcomed, practice.

Making Iago and Emilia an interracial couple could have served Scott's overall conception of the relationship between Iago and Othello by strengthening the image of Iago as an ambitious young man who is aggressively trying to advance in Venetian society. We learn at the outset that Iago's abilities, political and otherwise, have not gone unnoticed when he tells Roderigo: "Three great ones of the city, / In personal suit to make me his lieutenant, / Off-capped to him" (1.1.7–9). All he needed was a little extra help from the man he saw as a father-figure, who instead seems to thwart his ambitions. But a white Emilia would also undermine the essential premise of Iago's unnatural dependency on Othello by visually and psychologically weakening the sense of bonding in isolation, which is the armature supporting the entire production.

Besides preventing any dilution of the tensions of the Othello-Desdemona relationship, switching Emilia to match Iago also maintained

Emilia's subordination to Iago, making *her* increased isolation and dependency on her husband an additional motivation or cause of her betrayal of Desdemona, whether this betrayal was witting or unwitting. Having Emilia and Desdemona come from visibly different backgrounds could convey the message that under certain circumstances gender is a stronger source of affiliation than race or cultural origin. Or, if Emilia is conceived of as a character whose sense of identity depends on her associations with others rather than from an independent sense of self, the pained and angry insults she directs at Othello in act 5—"O, the more angel she, / And you the blacker devil!" (5.2.128–29)—could reflect internalized race and class hierarchies. Johnson-Haddad had wondered if Emilia, when she cried that Desdemona "was too fond of her most filthy bargain" (5.2.153), was "adopting the racist language of dominant white Venetian society and thereby participating in both Othello's and her own oppression (much as she colludes with the prevailing male language of domination when she calls Bianca a strumpet)."[81] Casting Emilia as black could sharpen the portrait of the traditional interpretations of the individual character—eager accomplice, neglected or abused wife—while contributing to the revised ensemble dynamics of the quadrangle formed with Othello, Iago, and Desdemona.

The Shakespeare Theatre production was a great success with general audiences and on the whole well received by professional critics as well. Most significantly, no one had any quarrel with the fundamental concept of having Iago and Emilia cast as black. It is therefore interesting that five years later, when another director, Penny Metropulos, staged a production where both Othello and Iago were played by black actors, the choice did provoke a highly negative reaction.

The Acting Company

The Acting Company's production of *Othello* directed by Penny Metropulos was performed at the Tribeca Performing Arts Center, May 16–25, 1995. Founded in 1972 by John Houseman and Margo Harley with members of the first graduating class of the Drama Division at Juilliard, the Acting Company has a three-pronged mission, seeking to revitalize the classics as it

- Develops the best young American actors by giving them an opportunity to practice their craft in a repertory of classic plays and new works

- Builds a discerning national audience for the theater by playing exceptional productions on tour nationwide for diverse audiences
- Educates students through master classes, student matinees, performance-based workshops of Shakespeare for younger audiences and Literacy Through Theater artistic residencies.[82]

Each year, the company performs in more than fifty cities, in the United States and abroad, reaching audiences totaling about 70,000. The company's general practice has been to tour for four or five months and then finish the season with a run in New York City. With the company's educational and outreach efforts aimed primarily at audiences who have had limited exposure to plays from the classic repertory, the Acting Company's productions tend to be more or less conventional in approach; publicity and program notes accordingly stress commonly received interpretations of the dramas rather than radical rereadings. Plays are most commonly performed in period costume and with minimal sets to facilitate easy transportation.

During the mid-1990s, the company was still made up primarily of younger actors. In Metropulos's production of *Othello,* Ezra Knight had the title role of Othello, Allen Gilmore was cast in the role of Iago, Karen Forbes played Desdemona, and Shona Tucker was Emilia. The production, along with *A Doll's House* with which it was being performed in repertory, was reviewed by the three major New York City daily newspapers. Clive Barnes's *New York Post* review was the most favorable, largely because he took into account the various constraints and objectives that had shaped the production. It was evident that he and Wilborn Hampton, the *New York Times* critic, had indeed seen the same production, but Barnes consistently put a more positive construction on the different elements of the production. For instance, concerning the overall quality of the performance, Barnes said, "The staging by Penny Metropulos . . . is swift and uninflected with any unnecessary scholarship, but is plain and comprehensible." He noted that this approach "admirably serves its purpose, as an introduction to Shakespeare, his piercing insights and his wildfire poetry. You can see Othello plain here—which cannot always be vouchsafed for productions 10 times as fancy."[83] Hampton, on the other hand, wrote: "Under Penny Metropulos's direction, the company's 'Othello' concentrates on the big scenes, as through the subtleties of the play were a nuisance. As a result, most of the performances are oddly incomplete, their motivation never fully established, and come to life only in the major confrontations."[84] Both singled out Allen Gilmore's Iago as a weak link. In Hampton's opinion, "As Iago, Allen Gilmore appears undecided about why he hates Othello so much. He speeds through the opening scenes as if he had somewhere else to go and is so pleasant and good-natured that it makes the whole tragedy seem just a misunderstanding."[85] Even here, Barnes softened his criticism by suggesting that the defects in the performance arose from what would be an asset in another context: "One very slight disappointment comes with Allen Gilmore's Iago. I have admired him in the past, but here his subtlety seems sometimes lost in the deep purposeless villainy of Iago's soulless night."[86] There was, however, one point on which the reviews coincided perfectly—neither mentioned that Allen Gilmore is black. With no photographs of Iago accompanying the text of the reviews, readers who had not watched the production would never have known that he was played by an African American actor.

This was not a point that escaped the attention of the *Daily News* drama critic Howard Kissel, who spent most of his column inches complaining about the casting of a black actor in the role of Iago:

> This is alas Clever Idea Shakespeare, and the Clever Idea here is to have Iago be black. This distorts the play considerably. If Othello is a black outsider in an otherwise white, racist society (in the very first scene, someone refers to him as "thick lips"), his plight is immediately understandable.
>
> If Othello belongs to an apparently integrated society, he is no outsider, and the play loses its force.
>
> Many classical plays are good candidates for nontraditional casting because the characters are larger than life and color doesn't matter. This play, however, is about color.[87]

These reactions stand in marked contrast to the reception accorded Scott's Shakespeare Theatre production. Whereas Scott's casting of a black actor as Iago was always commented on and favorably received (at least in principle), Metropulos's choice was either completely ignored or roundly condemned. Evidently there was fundamental disagreement over which conventions of reception to apply to the Acting Company production. Barnes and Hampton were treating the black Iago as a color-blind choice—a multicultural company's normal practice of casting without regard to race. In the absence of any evidence from the internal codes of the production, it was appropriate to assume that Gilmore's race did not perform any semiotic function and therefore was not a subject for comment. On the other hand, judging by Kissel's use of the term "Clever Idea," he assumed Metropulos was taking a conceptual approach, using Gilmore and Knight's common racial identity to remove race as a factor.

No such confusion had attended Scott's production. Onstage cues were provided by the costumes that made it clear that Othello, Iago, and Emilia were not just being played by black actors, but that we were to understand that all three were black African characters. Many, perhaps most, members of the audience would have been prepared by the considerable advance publicity. Beyond its normal educational value, offering the public insights into the director's and actors' processes is especially useful when nontraditional casting complicates the semiotic system of a particular production. In such cases, sharing the hypotheses underlying the production does not merely enhance audience appreciation, it signals to the spectators what protocols of reception to apply. In the *Asides* interview, Harold Scott was directly asked to speak about how the Shakespeare Theatre production related to his "overall casting philosophy as a founding member of the Non-Traditional Casting Board." Scott gave an answer indicating that his strategy for this production was to combine elements of the original "conceptual" and "societal" categories. Scott identified what he had done with *Othello* as "sociological casting . . . where certain characters are cast in another ethnicity in order to make a sociological comment." But it was important to Scott that the casting concept be historically justifiable based on the cultural history of the locations where the tragedy was set: "here, by definition, you can put a Black Iago, and a Black Emilia, and Black and Hispanic extras out there besides, because my god, once you see where Cyprus is on the map, to think that it's any pure culture would be folly."[88]

No comparable advance publicity or dramaturgical documentation paved the way for the production of *Othello* directed by Penny Metropulos for the Acting Company's 1994–95 season. Audiences attending regular Acting Company performances are not provided with the more elaborate explanatory materials available to spectators in theaters like the Shakespeare Theatre in Washington, with their larger budgets and relatively high-income subscription base. Therefore, when faced with a black actor playing Iago in the Acting Company's production, audience members and critics alike had to rely on various internal and external signals, such as previous experience and knowledge of the company's and the director's practices, to decide how to incorporate, or not to incorporate, this second black presence into the diegetic world of the drama. Although it seemed that in 1995 Metropulos's body of work was not well known to New York critics or audiences, her record reveals a director who is very sensitive to the implications of casting against tradition. Retrospectively, in the absence of any published accounts of the process of creating *Othello*, Metropulos's statement on her nontraditionally cast 2001 production of *The Tempest* for the Oregon Shakespeare Festival (cited and discussed above) may provide the most useful source of illumination for the earlier *Othello*. In *The Tempest*, new light was shed on the play's themes as the full implications of gendered difference emerged gradually during the rehearsal process, scene by scene, causing profound shifts in "the play's emphasis and its dynamics."[89] Having a black actor in the role of Iago could be expected to affect *Othello* in a parallel manner. Without making race more of an issue than it already is in the text—or a somewhat different issue (as Scott did)—the actors' social sensibilities would enter the production organically rather than conceptually through their interaction with the text and with each other during the rehearsal phase.

Such an approach to casting focuses on using the racial or gendered identities of the actors in the process rather than the product. The spectator is thereby given more freedom and also more responsibility to determine how to read the resulting performances. Not only must viewers decide on a semantic interpretation (the meaning of a particular performance), they must perform the trickier, and less familiar, task of selecting a semiotic interpretation (identifying theatrical conventions and codes). These levels or categories of interpretation were identified by Marco De Marinis, who underscores the vital importance of the latter form of interpretation: "While semantic interpretation focuses on the *meaning* of the performance . . . which is to say on *what* it is, semiotic interpretation . . . mainly focuses on *how* it is, which is to say on the theatrical *signifiers* . . . that constitute them."[90] Semiotic interpretation poses new challenges when nontraditional casting is applied because it is not enough to settle on the traditional *particular* conventions being followed—the conventions associated with given genres, periods, authors, regions, schools, and so on. The different forms of nontraditional casting—color-blind, conceptual, societal, and so forth—constitute relatively new additions to the codes of particular conventions. Providing spectators with the information needed to determine what particular conventions are being applied as far as the casting is concerned would let them know from the outset whether they should analyze how the corporeal signifiers fit in among the *unique* conventions of the performance they are watching.[91] By definition, unique conventions are "those that emerge from a given performance, that are present *ex novo,* and that can only be understood through that particular message and performance context. They can often be confusing and ambiguous due to their novelty and originality. This is one of the effects of the constitution or reestablishment of a new code."[92] Once audience members know that the casting of a black actor in the part of a white character has been endowed with semiotic value by the director, they can evaluate the semantic function of the casting choice.

In the case of Scott's production, the keys to the theatrical or conventional codes were made available to audiences ahead of time. Most importantly they were told how to interpret the production semiotically so that they could devote their full attention to interpreting it semantically. Left to their own devices in the case of Metropulos's Acting Company production, three highly competent spectators came to very different conclusions as to how they should perceive the signifiers, and their subsequent evaluations were profoundly affected by these preliminary conclusions. The case histories of the black Iagos confirm that racial positioning and life experiences always work in tandem with specifically theatrical competencies to shape an audience member's readings of productions like the unconventional *Othellos.* This point is made even more strongly when we consider the production cast in reverse.

The Photo-Negative Othello

Seven years after the Afrocentric *Othello* was presented in the theater at the Folger Shakespeare Library, the Shakespeare Theatre Company staged another production of the tragedy at their new home in the Lansburgh Theatre; the new production took an even more enterprising approach to nontraditional casting. In this version, Othello was played by a white actor while Desdemona, Iago, Emilia, and all the other speaking roles, except for Bianca, were performed by black actors. By all accounts, the original idea for this "photo-negative" production was Patrick Stewart's, born out of regret that by the time he had attained the professional experience and the maturity to play the part of Othello, it was no longer acceptable for a white actor "to put on blackface and to pretend to be African."[93] It occurred to him that it could be possible to "invert the racial topography of the original text by playing Othello as the only white character in a society otherwise comprised completely of blacks."[94] The intention was to allow Shakespeare's play to make the same observations concerning racism and prejudice as a "conventional" production of *Othello,* but in a more intense and provocative way. By replacing the black outsider with a white man in a black society, Stewart hoped to "encourage a much broader view of the fundamentals of racism, and perhaps even question those triggers—. . . color of skin, physiognomy, language, culture" that produce reactions of fear, suspicion or hostility.[95]

Three companies (two American and one British) turned down the idea before Michael Kahn, the artistic director of the Shakespeare Theatre in Washington, DC, enthusiastically adopted the proposal, recognizing the concept as a particularly appropriate one for the city: "It seemed especially right for Washington. The issue of race and racial difference is actively part of this city's dialogue, all the time, every single day. You can't say that about every city. But it's part of the fabric of life here and it concerns people deeply, not just intellectually. Washington seemed the most fruitful place for this project."[96] The director of the production, Jude Kelly, also pointed to the power dynamics in the nation's capital as they intersected with its racial demographics and its theatergoing patterns: "approximately 60 percent of the population is black, but it is the 30 percent white minority who hold most of the power and make most of the decisions. And go to the theatre." A British director known for her interest in work designed to provoke moral debates and to highlight "the social ramifications of private acts," Kelly did not hesitate to let the predominantly white audience know ahead of time that her production involved "a deliberate attempt . . . to make white audiences experience some of the feelings of isolation and discomfort that black people experience all of the time in their lives."[97]

In the actual production, the original simple "white Othello surrounded by an all-black cast" scheme apparently was modified by casting nonspeaking parts in a manner that underscored the social hierarchies and cultural divisions in the play.[98] Three members of Brabantio's household staff and the Cypriots, including Montano, were played by white or lighter-skinned African American actors. The production was therefore doubly "coded" through the casting: the vertical inversion of the white over black hierarchy that has historically prevailed when the two races occupy the same social space was supplemented by a horizontal reversal where the Venetian insiders were dark and the non-Venetian outsiders light.

In this revised schema, the fact that Bianca is played by a white actress, Kate Skinner, takes on triple significance. She is classified among the disempowered because of her sex, her class, and her culture. In tracing the evolution of interpretations of Cassio's mistress, Edward Pechter notes that she gained prominence when critical emphasis moved "away from dramatic characters conceived as though their speech and action were generated from particular desires and histories, and over to the concept of a unified design, to which the characters were only contributory effects."[99] While it was of course the normal practice for centuries to have Bianca played by a white actor, in the past couple of decades, it has become quite common for a black actor to fill the role. Black Biancas have appeared on both sides of the Atlantic—from Trevor Nunn's 1989 Royal Shakespeare Company production to Tony Taccone's 1999 production for the Oregon Shakespeare Festival; on screen as well as on stage—Oliver Parker's 1995 film with Laurence Fishburne and Kenneth Branagh; and even in the complete and unabridged edition of *Othello* presented in comic book format (1983).

While the decision to cast Bianca as black may be partially motivated by practical concerns in some cases—the need to find roles for a repertory company's black actresses—the part is so often selected for this purpose because it has the double advantage of being justifiable from a societal and historical perspective while at the same time offering interesting structural possibilities. Nunn wanted to make the contrast between Bianca and Desdemona striking in order to bring out Cassio's double standard in his dealings with women, placing one on a pedestal while using the other because she is sexually available and skillful with a needle. Casting to maximize the impact of visual difference would also provide a means of staging the structural mirroring between Othello's wife and Cassio's mistress observed by literary scholar Maynard Mack. He points out that it is precisely when Desdemona has been degraded to the level of a whore in Othello's mind that Bianca appears for the first time; both will be unjustly accused and protest their innocence in vain.[100]

Making Othello and Bianca the only two black characters may also serve to direct our attention toward the parallels between Bianca's actual situation and Othello's imagined one: Othello has begun to suspect that Desdemona's sweet words were superficially uttered words of seduction much like Cassio's endearments and promises to Bianca. For contemporary American audiences, the visual connection between the general and the courtesan hints at the irony of a situation where a military commander may prove as vulnerable as a courtesan because of the one trait they share in common—their racial identity. The oxymoronic casting of a black Bianca thereby promotes an estimation of Othello as a man who "has survived Venice's latent racism by cultivating a reputation and respect strong enough to hold back the tide of antiblackness," but whose "blackness is nevertheless susceptible to the dangers of white racism that erupt when he transgresses Venetian definitions of racial acceptability."[101] In Jude Kelly's production, the ironic commentary conveyed by the ocular link between Bianca and Othello—now two white outsiders whose fortunes depend on acceptance by a black society—would be inflected by the fact that the ill-used courtesan, fair skinned and blonde, was the only character who fit Othello's descriptions of Desdemona. Fittingly, but transgressively, Bianca now stood out among the ladies for "that whiter skin of hers than snow / And smooth as monumental alabaster" (5.2.4–5).

While Kelly's casting aggressively addressed the question of racial tensions in *Othello*, other aspects of the staging crossed racial and cultural lines to investigate the allied issues of masculinity and violence. Kelly stated that she was "interested in exploring what happens when you train men to be violent, prime them up for fighting and then leave them waiting. Where does all that energy get directed?"[102] One answer is that it gets directed against women. During the second act brawl in this production, several Venetian soldiers overpower and try to rape a female Cypriot soldier. Othello's arrival saves her and Desdemona rushes to her side. In 4.2, however, in his rising anger and jealousy, Othello rapes Desdemona as he denounces her as a whore and strumpet. Emilia comes to comfort her, just as Desdemona had gone to the aid of the female soldier. Emilia herself, once again played by Franchelle Stewart Dorn, was very clearly conceived of as a battered wife. Miranda Johnson-Haddad gives this description: "Though tall and attractive, this Emilia shrank into herself when Iago was around, clearly dreading the next blow, verbal or physical . . . and her pain at Iago's many jibes underscored her obviously desperate need for his affection."[103] Bianca, meanwhile, as realized by Kate Skinner, placed herself firmly in the company of all these "honest" women, giving force to her reproof to Emilia: "I am no strumpet, but of life as honest / As you that thus abuse me" (5.1.121–23). Witnessed in conjunction with the race-conscious casting, these gestures and actions, as Johnson-Haddad writes, "implied that the same social context that permits a culture of racism to develop also permits sexism and elitism."[104]

In Stewart's conception, his character's point of entry into this masculine world of violence is found in the line "Chaos is come again" (Act III, scene 3), uttered with a noticeable pause before "again." For him, those words constituted "the heart of the character because there is a mystery about him. . . . There are hints that seem to belong to that same world of chaos, of being taken by 'the insolent foe /And sold into slavery,' the 'distressful stroke / That my youth suffered.'"[105] His marriage to Desdemona represented the successful culmination of a long struggle to restore order to his life. From there, she came to mean everything to him, "in effect replacing what his life had been before."[106] In this production, the satisfaction and respite afforded by this hard-won stability were conveyed by the amplified strains of romantic comedy that run through the first two acts. Othello makes his entrance as a man literally and figuratively at peace, exhibiting a newly found joy and playfulness in his interactions with Desdemona. Once he suspects her of having betrayed him, his violence is a conditioned response, fostered both by his past history as a survivor and his military training. Kelly said of Othello's murder of Desdemona: "It is not a blind moment of madness as with many crimes of passion. It is a soldier exterminating an enemy."[107]

Stewart's conception, however, did not specifically stress Othello's need to survive as a black man in a white society or an African in a European society. The racial issues were to be raised semiotically rather than mimetically by the dislocation between signifier and signified that occurred when his other or other characters' lines described his white body as black, and by the frictions generated when racial epithets and stereotypes intended to denigrate black people to a white person. For black actors, even those who place race in an ancillary role, building the character without making race a central aspect of his psychological makeup has not been considered a viable option. Earle Hyman's interpretation of the play, built up over twenty-five years and more than 750 performances as Othello in ten productions (in English and in Norwegian), is representative in the relationship he sees between race and other factors. His study of the part led him to the conclusion that "*Othello* is not about jealousy or racism, although both these elements make the play more sensational and powerfully affecting. The play is about ego."[108] While "ego" rather than race functions as the keystone in Hyman's interpretation, race is understood to play a defining role in the process of ego formation. Hyman notes, "Even today, in a white-oriented society, a black man, in order to achieve success and any appreciable sense of security, has to make his services well-nigh indispensable. And the general and commander Othello *is* indispensable to Venice, one of the great city-states of all time. There is racism—a black man has to be *better* than a white man at the same job." Othello has managed to reach that level of success and security, but not without some profound reshaping of his psyche: "As a black man, [Othello] has a little more ego than he needs. Othello has to survive in a white society and therefore has to think more of himself, and about himself, than is really good for him."[109] Similarly, Paul Robeson considered Othello's murder of Desdemona to be a matter of honor, but it was a sense of honor shaped by his status as a cultural outsider:

> [Othello's] color is essentially secondary—except as it emphasizes the difference in *culture.* . . . Shakespeare's Othello has learned to live in a strange society, but he is not *of* it—as an easterner today might pick up western manners and not be western. Othello's personal, racial dignity is involved in his love. He might have been much slower to suspicion if his wife had been of the same background. But he is intensely proud of his color and culture; in the end, even as he kills, his honor is at stake, not simply as a human being and as a lover, but as Othello. The honor of his whole culture is involved. "It is the cause . . ."[110]

Kelly and Stewart were certainly aware that the British actor would not be bringing the same understanding of race relations to the part that a black actor would. Addressing this point directly, Kelly remarked: "What's fascinating for me is that you have 22 African American actors onstage who know what racism is about, and one white British actor who may know the effects of racism but has never experienced it the way they have. So the images of racial hostility flip back and forth. What it all means, I think, will depend very much on the color of the person who's watching."[111] Kelly's comments indicate that the production's provocations regarding race and racism were consciously left open-ended.

Not everyone was happy with a production that typically, in Robert King's words "both raised questions about race and held the answers back."[112] For some the resulting effect was preposterous. Toby Zinman, who had interviewed Patrick Stewart for *American Theatre,* thought "many of the play's nuances strike the ear as ludicrous: Desdemona's skin is decidedly not 'alabaster' nor is Stewart a 'black devil' with 'thick lips.'"[113] Others found that confusing effects vitiated any potential critique:

> For a white audience to see a white audience and character scorned in vicious racist terms could have been a scathing theater experience, but the whole issue just seems confused. What is the audience supposed to think when Stewart, an actor whose mouth is like a slit in his face, is derided with the remark "thick lips"? Or when, pale pate gleaming, he announces in the plummiest of English accents, "Haply, for I am black . . ."? Or when a black actor castigates Othello for his dark-skinned ugliness? If the purpose was to show how foolish and empty racial derogations are, how they're just words, the device misfires. Racial derogations end up seeming meaningless, even harmless—surely not what Kelly intended.[114]

Rose attributed the production's failure to shed new light on racism or on *Othello* to an unjustified emphasis on the subject of racial prejudice: "The stage couldn't be more obviously set for some daring, stinging race-reversal, but the potential dynamite fizzles—largely because race prejudice is only one of several dramatic elements in the script and won't stand up to being made into what the play is 'about.'"[115]

Peter Marks, writing for the *New York Times,* expressed a diametrically opposed view. For him, far from attempting to monopolize the interpretation, the casting functioned as a device that allowed the other elements to stand out in relief by neutralizing race as a factor. It was not so much that the dynamite had fizzled as that it had been successfully extinguished. In an echo of Rose's reaction to Harold Scott's production, Marks wrote, "the racial turning of the tables does not tilt the play toward ham-handed irony; rather it tends to take the racial issue off the table."[116] The one moment where he felt the casting had an undesirable effect was in act 1, scene 3, when Othello appears before the Venetian Senate:

> In traditional productions, surrounded by a roomful of white faces, Othello seems a figure of strength and sympathy. But when Othello is a white military leader—what more recognizable authority figure exists in Western culture?—it's hard to feel particularly sorry for him. It's an instance in which race reversal does not jibe with an audience's sense of the way the world beyond the theater works.[117]

These responses suggest several missed cues that go beyond the intended divergence in response. Some of the confusion can undoubtedly be attributed to the fact that the production had not reached a final form by press night and apparently continued to evolve significantly over the course of the two-month run. Miranda Johnson-Haddad, a scholar in residence at the Folger Shakespeare Library at the time and author of the program notes, watched three performances (the final dress rehearsal, the press night performance, and one about two-thirds of the way into the run) for her article on "The Shakespeare Theatre *Othello*" for the *Shakespeare Bulletin*. She found that "the show was constantly in metamorphosis . . . [O]n each occasion it was fundamentally different from the production I had seen (in one instance, only one week) before. Blocking, scene interpretations, line deliveries, and characterizations all changed from one performance to another, often radically. The only element of the production that did not change over the run was the set, although various props appeared and disappeared along the way."[118] When asked about this ongoing evolution in an interview, Patrick Stewart gave three reasons: Kelly's style of direction, which "did not depend on getting everything right on the first night and then just repeating it"; the short four-week rehearsal time; and his own approach to working that involved a continual exploration and investigation by remaining open to what both the play and the other actors were saying to him.[119] In particular, he mentioned that his relationship with Ron Canada's Iago underwent considerable development during the run.

As a matter of fact, the impression uniformly given by published accounts was that the actor playing Iago was groping rather than exploring, with inconsistencies evident not just across the run of the play but during a single performance. Although all three principal performances evolved, because of Iago's position as a partner in so many key duets (with Othello, Emilia, Cassio, and Roderigo), the static interference created by an indeterminate Iago may have blurred the impact of the experimental aspects of the casting. Iago, after all, is the character who most frequently calls attention to Othello's blackness, both to his face and behind his back. He alludes to Othello's black skin when he suggests that Desdemona's choice of Othello is symptomatic of serious defects:

Not to affect many proposed matches
Of her own clime, complexion and degree,
Whereto we see, in all things, nature tends—

Foh! One may smell in such a will most rank,
Foul disproportion, thoughts unnatural.

(3.3.233–37)

While Iago's language here is a calculatedly neutral and respectful echo of Brabantio's nastier "sooty bosom / Of such a thing as thou" (1.2.70–71), Iago has already proven that he can match and even surpass the racist invective of Desdemona's outraged father. Under the cover of darkness, he calls Othello in rapid succession "an old black ram," "the devil," and "a Barbary horse" (1.1.85–112). In Kelly's production, while Roderigo was letting Brabantio know that his "fair daughter" was in "the gross clasps of a lascivious Moor," Canada doubled the discourse with a simian pantomime, in which "Iago faces front in a half squat, sways, swings his drooping arms before him and whoops like a chimpanzee."[120] In his analysis of this moment, Robert King seems to have been more comfortable than his colleagues with the recommended mode of flexible reception:

> The offensive stereotype is undeniably racist, yet it is enacted by and for a black man. If it is meant to mirror the white audience's prejudices, it is little more than reverse racism, arrogant in its sweeping assumptions. Perhaps it is meant to be symptomatic of racism learned and absorbed by its victims. Whatever thoughts Iago's action prompted, we were thinking about race and participating in the performance, not waiting for a distancing classic to wash over us with placating truisms.[121]

This instance of felicitous reception is linked with King's understanding that the production drew our attention to race by undermining our confidence in "the ocular proof" we normally use as the basis for our categorizations of identity. In his review of *Othello*, which was part of a longer piece for the *North American Review* called "The Seeing Place," he points out:

> By the time Iago's influence begins to cloud Othello's vision, Stewart's whiteness has become a fact of performance, easy to overlook. So when he says to us in soliloquy, "Haply for I am black," we are reminded of a dramatic truth which our senses tell us is false: "I am black" is wrong because the speaker is obviously white; but white is

wrong because Othello is black. This disruptive moment, like others in the production, brings color to the forefront of our attention and makes us think about its dramatic and social weight.[122]

The photo-negative *Othello* invites us to analyze the construction not just of identity in general, but of whiteness in particular. Since the 1960s, directors, actors, and critics have placed black stereotypes in dialogue with the process of black subject formation in their interpretations of *Othello*. These artists used Shakespeare's tragedy to explore the fact that, as Stuart Hall has observed, "'black' has never been just there. . . . It has always been an unstable identity, psychically, culturally, and politically. It, too, is a narrative, a story, a history. Something constructed, told, spoken, not simply found. . . . Black is an identity which had to be learned and could only be learned in a certain moment."[123] By reversing the roles racially, the two-sided coin of racism has been flipped over so that we are now able to see the obverse: white subjectivity, privilege, and stereotypes. The moment singled out by Marks in his review is indeed an exemplary one. The casting strategy had worked eminently well if spectators were led to contrast the effect produced by the sight of a white commander surrounded by a roomful of black faces and the effect produced by a black military leader surrounded by a roomful of white faces. Having noticed that the reversed image of color and power did not coincide with their knowledge of "the way the world beyond the theater works," audiences were then meant to question the ways of the world that are at the bottom of such incongruities. Why indeed should the image of the white authority figure be such a familiar one? What forces or agencies confer an aura of security or invulnerability on such a figure?

In order to encourage audiences to engage with such questions, the photo-negative production of *Othello* had in effect employed devices most commonly associated with a Brechtian approach to the performance of a Shakespearean tragedy. Such a move runs counter to the late-twentieth-century American approach to performing Shakespeare, which continues to be dominated by the techniques of acting systematically developed by Stanislavsky. In fact, it is Stanislavsky's own account of his staging of *Othello*, translated and published in English in 1948, that exemplifies the application of his ideas and methods to a Shakespearean play. Past lives and given circumstances for the principal and supporting roles are recorded in detail. Interviews with the actors and directors make it clear that Scott's and Kelly's nontraditionally cast productions of

Othello followed in this tradition as far as the actors' creations of their roles were concerned. This approach to acting authorized audiences to have certain expectations for the production as a whole, according to the prescribed logic, which has been well articulated by Colin Counsell:

> Everything the actor does will visibly describe a link between himself/herself and the playworld's other elements, signaling to the audience that all are part of the same fictional reality. The elements of the production are thereby woven into a single whole, a fabric or "necklace" of objects/characters sewn together by the thread of deeds, utterances and all the minutiae of behaviour, so that the performances themselves "act" the production into unified text, a unified locus.[124]

These expectations were met in the case of Harold Scott's production. The given circumstances established by Scott and the actors provided sound sociological and psychological foundations for the utterance of racist remarks by a black Iago or a black Emilia. As we have seen, the new racial configurations may still have posed difficulties or divergences in reception. (Johnson-Haddad describes herself "turning increasingly athletic mental cartwheels in [her] attempts to explain discrepancies between the language of the play and the production itself.")[125] But, whether or not spectators liked the explanations devised by director and actors, the traditions of Stanislavsky's process were being respected. The newly imagined histories helped define each character's "through-line," which was melded into the binding superobjective of the work as a whole.

This was not the case with the 1997 Shakespeare Theatre production. While in all other respects, the production took a realistic approach to acting, the actors' efforts to create the illusion of actuality on stage were countered by the discrepancy between their racial identity and that of the characters they were playing. The physical aspects of embodiment, normally the material guarantor of the "truthfulness" of a portrayal, instead undermined the creation of the individual role. Ideally, whatever the casting might have subtracted from the individual portrayal would be compensated for by the clearer insights into social behavior and relationships so that a fundamental truth could emerge: "All of the many alienated characters who inhabit the world of *Othello* reveal a complex yet basic truth: that racism, far from being an isolated phenomenon, happens within an entire social context that permits certain individuals to wield power and influence at the expense of other individuals."[126]

If the messages generated by the production's core conceit amounted to a series of infelicitous speech acts for many spectators, the failure in communication may be attributed to what Timothy Murray has seen as a misplaced confidence in what can be expected from "a stress on bodily presence, in and of itself." Reiterating what black theater practitioners have long recognized, Murray noted the limitations of a black American theater, conceived of as "a drama of the presentation of black corporeal presence."[127] He cautioned that far from constituting a site for resistance or regeneration, "the empirical reduction of theatre's polymorphous structures to the primacy of corporeal presence might result in too strong a trust in phenomenological relations" and risk reinscribing the idealism of essence. While Murray was speaking specifically of African American theater and drama, the same could be said of nontraditional casting in which the mere physical presence of corporeal racial markers is expected to serve as a source of cultural criticism that is not otherwise relayed by the full material and affective resources of live dramatic performance.

This was to a certain extent the case with the Kelly-Stewart production. Interviews and program notes indicate that as the most influential figures, their creative efforts focused on the problem of violence. As seen above, Kelly was mainly interested in gender and violence. When he was interviewed for the *Washington Post,* Stewart said that he had conducted extensive research on violence and obsession. This included questioning psychiatrists and an expert who profiled serial killers for the FBI, whom Stewart asked to analyze the *Othello* "crime scene."[128] But the racial issues were dealt with only in the scenes or speeches where the text directly raised the question (e.g., 1.1, 1.3, 3.3). In between these moments, it was left to "mere bodily presence" to sustain the line of interrogation. The success of this procedure depended largely on each individual spectator's own experiences with racial matters. Those for whom questions of racial identity and relations exerted a formative and regular influence were most likely to import their own narratives to furnish some continuity between the moments of disjunction between speech and speaker when everyone in the auditorium would be forced into awareness. In the constant interplay between production and reception, this most unusual staging became part of a four-hundred-year-old tradition in which *Othello* was treated not just "as a product of a cultural milieu but also as a maker of cultural meanings."[129]

CHAPTER FOUR

Beyond Type

Re-casting Modern Drama and National Identity

What are the main characteristics of this form? We know it by heart, of course, since most of the plays we see are realistic plays. It is written in prose; it makes believe it is taking place independently of an audience which views it through a "fourth wall," the grand objective being to make everything seem true to life in life's most evident and apparent sense. In contrast, think of any play by Aeschylus. You are never under an illusion in his plays that you are watching "life"; you are watching a play, an art work.

—ARTHUR MILLER

While the various forms of nontraditional casting have come to be widely accepted in European classical tragedies and comedies, there continues to be greater resistance to racial mixing or cultural transposition in modern or contemporary domestic drama. The *Los Angeles Times* reporter covering the First National Symposium on Non-Traditional Casting posed these questions:

> Can a black actor be convincing in the title role of Shakespeare's "Henry V"? Can an Asian or Hispanic actor be believable as part of an Anglo family in Tennessee Williams' "Cat on a Hot Tin Roof"? Can any "ethnic" actor assimilate into the upper-crust, WASPish society portrayed in Philip Barry's "The Philadelphia Story"?[1]

By the time of the symposium, it was generally agreed that the answer to the first question was yes, but there was substantial disagreement as to the viability of the other examples. Racially mixed casts had performed in realistic European and American modern drama since the 1960s with mixed responses. A former member of the Guthrie Theatre Company recalled that when a black actor performed the role of the son in Douglas Campbell's 1966 production of August Strindberg's *Dance of Death,* in which the two parents were played by white actors, he was well received by Twin Cities audiences and critics.[2] Kenneth Washington, director of company development for the Guthrie, however, heard from older colleagues that there were also many patrons who could not understand or accept the idea of such mixed racial casting.[3] Earle Hyman, who has performed Ibsen in Norway and in Norwegian, was one of the first African American actors to realize these roles on American stages.[4] But in the 1980s, such casting remained frequently subject to criticism. When Gordon Davidson, artistic director of the Los Angeles Theatre Center, cast African American actor Lou Gossett as Vershinin in his production of Chekhov's *Three Sisters* for the 1985–86 season, the result was described as "unfortunate" and worse. As Davidson put it in retrospect, "I didn't think that was such a big deal, but the audience did."[5] On the other hand, the 1989 casting of Jeanne Sakata in the title role of *The Lady from the Sea,* for the Fountain Theatre, an organization "dedicated to providing a nurturing, creative home for multi-ethnic theatre and dance artists," received praise from *L.A. Times* drama critic Ray Loynd:

> Non-traditional casting in the major female role lights up Henrik Ibsen's psychological study of a woman's quest for freedom of choice in the tender "The Lady from the Sea" (1888).
>
> Jeanne Sakata's Asian Norwegian strongly serves the cause of colorblind casting as Sakata impressively dramatizes the quiet determination of a wife drawn to a mesmerizing sailor from the sea.[6]

In these productions, the approach was color-blind (although, as Loynd's expression "Asian Norwegian" reminds us, "color-blind" casting is never really color-blind). Libby Appel took a conceptual approach in her 1993 production of *The Cherry Orchard* for the Indiana Repertory Theatre. The serfs were played by black actors to transpose the play's power relations into an American context. While this staging was not subject to the same objections of implausibility as color-blind casting, the choice did raise objections much like those expressed when black actresses are assigned the role of Bianca—that legacies of racial inequality were being reinforced rather than critiqued or dislodged.

The controversies seem to have abated in recent years where late-nineteenth- and early-twentieth-century European modern drama is concerned. Over the past ten years, multiracial productions of European modern domestic drama have become far more common. These productions are usually performed by resident repertory companies whose members are familiar to audiences. Two recent West Coast productions of *The Three Sisters* typify the new situation. The Oregon Shakespeare Festival's 2002 season included *The Three Sisters,* also directed by Appel. The principal roles of Masha, Irina, and Vershinin were played by African Americans. In 2003, the American Conservatory Theater mounted a production of the same play. Artistic director Carey Perloff's staging featured four black actors (Chebutykin, Kulygin, Fedotik, Orderly) and one Latino (Andrei); all were core or associate members of the company, or were enrolled in ACT's MFA program. Reviews did not remark upon the race of the actors, and the productions were evaluated on the basis of the ensemble performance and the realization of individual roles.

Even when companies ventured to cast modern European dramas nontraditionally, there could still be reservations about having black, Asian, or Latino actors playing characters written as white in American classics. At the Oregon Shakespeare Festival, it was not until 2008, when Bill Rauch became artistic director, that nonwhite actors began to be regularly cast in revivals of works considered quintessentially American. Even when the works in question were not realistic domestic dramas, the inclusion of actors of color in the casts of works like *Our Town* (which featured Indian-born Mahira Kakkar as Emily Webb) and *The Music Man* (in which African American Gwendolyn Mulamba played Marian the librarian) still provoked some controversy. In Rauch's words: "It has been just a breath of fresh air for some audience members, and other audience members have really struggled with what they see as a lack of realism."[7]

The divergent reactions to these productions foreground the range of possible factors that affect responses to nontraditional casting in realistic modern dramas: the nature of the particular play; the effectiveness of the production as a whole; the quality of the individual performance; the aesthetic preferences of each critic; the company, the venue, and the regular audiences for both; and finally the spectators' perceptions of the cultural milieu of the play and the race or ethnicity of the actor. The criteria used for evaluating whether multiracial casting is appropriate present significant contrasts when compared to responses to nontraditional casting in classical tragedy or comedy. And the closer to the audience the action of a realistic drama draws in time and place, the more pronounced the differences in mode of reception and the stronger the resistance to breaks with tradition. Writing in the mid-1980s, *Village Voice* critic Robert Massa noted, "Theaters now seem willing, at least theoretically, to mix-cast classical plays, but they draw the line at contemporary family drama."[8] Casting director Barry Moss reiterates the frequently made observation that the decision-makers who draw this line feel they must accommodate audiences who have set expectations when they take their seats:

> In the classics, yes, you can do anything that you want and it is accepted by an audience. . . . On the other hand, if you are doing a contemporary play about a specific issue, casting an Oriental, black or Hispanic would change something that would confuse the audience. It would take 10 to 15 minutes for the audience to adjust. There are producers who are not willing to take that risk.[9]

Other formulations offer more precise indications as to what exactly it is about modern or contemporary domestic drama that makes it seem more resistant to experimental casting along racial lines. Maria Irene Fornes identifies the representational mode of modern and contemporary as a significant factor when she observes, "We can easily do the classics in whatever racial configuration that may occur. The question is of importance when we are doing plays that are realistic plays."[10] The *New York Daily News's* theater reporter, Don Nelson, stresses temporal distance when he writes that "people seem to accept ethnic actors more easily in a work of the past. There is a sense the cultures depicted were different from ours anyway."[11] Many who do not entirely preclude the nontraditional casting of realistic domestic dramas call for case-by-case evaluations. This is the position taken by director John Houseman as he recalls how a production he directed of *The Three Sisters* was received on the West Coast:

> At no point did any audience question that Frank Silvera was a black actor playing the part created by Stanislavski. Now, if this had not been Chekhov laid in Russia, if this had been a play laid in the deep South, would the same harmony, the same enormously successful

meld have taken place? One doesn't know. These are problems one has to study for each case. The artistic needs of the production make their own demands.[12]

Houseman's assessment also emphasizes the importance of proximity, in this case geographical as well as historical. Margo Jefferson outlines the complex interaction of generic and historical factors that figure into linking a directorial concept with casting choices:

> It's so obvious that these things depend on the kind of work, the style of staging. Take opera, since black people were allowed on the stages of major houses in the early '60s. Opera, even the most realistic opera, is non-naturalistic and can get away with it. So can Shakespeare, though there have been plenty of ugly little debates about that. I grant you, Tennessee Williams is not a strictly realist playwright, but some years ago they were thinking of doing *Cat on a Hot Tin Roof* with James Earl Jones as Big Daddy and Kathleen Turner as the daughter. This one would have been very hard to pull off, because as I recall there are a lot of specific references to the political power of Big Daddy in the state of Mississippi. Could I see an all-black *Cat on a Hot Tin Roof?* Sure. There were powerful, very segregated black leaders. I see why Ellen Holly wanted to play Blanche Dubois years ago. It makes perfect sense to me, it even makes sense in the tradition of the very light-skinned Creole of color.[13]

Implicit in Jefferson's statement is a continuing regard for the historical situation where realistic or naturalistic drama is concerned. Color-blind casting is posited as a possibility in opera and classical tragedy, but only forms of racially mixed or racially transposed casting that attempt to account for the presence of actors of color or else deliberately use visible racial differences as signifiers are readily accepted as viable options in American domestic drama.

These principles can be seen in operation in two prominent productions of Tennessee Williams plays performed with casts of African American actors: the Arena Stage's 1989 production of *The Glass Menagerie* and the 2008 *Cat on a Hot Tin Roof* that played on Broadway. *The Glass Menagerie,* starring Ruby Dee as Amanda Wingfield, illustrates the process of contextualization, if not adaptation, that takes place when "mono-racial" or "mono-ethnic" nontraditional casting is employed. The program notes offer historical justification for the racial change:

Ruby Dee and Jonathan Earl Peck in the 1989 Arena Stage production of *The Glass Menagerie*, directed by Tazewell Thompson. (Photo by Joan Marcus.)

In the period following World War I approximately one million African Americans migrated to industrial cities like Pittsburgh, Chicago, Detroit and St. Louis, hoping for better employment and education. In the late 1930s, African Americans constituted 11.4 percent of the population of St. Louis, a city which had been a haven since Civil War times. *The WPA Guide to Missouri* (1936) points out the variety of social customs, traditions and the particular idiom that greatly enhanced the culture of the city.[14]

Not all viewers were receptive to this attempt to contextualize the play's action in order to "naturalize" the casting. The Washington, DC, *City Paper* notes the contradictory responses elicited when a canonical American play is written with white characters but performed by a nonwhite cast, all of whom have the same racial background:

> As for questions of skin color, let's just note that in a mono-ethnic casting of any play, race is necessarily going to be largely irrelevant. That, of course, hasn't kept reviewers from waxing sociological about this production. Praise and condemnation have both come from unexpected quarters. The *Washington Times,* conceding that Dee was only "paraphrasing" her part, nonetheless called the evening "pure Tennessee Williams" and suggested that audiences "would swear [the author] always meant the play to be set in the black milieu." The *New York Times* took the opposite view, comparing Arena's production to a TV sitcom and myopically dismissing the existence of a real landed, post-Reconstruction black gentry in a sarcastic couple of phrases: "Forget the improbability that a black woman in the 1930s would recall long-ago beaux who were prominent young planters on the Mississippi Delta and who went on to become vice presidents of banks . . ."[15]

In the Broadway production of *Cat on a Hot Tin Roof* with James Earl Jones as Big Daddy, finally staged almost a decade after the idea was first proposed, there were minor textual and major visual modifications to keep the realistic illusionism intact. Significantly, this was not the color-blind production once envisioned, but one that made the play about a prominent family of black landowners in the Mississippi Delta. In order not to defy credibility, director Debbie Allen used the décor to move the time period twenty-five to thirty years forward from the original 1950s setting. The style of the furnishings and the electronic entertainment equipment placed the action in the late 1970s or early 1980s, when it would be quite plausible for a southern black family to own "twenty-eight thousand acres of the richest land this side of the valley Nile."[16] Minor modifications to the script, all approved by the Williams estate, were made to acknowledge the racial identity of the speakers and the racial order of the Deep South. These included the deletion of references to "Ole Miss" as the alma mater of Brick, Maggie, and Skipper, and a passage where Maggie tells how her "great-great-grandfather gave his slaves freedom five years before the War between the States started."[17] At the same time, certain lines or phrases acquired new meanings when spoken by black actors playing black characters. For instance, in one of his tirades, Big Daddy reminds Big Mama, "I quit school at ten years old and went to work like a nigger in the fields!"[18] In this context, as Howard Shapiro pointed out in his review, "the reference is no slur; it's about bucking white society's expectations."[19] Summing up the state of affairs in the mid-1990s, Simi Horwitz reveals the persistence of all of the above attitudes but also indicates that some progress had been made:

> Most advocates contend that the major classics are universal, belong to everyone, and therefore lend themselves to colorblind casting— families, dynasties, and serfs can be racially, ethnically, and culturally diverse without any voiced explanation in the text. . . .
>
> As for realistic plays, the advocates are a little more cautious, suggesting each work should be viewed individually and casting decisions made on a play by play basis. Still, there's an amazing degree of latitude, in terms of tolerating—indeed endorsing—racially mixed families on stage, even when it's not accounted for in the dialogue or action.[20]

All the above statements point to the complex factors involved in reactions to nontraditional casting. The common objections to nontraditional casting in any form of drama are invariably framed in terms of respect for theatrical tradition, historical authenticity, and biological laws. Opposition to nontraditional casting is grounded in the assumption that characters who are white should be played by actors who are white, and that the physical appearance of parents and siblings should not defy genetic possibilities. But if one looks at the common factor underlying all objections, they are ultimately about distance and difference, both theatrical and social, and maintaining a comfortable distance from difference.

The theatrical distance in question has been succinctly described by Michal Kobialka in his discussion of borders as they relate to theater:

> [T]heatre history and practice have a very specific reading of borders and border crossings. The separation between life and the imitation of life on stage, between the "real" and the "illusionary" conditions of the stage, between the way one functions in everyday life and the way

one acts on stage, or between the words one hears and the text one reads, has always been at the very center of any discussion concerning one of the most fundamental questions in theatre studies—what it means to represent.[21]

More than any other dramatic genre, late-nineteenth- and twentieth-century modern realistic and naturalistic drama operates by establishing minimal distance between the represented and representing worlds. Plays and productions strive to create an iconic or imitative representation of reality at all levels. Not only do the language, acting style, costumes, and décor aim at reproducing the details of contemporary everyday speech, gestures, and material conditions, but social institutions, economic structures, and familial relationships must also correspond to actuality. Long before nontraditional casting (as opposed to integration of American theaters) was a significant issue, Arthur Miller had provided a concise practical characterization of the realistic on stage in the passage quoted at the beginning of this chapter.

For mid- to late-twentieth-century audiences, modern realistic plays, no longer far removed in setting, situation, and language (as are classical or neoclassical tragedies and comedies), normally make relatively light demands on their competencies as theatergoers and cultural readers. The more or less familiar social structures and institutions, naturalistic speech, and realistic style of performance place spectators in a mode of reception that allows theatrical competencies to coincide with social competencies as much as possible. No special knowledge of theatrical conventions or glossed editions of texts is needed to facilitate comprehension. As far as acting is concerned, as Richard Hornby has pointed out in his essay "Interracial Casting," the naturalistic theory of drama requires the following set of assumptions:

> Basically actors play themselves. From the director's point of view, the ideal is to cast someone as close to the character being portrayed as possible. From the actor's point of view, the ideal is to replicate your real-life emotions on stage, honestly playing yourself rather than "hiding behind the character." From the audience's (and thus from the critic's) point of view, you are supposed to "reality test" the performances against our experience of everyday life. Thus, if a white man on stage purports to have a daughter who is in fact a black woman, lights flash in your head.[22]

This practice-oriented account of realistic theater receives strong reinforcement from Stanton B. Garner, Jr.'s characterization of realistic theater in terms of its phenomenal properties. His conception offers some of the most profound insights into understanding what it is about nontraditional casting that triggers "flashing lights," which may signal either unrelenting resistance to socially motivated innovations in theater practices or new revelations regarding the social construction of racial formations. By stressing the interrelations between spatiality and corporeality as they were redefined over the course of the nineteenth century, Garner readmits the body as "a site of political operation"[23] even without Brechtian antirealism:

> [R]ealism offers an unprecedented disclosure of the theatrical body as it physically inhabits its material and spatial fields. Precisely because verisimilitude and illusionism work at cross-purposes, the latter wavering as the former seeks to perfect itself, realism is characterized by a structural *instability* that allows the body to assert its radical actuality and thereby resist its subjugation within the conventions of stage illusion.[24]

As Garner points out, there is a radical dimension to the realist aesthetic, and it is this radical dimension that nontraditional casting explores and exploits.

Accompanying the refinements to the realistic mode of representation has been the culmination of a two-hundred-year-old shift to the concerns and perspectives of the middle-class family. The emphasis on psychological conflicts arising from nuclear family structures encourages and requires the spectator's ready identification of and identification with characters if the play is to be effective. The sense of distance between the spectator and the action and characters of the play must be minimized and, ideally, erased entirely. For theater practitioners interested in altering perceptions of racial difference and expanding audience members' capacity to identify with other human beings across racial lines, domestic drama therefore provides unique opportunities to effect social change through theatrical practice. In order to do so, directors who use color-blind or cross-cultural casting take advantage of the unique nature of theatrical communication. As Tori Haring-Smith has observed:

Theatre makes meaning by combining similarity and difference. The experience we see on stage must be familiar enough to be recognizable, but not so familiar that it is boring. It must show us what we know and teach us something new. The director's job is to negotiate these similarities and differences, offering the audience a recognizably truthful and yet interestingly new world.[25]

The point of contention, as far as casting is concerned, is at what point spectators are no longer able to recognize truth in the world being portrayed. For many members of the theater community—practitioners, audience members, and critics alike—the repositioning required by nontraditional casting in modern domestic drama represents an irreparable semiotic disruption. The expectation that a realistic play will mirror the social, natural, and historical worlds as they exist or once existed in actual life—regardless of whether these preconceptions are based on personal experience or prior representations—makes experimental casting untenable.

All-Asian Americas: Translation versus Diversification

In the case of American drama, the issue is particularly loaded because the plays of writers like Eugene O'Neill, Tennessee Williams, and Arthur Miller are considered the core of the American dramatic canon and key sites for defining a uniquely American national and cultural identity. The close interconnection between familial relationships and national identity in works by these and other playwrights is highlighted in Zelda Fichandler's description of *Death of a Salesman:*

> *Death of a Salesman* is a play about children and parents and the parents of those parents. It's a family play and contains profound information about primal relationships (mother and son, father and son, mother and father, sibling rivalry) as do all family plays—*Oedipus* or *King Lear* or *Raisin in the Sun*. It is also very specific. It centers on a family in a particular culture and the roles that different members of that family play. In its furthest extension, *Salesman* speaks about the American value system—about selling and about selling one's self, about America as a nation of consumers who are losing touch with the land, and about lying—to other people in order to make money and to one's self in order to go on pleasing mother and father and the rest of the world.[26]

This characterization emphasizes the simultaneous presence and the constant interplay of themes that are culturally specific and therefore enclosed by geographical and temporal borders, and themes that are not confined to a particular time and place and thereby cross such borders. New productions of a play must constantly negotiate between respecting and traversing boundaries between historical and contemporary perspectives, as is obviously the case whenever a play is updated and adapted for a different audience. Casting in a manner other than that originally intended can be seen as one of the newest means of shifting both theatrical and social boundaries.

The complexity of such shifts and the stakes involved as far as the definition of national identity is concerned become evident when we compare two situations in which plays considered to be "modern American classics" were performed by all-Asian casts: the 1983 Beijing People's Theatre production of *Death of a Salesman* and the National Asian American Theatre Company's 1997 stagings of two plays by Eugene O'Neill. On the face of things, if the expression is taken literally, the two productions look very much alike at first glance.[27] Since, for the reasons outlined in the opening section of this chapter, nontraditional casting in American theater is defined by the display of visible racial characteristics, I was intrigued by the fact that there was an entire category of production where the insertion of visible racial difference into a play's performance, far from inciting controversy or resistance, was uniformly welcomed. I am speaking of productions of plays that are translated into different languages and performed outside their country and culture of origin. By juxtaposing these two situations where nonwhite actors with the same racial features perform white characters in plays of the same genre and canonical status, I hope to shed light from new directions on some of the less obvious, or less readily acknowledged, sources of semiotic disruption that accompany decisions to cast nontraditionally.

The Beijing production of *Death of a Salesman* was organized by the Center for U.S.-China Arts Exchange. Privately funded, the Center was established in 1978 "to promote mutual interest in and understanding of the arts of the United States and China and to promote creativity in both countries."[28] The company used a Chinese translation of the play by Ying Ruocheng, who also played the part of Willy Loman and acted as chief interpreter for the Chinese cast, designers, and crew throughout the rehearsal process.[29] In addition to being covered by the *People's Daily* and over a dozen other Chinese newspapers, the event received widespread coverage in the American media. It was featured and reviewed in major daily and trade newspapers such as the *New York Times,* the *Washington Post,* the *Chicago Tribune,* the *Christian Science Monitor,* and *Variety* and in national newsmagazines like *Time* and *Newsweek.* It was also covered by major U.S. and Canadian television networks,[30] and the final rehearsals and the premiere were filmed by a CBS television news team for a half-hour special hosted by Bill Moyers. The production also received attention in international English-language papers including the *International Herald Tribune, China Daily,* and *Japan Times.* Opening night was attended by Zhou Erfu, vice president of the Chinese People's Association for Friendship with Foreign Countries, and Cao Yu, chairman of the Chinese Dramatists' Association. In conjunction with the opening, the Center for U.S.-China Arts Exchange organized a special two-week tour of China for prominent artists, writers, fashion designers, and patrons of the arts.[31] This unusual degree of attention was largely due to the fact that not only was Arthur Miller himself directing the production, it was the first time he had been fully involved in the staging of his most highly acclaimed work.[32]

By all accounts, including Miller's, the production was a great success, with Miller and Ying Ruocheng receiving a rare five-minute standing ovation at the end. In his journal, Miller recorded his memories of opening night: "the audience is passionate. At the end they would never stop applauding. Nobody left. . . . The gamble had paid off, the Chinese audience had understood *Salesman* and was showing its pride in the company."[33] According to Liu Hou-sheng, writing for *People's Daily,* "This is a play where the various departments of theatre arts showed their individual best and, at the same time, closely coordinated their efforts to attain a high degree of artistic integrity."[34] He went on to praise the play itself, the acting, and the set design. The *Chicago Tribune* United Press International story reported, "At the conclusion, when Willy commits suicide in a pathetic hope that the insurance payment would make his life amount to something, nearly everyone in the audience leaned forward, and several people wiped tears from their eyes."[35]

The Beijing production of *Death of a Salesman* followed protocols of cultural transposition that have been used in the European theatrical tradition since Greek tragedies and comedies were presented for Roman audiences: a play written by an author in one culture is translated into another language and performed by actors and for audiences in this second culture. Interestingly, the movement of a dramatic text across geographical boundaries often seems to authorize reinterpretation to a greater extent than movement over time within the borders of the play's country of origin; productions of a translated play are expected to involve adaptation or recoding. It is accepted that there will be gaps between the text in its original language and cultural context and its reincarnation in another language and "target culture." As Hanna Scolnikov reminds us, "The problem of the transference of plays from culture to culture is . . . not just . . . a question of translating the text, but of conveying its meaning and adapting it to its new cultural environment so as to create new meanings."[36] The protocols of viewing associated with translated plays are in fact so readily accepted that they provide an ironic contrast when objections to color-blind casting are made on the grounds of lack of realism. Richard Hornby's account of reactions to the casting of James Earl Jones in the role of Judge Brack in Ibsen's *Ghosts* seizes this irony:

> The critics' reaction was predictable: while some bent over backwards to be nice to Jones, they couldn't help pointing out that there were, in case you didn't know it, no blacks in nineteenth-century Norway. Casting Jones was a big mistake! At the same time, no critic took issue with the fact that the cast were speaking English, though I think nineteenth-century Norwegians actually spoke Norwegian. Speaking English was simply a convention, a neutral means for American actors to convey the play to an American audience, something that quickly slipped into the background if you thought about it at all.[37]

Operating along the same lines, in working with the Chinese actors, Miller sought to preserve the element of neutrality by refusing to allow them to adopt concrete bodily signifiers (what could be called "whiteface" makeup with rounded eyes and reddish wigs).[38] The ethnic origins and appearance of the actors were to be, like the Chinese language they were speaking, a "neutral means" for conveying the play to Chinese audiences. The underscoring of the element of neutrality or normality, so benign when discussing a play that is being produced abroad, takes on a contentious edge when inserted into discussions of nontraditional casting at home. This is a point Alan Nadel brings out in his contribution to moving the debates over casting practices "beyond the Wilson-Brustein debate":

America accepts its whiteness with neutrality. So when Wilson calls our attention to the "overwhelming abundance of institutions that preserve, promote and perpetuate white culture," he is attacking the idea that the neutral space is implicitly white and that white culture, all things being equal, does not depend on being perpetuated, only on being protected from defilement, assault, and dilution.[39]

The National Asian American Theatre Company's productions of *Long Day's Journey into Night* and *Ah! Wilderness,* like all its productions, reflect the mission of the company itself. The original impetus for forming the company was a very pragmatic one: in their careers as actors, the founding directors Mia Katigbak and Richard Eng had become acutely aware of the lack of opportunity they and other Asian Americans had to practice their craft fully. As they saw it: "At a time when diversity was being celebrated, we found ourselves severely limited, forced to conform to ethnic stereotypes in dramatic representation. . . . We had to contend with the fact that the very fundamental and basic theatrical repertory, the classics of the western canon, was not available to us, unless we followed the standard prescription of 'Asianizing' our presentations."[40] They therefore formed the National Asian American Theatre Company (NAATCO) in 1989 "to present European and American classics with all-Asian American casts."[41] In a departure from the usual practice of other Asian American theater companies, NAATCO intended to present these works without any transposition of the action to an Asian or Asian American context to accommodate or rationalize the race and ethnicity of the actors; nor was there any attempt to incorporate elements from Asian performance traditions.[42] In short, they are not interested in producing Shogun *Macbeths* or Kabuki *King Lears,* or transposing *A Doll's House* to an upper-middle-class Asian American household on Long Island, as the Pan Asian Repertory did in their 1992–93 season. In an interview, Katigbak recalled:

> When I was first thinking about forming the company, we had an informal reading of *The Glass Menagerie,* and no cultural transformation was necessary. That's why we do these plays as written, rather than assuming that people will only understand them if we reset them in Chinatown. I think that would be a step backward; it just perpetuates racism to make the setting that specific.[43]

The company's repertory to date has included works by Chekhov, Strindberg, Shakespeare, Albee, Wilder, Molière, Shaw, Yeats, Lady Gregory, Brecht, Lorca, Fry, Lope de Vega, Marivaux, and O'Neill.

Eugene O'Neill's *Long Day's Journey Into Night* and its sunny counterpart *Ah! Wilderness* were presented by NAATCO in the fall 1997 season. The plays were performed at the Mint Theatre, an Off-Off-Broadway venue, and reviewed in publications like *Back Stage* and *In Theater,* and on the Internet's *CurtainUp.* Both plays were well received, but judging by critical reactions, the company had mixed success in accomplishing its mission of having audiences both notice and not notice that the actors were all Asian American. Irene Backalenick commented, "Watching Asian performers recreate this quintessential American play is a bit of a jolt, especially when they resort to Irish brogue. Nonetheless the complex family relationships come across stunningly in the hands of these capable actors." At the same time, however, she saw the play as having been "translate[d] into Asian terms," despite the company's explicit rejection of such translations or transpositions.[44] An *In Theater* reporter also seemed slightly confused about the origins of the actors, beginning an article on the production with the comment:

> One might think that the kind of gross dysfunction displayed by the Irish-American Tyrone family in Eugene O'Neill's *Long Day's Journey Into Night* would be gladly repudiated by members of other ethnic groups. But a group of folks from the far East will claim the Tyrones' neuroses and substance abuse as their own when the National Asian American Theatre Company's production of the O'Neill drama opens.[45]

Although Miller's participation magnified the degree of attention given to the Beijing People's Theatre staging of *Death of a Salesman,* the perceived significance of such a production as compared to the work of domestic companies like the National Asian American Theatre Company productions is typical. When American classics are translated into other languages and performed in foreign countries by actors of different races, ethnicities, and nationalities, it is considered a sign of the significance and quality of a play, a confirmation of a work's high standing in the canon of American theater. This is in fact seen as a critical step in elevating a work from the standing of being just an American classic to a classic of world drama as well. The occasion further served as a reminder of the status of certain plays as icons of national culture and their situation in the larger context of international political and economic as well as cultural relations.[46]

In contrast, although there have been exceptions such as the Negro Ensemble Company, the Crossroads Theatre Company, and the East West Players, the great majority of culturally specific theater companies, like NAATCO, normally have their productions staged in small theaters, often without permanent homes. Although companies located in cities like New York or Los Angeles occasionally are reviewed in newspapers with national editions, their productions otherwise rarely receive national coverage and are of interest only to local newspapers or more specialized publications such as *Back Stage, In Theater,* the *Off-off-Broadway Review,* and the *Villager* or *CurtainUp.* This is consistent with the general situation in the United States where all-Asian, all-black, or all-Latino productions of works from the European and Euroamerican repertory are more often considered novelties, rather than events that enhance the reputation of a work. Theater companies created to represent a specific cultural group have in fact been subject to criticism from their own communities and professional critics for choosing to present works from the Euroamerican tradition, especially if there is no adaptation to "justify" the presence of nonwhite actors. When the East West Players (EWP) of Los Angeles presented an urbanized, but not "Asianized," version of *Godspell* with an all-Asian cast, several reviewers commented on the omission. John C. Mahoney of the *Los Angeles Times* remarked that the production failed to "inform the material with particulars from Asian-American experience or Oriental theatrical conventions."[47] After studying the full body of responses to EWP productions for her critical history of the company, Yuko Kurahashi found that this comment represented a common reaction. In her words, "if actors were Asian American, the audience often expects to see Asian elements in particular, even in a European American musical."[48]

Whether it is a question of color-blind, cross-cultural, or monoracial casting, as the twenty-first century proceeds, there is no sign that creative and enlightening applications of these possibilities will diminish, nor that the controversies over them will abate. Michael Portantiere concluded a *TheaterWeek* article by observing: "The one sure thing about nontraditional casting is that it will continue; with so many actors of color available for work, and so few roles written especially for them, there is probably no equitable alternative. At the same time, it does not seem unreasonable to hope that directors may retain the option to cast 'traditionally' without inciting anger more appropriate to an anti-apartheid protest; and that theatergoers will have the freedom to object to an all-black *Long Day's Journey into Night* on purely artistic grounds, with no fear of being labeled closed-minded or racist."[49]

What is only alluded to in this paragraph, the true root of the controversies, is made explicit by Margo Jefferson when she attributes the fierce nature of the casting quarrels to "the current environment, where everybody's enraged about political correctness, multiculturalism, and ethnic identity." In this environment, nontraditional casting in general and color-blind casting in particular become "a convenient handle, both highbrow and middlebrow, on the raging battle we're having now over who owns the culture, who has the right to determine what's canonically respectable, what's avant-garde, what's experimental—the larger culture wars."[50] Those fighting battles of the culture wars on theatrical terrain generally construe the relationship of art and society in two different ways: for the advocates of innovative casting, recognizing the racial diversity of American society and expanding the creative possibilities of American theater are inextricably linked processes; on the other hand, those who have resisted departures from traditional casting see attempts to alter long-standing practices as an inappropriate and diminishing intrusion of social politics into the artistic realm. In the next section, I will look more closely at the particular connections between art and politics that have been brought to the surface by developments in casting.

National Identity across Space and Time

The marked contrast between the celebration of an American play performed by an Asian cast abroad and the mild to hostile confusion that regularly greets all-Asian or all-black performances in the United States strongly suggests that the controversies over nontraditional casting practices in the United States are not simply about having actors of different races perform in works written by European/American writers but about majority-minority cultural dynamics within the United States. The wholesale transposition (language, ethnicity of actors, place of performance) of a play from one cultural context to a foreign one is readily accepted. Partial transformations—whether it be in the form of mixed color-blind casting, or a uniform cast of a different race with no corresponding change of language, setting, or performance site—has potentially disturbing effects. I would suggest that this double standard emerges because productions of the latter type ultimately upset the logic and ideology of coherent and homogeneous national identities and cultures. Productions like the Beijing *Salesman* arouse no controversy because they are consistent with long-dominant concepts of cultural identity—national and ethnic identity—that are articulated in predominantly spatial rather than temporal terms. These concepts of cultural identity are closely linked to the notion of national sovereignty, which in turn evokes "images of national boundaries" and a tendency to think geographically and synchronically. In other words, cultural identity is equated with geographical sites and is regarded as if it were "frozen in time." The point in time chosen as an originary reference is established by discourses of nationalism that posit a homogeneous population within well-defined borders. As John Tomlinson puts it: "One implication of this is to think of cultural identity as something 'static'—'Englishness' or 'the American way'—rather than . . . as something constantly changing and developing."[51]

The translation and transportation of a play across national boundaries is ultimately an affirmation of those boundaries, regardless of the fact that, as in Miller's case, the objective may be to transcend those boundaries. The exportation of *Death of a Salesman* was seen as a movement across space rather than time; Miller's account constantly emphasizes the need to reframe the American content of the play into a Chinese context. This was true for everything from the smallest details to the most fundamental issues. For example, in order for the attempt to impress the women at the restaurant by mentioning West Point to make complete sense to the Chinese actors, they had to think of an equivalent—having a young Chinese man claim to have a father in Hong Kong. To help the actor playing Biff answer the question, "What was [the] burden that only his father [could] help him unload?" Miller drew a complicated analogy with the Cultural Revolution in which Willy was compared to Jiang Qing, Linda to Mao Zedong, and Biff was like Deng Xiaoping who called for truth to be based on facts, not on ideology.[52] The rehearsal process entailed constant searches for Chinese references that would parallel events and ideas in the play. At no time, however, was there any discussion of temporal adjustments, of how to update 1950s material for a 1980s audience.

The National Asian American Company's stagings of O'Neill or Wilder present a very different situation. Here there is no movement across space—the plays are being presented within America's borders and in their original language; the settings are the ones O'Neill envisioned. Instead of reasserting a static, bounded notion of cultural identity, the cross-cultural casting makes a statement about the changing nature of American cultural identity over time. The company's mission statement very deliberately ties the company's approach to the Western theatrical canon to a larger project of defining "the changing face of America today." In the words of artistic director Katigbak, the situation on stage is intended to replicate all the cultural "cross-overs that define contemporary America." More particularly, "the superimposition of . . . Asian faces on a non-Asian repertory" is seen as a way of asserting an Asian American presence in American history and culture.[53] In contrast to the all-Chinese cast of the Beijing *Salesman,* the all–Asian American casts serve as corroboration of Stuart Hall's assertion that "Cultural identity . . . is a matter of 'becoming' as well as of 'being.' It belongs to the future as much as to the past. It is not something which already exists, transcending place, time, history, and culture. Cultural identities come from somewhere, have histories. But, like everything which is historical, they undergo constant transformation."[54] This perpetual state of flux entails a constant renewal of concepts, categories, and practices that not only reflect but actually constitute new cultural identities.

While analyses of national transformation have focused on racial and ethnic minorities, the dominant category of whiteness has by no means been exempt from this process of renewal and redefinition.[55] Resistance first to integration and then to multiracial casting has often been symptomatic of profound convictions that the national culture of the United States should be defined by its European heritage. As we have seen in the second chapter of this study, casting policies and practices have always simultaneously been structured by and participated in structuring the racial formations that have characterized American society. In the theater industry, the principal strategies that have supported white social privilege and cultural dominance have been the exclusion of artists of color from full participation and the control of representations of minority groups on stage. What might initially appear to be an obvious and straightforward remedy—the opening of the European American dramatic canon to actors of all races—has instead focused attention on more subtle ways in which cultural dominance may be reinforced.

For many advocates of multiracial casting, the principle that plays in which race or ethnicity is germane to the development of the action or characters should be seen as unsuitable for nontraditional casting is to be construed as narrowly as possible. In practice this stipulation is then applied exclusively to plays by black, Latino, or Asian playwrights or works involving interracial conflicts. Accordingly, almost all plays by white writers of canonical stature are considered eligible for racially mixed casting and cross-cultural adaptations. This would include the works singled out at the beginning of this chapter, *The Philadelphia Story* and *Cat on a Hot Tin Roof,* and comparable works set in specific sociocultural and regional milieus, where, in actuality, racist attitudes would have been prevalent. Using actors of color in such plays could be seen as an especially emphatic declaration of the values of a new era, a bold way for nonwhite actors to actively redefine national identity not only as individual artists but as representatives of their respective communities. On the other hand, it can be and has been just as well argued that such a broad move reinstates rather than destabilizes whiteness as the racial and cultural norm by reinforcing the illusion that white experiences, attitudes, and behavior exist outside history. As scholars interested in the construction of whiteness have repeatedly stressed, racial neutrality, the advantage of appearing unmarked, is the ultimate privilege conferred by racial supremacy. In her analyses of how whiteness historically has functioned in the United States as "a term of power, as socio-cultural currency," Ruth Frankenberg points out that "to view whiteness as 'unmarked marker,' as empty signifier, is to universalize a particular, and rather recent historical moment." She seeks to demonstrate that "a range of processes of inclusion and exclusion have gone into the making of the version of whiteness that has been handed down to us—whiteness as norm, as transparency, as national/natural state of being."[56] The centuries-old tradition of all-white casting was one of the most effective of these processes. As the case of casting shows, moreover, it is not a simple case of exclusionary practices protecting the status of whiteness as norm and increased inclusiveness redefining that norm; inclusion always carries the possibility or the risk of containment.

Directors who are sensitive to the paradox often deal with the problem by looking for historical justification rather than asserting the validity of a race-neutral approach. When Timothy Bond cast African American actor Andrea Frye as a biracial Martha in *Who's Afraid of Virginia Woolf,* it was important to him that an interracial marriage between her parents be plausible under the designated circumstances. Bond also looked for textual consistency and appreciated new dimensions the casting could bring to the dialogue. For instance, new innuendos could be introduced into the act 1 exchange when George tauntingly insults Martha's father by calling him "a great big white mouse."[57] Frye, who is also a director, says she has envisioned directing *A Streetcar Named Desire* as a "huge metaphor" for the shifting terrain of power in southern politics: "I see Blanche as the Old South and would cast her white. I see Stanley as the New South and would cast him black and Stella would be high tone color. I would love to see if that change in the political truth could resonate."[58]

The process of casting modern or contemporary drama against tradition acquires additional complexity when the playwright is living. Many writers are adamantly opposed to moves to change the race, ethnicity, or gender of the characters as they envisioned and wrote them. Ellen Holly, one of the first black actresses to perform regularly in integrated productions of Shakespeare in the 1960s and 1970s, recalls that Tennessee Williams opposed Joseph Papp's proposed staging of *A Streetcar Named Desire* with a black company, in which she would have played Blanche DuBois. In 1999, David Mamet refused permission for an all-female company, QuintEssential, to perform Off-Broadway in short plays selected from *Goldberg Street*. The letter from Mamet's representatives ordered them to "cease and desist from presenting any Mamet pieces with gender changes."[59] On the other hand, Albee approved of Bond's selection of Frye to play Martha—the first time a person of color was cast in a professional production of one of his plays. Sam Shepard agreed to a black cast (Pam Grier, Moses Gunn, Richard Lawson, and Henry Sanders) for *Fool for Love* at the Los Angeles Theatre Center in 1985. According to producer Diane White, "The idea had never occurred to him. He was neither wild about it nor against it. He thought it was OK to do it as long as we got a great cast."[60] A. R. Gurney, best known for his satiric chronicling of "the dramatically near-extinct world of upper-class WASPdom,"[61] has stated that a multiracial cast would be entirely appropriate for *The Dining Room*. The thinking behind his view is suggested in an "Author's Note" in which he says of his first nationally and internationally successful play: "Its setting may still be elitist, but its form is certainly democratic, and I hope that its subject matter in the sense that all families want to sit down and eat together, is universal."[62]

When Diahann Carroll and Paul Winfield first appeared in the Beverly Hills production of *Love Letters* in August 1990 (to be followed by Alfre Woodard and Blair Underwood a few months later), Gurney made minimal adjustments to lines of the play to accommodate black actors.[63] This, despite the fact that the original plays depict characters from wealthy WASP families who attended exclusive prep schools in the Northeast during the 1930s and 1940s. In one letter Andy (Andrew Makepeace Ladd III) writes to Melissa: "I got a letter from my grand-father telling me not to be first in my class because only the Jews are first. I wrote him and told him I wasn't first, but even if I was, there are no Jews here. We have a few Catholics, but they're not too smart, actually. I don't think you can be smart and Catholic at the same time."[64] The lines Gur-ney rewrote included direct references to racial features. In the original version, when Andy has an overseas love affair with a Japanese woman, Melissa passes on her psychiatrist's reassurance that "most American men have to get involved with a dark-skinned woman before they can connect with the gorgeous blonde goddesses they really love."[65] With African Americans in the roles, "dark-skinned" became "exotic" and "blonde" became "buxom." Where a white Andrew describes himself and Melissa as "two uptight old WASPs," a black Andrew and Melissa be-come "two uptight old farts." Director Ted Weiant was aware that making the characters black was somewhat problematical since black students were rarely if ever admitted to schools like the ones Andy and Melissa at-tended before the 1960s. His explanation was that the characters played by Winfield and Carroll needed to be seen as having been "plucked from their race and raised differently (from most blacks)." In this scheme of things, "their correspondence with each other reminds them of who they really are."[66] The casting director for the show suggested that "the important thing is you have to believe they went to school together. (A similarity in) age is more important than color."[67]

But if the logic of dramatic realism is to be applied, how can it rea-sonably be claimed that the letters "remind them of who they really are" when there is no mention of racial frictions? Well into the 1970s and be-yond, black students found elite white institutions inhospitable and fel-low students insensitive if not outright hostile. The true problem here is not dialogue that needs to be amended but silences that need to be filled. Cosmetic alterations to isolated snatches of dialogue do not re-configure the sociocultural structures that perpetuated and were per-petuated by exclusionary practices and prejudiced attitudes. In this par-ticular case, if these structures can remain sufficiently submerged so that the casting of black actors in roles that are in fact racially and culturally specific is not perceived as discordant, it is partly because the play does not depend on a realistic mode of reception. Performed as staged readings by celebrities, *Love Letters* becomes a vehicle where meaning is a function of presentation rather than representation. The actors are readers as much as characters and, as popular screen stars, rarely fully dissolve into their characters on stage anyway. This dimension of the performance is acknowledged by Fertig when he indicates that the producers were open to couples of all races and cross-racial pairings as well, as long as the actors would bring in audiences. In 1990 this apparently meant that Hispanic actors could be considered, but not Asians because of the lack of "Asian celebrities of box-office value."[68] Presumably if *Love Letters* were ever to be performed by Asian actors, some solution would be found to explain why Andy's realization that "those born to privilege have special responsibilities" entailed his rejecting a Japanese woman as a wife.

The case of *Love Letters* draws us back to a consideration of how connections between theater practices and contemporary social relations and racial formations shape limits for dramatic interpretation. The customary industry discussion of an actor's "box-office draw" presents this quality as the simple effect of exceptional individual talent and unusual personal charisma. The important part racialized attitudes play in establishing an actor's professional status is thoroughly discounted. In practice, however, only white actors have the privilege of ignoring racial identity as a significant factor in achieving professional success; in order for actors of color to achieve the same status on a national level, they must prove that they can attract the interest and empathy of audiences across color lines.

Like the Euroamerican actor, the modern Euroamerican dramatic text, enjoys many of the privileges attached to cultural dominance. The conditions of the text's own production and the cultural specificity of the action it represents may be occluded to the point where any implicit historical contradictions that arise from nontraditional casting are deemed irrelevant. This indifference is dependent upon an acceptance of the cultural neutrality of the text, which is then empowered to absorb racial differences without making any meaningful accommodation to truly acknowledge those differences. Of all the possible options, this is the one to be resisted on stage and in everyday life. This does not mean, however, that modern and contemporary American drama should be excluded from casting against tradition, or that only historically or conceptually justified approaches should be used. By deliberately changing the customary balance between the theatrical and the mimetic, a "color-blind" approach to modern drama can avoid the pitfalls of complicity with assimilationist projects by moving realist drama in the direction of a dialectical antirealism. By revising the codes of realistic representation and unsettling established protocols of reception, unconventional casting would ideally entail a heightened awareness of the processes of theatrical semiosis and of racial formation. If the silences and contradictions generated by multiracial casting are analyzed instead of masked, nontraditional casting has the potential to increase spectators' awareness of where the boundaries of neutral territory lie for each of us.

CHAPTER FIVE

The Theater, Not the City

Genre and Politics in Antirealistic Drama

Walk softly on your white feet. White? No, black. Black or white? Or Blue? Red, green, blue, white, red, green, yellow, what do I know? where am I?

—FÉLICITÉ

Here, it is the theatre, not the city.

—ARCHIBALD
JEAN GENET, *The Blacks*

The first American production of Jean Genet's play *Les Nègres,* closed on September 1, 1961, after 974 performances at the St. Mark's Playhouse on September 1, a run that broke all records for an Off-Broadway dramatic production. The same press release that announced the closing of the play also stated that a national tour was being planned. In February 1962, a cartoon inspired by these events appeared in the *Village Voice.* The cartoon shows the marquee of the St. Mark's Playhouse advertising *The Blacks.* Next to the entrance is a sign that reads "Casting Replacements Today 1–3 pm." Standing outside the doorway are five men, one of whom has apparently just emerged from an unsuccessful audition. He explains to his fellow actors, "They said I was too short for the role." The figure in question is indeed noticeably shorter than his competitors; he is also white whereas they are all black.[1]

While the self-evident humor of the situation can still be appreciated, the cartoon acquires new implications in light of the debates that have arisen around nontraditional casting practices. In another context, the cartoon could be seen as a comment on what critics of nontraditional casting have called the double standard or one-way street that calls for roles originally written for white actors to be open to actors of color, while "racially or ethnically specific roles" are reserved for actors of that race or ethnicity. We have seen how this position was articulated in relation to the *Miss Saigon* casting controversy. As recently as 2002, the issue surfaced in Oregon when two related articles appeared in the Sunday edition of the local paper: one was an interview with actor and director Andrea Frye, and the other a piece with the headline "Integration of Shakespearean casts made a belated entrance." The latter article notes, "Historically, black actors were lucky to be seen in black roles, let alone 'white' roles."[2] In her interview, Frye, who is also artistic director of Jomandi, an Atlanta-based company that is the largest African American theater in the United States, expanded on this point: "If a character is not culturally specific, there's no reason you can't cast somebody [black]. . . . Black actors should be allowed to play the roles that are there." As an example, she said, "Othello is culturally specific. . . . Take away that, and you've altered the story. Macbeth is not culturally specific."[3] A reader took exception to Frye's statement and OSF's casting policies in letters published a couple of weeks later:

> Actress Frye stated that the current placement of a black actor in the role of Macbeth, "is OK but a white Othello would not be." . . . Also in the current OSF repertoire, a black actor plays the Roman, Cassius, in the Bard's "Julius Caesar." No word from anyone at OSF about this character's "cultural specificity."

Two years earlier, another writer had raised similar objections, making the following proposal:

> In keeping with Ms. Appel's current policy, may I suggest a revival of "A Raisin in the Sun," with the red-headed Celt Dan Donahue in the role of Walter B. Younger in an otherwise all black production.

Such objections are in fact covered by the Alliance for Inclusion in the Arts' formulation, which makes it clear that it is not the static setting and racial, ethnic, or national identity of the character that is at issue, but whether or not race, ethnicity, gender, or physical capability is germane to the character's or the play's development.

Othello's blackness is an issue in Shakespeare's play; Hamlet's "Danishness" is not. Whether or not Macbeth's "Scottishness" affects the play's action or the character's development is a more complicated question: given the proximity and closely intertwined histories of England and Scotland, it very likely was considered a crucial factor in Shakespeare's time and would still have strong connotations throughout the United Kingdom today; but in modern U.S. contexts, the Scottish setting would do little more than provide local color. In contrast, Roman cultural identity is a central defining quality of the characters and the action of *Julius Caesar* and *Coriolanus,* yet these works have been performed with racially mixed casts. The Oregon Shakespeare Festival production of *Coriolanus* has already been discussed, and in 2005, a modern-dress version of *Julius Caesar* with a multiracial cast including Denzel Washington as Brutus played on Broadway. In contrast, an open dispute erupted between Joseph Papp and John Simon in 1989 over the casting of Mandy Patinkin as Leontes in *The Winter's Tale.* Simon maintained that "Patinkin is too ethnic to play the role of Leontes. You can't play the king of a Greek or Roman kingdom if you look too ethnic."[4] But this is a Roman identity imagined by and most often performed by descendants of northern European tribes the ancient Romans considered more barbaric than many of the African and Semitic civilizations with which they had contact in 44 BC. Which would be the greater stretch from an ancient Roman's point of view?

The title of the play alone would seem to affirm that *The Blacks* is not a suitable candidate for nontraditional casting. But is this necessarily the case? Genet's own views concerning the central theme of his play would seem to open the door to multicultural casting. According to Andre Gregory, producer of the St. Mark's Theatre staging of *The Blacks,*

Genet . . . believes hatred keeps the world running, that if people started to love they'd fall apart. He says Nazis hated Jews first, then Jews hated Nazis, blacks hate whites, whites hate blacks, yellows hate both and everybody hates yellows.

He isn't interested in racism as we think of it. He wouldn't understand the dispute between Alabama and the NAACP. He ponders the timeless struggle between oppressor and oppressed, between ins and outs. We think of ins and outs as political parties, but to Genet an in is a stratum of society strong enough to lash a weaker one which he would call the outs.[5]

Gregory also described Genet's vision of United States history as a never-ending series of turf wars between different ethnic and racial groups: "San Francisco to Genet is a battlefield for Orientals and Occidentals, although you and I know it isn't. He recalls that 50 years ago New York was a place of brick throwing between Irish and old settlers. He sees New York today as an arena for Puerto Ricans and whoever wants to fight them."[6] A multiracial cast could function as a powerful device for bringing out the broader resonance of Genet's classic ritual reenactment of cultural resistance and racial defiance. Just as unconventional casting has expanded the field of interpretation for plays about white characters, it could do the same for plays about black characters. Indeed the first line of the author's preface to his play states: "One evening an actor asked me to write a play for an all-black cast. But what exactly is a black? First of all, what's his colour?"

The only condition would be that the actors must be identifiable as members of a marginalized group that has suffered cultural repression. In the case of Genet's work, changing the color of the actors would not violate or confuse the work in the way a similar alteration of the casting would adversely affect plays like *A Raisin in the Sun* or any of August Wilson's or Wole Soyinka's dramas. *The Blacks*, like *The Balcony* and *The Maids*, is a play about the intersections of domination and repression with performance and illusion. The points of intersection are the bodies of the actors/characters. While the context is clearly colonial and post-colonial, the action takes place in no geographical locale—it transpires in the space of performance. This quality of abstraction was recognized in a rather backhanded way by Kenneth Tynan in his review of the Royal Court Theatre production that opened on May 30, 1961. The production was directed by Roger Blin, who had staged the original French production two years earlier at the Théâtre de Lutèce in Paris. In a remark that may say as much about the limited cultural variety of the English stage around 1960 as it does about the comprehensibility of the actors' speech, Tynan noted:

> M. Blin does not speak recognizable English, which may account for his failure to realize that many of the West Indian and African members of his London cast were not speaking recognizable English either. Their accents have a muddying effect on dialogue that could scarcely be called limpid to begin with.[7]

Evidently, authenticity was not considered an asset, as it presumably would be in a realistic drama about colonial empires. In Genet's work, as in all nonrealistic theater, there is a controlled rupture with mimesis and the sign refers first to itself and only peripherally to an external reality. *The Balcony* in particular destabilizes the notion of a coherent and knowable reality external to the performance space. The well-known opening stage directions for Genet's final work for the stage, *The Screens,* provides explicit indications as to the mode of theatrical denegation being employed: "Near the screen [on which objects are drawn in trompe l'oeil] there must always be at least one real object (wheelbarrow, bucket, bicycle, etc.), the function of which is to establish a contrast between its own reality and the objects that are drawn."[8]

If the play is to have any meaning, however, and escape dissolution into a vacuous display of surface effects, connections must be made between theatrical signs and social signs. The historical links between Africa, the Middle East, and Europe and the Americas must be acknowledged if plays like *The Blacks* and *The Screens* are to have any meaning. The connection, however, is not made through the automatic associations speedily delivered by mimetic representations, but through a conscious analytical effort that requires that the theatrical signs be decoded through an act of intellectual labor. As long as innovative casting increases rather than reduces the challenges to a spectator's theatrical competencies, an antirealistic play should be either unaffected or enhanced by racially mixed casting.

While one might therefore expect the relationship between nontraditional casting and nonrealistic works to be a harmonious and productive one free from negative criticism, this has been far from the case. When controversies have arisen, however, the grounds and terms of debates have differed significantly from those that have surrounded classical tragedy or comedy, modern drama, or, as we shall see, the Broadway musical. In the case of these forms, the objections to nontraditional casting share a common perception that generic conventions that guarantee the realistic illusion are being violated to such an extent that the spectator is unable to engage meaningfully with the author's work. There have been many cases where this logic has also been (mis)applied to nonrealistic plays as the viewer insists on judging the production according to standards of mimesis that are inappropriate when applied to essentially theatrical, rather than representational, forms of drama. As we shall see, however, such misreadings have not just exerted a conservative force, but been tactically used to promote the casting of minorities. In cases where antirealistic dramas are seen and heard on their own terms, objections are framed in terms of the violation of the *particular* conventions that have been defined by individual playwrights for their plays, rather than broad generic conventions. In general, the perceived problem is the reverse of that associated with predominantly representational forms, namely that the casting schemes pull antirealistic plays too far in the direction of realism by grounding the action in historical time and social space. Nowhere is this better illustrated than in the disputes involving plays by Samuel Beckett.

Re-casting Beckett

The most highly publicized disputes over casting in nonrealistic plays have involved the works of Samuel Beckett. The first and most prominent case was instigated by the 1984 production of *Endgame* directed by Joanne Akalaitis for the American Repertory Theater in Cambridge, Massachusetts. The author's objections centered on modifications to the setting, the addition of a musical score (by Philip Glass), and the casting of two black actors in the roles of Hamm (Ben Halley, Jr.) and Nagg (Rodney Hudson). Instead of a bare room with two small, high windows, the set represented a filthy windowless abandoned subway tunnel, filled with decaying train cars and other debris. A large puddle of water on the ground was constantly renewed by steady dripping from above. The ashbins, home to Nagg and Nell, were now large oil drums. Glass's music served as a prelude to the play and recurred a couple of times after the play had begun.

Apparently, Barney Rosset, president of Grove Press, Beckett's publisher and agent in the United States, had been alerted to these changes during the rehearsal period. Immediately following the first preview performance on December 7, 1984, Rosset, acting on the author's instructions, notified the American Repertory Theatre he would seek to bar any further performances. Beckett's New York lawyer, Martin Barbus, was ready to file suit in the U.S. District Court in Boston to halt the scheduled run of twenty-eight performances on the grounds that the author's copyright had been violated. Five days later an agreement was reached just in time for opening night. Akalaitis's staging would proceed, but

Beckett's name was to be removed from all advertising campaigns and a special two-page insert was to be added to the programs. The insert included Beckett's original stage directions and a statement from the author in which he called the production "a complete parody of the play as conceived by me" and commented that "anybody who cares for the work couldn't fail to be disgusted by this." Also included was Brustein's rebuttal arguing that "Normal rights of interpretation are essential in order to free the full energy and meaning of the play."[9]

Interestingly, however, the question of the casting was not raised in the first newspaper reports of the affair—only the set and music were cited as points of contention. Not until January 9 was it revealed that in a December 10 letter to Brustein, Rosset had written: "Two of the actors are purposefully black," contending that the purpose in question was for "us to know about miscegenation."[10] This aspect of the opposition to the ART production was only revealed to the public when the theater company's union representatives filed a grievance against Barney Rosset with Actors' Equity on behalf of the two black actors. On January 8, the governing council of Equity issued a resolution stating that the union "strongly abhors any suggestion that nontraditional casting is inappropriate in Mr. Beckett's 'Endgame,' which speaks to the universality of the human condition" and indicated their support of companies whose "casting practices reflect the realities of our society." Rosset responded by saying: "I don't disagree with what they're saying. All I'm saying is that taking all the factors together—that, the father and son were black and the mother was white—added a dimension to the play Beckett had not put there."[11]

Here, as in much of the ensuing discourse, the focus shifted from the fundamental problem—the shift from an abstract nonlocalized context to a historically and socially specific setting—to what should have been the insignificant, or more accurately nonsignifying, element of the actors' racial identities. The Equity resolution makes it clear that the actors took particular exception to the implication that they "were cast primarily for racial reasons and not because of their talents and abilities." The statement continues, "Mr. Beckett makes no reference to race in his stage directions, so A.R.T. makes no distinction in its casting of any play."[12] Certainly, Rosset was not the only one to find the mixed-race cast inappropriate or distracting. For instance, in her review of Akalaitis's *Endgame* for the *Wall Street Journal,* Sylviane Gold commented,

From the moment Mr. Halley removed the blood-soaked handkerchief that covers his face in the play's opening minutes, I wondered what color Nagg and Nell would be. They turn out to be half and half—Shirley Wilbur's Nell is white, and Rodney Hudson's Nagg is black. Whenever they start reminiscing about the good old days, we wonder why they were in Europe so much of the time.

Gold complains, "That's just one of the many details that Ms. Akalaitis's production fails to take into account. And every time we notice a discrepancy between what we see and what we hear, this 'Endgame' loses ground."[13]

Gold's objections would have been more understandable if they had been used to illustrate the core problem presented by the localizable set—that it made concrete and temporal what should have been abstract and outside of time, and encouraged the application of a realistic, literal mode of reading to an eminently nonrealistic play. But instead, the specific questions Gold raised draw our attention to the power of racial perceptions to displace or short-circuit normal modes of reception and interpretation. What exactly are the nature and origins of the discrepancies between seeing and hearing that she refers to? Why should the fact that this particular Nagg is black preclude the possibility of extensive sojourns in Europe? Long before 1985, there were substantial black populations in both Britain and France for whom English or French was a native language. Is the problem that this black Nagg is speaking with an American accent and so obviously not European? But when had two white actors speaking with American accents ever raised similar objections? If one were to continue down this path, it could be pointed out that historically, black Americans, especially actors and other artists, often encountered less discrimination in Europe and preferred to live and work there. An interracial couple, moreover, might well find relief from social pressures living abroad where they are outsiders to society anyway.

But the absurdity of any of these lines of reasoning should be clear when we recall that we are talking about two persons who are ostensibly spending their days and nights living in garbage cans, which no adult human being could actually fit in. If there is an offense to logic, it is here, not in the notion that a black person or interracial couple should have spent considerable time in Europe. To accept the fundamental premise of Nagg's and Nell's mode of existence means surrendering everyday logic and replacing it with a theatrical logic that applies only within the walls of the theater for the duration of the performance. In the case of *Endgame,* this logic is defined by the "particular conventions" of Beckettian drama. Casting actors of different races does not in itself violate those conventions; discussing the characters as if they were people we might run into on the street does.

Although the ART *Endgame* was the most highly publicized case of nontraditional casting in a Beckett play, having instigated a national debate over the role and rights of the author as opposed to those of the director, *Waiting for Godot* has tempted more directors to experiment with the staging and casting. The sex of the characters became an issue when Grimey Up North, a Manchester-based company, prepared to stage a production for the Edinburgh Festival Fringe in which Vladimir and Estragon were to be played by two women. Apparently it was only after preparations had been under way for several months that the company received the actual contract which contained a clause stating: "It is a condition that the play should be performed as written and the indications to the sex of the characters and performers must be followed at all times."[14] The company tried to persuade the Beckett estate by arguing that having women in the two key roles would demonstrate that the text transcended gender. Erin Ozagir, director of the company said: "We wanted to show that women suffer the same things as men and that two women can have the same relationship as two men. We wanted to show that this play is about the struggle of mankind and not just the struggle of men."[15] But they were not able to alleviate the estate's concern that the "production in drag" could bring ridicule upon the playwright. To Ozagir, it seemed "The Beckett estate just thought we were a gay rights group or that we had a political motive, but that wasn't the case at all."[16] James Knowlson, head of the Samuel Beckett Society at the time, further pointed out that because of the references to prostate problems, "it did not make sense to have the play acted out by women."[17]

Occasionally, a production that did not adhere strictly to Beckett's directions seems to have slipped under the radar of the playwright or his estate. A 1985 bilingual Arab-Israeli production by the Haifa Municipal Theatre presented Vladimir and Estragon as Arab day laborers who came over from the occupied territories to find construction jobs. Shoshana Weitz relates that "the production was given an Israeli context by altering Beckett's stage directions and making manipulative use of two languages: Hebrew and Arabic."[18] The *Jerusalem Post* reviewer, U. Rapp, wrote: "The stage floor is covered with sand and gravel. The tree was replaced by a scaffold. The bowler hats have been replaced by unmistakably Middle-East caps . . . [T]he play has become a parable about the ambiguous bonds which hold Jews and Arabs together."[19] There were two versions of the play. In the Arabic version, Vladimir and Estragon spoke Arabic; Pozzo spoke to them in Hebrew and to Lucky in faulty Arabic with an elementary vocabulary. Lucky delivers his monologue in Arabic, with an accent that distinguished him from Didi and Gogo. In the Hebrew version, Vladimir and Estragon spoke Hebrew with an Arabic accent. The production provoked strong negative reactions on two fronts: politically, the company was accused of using public funds to spread propaganda for the Palestine Liberation Organization. Weitz notes that "The director's intention to 'close' Beckett's 'open' text within a defined and bounded Israeli political context was publicly stated and is implied by the linguistic choices described above and the nonverbal elements such as the set, the costumes, and the properties."[20] Artistically, while most critics praised the production in general and the performances in particular, some did question "the artistic legitimacy of the interpretation and condemned the director for distorting and particularizing Beckett's universal message."[21]

It was not so easy for Joy Zinoman's exceptionally physical and theatrical 1998 interpretation for the Studio Theatre in Washington, DC, to escape notice. Although her original idea of casting a white woman as Lucky was rejected, Zinoman had no problem getting approval from the Beckett estate for the casting of two African American actors, Thomas W. Jones II and Donald Griffin, as Didi and Gogo respectively. In the course of her dealings with the estate, Zinoman learned that Beckett had once actually expressed a desire to see black actors in these roles. Indeed, in 1957, just seven months after the original Broadway run of *Waiting for Godot* had concluded, producer Michael Myerberg revived Herbert Berghof's staging of *Godot* at the Ethel Barrymore Theatre with an all-black cast: Mantan Moreland as Estragon, Earle Hyman as Vladimir, Rex Ingram as Pozzo, and Geoffrey Holder making his dramatic stage debut as Lucky. The production ran for six performances from January 21 to January 26. At the time, Beckett's work still mystified many, perhaps most, audience members and critics. In reviewing the black *Godot,* Brooks Atkinson observed: "Since no one knows what Samuel Beckett's rigadoon means, one should not say that the new version misinterprets the theme. Obviously a play has to be understood before the actors can be suspected of having muddled it."[22] Nevertheless, noting the irony of his critique, Atkinson went on to suggest precisely that. He wrote that while the actors were "good enough in their own right," " 'Waiting for Godot' is not so much of a minstrel show as it has become in Herbert Berghof's new style of direction."[23] With this production, however, the disagreement was over how to render the hybrid genre of "tragicomedy," not over the appropriateness of the casting. Atkinson felt this production overplayed the comedic aspects of the play, making it difficult to convey the work's "elusive" concern with "the suffering of mankind." If the production was shut down for one evening and required a court order for the curtain to be raised again, it was because of a dispute over the number of stagehands in the crew, not the color of the actors in the cast.[24] As Mel Gussow pointed out almost forty years later, as far as Beckett was concerned, "the question was not that of the actors but of the approach."[25]

With the Zinoman production, there was disagreement as to whether her casting concept constituted an approach that exceeded the boundaries of acceptable interpretation of Beckett's text. Jones and Griffin brought black American history and culture into the Studio Theater production. Vladimir and Estragon's predicament was seen from a distinctly African American perspective. In Jones' words:

> Every generation of black folks has been told that something big was coming. I think that's why we bought so heavily into the Christian ethic. Someone was coming to deliver us. First we moved to the North but nothing got better. Then it was education: We got educated but nothing really changed. So waiting became our historical motif. . . . When we accept that nobody's coming, we take our destiny into our hands.[26]

If these connections had remained implicit, the production would have completed its scheduled run without incident. But Zinoman drew heavily on the diverse talents of Jones and Griffin as stand-up comedians, vaudevillians, jugglers and wrestlers as well as dramatic actors. Their virtuosity became an exploration of "the waiters' existential predicament in terms of the possibilities and limitations of performance."[27] In an interview with the *Atlanta Journal and Constitution*, Jones and Griffin jokingly foresaw the trouble their performances might stir up:

JONES: . . . We push some boundaries. Old Sam might just climb out
of the grave and come after us!

GRIFFIN: Nah, he can't mess with us now.

JONES: I don't know, he might say, "I wanted to see it black, but not
this bad!"[28]

Ironically, it was the success of the small theater's production that almost led to its demise. Two weeks after the opening, Peter Marks's
largely enthusiastic review appeared in the *New York Times,* marking the
first time that a Studio Theatre production had been reviewed in that paper. The third paragraph alone could not have been more effectively
crafted to goad the late author's New York–based American agents into
taking measures to shut down the production: "in Ms. Zinoman's liberty-
taking and immensely enjoyable production, Godot is practically superfluous. Who needs the intrusion from that metaphysical no-show?
Didi and Gogo . . . are happy to keep themselves occupied with their own
skills as performers, even if their performance space is as experimental
as they come: the middle of nowhere." The "nowhere" in Russell
Metheny's set, moreover, had become "the symbolic edge of America's
vast cultural wasteland: . . . a bare tract behind a drive-in movie screen so
big it blacks out the sky."[29] Marks let on that the production opened with
music ("a few jazzy notes on a saxophone") and that Didi and Gogo "perform bits of hip-hop and, in the kinds of improvisations that would have
driven Beckett up the wall, embellish the text with caustic asides, resort
to black slang and even flirt and banter with the audience." After expressing some reservations concerning the absence of a bridge between
the actors' virtuosic riffing (including imitations of Martin Luther King
and Jesse Jackson) and the darker dimensions of the play, Marks closed
by remarking: "Still, Ms. Zinoman and her excellent players have performed a vital service, liberating 'Waiting for Godot' from the airlessness
and pretension that often afflict productions of Beckett."[30]

In the first move in a miniwar that would ensue, the literary agency
that represents the Beckett estate, Georges Borchardt, Inc., directed
Samuel French to issue a cease-and-desist order to the Studio Theatre.
Zinoman, artistic director of the company as well as director of the production, defied the order and would even extend the run an extra four
weeks to meet audience demand. She argued that the interactions with
the audience and the ad-libbing that were a primary source of contention were authorized by the text, occurring at points where the stage

directions indicate the characters should "turn toward the auditorium" or that "Vladimir and Estragon protest violently" or that there is a "general outcry." According to Serge Seiden, the director of production at the Studio, in a telephone conversation, a Borchardt representative had gotten the impression from reading reviews that the actors were performing in whiteface to inject race into the play.[31] In fact, the makeup in question was meant to recall that used by black vaudevillians, which would be entirely consistent with the style of *Waiting for Godot.* After several exchanges and a transatlantic telephone conversation between Zinoman and Edward Beckett, the playwright's nephew and executor of the Beckett estate, Borchardt agreed to send down a representative to see the production rather than relying on secondhand accounts. Following this visit, the ban was to be rescinded if Zinoman signed an affidavit promising to eliminate the ad-libbing and interactions with the audience. She refused to sign and after an in-person conversation with the Samuel French licensing agent, the conflict seemed to have been resolved and the extended run was completed without further incident.

In the prologue to his classic study of Beckett, Vivian Mercier remarked that the 1957 black production, constituted "an early proof of the universality of the play."[32] This kind of claim, now made overly familiar by theater company publicity departments, has already been challenged by scholars who have stressed the grounding of Beckett's ideas and themes in traditions of Western philosophical thought going back to the seventeenth century. In the original 1961 preface to his own groundbreaking study, which was dedicated to Mercier, Hugh Kenner recalled that Beckett had once suggested to him that "overinterpretation . . . arose from two main assumptions: that the writer is necessarily presenting some experience which he has had, and that he necessarily writes in order to affirm some general truth."[33] More recently, in his essay "Beckett's Stage of Deconstruction," Lance St. John Butler observes that Beckett's plays "are first and foremost, no freer than any other cultural objects from the historical moment in which they were produced. They are situated at a particular point in the 'general text' of twentieth-century culture, and speak the language of their environment."[34] From the intellectual perspective of the mid-1990s, Butler proposes that "Beckett, as much in his plays as in his fiction, is best seen as offering an artistic version of the most recent philosophical expression of the void, poststructuralist relativism."[35]

Nontraditional casting and staging offer practical corroboration of the abstract demonstrations of the cultural, historical, and intellectual moorings of Beckett's drama by calling attention to the limits of any purported universality. Some tugging at these moorings, as would be almost inevitable when the play is performed outside Europe or North America, seems to be acceptable, perhaps even welcomed. Color-blind casting, and even "multicultural casting," that acknowledges that actors of color bring different sensibilities, experiences, and points of access to the characters pose no problems as long as the text and the approved mode of performance are respected. This would seem to have been the case with the production that Athol Fugard directed for Cape Town's Baxter Theater. The production, featuring John Kani (Vladimir) and Winston Ntshona (Estragon), was brought to New Haven's Long Wharf Theatre in December 1980.[36] Mel Gussow's review noted minimal alterations including the substitution of a hilly landscape for the usual open plain, some added stage business, and the introduction of an African tune for Didi's second act song. His comments on the casting convey the nature and extent of its impact: "With a multiracial South African cast, the play assumes different tonalities, but the core of the tragi-comedy remains perdurable. Two tramps, born 'astride of a grave,' wait out their lives, sharing familiar routines and rituals while looking to the unseen Godot for promised release."[37] Recalling the performance five years later, he offered a more explicit appraisal of the balance the production had achieved between respect for Beckett's text and sociopolitical grounding:

> That production was faithful to Beckett and also, with no gratuitous changes but with a slight shift in accent, illuminated aspects of the black South African experience. Watching the performance, one could sense the inertia of time passing without progress, which seems so endemic to south Africa . . . the Ntshona-Kani "Waiting for Godot" was a challenging act of political theater.[38]

Rather than attempting to suggest that this successful expansion of *Godot*'s field of interpretation constituted proof of a universal human condition, Gussow paid tribute to *Godot* by incontrovertibly characterizing the play as "a true international masterpiece" that can "adapt itself to different languages, environments and acting styles."[39]

In contrast to the acceptance accorded Fugard's staging, cross-cultural productions like Zinoman's that anchor the play's meaning in cultural traditions and historical concerns that fall outside the intellectual and philosophical field of play that interested Beckett are actively resisted. While Zinoman, like Akalaitis and Brustein, might legitimately claim faithfulness to the text, Thomas Jones's insights into the appeal of *Waiting for Godot* reveal how difficult, even impossible, it is for any cross-cultural transposition that is not merely decorative to fall within the orthodox range of interpretation. When asked if he thought black audiences would come and connect with the Studio Theatre production, Jones replied: "I wish I knew. Connecting with this play shouldn't be a big leap for anyone, though. It has tons of humor. It deals with issues of power and class that resonate with Jews, resonate with women, resonate with the Irish. This isn't a production about race but man's inhumanity to man."[40] Zinoman also maintained that the play was not a political statement about race, but her conceptions seem to proceed from religious and emotional bases that are foreign to Beckett's dramaturgy of the metaphysical explored through the material: "The play scared me to death at first until I began to approach it not as a cosmic work about salvation, but a story in which redemption and meaning are found in the friendship of two valiant vagrants."[41] There is a confidence and optimism in these readings that does not hold up when *Godot* is placed in the full context of Beckett's plays, novels, and other writings. But Jones's thematic shift to questions of class and power and Zinoman's affective shift to a mood of happy resolution are the bridges that allow "this 'Godot' [to] happen in a black world" (whether in the United States or Fugard's South Africa), where, as Jones declared, the final realization must be that the waiting must come to an end.

The affirmative cast of Zinoman's Studio Theatre production also marked the third American all-black production of *Waiting for Godot* by a professional theater group. This production was staged by the Classical Theatre of Harlem in June 2006. The play was directed by the company's cofounder, Christopher McElroen, and performed at the Harlem School of the Arts. The setting did not at all correspond to Beckett's stage directions; instead Troy Hourie's set placed the action not on a lonely country road but in a flooded wasteland created by 15,000 gallons of water out of which rises the roof of a submerged house.[42] The platform created by the roof serves as a refuge for the characters and a stage for the actors. An image of two men floating on a door to survive the Hurricane Katrina floods of 2005 had inspired McElroen to use the aftermath of the hurricane as a central metaphor for interminable waiting with no end in sight. As in Zinoman's production, the vaudevillian elements were supplemented or supplanted by contemporary African American popular cultural forms such as rap. This time, however, there was no controversy and no opposition from the Beckett estate.

Nor was there any protest when the connections with the New Orleans disaster—in particular the failure of government agencies to provide effective assistance to displaced victims and to rebuild the city's largely black neighborhoods that had suffered the worst damage—became even more pronounced eighteen months later when the production was restaged as site-specific performances in the Lower Ninth Ward and the Gentilly neighborhood of New Orleans.[43] These performances were produced by CTH, Creative Time (a New York public arts organization), and digital media artist and political activist Paul Chan, who initiated the project; they worked in collaboration with local community and educational institutions. The performances, which took place at a street intersection surrounded by ruined homes in the Ninth Ward and on the front porch of an abandoned house in Gentilly, were free to the public. The localized associations were musically as well as visually reinforced by rhythmic, vocal, and choreographic elements: Vladimir, played by Wendell Pierce, opens his song about the dog in the kitchen with a Mardi Gras Indian call and delivers it with a street band beat; Tyrone Smith as Pozzo wears crushed beer cans on his shoes as taps and dances out the cadences. For Pierce, whose parents live in New Orleans and lost everything to the floods, the new performance context gave added weight and new inflections to many of the lines, notably one of Vladimir's speeches from act 2:

> It is not every day that we are needed. Not indeed that we are personally needed. Others would meet the case equally well, if not better. To all mankind they were addressed, those cries of help still ringing in our ears! But at this place, at this moment in time, all mankind is us, whether we like it or not. Let us make the most of it before it is too late![44]

When placed in the concrete spatial and temporal frame of post-Katrina New Orleans, the futile earnestness of the existential lament or the empty irony of the postmodern conundrum is transformed into a call to action. This result would seem to be antithetical to the commonly accepted understandings of his work—Beckett after all is not Brecht; his audiences are not expected to leave the theater ready to change society.

For the artists of the Classical Theatre of Harlem, however, and apparently the representatives of the Beckett estate as well, there was no contradiction between Beckett's fundamental conception of *Waiting for Godot* and their interpretation. The grounds for compatibility are suggested by Pierce in an interview published in the *Observer:*

> People identified Godot as FEMA [the Federal Emergency Management Agency] in its lack of response to the crisis. But we knew that Godot also symbolised our very existence which had disappeared; our neighbourhood was no longer there, and we feared it would not return. After Katrina, many survivors were asking "Should I give up?" and "Waiting for Godot" offered the answer, "We must go on."[45]

While the New Orleans *Godot,* much like the productions by the Haifa Municipal Theatre and the Cape Town Baxter Theater, may have clearly indicated a locale somewhat different from the one described in the stage directions, the material modifications allowed the message of the parable to be conveyed to a new audience more immediately than strict adherence to the original directions might have. (Although, as creators of the original indoor CTH production pointed out, the road was still there—it was just underwater.) Furthermore, the work of the directors and actors involved in these productions brought out an aspect of in Beckett's work that has been omitted from more canonical approaches. These three examples of cross-cultural casting and staging remind us that nontraditional casting at its best constitutes an intervention in the field of dramatic criticism: the very fact that the play lends itself so successfully and meaningfully to cultural transpositions provides a counterbalance to the recent trend to emphasize the postmodern dimensions of Beckett's oeuvre. According to these arguments, the primary contribution of Beckett's plays and novels has been to stage the collapse of discursive narratives and other structures of meaning; it is not considered terribly relevant that the writing and original staging of *En Attendant Godot* took place amid the devastation of an as yet unreconstructed Europe. The author's identity as an Irishman and his experiences as a member of the French Resistance during World War II are considered background biographical information rather than factors that affect the meaning of his plays, a view that Beckett himself strongly endorsed. As Mel Gussow wrote on the occasion of Beckett's eightieth birthday:

> Beckett is, in fact, one of the most autobiographical of writers, pulling
> his art from his own experiences while concealing all personal ele-
> ments. For Beckett, as it should be, art must speak for itself, above and
> beyond autobiography. To potential biographers, he is inactively dis-
> couraging, proposing neither to help nor to hinder, but insisting that
> his life is "devoid of interest." Insofar as the life is the work, the life is
> of astonishing interest.[46]

That life, however, would suggest that the strain of hope that persists in
Beckett's plays, especially *Godot,* may derive in part from his awareness
that resistance is not futile and under certain conditions, action must be
taken. This observation evidently found its way into his text, to be articulated and heard by certain people, in certain places, at certain times.

The full record of Beckett's resistance toward unorthodox productions of his work affirms that it was fundamentally revised interpretations
rather than the race of the actors that were the target of his opposition.
With this in mind, one wonders how he would have reacted to another instance of very nontraditional casting in the Washington Stage Guild's
production of Don Nigro's dark comedy *Lucia Mad.* The mad Lucia in
question is James Joyce's schizophrenic daughter, who developed an in-
fatuation with her father's secretary, Samuel Beckett. Beckett was played
by Morgan Duncan, who was described in the *Washington Post* review as "a
slender handsome African American."[47] With *Lucia Mad* opening in January 1999, just two months after the Studio Theatre's *Waiting for Godot*
had closed, the casting took on a special resonance for Washington theatergoers. Given his own ironic sense of humor, it does not seem inappropriate to believe that Beckett himself would have enjoyed the gesture.

Re-casting Brecht

If the main objections raised against nontraditional casting of Beckett's
plays were that changing the race or gender of the actors politicized the
works by grounding them historically and socially in a manner the author had not intended, the same protests could hardly be made with regard to Bertolt Brecht's plays.

John Rouse's characterization of the Brechtian conception of the social function of theater and of the director's and the actors' roles in exe-
cuting that function accentuates the principles that make Brechtian
drama an ideal host for race-conscious casting:

The Brechtian theatre's most fundamental principle is its commitment to social change. The dramaturgical principle most basic to fulfilling this commitment is, in turn, that the theatre must attempt to present society and human nature as changeable. Theatre does not, however, depict either society or human nature directly, but rather through interpretive examples. As Brecht defines it, theatre "consists of the production of living illustrations of historical or imagined occurrences between people."[48]

Rouse further points out that for Brecht this project required the "fable" to take precedence over individualized characters, but not in a manner that precludes emotional identification as a significant factor in the creation of a role: "the actor's ultimate goal in performance is to achieve a dialectical unity between the gestural presentation of the character in his social relationships and a realistic emotional foundation won through identification."[49] This process draws on actors' social, cultural, and personal experiences—not just their outward appearance. An actor's background, shaped by a full array of group affiliations, makes a profound rather than superficial difference in the performance text.

From a technical point of view, Brecht's prescription that actors demonstrate their roles in order to foreground the artificial nature of the performance rather than strive for mimetic illusionism is supported by innovative casting. The "gestic split" that stages the separation of the character into the actor and the role naturally accommodates diverse casting, which therefore is very much in the Brechtian tradition. Colin Counsell's semiotic analysis of gestic performance elucidates the source of nontraditional casting's exceptional compatibility with the Brechtian notion of gestus: "In most forms of acting the performer presents the audience with a single coherency of signs, the character which acts as the sole source of utterance. But with the gestic split we have signs emanating from two different coherencies, albeit that they occupy the same bodily space. Moreover, these function in different registers: the actor encompasses artifice and so is of the Concrete; the role exists only within the locus and is of the Abstract. The audience, then is presented with two mutually exclusive ways of viewing the performance text."[50] With spectators already being challenged to navigate the simultaneous interpretation of two streams of signs—"signs emanating *from* the character and signs *of* the character from outside its world"[51]—the additional task of incorporating an actor's racial or cultural identity into the configuration of concrete or theatrical signs requires minimal effort. With the possible exception of *Galileo,* with its historical European figures, directors have therefore been free to explore the casting possibilities offered by Brecht's plays without any outcries from critics or audience members.

Since the 1980s, *The Good Woman* or *Good Person of Setzuan* (or *Szechuan*) and *The Caucasian Chalk Circle,* parables that portray communities in mythic locations, have inspired some particularly original casting and staging choices. In 1985, Washington's Arena Stage presented Brecht's *Good Person of Setzuan,* moving the action from a fictional town in China to an abandoned lot, where weeds poked up through fissures in the broken concrete. As David Richards pointed out in his review, the play was being interpreted as "a 20th-century urban parable."[52] Despite this contemporary focus and the multiracial demographics of late-twentieth-century American cities, exemplified by Washington, DC, itself, only two of the twenty-one members of the cast were actors of color— African American actors played the Sister-in-law and the Niece. Missed opportunities such as this led to strong criticism of Arena on the part of the black artistic community. Part of Arena's response was to appoint African American director Tazewell Thompson as an artistic associate. One of Thompson's first productions was Brecht's *Caucasian Chalk Circle* (1990), now strongly multiracial and multicultural. The designers, composers, and musicians as well as the actors came from a variety of racial and ethnic backgrounds. In something of a "pan-national folk festival," setting, costumes, and music contained references to China, India, Mongolia, Africa, the West Indies, and Polynesia.[53] In conjunction with the production, Arena organized a program that brought together Native American and African American historians and scholars to discuss how spiritual and legal rights to own property and build have been defined by different cultures and communities, often in incompatible ways.

Later that year, George C. Wolfe's staged the same Brecht play at the Public Theatre. Thulani Davis's adaptation moved the action from Georgia to the Haiti of Papa Doc Duvalier, which materialized in a set by Loy Arcenas (who had also served as scenic designer for Thompson's production). When interviewed by Suzan-Lori Parks, Wolfe revealed that he had been "looking for a Western play that [he] could, in many respects, colonize" in order "to deal with the process of colonization as it impacted on people color."[54] Unlike his colleagues who sought to modify Beckett's plays, Wolfe needed no authorization to cut the socialist prologue of Brecht's drama at the same time that he proclaimed the political nature of the project: "It's political . . . because to be a person of color and to be alive in 1990 is a political statement. What you're doing is defying a whole series of structures that say no to you. Every single character in 'Chalk Circle' is completely and totally aware of how they fit into the power structure—even if they're powerless—whereas most people without power have no idea."[55]

On the highly multicultural West Coast of the 1980s and 1990s, multiracial and multiethnic casting of Brecht's works was readily accepted. The case of the Berkeley Repertory Theatre's 1987 production of *The Good Person of Szechuan* offers indirect corroboration of how natural nontraditional racial casting could seem, especially when contrasted with other uncommon casting decisions. In this production, codirected by Timothy Near and Sharon Ott, the principal role of Shen Te / Shui Ta was quite literally split: while a hearing actor, Sharon Omi, spoke the lines of dialogue, Freda Norman, a deaf actor, performed the movements and communicated the text in American Sign Language. Omi, wearing simple black cotton pants and top, communicated using speech alone, without expressive gestures and standing mostly around the edge of the playing space. Occasionally, she shadowed her mobile double, but still remained outside the circle of physical interaction. Norman, wearing costumes suggestive of the fictional world of Szechuan, moved freely and expressively about the stage; her speaking counterpart delivered the dialogue as if it were narration, acting as a detached observer at the same time that she was a participant. The rest of the multiracial acting company, twenty-three hearing actors, spoke their lines and performed the gestures and movements. At some points, they would simultaneously speak and use limited signing.

Two Bay Area reviewers who found the splitting of the title role to be very effective were less enthusiastic about the selective signing employed by the rest of the actors. For David Armstrong, staff critic for the *San Francisco Examiner*, the "sometimes cumbersome mechanics of having actors speak and sign simultaneously . . . threaten[ed] to produce information overload."[56] Bernard Weiner of the *San Francisco Chronicle* was stronger in his criticism:

> The problem comes with the signing by the other actors. They do not use ASL, but some odd kind of inconsistently applied shorthand. Indeed, one could even question the necessity for this signing, within the context established by the directors, especially since the show is

not designed for deaf audiences. . . . All that gesturing and motion soon becomes superfluous, distracting, annoying and finally, overkill.[57]

Weiner's comments initiated an exchange with Sharon Ott, who had directed the production with Timothy Near. Ott pointed out that, for Freda Norman, the signing by the hearing actors was not a superfluous "doubling" of communication, but the only means by which she could receive her cues and track where the other actors were in their speeches. Without the incorporation of signing by the other actors, however sporadic, it would have been very difficult for Norman "to deliver a performance at all, especially one with any spontaneity or life."[58] In responding to Ott's objections to his critique, Weiner conceded, "it's quite possible I'm missing the forest for the trees, that I'm so hung up on theatrical logic and realism that I can't suspend my disbelief and just let go for a semi-Brechtian device." Apparently, however, Weiner's sense of theatrical logic and realism was not upset by the color-blind casting, which included having a Japanese American actor and a European American actor share the same part. Whether because of the cultural diversity of the Bay Area or the widespread use of multiracial casting, or a combination of the two, it was the unfamiliar sensory experience of having signed utterances appended to speech and to uncoded gestures that proved alienating rather than the racial composition of the cast.

In 1994, the La Jolla Playhouse commissioned a new adaptation of *The Good Person of Setzuan* from Tony Kushner. Kushner's version would move the parable from the fictional Chinese city of Setzuan to "an unspecified but distinctly Mexican-American milieu" in Southern California.[59] Original music and lyrics adapted from Brecht's songs were composed and performed by David Hidalgo and Louie Perez of Los Lobos. The casting was, as one *San Diego Union-Tribune* arts critic put it "multicultural to the max"[60] with the roles being divided among Latino, African American, Asian American, Anglo American, and multiracial actors. Charlayne Woodard (who had played Grusha in Wolfe's *Chalk Circle*) and Lou Diamond Phillips were chosen for the leading roles of Shen Te / Shui Ta and Yang Sun. Director Lisa Peterson explained:

I wanted the production to deal with the border. What I didn't want to do was set the play in Tijuana and use all Latino actors. But I certainly wanted it to be a mixed world, since that's what Southern California is about. . . . It wouldn't make sense to do this play in La Jolla with only Anglo actors. That would only be interesting if I wanted to do a very German production of it. Because I wanted to do an American production, it was more potent this way."[61]

Peterson sought actors who also had experience in presentational rather than representational forms of performance—performance art or stand-up, street, and musical performance.

The Cornerstone Theater Company's mission of celebrating communities by involving residents in theater productions was ideally served by Brecht's two parable plays. After establishing residency in Los Angeles in 1992, the company began a series of urban community collaborations. The 1994–95 season focused on building bridges between African American and Latino residents of Watts. The culminating project in the four-play sequence was *The Central Ave. Chalk Circle*. In Lynn Manning's adaptation, a young janitor saves an abandoned baby as California secedes from the United States, and then must face a comic judge's idiosyncratic notions of justice. In a commissioned collaboration with the Long Wharf Theatre, Cornerstone staged *The Good Person of New Haven* in May 2001. Plans for developing "a play custom-fitted to the realities and concerns" of New Haven were initiated by Doug Hughes shortly after he became artistic director of the Long Wharf in July 1997.[62] Brecht's text was adapted by Alison Carey and directed by Bill Rauch. The actual performance, which used a cast of ten professional actors and twenty-four New Haven residents, was preceded by eighteen months of workshops, community outreach activities, and conversations with community leaders that shaped the final production. As one reporter observed, "the very idea of community is at the core of both the play and its successful realization."[63]

The locations evoked by Lynn Jeffries' sets included a minimart (the tobacco shop of the original play), a laundromat, New Haven Green, Yale University, and an I-95 overpass. Costumes (David Zinn) both updated and derealized the characters and action. The three gods were transformed into three angels; Shen Te / Shui Ta was renamed Tyesha Shore / Taiwo Highwater (played by Patrice Johnson, who had been Desdemona in the Washington, DC, "photo-negative" *Othello*); Fong the water seller became Quinn (Christopher Liam Moore), a homeless man who collects discarded soda cans in a shopping cart; Yang Sun the pilot turned into Eddie the unemployed railroad engineer; the good neigh-

Cornerstone Theater Company's production of *The Good Person of New Haven* (2001), created in collaboration with the Long Wharf Theatre. Patrice Johnson (Tyesha) and Raul E. Esparza (Eddie). (Photo by T. Charles Erickson.)

bors who lend Tyesha money were a gay couple in their sixties, and Mr. Shu Fu became the Reverend Marsh, a wealthy African American preacher and slumlord. The multiracial and multiethnic cast ranged in age from nine to eighty-three. The score composed by Shishir Kurup drew on different musical traditions, with especially noticeable elements of salsa, calypso, gospel, and jazz. For the role of Eddie, Raul E. Esparza's bilingual abilities were used to convey the character's duplicity—he spoke in Spanish when he wanted to hide his intentions from his fiancée. (Unlike Tyesha, audience members who did not speak Spanish had the

Cornerstone Theater Company's production of *The Good Person of New Haven* (2001), created in collaboration with the Long Wharf Theatre. Martiza Cordero (Sister-in-Law) and Michael Gaetano (Junior). (Photo by T. Charles Erickson.)

benefit of simultaneous translation.) The theme of good was brought home to New Haven by Quinn's chanted recital of local community service agencies, and the adapted text was peppered with insider jokes referring to civic concerns and local history.

The approach to nontraditional casting defied boundaries by incorporating elements of cross-cultural, color-blind, and conceptual casting.

The most notable instance of the last approach involved the casting choices for the three angels. In a workshop production the previous summer, the angels represented different racial groups, extending the casting logic applied to the mortal characters. For the finished production, however, Rauch decided to make all three white and English-speaking in order "to make a separate political point about [the] traditional imbalance of power."[64] Dressed like tourists in Hawaiian shirts and Bermuda shorts, the angels became privileged sojourners who could decide on the fate of a community with which they had minimal contact and of which they had even less understanding.

In over two dozen reviews, mostly favorable and many enthusiastic, the adaptation was generally regarded as being faithful to the plot and spirit of Brecht's work and commended for giving a potentially outdated work new relevance. In fact, some critics praised the *Good Person of New Haven* for managing to avoid the heavy-handed moralizing and didacticism often associated with stagings of Brecht's dramas. Only one critic took exception to the mode of adaptation, pointing out that "site specificity is antithetical to Brechtian beliefs."[65] Such an argument could have provided the most plausible defense in the only controversy over casting in an American production of a Brecht play that involved legal action. In 1972, a group of Asian American actors[66] filed a complaint against the Repertory Theater of Lincoln Center with the New York State Division of Human Rights alleging discrimination against Asian actors. The complaint cited two productions: the fall 1970 staging of *The Good Woman of Setzuan* and the winter 1972 production of Edward Bond's *Narrow Road to the Deep North,* a denunciation of the inhumanities wrought by tyranny, imperialism, and religious institutions. The Brecht play had an all-white cast except for a child played by Toby Obayashi. The cast included Colleen Dewhurst as Shen Te / Shui Ta (a fact that some critics of Equity's position would bring up years later in the *Miss Saigon* casting debates). Bond's work, strongly influenced by Brecht's theories of theater, was set in "Japan of the seventeenth, eighteenth or nineteenth centuries." The characters included historical as well as fictional Japanese and Western figures, although as one critic noted, "The Japanese setting would appear to be largely an excuse to make use of some of the exotic techniques of Japanese theater, since what happens in the play has only a superficial relationship to Japanese culture or history."[67] This time the cast included two African American actors—Cleavon Little in the major role of Shogo and Robert Christian in the smaller part of Heigoo—but not one Asian American. There was no attempt to use "yellowface" makeup in either production, although the Commodore in *Narrow Road* was made up in whiteface to suggest the caricatured depiction of westerners in nineteenth-century Japanese prints. The costumes of *Good Woman* were clearly modeled on Chinese forms of dress, and the program of *Narrow Road* contained several examples of Japanese prints and poems. Therefore, while it could conceivably be argued that to have all the "Chinese" or "Japanese" roles played by Asian actors would diminish the gestic qualities of the play so essential to their social and political critiques, there was evidently no objection to using Asian elements indexically rather than iconically.

Taken as an isolated case, the Repertory Theatre's productions may not seem to have been the best ground on which to make a case for discrimination against Asian American actors. But seen in the broader context of casting policies in all types of drama and dramatic mediums, the failure to cast any Asian American actors in the Brecht and Bond plays exposed the roots of Asian exclusion, which did not engage the subtleties of generic considerations. Up through the 1970s, Asian American actors had very limited opportunities because of the small number of parts written for Asians and the fact that they were not even guaranteed those roles. When major Asian roles did come up, they were invariably given to Caucasian actors with greater box office draw, leaving Asian American actors with largely stereotypical minor roles. Furthermore, as actor Sab Shimono pointed out, "If they decide to cast a white actor as a star, they are very hesitant to put an Asian in there because if you put an Oriental in there the white man stands out" and the artificiality of the eye makeup becomes glaring. The advent of color-blind or race-neutral casting did not improve the situation for Asian actors, who found that "producers and directors viewed them not as actors, but as Asians and hence did not assign them non-Asian roles."[68]

The Human Rights Division initially ruled against the actors in September 1972, but that decision was unanimously overturned by the four-member Appeal Board eight months later. The Repertory Theater of Lincoln Center was found "guilty of discrimination because it 'systematically failed to give equal opportunity' to Asian-American actors, 'particularly as evidenced by the regular awarding of Oriental parts to non-Oriental actors.'" Commissioner Albert S. Pacetta, said that he hoped "enough pressure can be brought upon theater people to give due consideration for Oriental actors, particularly, but not exclusively, for Ori-

Narrow Road to the Deep North (1972). Repertory Theatre of Lincoln Center. Directed by Dan Sullivan. Sydney Walker (Commodore), Robert Christian (Heigo), James Tolkan (Tola), Lawrence Wolf (Breebree), Andy Robinson (Kiro). (Photo by Martha Swope.) Billy Rose Theatre Division, The New York Public Library for the Performing Arts, Astor, Lenox and Tilden Foundations.

ental parts."[69] He added that the Board also recognized that the exclusion of Asian actors from theater, film, and television was not just a matter of job discrimination but permitted the reinforcement of negative stereotypes of Asians. While this event received considerably less publicity than the *Miss Saigon* debates twenty years later, it marked the first major step in the efforts to make the casting of Asian actors in Asian roles traditional casting and to have Asian American actors seriously considered for racially mixed productions. The New York State Human Rights Appeal Board decision may in fact have set the stage for the *Miss Saigon* controversy by making it, if not necessary, certainly prudent for the entertainment industry to employ the "Eurasian stratagem" in order to continue the practice of casting Caucasian actors in the lead roles of stage, film, or television dramas using Asian subject matter.[70] From a generic or dramaturgical point of view, citing inauthentic casting in Brecht's *Good Woman of Setzuan* or Bond's *Narrow Road to the Deep North* as instances of racial discrimination may not have been the soundest choice; but using the work of writers who never found the union of art and politics problematical to effect changes with significant social as well as artistic consequences was a most befitting gesture.

Re-casting *Our Town*

Nowhere is the deep entanglement of responses to nontraditional casting and preconceived ideas of a play's generic properties better illustrated than with nontraditionally cast productions of Thornton Wilder's *Our Town*. The play's title and subject make it ideal material for casting that seeks to redefine an American national identity and iconography. Looking back from the vantage point of the late 1930s, when the play was written and first performed, the Grover's Corners of 1901 nostalgically recalled a pre-Depression New England where everyone was white and those of good Yankee stock need not concern themselves with the social and economic marginalization of the East European immigrants and Catholics who lived on the "other" side of the tracks. Advocates for a multiracial and multiethnic Grover's Corners argue that if *Our Town* is to have any claim of representing "every town" at the turn of the twenty-first century, it must acknowledge the diversity of the United States as a whole. Such a broadened and idealized context is in fact sanctioned by Wilder's text. At the end of act 1, we learn that one of the town's (Protestant) ministers once wrote a letter to an ailing parishioner and addressed it to

> Jane Crofut; The Crofut Farm, Grover's Corners; Sutton County; New Hampshire; United States of America; Continent of North America; Western Hemisphere; the Earth; the Solar System; the Universe; the Mind of God.

These are directions for the spectator as well as the postman—the particular and local are to be used as a point of access to the universal and the divine, rather than being perceived and evaluated as an historical recreation. Grover's Corners is meant to be comprehended as a metonym and a metaphor rather than as a mimetic representation.

These qualities have attracted a number of directors to revisit the play in recent years and use nontraditional casting to enhance the scope and contemporary relevance of the play. In 1990, Douglas C. Wager directed a production for the Arena Stage. An essay by Malcolm Goldstein, commissioned for the program notes, was entitled "*Our Town* and Everytown." Goldstein wrote, "Wilder tells, not just the story of one remote town in the American Northeast, but of all towns, large and small, and all their inhabitants. . . . It is not just the Gibbs and Webb families of Grover's Corners we observe as their history unfolds, but every family, 'in every time, place and language.' "[71] The diversity of the cast of twenty-six actors (eighteen were European American, seven African American and one Latino American) was intended to support this perspective. Rebecca Gibbs, Wally Webb, Sam Craig, Howie Newsome, a baseball player, and various townspeople, alive and dead, were played by the African American actors. In the role of Dr. Gibb, Jaime Sanchez spoke with a noticeable accent.

Wager's casting was criticized in two pieces published in the *Washington Post,* but for diametrically opposing reasons. Megan Rosenfeld felt that the multicultural casting solved one of the major limitations of Wilder's play: "that the mankind it writes of is limited to white Anglo-Saxon Protestants from New England." In her opinion, however, Wager had not gone far enough:

> But in expanding this vision of the family of man, Wager does not take a strong idea far enough. Why not a handicapped actor, or an Asian one? A Native American? A Caribbean. Once the traditional casting barriers are breached, it feels incomplete not to develop the metaphor fully. This leads some, I fear, to focus on questions like "Why does Doc Gibbs have a Spanish accent?" rather than getting the Big Picture.[72]

One of the people distracted by Dr. Gibb's accent was Rosenfeld's colleague Jonathan Yardley, who used this and other Arena Stage productions to express his views on nontraditional casting. Yardley stressed that he did not object to nontraditional casting in general, only to its inappropriate use in specific plays. In his mind, *The Caucasian Chalk Circle* was a play that benefited from diverse casting. *Our Town* was not. For Yardley, Brecht's play "transcends, in setting and cast of characters, most cultural and racial considerations. Arena's production turned the play into a spectacularly diverse human tapestry, in so doing emphasizing its essentially fabulous nature and making it into a better play than it really is."[73]

Although, as Yardley acknowledged, *Our Town* was also a fable, he believed it was important to remember that Wilder was making a strong point of speaking to the universal through the specific:

> If [*Our Town*] speaks to the universal, as certainly it does, it speaks all the same through the medium of a New Hampshire Yankee town, in the language of the people who inhabit such a town and in customs such as would have been encountered there from 1901 to 1913. . . . Clearly one of the play's themes is that even in a place as remote and provincial and homogenous as Grover's Corners, we can find a microcosm of the world or, if you like, the universe; but its homogeneity is essential to its character, indeed may well be essential to Wilder's message, and to fudge it is to fudge the play itself.[74]

Yardley then went on to voice more conventional objections to the casting: the presence of interracial siblings in both the Gibbs and Webb households and the lack of historical accuracy. To support his arguments in the second category, Yardley cited 1980 racial demographics for the state of New Hampshire (less than .5 percent black and .005 percent Hispanic) and concluded, "New Hampshire . . . even now comes about as close to being lily-white as any of the American states, so to represent it otherwise may be noble but it is also preposterous."[75] He characterized the Arena production as an "attempt to turn 'Our Town' into a vehicle for the new political correctness." As far as he was concerned, the "wildly inappropriate example of 'nontraditional casting'" had "turned this melodrama about turn-of-the-century white New England Protestants into a multiracial and multicultural extravaganza, in the process making it into something it simply is not."[76] He compared the multiracial casting of *Our Town* to the casting of a white actor in the role of Lena Younger, not taking into account the fact that *A Raisin in the Sun* is a realistic drama about African American experiences, while *Our Town* is avowedly antirealistic in order to facilitate the transcendence of historical and geographical contingencies.

In responding to Yardley's criticism in the editorial section of the *Post*, Wager referred to Wilder's 1941 essay "Some Thoughts on Playwriting," in which the author had stated that theater is "'a world of pretense,' replying on conventions or lies . . . created by the playwright and accepted by the audience."[77] He contended that by holding up productions of *Our Town* to the standard of New Hampshire's population statistics, Yardley was refuting "Wilder's central notion of theater as a narrative form that sets us free from reality." Wager also quoted Alan Schneider, who had directed a much earlier multicultural production of *Our Town* for Arena in 1973. In his notes on that production, Schneider had written, "somewhere deep inside we are still the 'family of man,' whatever lurks in our outer skins. We are all related by birth—and death—sons and daughters and parents of each other."[78]

As the turn of the century approached and passed, however, the same debate over the play set in the northeast corner of the country was being rehearsed in the southwest corner. In 1998 the South Coast Repertory performed a multicultural production of *Our Town* directed by Mark Rucker, and three years later the La Jolla Playhouse's former artistic director Michael Greif returned to stage the play for that company. The South Coast production made Grover's Corners a racially mixed community. The Stage Manager was played by an African American woman, the milkman and Mrs. Webb by Japanese Americans, and Mr. Webb and George and Rebecca Gibbs by Latino actors. Rucker described the diverse casting as the natural extension of Wilder's idea of staging the lives of the residents of Grover's Corners as a play within a play. The multiracial casting therefore reflected the composition of a late-twentieth-century theater company performing the play:

> The (original production) showed a group of contemporary actors and a Stage Manager in a typical 1938 theater company looking back at a very specific time and locale. What I've tried to do is expand that and (show) the 60 years since it was writtten.
>
> My group of actors looks more like what America is now, as opposed to 1938. Our Stage Manager looks more like a present-day stage manager. She's a woman, because so many of them are.[79]

Avoiding any duplication of the effects of Rucker's production, Greif did not use color-blind or ethnically neutral casting. The only obvious instance of nontraditional casting was selecting Lizann Mitchell to be the Stage Manager. The three young baseball players who make a mildly disruptive sortie onto the stage during the wedding were played by University of California at San Diego acting students, whose names but not necessarily their physical appearance reflected their Latino or Asian ethnic backgrounds. These parts involved no family connections, have no scenes in which they are portrayed as integral parts of the community, and have no sustained one-on-one interaction with other characters. The Stage Manager's brief foray into the dramatic action is ceremonial rather than personal. Greif's choices were not greatly appreciated by Paul Hodgins, the theater critic of the *Orange County Register,* who labeled Rucker's production a misguided "Rainbow Coalition *Our Town.*" In his opinion,

> It didn't work—one of the few instances in which so-called blind casting drew unwanted attention to itself and undermined the play's intent. Grover's Corners, for better or worse, is overwhelmingly white, Protestant and Republican. The Stage Manager (the play's narrator) tells us so. The minorities are mentioned briefly, and it's clear they have been relegated to the margins of this tiny society. The Catholic church is on the other side of the tracks, and the Poles have their own neighborhood that's well separated from the characters' tight, blindered little universe.[80]

In contrast, Hodgins praised what he saw as Greif's more conservative treatment. "Grover's Corners, N.H. hasn't changed much over the years. To his credit, director Michael Greif doesn't drag it into the 21st century. His superbly cast and restrained production of 'Our Town' at the La Jolla Playhouse leaves the source unmolested—not an easy task in this era of radical reinvention. The thing is, the place can't change."[81] Hodgins underscored the appropriateness of making the Stage Manager the only noticeably nonwhite figure, noting that "the Stage Manager isn't really part of this world, after all; casting a black woman in the part simply reinforces the character's quality of insularity and omniscience and reminds us of the setting's homogeneity."[82] The headline read "'Our Town' like home, sweet home; La Jolla's respectful production doesn't try to alter a classic's timeless messages."

It is not at all certain, however, that Wilder would have agreed with this assessment. In his synopsis, "Story of the Play," Wilder himself tells us that like Emily, we should learn "how impossible, how futile it is to return. The past cannot be re-lived. . . . Truth is to be found only in the future."[83] This would seem to be a message that could be even more strongly conveyed by casting that is not dictated by a frozen past, which moreover was never meant to control or dominate the presentation of the characters and episodes.

Although Jonathan Yardley's argument was more complex in that he brought together sociological and dramaturgical considerations, he, Hodgins, Alvin Klein (who objected to the casting of a black and an Asian actor in a 2002 Bay Street Theater production on Long Island), and others who considered nontraditional casting an unforgivable violation of Wilder's play all seemed to have disregarded the playwright's own recommendations concerning the meaning and staging of his work. In offering "Some Suggestions for the Director," Wilder observed:

> It has already been proven that absence of scenery does not constitute a difficulty and that the cooperative imagination of the audience is stimulated by that absence. There remain, however, two ways of producing the play. One, with a constant subtle adjustment of lights and sound effects; and one through a still bolder acknowledgment of artifice and make-believe: the rooster's crow, the train and factory whistles and school bells frankly man-made and in the spirit of "play."[84]

While he allowed directors considerable latitude in deciding which style to choose, Wilder himself indicated a preference for an approach that foregrounded the artificial and theatrical nature of the performance: "I am inclined to think that this latter approach, though apparently 'amateurish' and rough at first, will prove the more stimulating in the end, and will prepare for the large claim on attention and imagination in the last act." He closes with a prescient statement that would seem to offer the definitive counterargument to those who oppose multiracial casting on the grounds of historical and biological realities: "The scorn of verisimilitude throws all the greater emphasis on the ideas which the play hopes to offer." In a telling gesture, Thornton Wilder identified co-ordinates of latitude and longitude for Grover's Corners that place it not in the state of New Hampshire but in the middle of the Atlantic Ocean.

CHAPTER SIX

Chasing Rainbows

Re-casting Race and Ethnicity in the Broadway Musical

I haven't had a single complaint that the hillsides of Maine are represented by a carpet, or that the Atlantic is represented by blue linoleum.

—NICHOLAS HYTNER

While verisimilitude is by no means scorned in the uniquely American form of theater known as the Broadway musical, many works falling into this category cultivate the borderlands of fantasy and luxuriate in the unlikely. This highly composite form of theatrical performance threads a fully developed dramatic narrative through scenes of spoken dialogue and naturalistic gestures and episodes of full-voiced singing and full-bodied dancing with equal aplomb. As Stacy Wolf suggests, the uniqueness of the Broadway musical as a theatrical form lies in the ways in which the spectator's attentiveness, involvement, and identifications "have less to do with the characters and the narrative and more to do with bodies shaped through song and dance":

> The pleasure of the musical is not that the boy gets the girl but that they sing about love. The pathos of the musical is not that she longs for him but that she dances that desire. Whatever the dialogue, the musical is fundamentally structured by way of song and dance, by overt displays of vocal aptitude and physical prowess—that is, by its own pleasure in its own performance. The performers' virtuosity is always evident and part of the musical's pleasure.[1]

It would therefore be reasonable to expect that American musical theater would rank highly among the forms that most readily and effectively accommodate the substitution of one body for another regardless of the racial characteristics borne by those bodies.

In practice, however, this has not been the case. Nontraditionally cast productions of Broadway musicals have in fact provided some of the most widely publicized reminders of how unhappy audience members can become when the customary foundations of realism are rocked, even when those foundations support an imaginary universe that corresponds only intermittently to any lived or historical reality. The modern American musical subscribes to what theater semioticians have characterized as a "regime of verisimilitude" that makes it "appropriate, therefore probable—therefore intelligible, therefore believable" that characters will spontaneously burst into song or dance.[2] Linear coherency along with measured infusions of psychological and material realism are instrumental in creating an impression of familiarity that enables spectators to believe the unfolding action and the display of emotions. The history of reactions to nontraditional casting in musicals indicates that this sense of belief—notoriously fragile yet always resilient—can be disrupted as easily for musicals as for classical tragedy and comedy or modern realistic drama. Even in the twenty-first century, many audience members continue to be unsettled by or resent any interference with the phenomenal experience that defines traditional musical theater spectatorship.

Reactions to Nicholas Hytner's use of color-blind casting in his 1994 production of Rodgers and Hammerstein's *Carousel* typify the controversies over cross-racial casting in musicals. In the production that opened at Lincoln Center's Vivian Beaumont Theatre on March 24, 1994,[3] thirteen of the forty-four roles were played by actors of color. Most prominently, African American singers and actors Audra MacDonald and Shirley Verrett were cast respectively in the featured roles of Carrie and her cousin Nettie Fowler. By this time, the different positions supporting or opposing casting against convention followed a familiar pattern. The opinion that nontraditional casting was largely political correctness asserting its ascendancy over artistic integrity persisted. *Hollywood Reporter* columnist and critic Robert Osborne wrote: "'Carousel' has been made so politically correct with interracial casting it becomes both jarring and a nuisance." More specifically, he called attention to the contradictions of history introduced by the casting decisions: the heroine Julie Jordan is white, and she's the cousin of Nettie Fowler, who's black; Julie's best friend is Carrie, who's black and courted by the uptight and rigid New Englander Mr. Snow, who's white. After they wed, the Snows have eight children who are played by a mix of Caucasians, blacks and one Chinese boy. Allowing that such relationships would not be inconceivable in cosmopolitan cities of the 1990s, Osborne found them ludicrous in a small New England fishing village of the 1870s.[4] John Simon objected to the illogical alterations that would be made to the internal dynamics of the script if one assumed a harmonious multiracial community, pointing out that "if a small 19th-century fishing town was so liberal and liberated, the country carnival barker Billy Bigelow, who is at best a bit of a rebel without a cause, is diminished into an almost totally gratuitous malcontent."[5]

Implicit rebuttals were offered by the many reviewers who did not even mention the multiracial casting. Among those who commented on the casting explicitly but not unfavorably was William A. Henry III, who felt that "the race-blind casting, if historically inaccurate, does not jar because this is clearly a fable."[6] Two of the most distinctive scenes of *Carousel* are after all the ones where Billy appears before the gates of Heaven and then returns to earth, where he appears selectively to the loved ones he left behind. Hytner, besides offering the remark cited at the head of this chapter, acknowledged that historical accuracy was an essential factor—but the historical reality of the time of the production rather than the time of the action: "This is so quintessentially an American show that it would have been odd to have excluded a large part of America from it. . . . What I would have to justify is racially exclusive casting."[7]

So far, these arguments have essentially replicated those made in regard to dramatic forms of theater. What has separated the situation for Broadway productions from that of Off-Broadway venues and not-for-profit regional theaters are the commercial pressures exerted when the need to produce the maximum returns on capital investments are undiluted by any educational mission. The brief update on the status of nontraditional casting practices in the mid-1990s[8] that Weber appends to his summation of the *Carousel* controversy contrasts the situation on and off Broadway:

> The notion of a changing theater is especially pertinent on Broadway, where the most money is at issue. Indeed, Off Broadway, both critics and audiences have long accepted race-indifferent productions. "Richard II" opened last night Off Broadway at the Joseph Papp Public Theater, with Andre Braugher and Earle Hyman, two black men,

in the roles of Bolingbroke and John of Gaunt. (Did anyone notice?) The fear exists that producers and directors are excluding minority actors from roles they are suited for because of the fear that the tra-ditional—i.e. white—Broadway audience will shy away.[9]

Given these close-of-the-century concerns, it is interesting to note that the first prominent applications of a nontraditional casting ap-proach to Broadway musicals were, in the opinion of many, motivated primarily by commercial interests. The productions in question were stagings of *Hello, Dolly!* and *Guys and Dolls* with all-black casts. A closer ex-amination of the production history and public discourses surrounding these two productions, a 2006 staging of *Hello, Dolly!,* the National Asian American Theatre Company's *Falsettoland,* and the 2004 Broadway re-vival of *Fiddler on the Roof* reveals a much more complex situation in which generic traits intersect with sociocultural conditions to negotiate racial, ethnic, and national identities in ways distinct from the dramatic forms considered thus far. It is with the Broadway musical that the cate-gories of race and ethnicity intersect most prominently. The questions about the ethnic, namely Jewish, specificity of central characters and cul-tural experiences raised by the cross-racial casting of these four musical demonstrate the porous and mutable nature of these concepts. At the same time, it becomes clear that as a practice, nontraditional casting re-lies on and reinforces conceptions of racial categories that are defined by visual and visible distinctions.

So Nice to Have You Back Where You Belong: *Hello, Dolly!* with an All-Black Cast

The 1964 musical based on Thornton Wilder's *The Matchmaker* (1954), already a revised version of an earlier play, *The Merchant of Yonkers* (1938), achieved a degree of commercial success and long-lived popu-larity that was unprecedented at the time. In the opinion of many critics, this success could not be explained by the show's artistic merits or any claim to innovation. In fact, in his book *The Rise and Fall of the Broadway Musical,* Mark N. Grant gives Gower Champion's greatest Broadway hit the dubious distinction of having sounded the death knell of the inte-grated musical as exemplified by the work of Richard Rodgers and Oscar Hammerstein. He writes:

Hello, Dolly! was the first megahit, long-running book musical that wasn't in the R&H mold, that is to say, it was the first in which production aspects were more important than the integration. *Hello, Dolly!* certainly has a plot and characters, but not only are they subordinate to gestures of staging, they are enveloped and overwhelmed by them. . . . *The King and I* was also a show of exorbitant physical production. . . . But *The King and I*'s intimate drama was never sacrificed to spectacle. *Hello, Dolly!* and other Champion shows reversed this balance, and through an influence ingeniously sustained through a long run by the producer David Merrick, ultimately helped the Broadway musical to regress from a *Gesamtkunstwerk* to the equivalent of a pre-1920 song-and-dance show with a mere excuse for a plot.[10]

It was, however, perhaps this very aspect of *Hello, Dolly!* that assured its endurance, enabling the work to serve as a showcase for a succession of female stars: first and foremost Carol Channing, followed by Ginger Rogers, Martha Ray, Betty Grable, Eve Arden, Ethel Merman, and Mary Martins (London). Of the many distinguished women who played the part of Dolly Levi on Broadway, however, only Pearl Bailey came close to making the role her own in a way that rivaled Channing's iconic association with the character. As the *New York Times* music critic John S. Wilson pointed out, Bailey's success was linked to her ability to capitalize on the presentational dimensions of the show, creating a Dolly Levi who was "an extension of the character that she [had] been projecting for years in her night club and vaudeville appearances." Wilson notes the fortunate matches between Bailey's nightclub persona and the character of Dolly: "Pearl and Dolly are both women who manage to keep their hands in practically anything that comes along—and Miss Bailey settles into her Dolly characterization with complete ease, using her own gestures, inflections and phrases to bolster it."[11]

Bailey took on the role of the widowed matchmaker in November 1967, after the show had been running on Broadway for nearly four years. This was not, however, a simple substitution in the key role. The entire cast was changed so that Bailey would be starring in an all-black production of the musical. In the original cast, other leading roles were played by Cab Calloway (Horace Vandergelder), Roger Lawson (Ambrose Kemper), Sherri Peaches Brewer (Ermengarde), Emily Yancy (Irene Molloy), Jack Crowder (Cornelius Hackl), Winston DeWitt Hem-

Pearl Bailey and cast in *Hello, Dolly!* (1967). Billy Rose Theatre Division, The New York Public Library for the Performing Arts, Astor, Lenox and Tilden Foundations.

sley (Barnaby Tucker), and Chris Calloway (Minnie Fay). The new production began with a short run in Washington, DC, starting on October 10 and then moved to Broadway's St. James Theatre to open on November 12. None of the details of Michael Stewart's book or any of Jerry Herman's lyrics were changed: the names of all the characters remained the same, the action took place in Yonkers and in Manhattan, and the time was the 1880s. By all accounts, the production brought down the house and received nothing but rave reviews, which praised the production for giving new life to the long-running musical. The *New York Post* critic, Richard Watts, Jr., went so far as to say, "You really haven't seen 'Hello, Dolly!' unless you've seen it in the production headed by Pearl Bailey and Cab Calloway."[12] Clive Barnes could have been speaking for all his colleagues when he described Bailey's opening night performance as "a Broadway triumph for the history books."[13] The only complaint consistently made was that the role of Horace Vandergelder did not offer Calloway enough opportunities to take center stage. The triumphant Broadway run was followed by a national tour extending through 1970.

Apparently, in his early discussions with Pearl Bailey, producer David Merrick had not mentioned that he envisioned what at the time was called an "all-Negro" cast. In an interview that appeared shortly after her casting was announced in July 1967, Bailey said she had learned of Merrick's plan only from reading about it in newspaper reports.[14] She had no objections to the proposal and made it clear she did not agree with black artists or others who objected to the all-black casting on the grounds that it was a form of continued segregation. While Bailey declined to discuss the production in terms of its racial composition for a feature article published in the January 1968 issue of *Ebony* magazine—"Hello, Dolly! Pearl Bailey, Cab Calloway Lend 'Black Magic' to Show"—the controversial aspects of the production were brought out in the final paragraphs of the article:

> When it was first announced that David Merrick was planning on an all-Negro version of *Hello, Dolly!*, many people questioned his motives. Most were the so-called white liberals who felt this would be a relapse to the all-Negro shows of an earlier, less-enlightened era. Cynics contended it was just a gimmick to attract people who had already seen the show, and the Women's National Democratic Club voted down a proposal to engage the show for a benefit because the cast was "segregated."[15]

Other actors were willing to comment on the question, including Jack Crowder, who first asked, "Why is there so much discussion any time Negroes work?" He applauded Merrick's decision and also stressed that the concept was not inconsistent with historical realities: "Every character is valid as a slice of black society in early New York. . . . Isn't it unrealistic for people to be asked to believe that all Negroes do nothing but crusade and protest?"[16] The celebrated calypso singer Josephine Prémice was disappointed by Merrick's decision not to have a racially mixed cast. Prémice had had a key role in another highly successful Merrick-produced Broadway musical, *Jamaica,* which had run from October 1957 to April 1959 and earned Tony nominations for its principal actors Lena Horne, Ricardo Montalban, and Ossie Davis. While she expressed enthusiasm about the casting of Bailey, she felt that as "one of the few producers who can afford to be adventurous," Merrick had missed an opportunity to do something revolutionary for the Negro performer and the theater in general by introducing multiracial casting into an established work originally written for and performed by an all-white cast.[17]

Actors' Equity also focused on the extradiegetic implications of the casting decision rather than questions of internal representational logic.

Frederick O'Neal, president of the organization at the time, was concerned about the reverse discrimination implied by the racial uniformity of the production: "this seems to be a favor in reverse. It's very difficult for our policy to get through to producers—casting should be done according to ability. . . . Having an all-Negro cast—or an all-Jewish or all-Chinese one, for that matter—is not the idea at all. . . . Of course, Negroes need the work they will get in the new production of 'Hello, Dolly!" But we are sacrificing our principles for a few bucks."[18]

Once the show actually opened, the initial reservations of some critics were apparently overcome by the quality of the performances in all the leading and supporting roles, and the effectiveness of the production as a whole. Barnes addressed the issue most directly, expressing initial reservations about the musical itself as well as the way in which it was cast: "Let me admit that I went prejudiced. I had not been bowled over by it earlier, and frankly my sensitive white liberal conscience was offended at the idea of a nonintegrated Negro show. It sounded too much like 'Blackbirds of 1967,' and all too patronizing for words. But believe me, from the first to the last I was overwhelmed."[19] Alan N. Bunce, writing for the *Christian Science Monitor,* also dismissed the notion that the production could be thought of as an elaborate novelty act, asserting that "The show's attraction lies not in any 'exotic appeal' of an all-black cast. It rests on material and performers, pure and simple."[20] While the all-black cast was mentioned by all the reviewers of the 1967 opening, many reviewers merely noted the fact without further comment regarding any special significance or possible controversy.

Some of the most judgmental remarks surfaced retrospectively, when the casting scheme of the 1967 production was compared to that of the 1975 revival, which had a racially mixed chorus of singers and dancers. This new touring production staged by Lucia Victor (after Gower Champion's original direction) made its next-to-last stop at the Minskoff Theatre on Broadway. The production featured Bailey with a new leading man, Billie Daniels, and a new supporting cast. The show's final New York performance, a Sunday matinee in December 1975, was also Pearl Bailey's farewell performance on a New York stage. The production moved on to the Kennedy Center in Washington, the city where the all-black production had first opened nine years earlier, for a final month of performances. For the most part, this show was less enthusiastically received than the original 1967 Bailey-led production.[21] Several critics commented that the scenery and costumes seemed designed for portability and fell below the usual standards for a Broadway musical, and also noted that the cast seemed visibly tired, having arrived in New York after a long road tour. There was general agreement that the Bailey persona had come to overshadow the character of Dolly. Apparently, the ad-libbing and direct audience engagement, which had been lightly sprinkled through each performance in the 1960s, had now evolved into a more pronounced breaking of character. Opinion was sharply divided as to whether this appropriation was the most appealing, or indeed only redeeming, quality of the production or just the most obvious instance of a pervasive lack of professionalism. The flaws of the revival provided reviewers with openings for barbed comments about the musical itself and its earlier incarnations, including the *Dolly* with the African American cast. Martin Gottfried wrote in the *New York Post:*

> The only thing good about the revival is that the engagement is limited. No. One more thing. It isn't the segregated modern day minstrel show that Pearl Bailey's original "Hello, Dolly!" was. This is a fully integrated company rather than that one whose main identity was not the show, or even the star, but the fact that everyone in it was black. Could a black actor work only in an all-black show? And what in the world did "Dolly" have to do with a completely black setting? This Bailey version is admirably interracial.[22]

Reactions to the cross-racial casting of *Hello, Dolly!* still followed the prevailing pattern set in the early 1960s: the racially homogenous minority cast was seen in terms of segregation while a mixed company of black and white actors was identified as an integrated group. Where controversy arose, it always concerned the implications of that homogeneity as an employment practice and a social or political statement. The reviews and interviews I have cited are typical in evincing relatively little concern with the representational or diegetic implications of an all-black cast. In the sociopolitical climate of the late 1960s and mid-1970s, a period when the quest for social and economic equality retained its urgency, the question of the historical plausibility of the cultural transposition could easily seem to be a matter of secondary importance.

In the case of *Hello, Dolly!* other factors undoubtedly contributed to the absence of any extended debate over the switch from a white to a black American milieu. One key factor, as suggested at the beginning of this section, was the highly presentational or theatrical as opposed to representational or psychological nature of the musical, in part due to its roots in nineteenth-century farce. The broad character typing created matrices that could easily be filled by different bodies. The performers' ability to relate to the audience, their sense of comic timing, and the rapport they established with each other to create the feeling of a close ensemble were more important than historical authenticity. To the extent that realism figured into the equation, as Jack Crowder pointed out, only one of the two locations for the action required any stretch of the imagination since there were black neighborhoods in Manhattan by the late nineteenth century. (African Americans did not begin to move from New York City up to Yonkers until after World War II.) Certainly, the subject matter of matchmaking and mating, a preoccupation common to all human cultures in one way or another, was easily shifted to a different cultural group.

Given the central theme of *Hello, Dolly!* it is surprising that one central question was never raised, at least publicly, by those objecting to a segregated cast. Was there a feeling the producers had eschewed a black and white cast in order to avoid dealing with the issue of having an actor of one race playing a character romantically pursuing a character played by an actor of a different race? It seems curious that critics would call attention to the fact that the 1975 Bailey *Dolly* was integrated or racially mixed, even laud the change, when that move affected only the chorus performers who sang and danced together, but had no dramatic interaction with one another. The question was never asked and no explanation was ever given as to whether this decision, or the one originally made in 1967 to have an all-black cast, was motivated by the desire to preserve the impression of a coherent community that constitutes the sphere of influence of any successful matchmaker, while bowing to calls to integrate the production, or whether the producers simply were not prepared to take the risk of having some audience members offended by the appearance of interracial romances. It may very well have been that the exceptional theatricality of a musical more than tinged by farce would have dampened the incendiary potential of such pairings, but in 1967 producers did not consider trusting to the niceties of generic conventions to calm social tensions that had seeped into the theater.

Whatever the concerns of the producers may have been, once the project was under way, by all accounts, the black cast with the exemplary leadership of Bailey took ownership of the stage. The success of a black cast in a Broadway musical without a complete cultural transposition and minimal if any rewriting contributed to shaping the contours of a post–civil rights era African American presence on Broadway and opened the way for a wide range of Broadway musicals to become part of the standard repertory of black performers.

Rockin' the Boat: *Guys and Dolls* with an All-Black Cast

Despite the critical and popular success of the "all-Negro" production of *Hello, Dolly!* it would be nine years before the scheme of having an all-black cast perform an acclaimed Broadway musical with minimal or no modifications to the words or music would be employed again. The proposal for an all-black revival of *Guys and Dolls* was advanced by choreographer and director Billy Wilson, who had just completed work on *Bubbling Brown Sugar.* The 1950 musical with a book by Jo Swerling and Abe Burrows and music and lyrics by Frank Loesser had not been performed on Broadway since its initial run from 1950 to 1953, and Wilson believed the New York setting and characters taken from stories by Damon Runyon could be readily transposed to a black cultural milieu. The new production, directed as well as choreographed by Wilson, opened in New York on July 21, 1976, at the Broadway Theatre following well-received out-of-town runs in Philadelphia and Washington, DC. It ran until February 13, 2007, for a total of 239 performances. The principal roles were played by Robert Guillaume (Nathan Detroit), Norma Donaldson (Miss Adelaide), James Randolph (Sky Masterson), and Ernestine Jackson (Sister Sarah Brown).

Changes to the original book, lyrics and score were minimal—indeed, considerably less than the new director and cast would have liked, as will be discussed subsequently. The adaptations were for the most part localized revisions: Mindy's famous cheesecake and strudel became apple pie and strawberry shortcake, the most obvious "Yiddishisms" such as "nogoodnik" were eliminated, while black expressions like "Oh you jive turkey" were occasionally inserted, and location and product names that reflected a social hierarchy established by white Anglo-Saxon Protestant tastes and values were replaced by culturally neutral terms. For instance, when Sky Masterson taunts Sister Sarah about her ideal love, his original words are:

You have wished yourself a Scarsdale Gallahad
The breakfast-eating Brooks Brothers type!

Guys and Dolls (1976). Directed by Billy Wilson. Robert Guillaume (Nathan Detroit) and Norma Donaldson (Miss Adelaide). Billy Rose Theatre Division, The New York Public Library for the Performing Arts, Astor, Lenox and Tilden Foundations.

In the revised version, Masterson provokes Sarah by telling her:

You have wished yourself a real dumb character
A square-thinking, pencil-pushing type!

The musical arrangements were altered by Danny Holgate to incorporate jazz and swing orchestrations and rhythms from rock and disco music. The Latin numbers were made more percussive, the nightclub dances, in Wilson's words, "more hip," and Nicely-Nicely Johnson's revival meeting testimonial "Sit Down You're Rockin' the Boat" exploded into a full-blown black gospel celebration that rocked the house. The extraordinary success of returning the number to its African American roots was echoed in the 2009 Broadway revival directed by Des McAnuff. In this production, Tituss Burgess, one of four African Americans in the cast, was featured as Nicely-Nicely.

In contrast to the overwhelmingly positive reception accorded the all-black production of *Hello, Dolly!*, critical opinions regarding the merits and the appropriateness of this revival of *Guys and Dolls* were markedly divided. Reviewers who maintained that the re-casting was immaterial were in a distinct minority. Suggesting an explicit connection with the earlier musical, Clive Barnes found the results comparable: "The present producers, possibly taking a leaf out of David Merrick's book for '*Hello, Dolly!*', have made this '*Guys and Dolls*' entirely black. It doesn't seem to matter at all. The musical works as admirably black as it worked admirably white."[23] Ernesto Leogrande went even further in his review for the *Daily News,* envisioning yet other casting possibilities: "The characters remain just as they are, a lovable, misguided crew, and the fact that they are black in this case is only incidental. This could be an all-Asian cast and the factor of importance still would be only: do they have the talent to make the show work all over again."[24] In contrast, the majority of their colleagues viewed the racial transposition as significant. Whether or not a reviewer thought the transposition from a white cast to a black one was a viable move was invariably linked to the degree to which *Guys and Dolls* was perceived as an ethnically specific work. Place, time, and language were evoked as indicators of diegetic limits that were either seen as broad enough to encompass characters of any race or ethnicity or else defined in so constricted a manner as to admit only facsimiles of the original conception and staging.

The first question about the location was the fundamental one raised in regard to all musicals: does the action take place at specific geohistorical coordinates or in a realm of theatrical fantasy? Leogrande's expansive vision is predicated upon a script set "in a never-never land in a never-never time." He asks, "Whoever believed those romantic gangsters, con artists, chorus girls and mission lassies were real life anyway?" His own answer to his not quite rhetorical question is, "Not even Runyon."[25] In a similar vein, and perhaps with an added investment in the topic as the theater critic for the *New Yorker,* Brendan Gill commented,

> I still hope to overhear Runyonisms in Times Square, knowing that in forty years I have not encountered a single one. The extreme fictitiousness of Runyon's characters makes them ideal for the purposes of musical comedy. These hoods and gamblers are the murderous scum of the earth, yes, but they are also as little dangerous as Winniethe-Pooh. Their gross misconduct makes us happy because it has been purged of the least taint of plausibility.[26]

Michael Feingold points out that *Guys and Dolls* bears a subtitle that identifies it as a "musical *fable* of Broadway," a descriptor that in his view "means we can accept anything happening . . . within the terms of the story." Likening the relationship between Miss Sarah Brown and a real Salvation Army worker to the one between a Marivaux shepherdess and "a real girl on a sheep farm," he concludes "it does not matter so very much if she is white or black—fantasy can be any color."[27]

On the other hand, when the characters, situations, and events were perceived as being anchored, however lightly or solidly, in a sociohistorical reality, reactions were organized along lines of logic that originated at the same point but quickly diverged. The most uncompromising position was that *Guys and Dolls* was both "very white and very Jewish," and could not and should not be altered to accommodate a cast of actors who were not themselves white and so would be inconceivable as Jewish characters. Martin Gottfried argued: "The songs, the jokes and the dialogue that create the show's very nature are Jewish through and through. . . . Even as one tends to adjust to any show as it proceeds, this one again and again reminds you of the inconsistency between the white material and the black company."[28] In articulating similar views, John Simon noted that while *Guys and Dolls* was hardly an example of photographic realism, it had "a mythic reality" and "a fictional solidity," and consequently derived much of its effectiveness from "certain authentic social observations that are embedded in time and place and ethnicity." He referred to the musical's long-engaged couple to illustrate his point: "Both Nathan and Adelaide speak with the syntax and inflections of Brooklyn—a fantasy Brooklyn, perhaps, but a very vivid and Semitic one. It is fairly preposterous for a black to sing repeatedly, 'Alright, already.' "[29]

Wilson, working with Abe Burrows, had in fact been very conscious of the need to eliminate the most obvious "Jewish ethnic phrases" from the spoken dialogue and the lyrics of the songs. As reactions demonstrated, however, what seemed "obvious" depended to a large degree on the listener's level of familiarity with the speech of New York's Jewish community, composed largely of Yiddish-speaking East European immigrants and their descendants. For instance, in the song "Sue Me" Nathan's original lines were:

> Alright, already I'm just a no goodnick
> Alright, already it's true, so nu?

In the black version, Robert Guillaume sang:

> Alright, already I'm just a big zero
> Alright, already it's true so true.

Apparently, "no goodnick" and "nu" were considered too ethnically and linguistically specific by Wilson and Burrows, while "alright, already" was treated as one of the many "Yiddishisms" that have been adopted by non-Yiddish and non-Jewish New Yorkers.

While the language, whether identified as "Jewish" or "white Broadwayese," was invariably considered the source of the most striking incongruities between the script and the black cast, it did not constitute an insurmountable obstacle to cultural transposition in the eyes—or to the ears—of all reviewers. In some cases, this was because the speech of New Yorkers in general and its underworld characters in particular, especially as manifested in popular cultural forms, was recognized as being already a composite of dialects. Michael Feingold points out: "Many of the mannerisms of Runyon's white underworld were adopted from the black underworld in the first place; in effect, they are being sent black [*sic*] where they came from."[30]

In other cases, the black casting was considered a successful move because critics felt that Wilson and his actors had found an equivalent form of delivery in African diasporic culture. In his enthusiastic account of the revival in *New York* magazine, Alan Rich discerned compatible features in the source and target dialects:

> I had my doubts about Damon Runyon's peculiar brand of Times Square lingo—distinctly Jewish in its tendency toward the elegant variation, and in its grammatical prissiness that favors complex construction over contraction—becoming congruent with black jive. But with only the slightest alteration in Jo Swerling and Abe Burrows's

original book, and with some splendid work by his wholly inspired cast, Billy Wilson has achieved the translation gracefully and easefully. The Runyonese, he has found, works best when delivered with a warm, deliberate Jamaican inflection.[31]

In most of the positive reviews, however, the author was concerned less with specific linguistic correspondences than with general inflections and the attitudes they conveyed. In his highly favorable review for the *Christian Science Monitor*, John Beaufort wrote: "the change from white New Yorkese to Afro-American is not so much a matter of altered accent and idiom. It is rather the replacement of one kind of city sharpness for another."[32]

Implicitly or explicitly, when *Guys and Dolls* was not perceived as taking place in a never-never land or a generic New York of the imagination, historical plausibility was used as one of the standards against which to measure the merits of the revised staging. But there was a difference of opinion as to whether plausibility necessarily entailed moving the locations about eighty blocks north on Broadway. Some reviewers seemed to assume this was the case: Barnes observed that the successors to the characters first embodied by Vivian Blaine, Sam Levene, Stubby Kaye, and Robert Alda seemed "perfectly at home in Harlem,"[33] while Hobe presumed audiences for the revival were watching "Harlemites of the 1970s."[34] Other comments, however, indicate that these were indeed assumptions. Beatrice da Silva tantalized *Villager* readers with the remark, "Maybe the 'oldest established permanent crap game in New York' resides these days in Harlem, but perhaps it does not."[35] The same sense of ambiguity appeared in a complaint about the scenery; Kissel attributed the "thoroughly unimpressive" physical production to the fact that "no one made a firm decision about whether the show is still set in Times Square or further uptown."[36]

The lack of a clear commitment to a black neighborhood setting was just the most superficial dimension of a larger problem that proved to be as much a point of contention as the casting decision itself. Many of the critics who were open to the notion of an all-black cast remained receptive only as long as the transposition went more than skin deep. In some cases, objections were raised out of a sense of respect for the status of the original work, which was considered by many of the writers to be not just another classic American musical but one that was unsurpassed for its seamless integration of dialogue and lyrics, with the latter contributing as much to character and plot development as the former. Any alterations should therefore reflect the same degree of commitment to the integrity and distinctiveness of milieu, character, and language. As da Silva put it very succinctly and colloquially, "why did they choose to exploit a tried-and-true musical with a fine Jewish heritage and transform it into an all black performance that ain't got no soul?"[37] More than one critic went so far as to compare the end result to a production in blackface. In *Newsweek,* Charles Michener wrote:

> But the most troubling interference is the blackface. It's not that the show's original Jewish flavor proved ineradicable, for its essentially showbiz idiom flows just as naturally from blacks as it did from whites. But of the four principal characters, only lovable slippery Nathan Detroit seems completely himself in the person of Robert Guillaume. . . .
>
> This "Guys and Dolls" has acquired a black cast but, for the most part, the cast is just a cast—a darker shade of make-up uneasily applied over white characters.[38]

Expanding upon his criticism of the all-black casting in *Hello, Dolly!,* Gottfried thoroughly denounced the practice as racist and commercially motivated, drawing analogies to minstrel shows:

> It's become wearisome to keep pointing out the offensiveness of all-black versions of white shows. There is a basic racism to them: the blackness of the actor is being used as a theatrical motif. It is a condescending exotica attitude that was supposed to have passed with minstrel shows and "Carmen Jones." However, the commercial value of today's all-black shows, as with all commercial values, rides roughshod over that.
>
> All-black versions of white shows also make as much sense as all-white versions of black shows. Material that was specifically written for one milieu is recklessly stretched to fit another or, as is more commonly the case, is simply ignored.[39]

The reviewers who found fault with the black production on the grounds that it was not black enough invariably joined their more satisfied colleagues in singling out one number for praise—Ken Page as Nicely-Nicely leading the revival meeting in "Sit Down You're Rockin' the Boat."

The public debate over the degree of cultural transposition that was necessary or desirable was the efflorescence of a fundamental point of disagreement between Abe Burrows and Billy Wilson. Abe Burrows, when asked, why do an all-black *Guys and Dolls,* replied laconically, "Why not?"[40] Elsewhere, he elaborated: "There are a couple of new thoughts, a couple of new lines. But it's not a show that's confined to a particular time and place. None of my shows are." In contrast, in an interview that appeared a few days before the show opened, Wilson stated that while there were never any big fights, "I do disagree with Abe on one point, though. He says it makes no difference what color of people do 'Guys and Dolls,' but I take exception. The moment black people are doing anything, or Jewish people or Indians, the show must take on the flavor of it."[41] The official program and all other publicity credited Wilson as the director and choreographer and noted "Entire Production Under the Supervision of Abe Burrows." This announcement may have been intended to function as a seal of approval from the surviving creator of the original, who, along with Loesser's widow, held the rights to the book, music, and lyrics; but in retrospect it serves to identify the source of what struck many critics as "an uneasy compromise."[42] Wilson recounts that his efforts "to tak[e] chicken soup and mak[e] it a little more gumbo"[43] were curbed, mainly while the show was in the rehearsal stage. It was only after the production opened to good reviews in Philadelphia that he "had more freedom to 'stretch the show and make it blacker.' "[44]

While many of the issues raised by the nontraditional casting of *Guys and Dolls* were the same as those raised during the 1960s, the public discourse had undergone marked changes. The terms *integration* and *segregation* were no longer in evidence no matter what the position or sentiments of the writer. The key terms of the mid-1970s lexicon appear in Gussow's essay, "Casting by Race Can Be Touchy":

> The crucial question is whether a play should be cast entirely with black performers or with a mixed company. The former can seem racist if there is no artistic validity for the switch in color. Then its only justification is to give minority actors employment. The mixed company makes far more sense, but there are those special cases, such as "Guys and Dolls."[45]

The new terminology moved theater practices away from being equated with sociopolitical policies and legislation. This move had both progressive and conservative incentives and effects. On the conservative side, the separation reflected an impulse to seclude theatrical activity from contemporary social controversies and contests and deny unwelcome external pressures. At the same time, the conversion to less politically charged terminology both reflected and enabled a shift to conditions where ideas and practices could begin to take on inflections particular to specific cultural forms. In the case of theater, this meant, as we have seen with *Guys and Dolls,* going beyond a bold but unidimensional gesture of casting actors of a different race as an end in itself—even when this entails making surface adaptations to text or staging—to reconsidering the work itself both as an aesthetic entity and a cultural product. This is the process that Gussow describes in his meditation on race-based casting, as he reconsidered the music and book of *Guys and Dolls* and recognized elements that had not been brought out before:

> Perhaps the most surprising conclusion about Loesser's score, as performed at the Broadway Theater, is that it has a definite line of black sensibility and rhythm. . . .
>
> "Sit Down" is the clearest, although not the only example of the blackness that has been discovered within "Guys and Dolls"—largely, one assumes by director-choreographer Billy Wilson.[46]

Turning to the book, he found that although at first sight the book presented "something of a problem," with "only a few minor—and interesting alterations, the story turns black." He concluded by observing that "there are times when a black company can itself act as a re-interpretation of a show," with the reinterpretation taking place on all levels of expression—spoken words, songs, characters, music, and performance style—and taking into account the particularities of each musical:

> Pearl Bailey's "Hello. Dolly" would have made much more sense if the production had not been all black. We kept wondering what all those blacks were doing in Yonkers at that time. Yet a black Dolly is imaginable if she has the force of personality of a Pearl Bailey. "Hello Dolly" is *about* its star's force of personality, whether that star is Miss Bailey or Carol Channing. There is no reason why a strong black performer could not play "Gypsy" or Sally Bowles in "Cabaret." If the King of Siam could be played by Yul Brynner, why could the role not also be played by a black man?[47]

The most significant change reflected by the withdrawal of the term *segregation,* however, concerned the new contexts for the presence of black artists and productions on Broadway. The primary cultural corollaries of the political and social reforms brought about by the civil rights movement were the recognition of African American contributions to the history and culture of the United States and a burgeoning of black artistic expression at sites that, with rare exceptions, had previously been closed to racial minorities. By the mid-1970s, an all-black cast was no longer a sign of containment but the assertion of a continuing black tradition of musical theater. *Guys and Dolls* followed *Purlie* (1970), *Raisin* (1973), *The Wiz* (1975), *Bubbling Brown Sugar* (1976), and would be succeeded by *Ain't Misbehavin'* (1978), *Eubie* (1979), *Dreamgirls* (1981), and *Sophisticated Ladies* (1981).

While a racially mixed cast would have made an overt, highly visible statement regarding integration as the new social norm, from the performers' (and in the case of *Guys and Dolls,* the director-choreographer's) point of view the racial uniformity afforded an experience of camaraderie and unity that would have been dissipated by mixed casting. Shared cultural experiences unique to members of African American communities could become part of the finished product through the process of creation and the performance experience only with an all-black company. This is evident in Wilson's directions to his actors concerning the critical issue of language:

> It's not so much the phrasing of words that makes the difference. . . . It's the delivery. We have such rich attitudes among blacks. It's something that's intrinsic with us. . . . The cast at the very beginning was very anxious about what I was going to do to help make the show their own. My biggest point of direction to them was, "find the equivalent in your own experience, and go from there. Get the rhythm, the way you would really say that."[48]

This was a far more subtle and sophisticated approach, both culturally and artistically, to redefining what is undeniably a quintessential American cultural form, the Broadway musical, than the injection of almost stereotypically black American elements that several reviewers seemed to be seeking. In an interview with the *Philadelphia Inquirer,* Billy Wilson pointed out, as August Wilson would two decades later, that the black theater artists' cultural heritage included forms and genres developed by

European and Euroamerican artists and institutions: "Everything that happens in this country is part of my experience. I have my African heritage, the European culture that was imposed on me, and what I have become is an American."[49] By physically inhabiting classical roles and works, African American artists were redefining both black culture and American culture.

While the all-black casting may not have presented a picture of integration on stage, it had perhaps an even more important effect in promoting racially mixed audiences in a way that color-blind casting could never have. Musicals created or performed by black artists had a noticeable impact on audience composition throughout the 1970s. The growing African American theater audience was a nationwide trend, attributable in large part to the increase in touring productions that originated on or were destined for Broadway. Such productions appealed specifically to middle-class African Americans who had the financial means to attend the theater but previously had not found material playing in their cities' cultural centers that related to black American culture and experiences. A survey of dozens of theatergoers showed that the wave of black-oriented Broadway productions filled cultural gaps left by black community theaters, which focused largely on socially and economically deprived communities, and the blaxploitation films of the decade, which appealed to younger audiences.[50] For Norma Donaldson, who played the part of Adelaide, the concern for building a sense of black community and entertaining a multiracial audience were not mutually exclusive goals: "An all-black cast is valuable in terms of identity. . . . It gives black people dignity. When I see black people turn out for 'Guys and Dolls,' I'm thrilled . . . and what gives me an even better feeling is that both races are leaving the theatre saying they had a good time."[51]

Guys, Dolls, Dollys, and Ethnicity

While casting *Hello, Dolly!* and *Guys and Dolls* with black performers naturally directed the public discussion toward questions involving black-white social and cultural relations, these particular works are also notable for having engendered discussions about defining ethnicity on Broadway stages. As already indicated above, Billy Wilson's production of *Guys and Dolls* raised questions not just about the "whiteness" of the work but its inherent "Jewishness" as well. In the case of *Hello, Dolly!* a 2006 production at the Paper Mill Playhouse starring Tovah Feldshuh illustrated the process through which a character's ethnic identity was heavily derived from the ethnic identity and repertoire of the actors associated with the role.

The obvious cross-casting approach of the all-black production of *Hello, Dolly!* exempted the production from any obligation to justify the cultural transposition historically or genealogically. It is curious, however, that, given the title character's full name, Dolly Gallagher Levi, the character's ethnic or religious identity is never explored in the script of the musical, and the matter was never treated as problematical or intriguing by performers or critics. As an obvious index of Irish and Jewish cultural origins and affiliations, the name suggests Dolly is an Irish American (at least on her father's side of the family) who married a Jewish man, Ephraim Levi. Indeed, Dolly's first line is "That's right, Mrs. Dolly Levi, born Gallagher." While such an interethnic marriage would have remained a social anomaly from the late nineteenth century up through the 1930s when Wilder wrote *The Merchant of Yonkers* (1939), Irish-Jewish marriages were in vogue on stage and screen in the 1920s and 1930s. Ephraim and Dolly would have followed a long line of couples beginning with the central characters in Ann Nichols's Broadway play *Abie's Irish Rose* (1922). Between 1922 and 1927, seventeen films featuring Irish-Jewish couples appeared, the most memorable of these being *The Cohens and the Kellys* (1926), which spawned several sequels including *The Cohens and Kellys in Africa* (1930). These films were designed "to encourage assimilation and to critique what was considered the stubborn separatism of immigrant groups."[52] While Dolly represented the Irish side of the family, on the New York stage and in American popular culture, it would be Dolly's married, not maiden, name that would define her ethnic identity.

Dolly clearly seems to have acquired her indelibly Jewish ethnic identity when her story made the transition from farce to musical. Neither the text nor the performance history of *The Matchmaker* cultivated an image of the figure as a Jewish woman, and her pedigree reaching back through nineteenth-century Austria to seventeenth-century France to ancient Rome certainly could not have predicted a descendant emerging from a cultural community that had yet to be imagined, much less exist. Yet the most prominent and enduring portrayals of the musical Dolly—Carol Channing's iconic stage creation of the role and Barbra Streisand's film performance—both presented her as a distinctly New York Jewish matchmaker. Carol Channing offered a simple explanation from her own life when asked why she had decided to play Dolly as a Jew, stating that "from my own personal experience [of having married into a Galician, Yiddish-speaking family], I've found that you turn Jewish when you're married to a Jew."[53]

The characterization of Dolly as Jewish was reinforced when Barbra Streisand starred in the 1969 film version of the musical. Although the film and Streisand's portrayal were widely criticized, once she had inhabited the role, Streisand stamped it with her celebrity persona. As Stacy Wolf very emphatically points out, this persona was inseparable from her identity as a Jewish performer: "Streisand's star persona—her appearance and behavior, her multimedia superstardom—not only signifies Jewishness but powerfully remakes the meaning of Jewishness for American culture. She is the Jewish Woman and the Jewish Woman is her."[54] Ironically, Streisand's identification with Jewish roles was being forged on Broadway at the same time Channing was defining what would become her signature role as a Jewish character. *Funny Girl,* in which Streisand starred as the Jewish American actress Fanny Brice, opened on March 26, 1964, just three months after *Hello, Dolly!*'s January 16 premiere. The year 1964, moreover, was also when Jerry Bock and Sheldon Harnick's *Fiddler on the Roof* opened, with its archetypal matchmaker Yente. Yente, like Dolly, is a widow who spends her empty hours thinking of her departed husband and meddling in the lives of others. The popularity of "Matchmaker, Matchmaker," the song that lamented the yawning gap between Yente's pragmatic notion of suitable matches for young women and their own romantic ideas, further served to weld together the ethnic and professional dimensions of the Jewish matchmaker. The fact that all three of the 1964 musicals were made into films assured the longevity of both the character and actor types.

With such a cultural history to contend with, the significance of the "Gallagher" was never foregrounded as a dramatic element until Tovah Feldshuh was cast in the role at the Paper Mill Playhouse in 2006. Feldshuh could easily have been expected to continue the tradition begun by Channing and reinforced by Streisand. Feldshuh, who had chosen to acknowledge her Jewish heritage by replacing her given name "Terri Sue" with a Hebrew first name when she was in college, was well-known professionally for her work in plays with Jewish themes. She had first gained national recognition in the 1970s as the title character in a dramatic version of Isaac Bashevis Singer's story "Yentl" (1975–76), earning her first nominations for Tony and Drama Desk awards, and she was nominated for an Emmy award for her role as a Czech freedom fighter in the TV miniseries *Holocaust* (1978). Her last project before taking on the lead role in *Dolly* had been playing Israeli prime minister Golda Meir in the one-woman show *Golda's Balcony,* which ran both off and on Broadway from 2003 to 2005; she received Drama Desk and Lucille Lortel Awards and a Tony nomination.

Feldshuh considered the choice of playing Dolly as a Jewish match-maker a misguided one, since she had acquired the Jewish surname only through marriage. Instead the actress imagined a detailed backstory for the character. Her Dolly was born in Connemara in 1850, in the western part of Ireland that was hit hardest by the potato blight of the late 1840s. At the age of twelve or thirteen, she emigrated to the United States with her Irish-Catholic family (including twelve siblings) to escape famine and poverty. Growing up in the "melting pot" of the Lower East Side of Manhattan, Dolly met and married a Jewish young man whose parents were East European immigrants. For Feldshuh, viewing the nineteenth century as the first great era of mass migrations to the United States was central to creating the context for the story. Dolly was not a brassy exhi-bitionist but "a first-generation immigrant who is trying to fit in and has been struggling to get by since being left a widow."[55]

Although Feldshuh did not continue the tradition of portraying Dolly as Jewish, she did continue the tradition of ethnic impersonation, which is primarily a function of speech.[56] Feldshuh concluded that with her speech patterns already formed by the time she arrived in New York, Dolly would speak English with an Irish accent. For Feldshuh, this was the key to her interpretation: "I find the character by the sound. When I found the sound of her, I found her."[57] The sound included a marked Irish brogue evident in both the dialogue and the songs. If Dolly is un-usually talkative, it is no longer because she is a "yenta" but because she has "the blarney." As the headline for Neil Genzlinger's article for the New Jersey edition of the *New York Times,* "A Brogue Helps Keep the Spir-its at Bay," suggests, the ever-present (and apparently somewhat carica-tured) accent served to discourage the audience from associating Feld-shuh with her previous roles and, more importantly, from associating Dolly with her previous celebrity interpreters.

While all the interviews and reviews of the Paper Mill Playhouse pro-duction devoted considerable attention to Feldshuh's departure from previous conceptions of the role and most mentioned the special place Jewish roles had played in her extensive career, only the reporter for the *New Jersey Jewish News* asked her directly, "How does being Jewish affect the way you play this role and how people respond to you in this role?" Her answer was: "The biggest trap is to play Dolly as a Jew. Only Carol Channing—a Christian Scientist married to a Jew—can afford to do that. . . . As a Jew I feel a kinship with Dolly. As Jews have suffered, so has Dolly. She had the potato famine and the English to contend with [in her past]."[58]

While Feldshuh's conception of the role was a topic of interest, it was never suggested that because she herself was not of Irish descent it was inappropriate or even offensive for her to play Dolly as an Irish American, or a denial of her own cultural heritage. As I have argued elsewhere,[59] the double standard for cross-ethnic as opposed to cross-racial casting lies in the difference in the principal means for performing ethnicity as opposed to race on stage or on screen. Race is most readily defined by physical features that are by nature immutable over the course of an individual's life—skin color, eye shape, facial features, and bone structure. Any alteration must therefore be artificial and whether achieved through cosmetic surgery, chemical treatments, or makeup and prosthetics, leave traces ranging from a sense of the unnatural to an impression of disfigurement or mutilation. In the case of speech, however, it is in the very nature of the speech organs to be trained and re-trained, part of their natural function to control the flow of air in different ways to produce the range of sounds and sound combinations particular to different language systems. As Robert Hodge and Gunther Kress put it very dramatically, the phonological code for any given language is "the narrative of the journey of air from the lungs to the outside, past various obstructions, making use of various opportunities along the way."[60] Since accents are the primary markers of ethnicity for the actor, it follows that it is possible for skill and technique to reproduce a "real accent" rather than a stereotype. This is, after all, just a highly concentrated version of a natural process that takes place over years when a person migrates and resettles in another country or region.

Accordingly, in the case of *Guys and Dolls,* the casting of non-Jewish white actors, notably Frank Sinatra in the part of Nathan Detroit in the film, or non-Jewish white actresses in the part of Adelaide, never excited critical comment. In fact, neither these characters nor *Guys and Dolls* as a whole work were ever identified as Jewish until the black cast was introduced. With this change, the process of cultural discovery and cultural claiming initiated by the transposition to a black cast and black milieu proved to exceed the uncovering of African American elements in *Guys and Dolls;* it also instigated the public declaration of the Jewish identity of the characters, language, and plot elements. For while much was made of the Jewish and Yiddish origins and nature of the musical, as I've indicated, when the black production was staged in 1976, no such identification was made when the original production opened in 1950. In thirty-five press reviews or features on the director and actors, the adjectives *Jewish* or *Yiddish* were never once used to describe the creators, the characters, the language, the milieu, or the narrative—not even when Sam Levene, the actor who created the role of Nathan Detroit, was being interviewed or discussed, and his one song, "Sue Me," singled out.

Even the critics writing for publications that might be supposed to have the greatest interest in claiming cultural ownership of the acclaimed new work for their targeted readership did not view *Guys and Dolls* possessively. In the *American Jewish Review,* Harold Stern proclaimed the new musical the "Year's Biggest Smash Hit"; the only information imparted to his readers about the fictional figures was that they were "based on the stories and characters of Damon Runyon's 'Broadway Mob'" and they spoke using "their indigenous Broadway lexicon."[61] Similarly, the *Brooklyn Eagle* critic, Louis Sheaffer, did not identify key characters as unmistakable natives of his newspaper's home borough, as some of his successors would twenty-six years later, but instead praised the writers and actors for "capturing the Runyon accent and flavor," the hallmarks of imaginary beings who "were virtually cut from the whole cloth of Mr. Runyon's imagination."[62] It was not that Runyon's repertoire of characters did not include obvious ethnic types and stereotypes—the most prominent Jewish ones being Sam the Gonoph, Charley Bernstein, Little Isadore, and, least subtly, Jew Louie—but like all his creations these figures did not correspond mimetically to any living persons. In Sheaffer's estimation, only "innocent natives in the hinterlands" could possibly imagine that "Nicely-Nicely Johnson, Harry the Horse, Angie the Ox, Rusty Charlie, Big Jules [*sic*] and their like are carbon copies of the sort of flashy gentry you actually find hanging around Broadway."[63] With regard to their manner of expressing themselves verbally, he remarked: "The actual gab of the characters around Broadway bears as much resemblance to the colorful Runyon dialogue as every-day talk does to Christopher Fry's effervescent wit in 'Ring Round the Moon' or 'The Lady's Not For Burning.'"[64]

Runyon's New York stories and characters reflect the cultural diversity of New York City, with its immigrant communities from different parts of Europe—the Irish American presence being as significant as the East European Jewish one, supplemented by Hispanic, Greek, and Italian characters—as well as migrants from the western parts of the United States like Sky Masterson. In terms of language, Runyon scholars have identified a complex mixture of street, stage, and newsprint languages and rhythms in the speech the author crafted for his characters. In his study of Runyon, Daniel R. Schwarz analyzes the style and sources of Runyonese in considerable detail and finds "gangster argot, the rhythm and sounds of jazz, and the pace and tempo of burlesque comedians." He describes the gangster argot as having been "homogenized from Jewish, Italian, and Irish immigrants who did not have much formal education."[65] Similarly, while William R. Taylor specifically mentions "the richness of Jewish humor and the Yiddish Theatre" as being one of the sources for the "slanguage" spoken by the denizens of the Times Square area, he stresses that this was an amalgam of languages.[66]

The perceived Jewishness of the characters and language therefore seems to have accrued markedly when "The Idyll of Miss Sarah Brown" was transformed into *Guys and Dolls* by the words and music of Frank Loesser and Abe Burrows, the direction of George S. Kaufman, and the performances of various actors. By 1950, the very genre of the Broadway musical had been defined almost exclusively by Jewish writers, composers, and directors, with Cole Porter being the only major exception in a long list that includes Irving Berlin, Jerome Kern, Richard Rodgers, Oscar Hammerstein II, George and Ira Gershwin, Lorenz Hart, Moss Hart, Alan Jay Lerner, Frederick Loewe, Dorothy and Herbert Fields, as well as Loesser, Burrows, and Kaufman.[67] Various studies including Steyn's have discerned a signature relationship between traditional Jewish music and the Tin Pan Alley "standard" songs—songs for a single voice that privilege melody—and the vocal form that lies at the heart of Broadway musicals.[68] In contrast to the case of *Dolly,* with *Guys and Dolls* it was not the cultural identity of the title actor, but the cultural identity of the writers and composers, their words and their tunes, and the genre itself that imprinted the cultural label of Jewishness on the musical as a whole in the minds of many spectators, particularly those residing in New York City.[69]

The perceived Jewishness of the work was not invoked, however, when a very famous non-Jewish actor in the role of Nathan Detroit for the 1955 movie. Frank Sinatra would be only the first of a very long line of actors, both prominent and obscure, who did not come from a Jewish background to pass in the part without arousing any qualms. In fact,

Samuel Goldwyn had apparently decided not to have Sam Levene reprise his highly successfully stage performance because, as he said to Burrows's wife, "I don't want him to be Jewish."[70] It was only the switching of the race of the cast and characters not toward a neutral whiteness but to a markedly different cultural milieu, with corresponding modifications to the language and music, that provoked several critics into certifying the Jewish roots of *Guys and Dolls* and arguing for the immutability of this cultural identity.

On the surface, the resistance to the transposition placed the defenders of the original version in opposition to the creators and supporters of the black adaptation. But another interpretation would be to see the conjunction of the African American production and the emphatic declarations of the heretofore unrecognized Jewish American identity of Loesser's musical as parallel developments arising from the same conjunction of historical forces. As recent studies of Jewish American history of the first half of the twentieth century have demonstrated, this period was marked by constant negotiations between the pressures of retaining a distinct ethnic and cultural identity and being accepted as white Americans. The predominant direction was a multithreaded yet consistent drive toward successful assimilation up though the end of World War II. This proved to be a relatively successful enterprise, but one that came at a price.[71] A numerically disproportionate and exceptionally influential Jewish creative presence in various fields of commercial entertainment made Broadway theater and Hollywood film prime sites for enacting a process of cultural formation that was, at the very least, double-coded and that performed, at the very least, a dual function. As Neal Gabler[72] and Andrea Most have argued in regard to the cultural institutions of Hollywood and Broadway respectively, the idealized visions of America depicted in works now regarded as classics were largely created by members of a minority who were themselves excluded from the actual sites, institutions, and ways of life being portrayed. These locations and ways of life, moreover, often gained iconic status only through the work of the Jewish producers, directors, writers, composers, and performers. Most writes:

> The Broadway stage was a space where Jews envisioned an ideal America and subtly wrote themselves into that scenario as accepted members of the mainstream American community. Remarkably successful, the Jewish creators of the Broadway musical established not only a

new sense of what it means to be Jewish (or "ethnic") in America but also a new understanding of what "America" itself means.[73]

Bial goes on to stress that ultimately, "it is the presence of the recognizably Jewish code, not the artist's intent, that determines an audience's ability (or inability) to recognize (or imagine) Jewishness in a performance."[74]

The case of *Guys and Dolls* would seem to fall between a work like *Oklahoma!* and *Fiddler on the Roof* in the extent to which the Jewish themes, narrative, or character portrayals would stand out only to those from or familiar with Jewish cultures and communities. In *Guys and Dolls* the stage is populated with several Jewish characters, but their ethnic origins are never foregrounded, nor is their religious background. Indeed, the fact that all the underworld characters are seriously in need of moral reclamation is central to the comic structure. For casts and audiences far removed from New York City, however, the Jewish elements, with the probably exception of Nathan Detroit's "So nu," would dissolve into the second- or third-generation multiethnic mix of immigrant cultures. In productions staged well outside of the Tri-State area, any regional speech accent would mostly likely be thought of as a "New York accent" without being specifically associated with the Lower East Side of Manhattan or Brooklyn, much less particular ethnic groups residing in those neighborhoods. Consequently, when with the all-black cast the musical was performed by actors who could not pass for Jewish, the elimination of the Jewish text was felt most acutely, perhaps even solely, by Jewish spectators and native or longtime New York residents.

While it often seems that where professional critics are concerned, absence or loss is more likely than presence to elicit comments, it seems safe to suggest that there is another reason for the cultural identification or claiming that took place in 1976 in contrast to the silence about the inherent Jewishness of *Guys and Dolls* when it first opened in 1950. The musical first appeared during an era still marked by residual reticence about claiming or calling attention to an individual or collective Jewish identity in mainstream social situations. As Bial observes:

In the immediate aftermath of World War II, Jews in the American entertainment industry were faced with an identity crisis. It was no longer possible to ignore one's Jewishness in the face of the annihilation of European Jewry; nor was it possible to take comfort in the apparently secure position that Jews had established in the United States. At the same time, "assimilation" had been very good to the Jews in terms of social mobility, especially in the realm of theater and film. In fact, the widespread perception among anti-Semites that Jews controlled the American entertainment industry caused many Jewish actors, directors and playwrights to feel deeply ambivalent about publicly acknowledging their Jewishness.[75]

In this climate, there was understandable concern that identifying a play as Jewish could diminish public interest and hurt the production financially. By the mid-1970s, however, the strong shift in Jewish American attitudes toward individual and group identities that had emerged in the previous decade became firmly established as "the legitimization of a number of new identity-based movements . . . lessened pressures on American Jews to downplay their Jewishness."[76] Seen in this light, the seemingly competing claims to black or Jewish American ownership of *Guys and Dolls* were not purely oppositional but in fact operated in tandem to mark a new era when cultural differences are affirmed rather than obscured.

The Final Frontier? Goyim in Falsettoland and on the Roof

Amid the myriad disagreements over the merits and parameters of nontraditional casting, the single most readily accepted principle has been that such approaches should be restricted to works where race or ethnicity is not central to the action or the characters' development. In the past decade, two notable productions have tested, some would say transgressed, these limits: in 1998, the National Asian American Theatre Company staged an all-Asian production of William Finn and James Lapine's *Falsettoland* and in 2004 David Leveaux's Broadway revival of *Fiddler on the Roof* deliberately sought to "universalize" the musical's themes by removing or downplaying ethnically specific characteristics. While the question of Jewish identity and casting had been raised in relation to the nontraditionally cast productions of *Hello! Dolly* and *Guys and Dolls,* the situation was of course very different with *Falsettoland* and *Fiddler on the Roof.* It is no longer a question of subtle or isolated references that can be expunged by minor editing. Jewish American culture and Judaic traditions are foregrounded in the narrative and lyrics of Finn and Lapine's chamber musical, while *Fiddler* is deeply embedded in a tradition of Jewish history and culture going back to the East European pogroms and Sholom Alecheim's Yiddish stories.

Falsettoland, which premiered in 1990, was the third in what would come to be known as Finn's trilogy of "Marvin Musicals"—three short musicals about the eponymous character's evolving relations with his family and closest friends as he moves from adolescence to adulthood and from heterosexual to homosexual relationships. These explorations are intertwined with the protagonist's ethnic and religious identity as a Jewish American. The first of these plays, *In Trousers,* premiered in 1979 and was revived with substantial revisions and additional songs in 1985. After a decade of seemingly happy marriage, despite "a wife who's perfect in many ways" and "a dazzling son," Marvin increasingly feels something's missing in his life. Finding himself constantly fantasizing about making love to men, he takes a male lover, Whizzer, and realizes that he feels "alive-er" than he's ever felt before. Feeling "a little unlawful but a lot relieved," Marvin decides to pack up and move in with his boyfriend, leaving his wife Trina on the brink of breaking down.

The second installment, *March of the Falsettos,* opened just two years later in 1981. Marvin and Trina have gotten a divorce, but Marvin continues to want "a tight-knit family" that includes his ex-wife, his son, and his lover. He encourages first his wife and then their son Jason to see his psychiatrist, Dr. Mendel, who is instantly attracted to Trina. They eventually decide to get married—a development that was not part of Marvin's vision for a reconfigured family. At the same time, after nine or ten months of their living together, his own relationship with Whizzer has begun to founder as everyday differences replace initial passions. As the adults around him fight and their relationships permutate, Jason deals with the fact that his "father's a homo" and wonders if the trait is passed on by chromosomes. At the end of *March,* the father-son relationship is the only one Marvin is able to repair as he counsels Jason, "Father to son, I for one would take love slower. / I've made my choice. You can sing a different song."[77]

Although it would be another nine years before the sequel *Falsettoland* appeared in 1990, the action resumes less than a year after the closing scene of *March of the Falsettos.* An equilibrium has been established, but it is about to be unsettled by Jason's upcoming bar mitzvah and the reconciliation between Marvin and Whizzer, who meet again at one of Jason's Little League baseball games. While Marvin and Trina drive Jason crazy bickering about the music and the food, Mendel reassures him that "everyone hates his parents." A second single-sex couple joins the original cast of characters: Dr. Charlotte, an internist, and her lover Cordelia, a nouvelle-Jewish-cuisine caterer. At her hospital, Dr. Charlotte is seeing a growing stream of sick and frightened "bachelors" suffering from a mysterious terminal illness. It soon becomes apparent that Whizzer has become one of them. Instead of being a source of division, Jason's bar mitzvah becomes an occasion for redefining the nuclear family when he decides to celebrate it in Whizzer's hospital room. The ritual not only recognizes his identity as "son of Abraham, Isaac and Jacob" but also as "son of Marvin, son of Trina, son of Whizzer, son of Mendel" and "godchild to the lesbians from next door."[78]

In April 1992, a combined version of *March of the Falsettos* and *Falsettoland* opened on Broadway at the John Golden Theater under the title *Falsettos*. The show in its full-length version was well received by audiences and critics. *Falsettos* received Tony nominations in several categories for new musicals (best musical, book, score, director, leading actor, featured actor, featured actress) and won the awards for best book and best score. Like the individual productions, the combined version was greeted as the first musical to present the dynamics of homosexual relationships and families in the same terms as heterosexual ones. Conventional family values were being preserved by unconventional family units. Finn's original directions for the male quartet *March of the Falsettos* specified that everyone should be "very serious and very manly. And very falsetto." In interviews, Finn explained the meaning of the musical analogy: "Falsetto is the voice you use outside the normal range, and at that time this family was way outside that range. What's happened since is that the normal range has expanded so that this kind of family is right in the center."[79]

With each of the three segments, the fact that the family in question is a Jewish one becomes increasingly prominent. In *In Trousers,* only the reenactment of Marvin and Trina's wedding draws attention to the couple's religion: a rabbi presides and the ceremony concludes with the ritual breaking of the glass—except that it is Trina who performs the gesture after Marvin tries and fails. The rousing opening number of *March of the Falsettos* is unabashedly entitled "Four Jews in a Room Bitching" and enthusiastically sung by Marvin, Mendel, Jason, and Whizzer. Each in turn proclaims "I'm Jewish" except for Whizzer, who can only lay claim to being "half Jewish." Here, the declaration is social and cultural rather than strictly religious. They characterize themselves and each other:

Four Jews talking like Jew-ish men.
I'm neurotic, he's neurotic.
They're neurotic, we're neurotic.

Later, a menorah provides the light for a scene in which Trina and Mendel sing about making a home. *Falsettoland* brings together the religious and sociocultural dimensions of being Jewish primarily through Jason. The preparations for his bar mitzvah evoke centuries of Jewish tradition and a contemporary ethnic community as Jason practices the Hebrew blessings and scriptural passages he will recite and Cordelia plans the menu from her *New Jewish Recipes* cookbook. This celebration is preceded by an important secular family event, where everyone attends a Little League game to watch "Jewish boys / Who cannot play baseball / Play baseball." As Jason and his teammates make "the most pathetical errors," they are urged to emulate Sandy Koufax and Hank Greenberg and to remember that "it's not genetic."[80] Jason attempts to strike a bargain with God, praying for "a miracle of Judaism" to cure Whizzer of AIDS and Mendel cites the Torah as the ultimate authority for his contention that it is natural and inevitable for children to hate their parents.

When the various New York productions of the one-act and full-length versions were reviewed, critics devoted almost all of their column inches to the new ground being broken by the musicals with their open, affirmative, and lighthearted treatment of the experiences of homosexual individuals, couples, and families. The fact that Finn, who is descended from Russian Jews on both sides of his family, was very consciously drawing on a Jewish model of family life and adolescence was usually barely mentioned and never extensively discussed. With *In Trousers* and *March of the Falsettos*, acknowledgment of the Jewish cultural milieu came almost in passing in the form of a single adjective or through the mention of a song title or brief citation of lyrics. In the case of *Falsettoland*, readers were often left to conclude from the plot summary that the musical was about a Jewish family. The most direct indication of the degree to which Finn was satirizing Jewish family dynamics and rituals was expressed in Frank Rich's comment that "The evening builds to a bar mitzvah in the Philip Roth mode."[81]

The perceived or acknowledged "Jewishness" of the musicals seemed to increase as the site for performance and discussion moved farther away from Manhattan to locations where one is less likely to find audience members who fit the description of Marvin as an "urban, neurotic,

Jewish, gay New Yorker."[82] Critics reviewing touring productions or revivals outside of New York City were far more likely to identify the plays
as culturally specific, with Woody Allen films often serving as a point of
reference. Among typical comments were the following:

> The whole thing is very New York and very Jewish, smart, sophisti-
> cated and not-so-secretly tenderhearted. Think of a Woody Allen
> movie set to music of Sondheimian virtuosity.
> —EVERETT EVANS, *Houston Chronicle*, JUNE 7, 1997

> "March of the Falsettos" is a musical about bad things happening to
> people with Upper West Side co-ops. We're in Woody Allen's old ter-
> ritory, where the characters are smart, rich, Jewish, neurotic and re-
> ally, really articulate.
> —LLOYD ROSE, *Washington Post*, JUNE 24, 1997

> The show is certainly not for the blue-nosed or the anti-Semitic.
> —ERIC E. HARRISON, *Arkansas Democrat-Gazette*, MAY 27, 1995

Given the distinctly ethnic nature of the musical, *Falsettoland* seemed
like an unlikely choice for Alan Muraoka to suggest for the National
Asian American Theatre Company's 1998 benefit performance. In the
director's note included in the program for the revival mounted in 2007
for the inaugural Asian American Theatre Festival, Muraoka writes that
he proposed Finn's work because of his frustration with the limited opportunities in musical theater available to Asian American actors. As an
ensemble chamber piece, *Falsettoland* was well suited to the small company and provided the actors with dramatic and musical challenges beyond those afforded by the few Broadway musicals like *The King and I,
Flower Drum Song,* or *Miss Saigon* that include significant Asian roles.[83] In
a 2007 interview, NAATCO director Mia Katigbak recalled that in addition to the practical advantages and musical opportunities afforded by
Falsettoland, Muraoka was also attracted to the work by "its strong affirmation about family—gay and straight, Jewish and gentile."[84] Although
William Finn was apparently somewhat skeptical at first, he gave his permission for the company to perform the musical and attended the opening night as the guest of honor. In July 1998, five months after the successful fund-raiser concert performance, the production was fully staged
for a general audience at the Vineyard Theatre.

There were only two differences in the 1998 and 2007 productions that could be considered significant from the point of view of the cross-ethnic casting concept. In the earlier version, the substitution of Asian actors for actors who were either Jewish or could pass for Jewish was considered strange enough to warrant the insertion of a prologue in which the actors were hypnotized so that they could fully inhabit their new identities. The success of the initial run obviated the need for such a device in 2007. The second change was more subtle and never mentioned in interviews or reviews. All the members of the first cast were Chinese or Japanese Americans. In the revival, Manu Narayan, who had played the starring role of Akaash in the Broadway production of *Bombay Dreams,* joined the cast as Whizzer Brown. With the other parts still being played by actors with East Asian backgrounds, Narayan's Indian ancestry made him stand out visibly as the only half-Jewish character, whose non-Jewish heritage set him apart from the other men, allowing him, among other things, to be good at sports.

Both productions were well received, not just by audiences—a largely self-selected group who could be expected to be enthusiastic and supportive—but by professional critics as well. Writing for the *New York Times,* Peter Marks addressed the issues raised by attempting cross-racial/ethnic/cultural casting in this "lyrical paean to Jewish angst, with its aggressively Jewish New York sensibility and multiple references to gefilte fish." Noting that the cast did in fact have difficulty handling the "send-ups of the ritualized neuroses of Jewish New Yorkers," he nevertheless concluded: "It's surprising how rapidly your mind adjusts for superficial incongruities" such as cast members in yarmulkes and prayer shawls.[85] Similarly, *Back Stage*'s Victor Gluck agreed that "after the initial surprise of the all Asian-American ensemble, the viewer quickly forgets and settles in to watch this cleverly directed, beautifully sung, and excellently acted revival."[86] Nine years later, *CurtainUp*'s Les Gutman continued to find that the "winning performances throughout make one quickly stop thinking about how Asians can play Jews and the like."[87] For *Time Out* critic Adam Feldman, however, the visual incongruities were not so much factors to be overlooked as semiotically significant elements: "Because the characters are drawn so specifically, NAATCO's cross-racial casting is able to add layers of new connotations to the piece without eroding the integrity of the story."[88] It would seem that, for some viewers at least, the Asian casting had transformed *Falsettoland* from a Jewish American musical into a more broadly multicultural one.

Should the ready acceptance of NAATCO's *Falsettoland* be taken as a

The National Asian American Theatre Company's production of *Falsettoland* (2007), directed by Alan Muraoka. Jason Ma, Francis Jue, Manu Narayan, Ann Sanders, Ben Wu, MaryAnn Hu, Christine Toy Johnson. (Photo by Bruce Johnson.)

sign that the time has come when nontraditional casting can and should be applied to works where race or ethnicity are germane to the action? Or are there specific factors that made such casting possible and appropriate in this particular case? I think that further examination of the situation shows that *Falsettoland* must be seen as the exception that proves a few rules. In the first place, this ethnically specific play was being produced by an ethnically specific company whose modus operandi is to match Asian actors with non-Asian roles. Audiences who attend their performances have at the very least made the decision beforehand to keep an open mind; most spectators go well beyond this to actively support the company in its three-pronged mission:

- Promote and support Asian American actors, directors, designers, and technicians through the performance of European and American classical and contemporary works

- Actively develop an Asian American audience and encourage Asian Americans to become a significant part of a more diverse audience in American theater
- Cultivate in non-Asian Americans an appreciation of Asian American contributions to the development of theater arts in America today.[89]

These factors also resulted in the preselection of the cadre of critics who reviewed the productions. The only major daily newspapers to review the performances were New York City publications like the *New York Times* and *Daily News;* the other reviews appeared in publications or on websites that specialized in covering theater and other entertainment events (e.g., *Time Out, Back Stage, CurtainUp*). Like other NAATCO productions, *Falsettoland* did not receive coverage out of town or in national magazines. The audience, both professional and amateur, was therefore largely composed of people who were interested in new theatergoing experiences or interested in ethnic American, especially Asian American, culture.

Given this institutional context, the casting arrangement, which brings together two distinct ethnic and cultural groups, draws our attention to the significance of cultural differences rather than away from it. Placed in juxtaposition, neither the Jewishness of the characters nor the Asianness of the actors can be taken for granted. The fact that *Falsettoland* is a musical and, moreover, one that relies on a heavily presentational rather than representational mode of performance also makes the piece an effective host for unconventional casting. The structure of all three parts of the Marvin trilogy is episodic, with the scene changes carried out by actors moving around minimal furnishings and props. Recalling Nicholas Hytner's response to doubts about his multiracial *Carousel,* actor Welly Yang (Whizzer in the 1998 production) drew an analogy between the scenery and the actors as signifiers. After acknowledging that it was "weird when a bunch of Asian-Americans walk in wearing yarmulkes," he continued, "But if you can believe this blue background on the stage represents the sky, then you can believe these Asian-Americans are Americans who are Jewish."[90] Most of all, the performance style of the musical numbers is presentational, with the actors often directing their words and gestures toward the audience rather than each other. The actors occasionally adopt narratorial functions as well as dramatic ones as they set a scene and announce what it will be about (e.g., "Whizzer: A day in Falsettoland. Doctor Mendel at work"). In corroborating the strong impression made by the artistic abilities of the cast, Marks confirms that he mainly appreciated the performers qua performers, rather than as actors who dissolved into the characters they were playing:

> What one approaches nervously as a potentially embarrassing put-on is in reality a rather loving tribute to, among other things, the joy of being in a musical. Here are seven singing Asian actors who seem to be declaring to audiences and casting directors alike that they would like to be considered for parts in musicals other than "Miss Saigon" and "The King and I."[91]

By encouraging, even forcing, the audience to see the persons on stage as performers as much as characters, the NAATCO production both benefited from and reinforced the already predominant theatrical qualities of *Falsettoland*. Such distancing would be counterproductive, even disruptive, in a straight dramatic play. The same would hold true for a book musical where the balance between mimetic illusionism and theatrical effect was heavily tipped toward the former and narrative continuity was maintained by seamless passages between scenes and into and out of musical numbers. In the case of Finn and Lapine's piece, however, the nontraditional casting underscored inherent qualities of the work.

The discussions surrounding the Asian American *Falsettoland* confirm that nontraditional casting is ultimately about identities that can be visually verified. While the conundrums posed by an all-Asian production of a Jewish American musical received ample attention, the question of whether the sexual preferences of the actors corresponded to those of the characters and how that might affect their performances was never raised. No one has ever considered whether a *Falsettoland* performed by gay and Lesbian Asian Americans would be more "authentically" cast than a *Falsettoland* performed by heterosexual non-Jewish white actors. In the original Playwrights Horizons productions of *March of the Falsettos* and *Falsettoland*, three of the key characters—Marvin, Whizzer, and Mendel—were played by the same actors—Michael Rupert, Stephen Bogardus, and Chip Zien respectively. Shortly after *Falsettoland* opened in June 1990, the actors were interviewed and asked how the changes in society and their own lives during the intervening decade had affected the way they reprised their roles. The subject of any form of "cross-"casting in terms of sexual orientation, religious affiliation, or ethnic background was never raised. Readers were left to infer from surnames or the mention of wives and marriages whether or not the actors might share the same sexual and ethnic backgrounds as the characters they were playing.

A telling contrast to the case of *Falsettoland* was provided by the 2004 Broadway revival of another musical far more closely identified with Jewish culture—*Fiddler on the Roof.* The fortieth-anniversary production was directed by a British director, David Leveaux, who was best known for his stagings of contemporary drama. For the first time on Broadway, the role of Tevye was played by an actor who was not Jewish—Alfred Molina. The key supporting roles of the three oldest daughters, Tzeitel, Hodel, and Chava, went to three actresses—Sally Murphy, Laura Michelle Kelly, and Tricia Paoluccio—whose names, in the words of one critic, "read like an attendance sheet at a Catholic girls' school"[92] and who "looked more like Irish colleens than Ukrainian Jews."[93] The impact of these casting choices was compounded by the deliberate (although not uniform) excision of the strong Yiddish accents and speech inflections that had heretofore been considered integral and essential components of any performance of the musical. These changes represented the first significant break with the production concept and performance traditions that had been established forty years earlier when Zero Mostel first created the role of Tevye on Broadway.

The emotional protests excited by these alterations reflect the iconic status of *Fiddler on the Roof* as a work that did not so much commemorate a mythic Jewish past as create it. The second-generation Jewish Americans who fashioned *Fiddler*—Joseph Stein, Jerry Bock, and Sheldon Harnick—experienced East European Jewish culture through their parents and grandparents who had emigrated to the United States. Librettist Joseph Stein's parents moved to the Bronx from Poland, and Yiddish was the first language in their home. Stein wanted this heritage to be apparent but not dominant: "I was very careful not to have any Yiddish words or phrases in the script—and there are only one or two Yiddish words in any of the songs. But through the quality of the talk, the construction of sentences, there is a kind of ethnic rhythm without any Yiddishisms."[94] Similarly, when composing the score, Jerry Bock drew on his own memories of the Russian and Jewish folk songs his grandmother sang to him when he was growing up. For him, Yiddish and Russian music were essentially indistinguishable.[95] Bock never felt he needed to research the score, because the music was already inside him. Speaking for the creative trio, Bock said: "I'm sure Sheldon and Joe had he same inner sense of the material's being right for the writer. It's not that any of us is Orthodox; it was the association, the comfort of having that instinctive knowledge about things."[96]

Given the fact that the creators' knowledge of peasant life in Eastern Europe was gleaned secondhand from stories, songs, and memories, it is not surprising, as many critics have pointed out, that Anatevka and its inhabitants ended up bearing a greater resemblance to Brigadoon than to any Russian shtetl that actually existed.[97] It was, however, the very lack of documentary authenticity that allowed the musical to attain iconic status and function as a community-defining cultural work—not for East European Jews but for post–World War II Jewish Americans. In his study of Tevye as a figure who, since his first appearance in 1895, has continually evolved to recast Jewish cultural history in response to successive historical traumas, Seth L. Wolitz argues that in his American musical incarnation,

> Tevye reflects the efforts of Yiddish and Jewish American artists to capture different stages and ideologies of their group's acculturation to Western secularism. In reworking the character of Tevye to fill the needs of Jewish cultural adaptation, these artists over the course of one century manipulated yearnings for a lost "pastoral" past, acknowledged surreptitiously the wounds of the Holocaust, and expressed the need for historical-cultural recognition and legitimation. The Americanization of Tevye expressed the validation of Jewish-American participation in American life.[98]

Wolitz goes on to demonstrate how Tevye became the personification of the Jewish immigrant and "the universal grandfather of Jewish America."[99] Over the course of the evening the Tevye moves from the traditional values of the opening number to the American ideals of tolerance and individual rights, notably the right to pursue (personal) happiness. In summarizing "How 'Fiddler' Became Folklore," Alisa Solomon notes the confluence of three historical events or movements that coincided with the emergence of the musical: the civil rights movement, which "lent urgency to the theme of tolerance even as it ignited a widespread passion for reclaiming ethnic roots";[100] the trial of Adolf Eichmann, which received extensive media coverage in the early 1960s and served as a focal point for Jewish communities that were just beginning to come to terms with the Holocaust; and the ethnographic interest in East European Jewish culture generated by the 1952 publication of *Life Is with People: The Jewish Little-Town of Eastern Europe,* by Mark Zborowski and Elizabeth Herzog (reprinted in 1962 with the subtitle changed to *The Culture of the Shtetl*). This study, which was largely responsible for promoting the popular notion of the shtetl as a hermetic Jewish world, was a key reference for constructing the universe of Anatevka.

Along with Wolfitz, several theater critics have pointed out that *Fiddler* appealed to middle-class Jewish Americans as both a commemoration of the Jewish immigrant's rise in social status and economic security, and as an expression of nostalgia for the cultural roots from which suburban Jewish Americans were increasingly separated. If *Fiddler*'s ties to the music and folk culture of rural Russia at the close of the nineteenth and opening of the twentieth century were tenuous, however, its integration into Jewish American folk culture was not. It was not "The Sabbath Prayer" (essentially a translation from the Hebrew of the traditional Shabbat blessing for children) or the klezmer music or cantorial chants that wove together popular culture and Jewish community life but songs like "Sunrise, Sunset" and "Matchmaker, Matchmaker," which came to be played and sung at both religious and secular family celebrations— bar and bat mitzvahs, weddings, and graduations. The 2004 revival brought out accounts of spectators for whom *Fiddler on the Roof* did not so much evoke a nostalgic genealogical past, as itself become the object of powerful nostalgic associations. Peter Marks, the same critic who had welcomed the Asian American *Falsettoland,* had a strong and telling negative reaction to the 2004 revival directed by Leveaux. He began a review titled "A 'Fiddler on the Roof' Hopelessly Out of Tune" with the following reminiscences:

> In the secular Jewish home of my childhood, about the closest we ever came to spiritual sustenance was "Fiddler on the Roof." . . . [Our hi-fi] seemed to be a shrine to the song stylings of Jerry Bock and Sheldon Harnick, grinding out "Sunrise, Sunset" from dawn till dusk.
>
> We had our rituals: My father could be counted on for a driver's-seat rendition of "If I Were a Rich Man" at least twice on every road trip. Our iconic images: My piano teacher . . . kept a portrait of Marc Chagall's fiddler over her piano. Our expressions of worship: My brother, Jamie, played Tevye in a boffo Camp Leonard production.[101]

Leveaux had deliberately rejected the notion that *Fiddler on the Roof* was first and foremost a nostalgic Jewish musical and the allied conception of Tevye as an extroverted folk figure. Focusing on the text, both spoken and sung, rather than the performance tradition or the original cultural context, Leveaux sought to interpret the work for contemporary audiences. He was interested in the story on two levels: first, as the story of a family where a father and his daughters and a husband and a wife are redefining their relationships and ideas of love; and second, as the story of a community whose culture is being threatened with eradication.[102] To Leveaux and producer Stewart F. Lane, the usual lively musical comedy performances and "bravura theatricality" exemplified by Mostel were at odds with the darker aspects of the story—the pogrom and the final enforced exile that signaled the extinction of this way of life.[103] Their aim was to produce a show that would be firmly rooted in reality. Actor Stephen Ward Billeisen, who played one of the Russians, recalls: "We were not told don't act Jewish, we were told, don't act over the top, it's a real story, focus on the words of the piece and the music of the piece, don't overdo it."[104] In many ways, this translated into shifting the conventional modal balance between realistic and antirealistic qualities that defines Broadway musicals and approaching the work more as a naturalistic drama. The Russian setting and literary and artistic connections became as relevant as the Jewish ones. Overtones of Chekhovian resignation infused Molina's performance of Tevye as an essentially reflective man, an interpretation that was either praised for bringing subtlety and shades of gray to the role or criticized for being unduly subdued and somber. A forest of living birch trees as well as a more somber mood evoked Chekhov's renderings of provincial communities undergoing profound transitions around 1900. While *The Cherry Orchard* was the most obvious point of reference, some critics also found elements reminiscent of *The Seagull* and *Uncle Vanya*.

While Pye's set was almost universally admired for its beauty and elegance, the sense of refinement that pervaded Leveaux's production—leading one critic to suggest that a more appropriate title for the show would be "Violin on the Verandah"[105]—could be seen as symptomatic of the root revisions that stirred deep emotions.[106] A *Los Angeles Times* article by novelist, essayist, and law professor Thane Rosenbaum received widespread attention and was often seen as having initiated the controversy that ensued, even though many theater critics expressed similar views in their reviews of the production. As a commentary based on a preview performance rather than a formal theater review, however, the essay was able to appear a good eleven days before the official opening night. (In retrospect, it was as much the premature appearance of the essay as its contents that provoked the angry response of Leveaux.) The headline read: "A Legacy cut loose; Unmoored from the dark particulars of history, a new 'Fiddler' has become an Everyman saga—and seems to have lost its soul."[107] While he recognized the talent of the cast and praised the show's fresh look, Rosenbaum challenged the philosophy or vision underlying the production: "This production is trying to emphasize the universal elements of the show and, in so doing, has stripped away the authentic Jewish elements." While he understood the desire to elevate the universal themes, he objected to this being done at the expense of "the truer feelings of that old, vanished *shtetl* life."[108] More rhetorically inflammatory versions of Rosenbaum's objections described the show as having been "ethnically cleansed"[109] or "de-Jewed."[110] The more common laments, however, echoed Rosenbaum's complaint over the loss of the Jewish "soul" or regretted the absence of the "ethnic flavor" that imbued previous productions.

The soul and flavor resided first and foremost in the actors' performances of ethnic identity, to be distinguished from their actual ethnic identity or religious affiliation. As Harnick—who along with his partners had stressed the broad reach of the musical since its creation—noted that the percentage of non-Jewish actors was about the same as in the original Broadway production, and pointed out that "The show has been done around the world, and 90% of the Tevyes have not been Jewish. . . . We always approached this show looking for the universal aspects of the story."[111] Never, however, had a non-Jewish actor played Tevye on Broadway, and, in the original production, actors who were not Jewish at least had to look like they *could* be East European Jews. At a 1983 symposium sponsored by the Dramatists Guild, Harnick recalled that "We wanted people who would look as though they could conceivably be linked with this community at that time."[112] The non-Jewish actors, moreover, were directed and coached to *act* Jewish and understand the East European Jewish experience of persecution. In the original production, this went beyond speaking with Yiddish inflections or accents; Jerome Robbins conducted exercises intended to help actors internalize the history of persecution that culminated in the Holocaust.[113]

For Leveaux, far from denoting authenticity, the accents and gestures after forty years had "become so clichéd they're an advertisement for the culture, not the culture itself."[114] While Leveaux wanted to remove the more stereotyped elements, his choice of Alfred Molina to play Tevye suggests he was not indifferent to the cultural specificity of *Fiddler.* As a British actor with a multiethnic background—his parents were Spanish and Italian and he grew up in a section of London with a high population of immigrants from Ireland, the West Indies, Poland, and Africa—Molina had been cast in a wide range of "ethnic roles": Iranian, Russian, Cuban, French, Mexican, and Belgian. In this case, however, this concession to traditional expectations of how Tevye should look, act, and sound was negated by the fact that he did not sound "ethnic." Molina did adopt an accent that was not his own, but this accent was incontrovertibly standard American, with the speech rhythms that characterized the English of native Yiddish-speakers completely evened or flattened out. This choice was consistent with Leveaux's overall production concept, which foregrounded the realistic or naturalistic aspects of the Broadway musical as a genre. American audiences were being positioned to imagine that they and the inhabitants of Anatevka lived in the same world and spoke the same language, so that no "foreign" accents were discernible. Unfortunately, as even the cast album clearly reveals, not all the actors made the same choices with regard to accent or inflection. All the younger-generation principals, like Molina, spoke and sang in straightforward standard American, but there was considerable variation in the speech patterns of actors playing older-generation Anatevkans. For instance, although Nancy Opel and David Wohl in the roles of Yente and Lazar Wolf also avoided distinct Yiddish accents (or the Queens-Brooklyn Jewish accents that have often substituted for Yiddish accents in both amateur and professional productions of *Fiddler on the Roof*), their words bore traces of a generic nonlocalizable foreign accent. Most importantly, they retained the original rhythmic patterns of the dialogue. Under these circumstances, Molina's American dialect did not convey cultural neutrality, but stood out as a discordant element that drew attention not so much to Molina's choices as an actor but to his own cultural background.

When asked for his reaction to the objections raised over a non-Jew being cast as Tevye, Molina replied: "I don't have to be Jewish to play a Jew. I don't have to have that experience. My job is to give the audience that experience."[115] The problem was that evidently for many spectators, Molina's performance did not give them that experience. The question remains open as to whether reactions would have been different if Molina and the rest of the cast had met audience expectations by "acting

Jewish"—which in this case seems to have meant speaking English with a Yiddish accent and moving toward the "over-the-top" performance style established by the original production. Would the ethnic and religious background of the cast members then have become irrelevant? The change of actors in the lead offers no enlightenment on this question since Harvey Fierstein, who took over the role of Tevye in January 2005, is Jewish and, like Mostel, his reputation as a performer was based largely on his talents for broad comedy. He had moreover the perfect cultural credentials for the role. He grew up in a "High Holy Days" Jewish family and his father spoke Yiddish; the family lived in a Jewish community in Brooklyn across the street from the rabbi. Finally, as he told a reporter, "'Fiddler on the Roof' meant everything to us. . . . It was sung at every bar mitzvah, every wedding. My father sang 'Sunrise, sunset' at my graduation. This show means something to our heritage. Being Jewish is not just a religion. It's a people."[116] With Andrea Martin, "another member of the tribe,"[117] taking over as Golde, complaints about the lack of ethnic authenticity were silenced.

Critics of Leveaux's revival were appeased not just because of Fierstein's and Martin's cultural origins, however, but because they returned the missing Yiddish inflections to the dialogue and lyrics. Besides restoring these traditional indications of authenticity, the use of accents had an additional benefit. With both parents now speaking in accented English while the daughters and their suitors continued to use standard American English, the variations in speech no longer seemed random or discordant. Instead, the aural qualities of spoken language became a way to accentuate one of the central themes of the musical—the divide between the generations. The older generation's accented speech contrasted with the unaccented pronunciation of the sisters and their suitors to underscore the contrasting ideas and values being expressed. The effect was achieved, however, not because the contrast illustrated generational differences in provincial Russia but because it replicated language patterns found in the typical American family, where the parents were first-generation immigrants and their children were born or raised in the United States.

The casting of Fierstein as an archetypal pater familias, however, crossed identity lines in another way. Fierstein came to the role as an openly, even "famously, jubilantly gay actor" known for playing roles in drag; reviews and interviews commented freely on this new dimension of cross-casting. According to Fierstein, when it was announced that he would replace Molina, he was asked: "Is it going to be a strain for you to play a heterosexual?"[118] The headline of the *Daily News* review read "Playing It Straight: Harvey Fierstein Takes On 'Fiddler' Tevye?!" and in the *New York Post*, Clive Barnes declared, "Now we have a gay Tevye, with the uncloseted Harvey Fierstein."[119] Although several critics who had found Molina's pensive and introverted Tevye overly morose thought Fierstein had overshot the mark in reinjecting bursts of exuberance and comic effects into his characterization, there was never a suggestion that because of his own sexual orientation he couldn't relate to the experiences of a heterosexual father of five daughters.[120] Alisa Solomon summed up the contrasting reactions to Molina and Fierstein very succinctly: "when it comes to the role of Jewish patriarch, gay beats goy, it seems."[121]

What is most striking from the point of view of this study is that amid all the debates over casting and ethnicity never did anyone come close to suggesting that Leveaux's production of *Fiddler* had employed nontraditional casting. Instead, Leveaux's unconventional choices were characterized as "dogged miscasting."[122] The mixed cast of Jews and non-Jews was never described as "multiethnic" or "multicultural." Even though it was obvious that some of Tevye's daughters were "a couple of gene pools removed from his own,"[123] because the gene pools in question are commonly perceived as falling into the same racial category of "white," the terminology and discourses associated with nontraditional casting were not invoked. It would seem that whether or not *individual* actors could convincingly portray a character of a particular religious or ethnic group was not the issue. Molina can and has successfully played Jewish and Russian characters. On the other hand, Sally Murphy could never have been mistaken for a girl from an East European shtetl. Nevertheless, her inclusion in the cast did not elicit the same reactions that the casting of a black or Asian actress in the role would have. Unlike the casting of Audra MacDonald in *Carousel,* it was never suggested that having an actor who was very visibly of Scots-Irish descent playing Tzeitl would bring down the facade of realistic illusionism that enabled an audience's intellectual and emotional engagement with the musical. The casting of Murphy as Tzeitel was treated as a matter to be overlooked rather than one to which the audience needed to turn a blind eye. As a homologous reproduction of prevailing categories of thought and social formations, the case of the 2004 revival of *Fiddler on the Roof* reflected the continued dominance of racial categories defined by "color" in the United States of the early twenty-first century, even in situations where more specific ethnic or cultural identities were at stake.

It is hard to imagine a more appropriate work to close with than *Fiddler on the Roof* with its exploration of the sometimes volatile but always creative tensions produced by the mutable qualities and the stabilizing functions of traditions. What was once unheard of or seemed absurd has become commonplace even if not universally accepted. Whether in social or casting practices, as the limits of what is conceivable are stretched, there always will be varying degrees of acceptance of or resistance to the changes. But once the first thread is pulled, as Tevye learned, there is no going back.

Afterword

The theater can play only a small part in the vast change that is certainly coming. It is under no special obligation to lead. By nature, theater is a somewhat sluggish form, always a bit behind the underground pressures moving society as a whole. Because it is a public form, addressing itself nightly to diverse minds, it lags behind agile minds working in private. It is forced to unite and move an exceedingly diversified mass in no more than two-and-a-half hours, and that is a difficult thing to do. It has never been a disgrace for the theater to wait until a wind has become a prevailing wind before reproducing its sound for all comers.

But there is already an urgency inside it, echoing the urgency that is on the streets. indeed, it is a measure of how far the streets have gone to see how quickly the theater is catching up. a solution is wanted now.

—WALTER KERR

Since multiracial casting first became a regular part of the American theater scene a half century ago, the practices have prompted myriad debates, discussions, and developments. Theater professionals, critics, and audiences have been led to articulate or to reexamine their assumptions concerning fundamental theater practices and the relationship of theater to contemporary society. Productions cast nontraditionally have foregrounded questions about the parameters for representation attached to dramatic genres, the bases for establishing different modes of reception, the function of the actor and the nature of acting as a semiotic activity, the expression of ideological values through artistic practices, and the continuing part dramatic performance has to play in defining a national cultural identity. Particular theater productions have been seized as opportunities for artists, spectators, critics, and even people not normally interested in the theater to make political or ideological statements, both progressive and conservative.

Experiments in casting, like all innovations, have demonstrated the flexible and contingent nature of the classifications and conceptions that are integral parts of complex systems of meaning. Nontraditional casting practices materialized the deeply ingrained conventions of realism and naturalism that pervade *all* genres of contemporary Euroamerican theater, except avowedly antirealistic works, and the attendant habits of spectatorship. Walter Kerr gives a vivid account of these habits in action:

> Naturalism has developed in its audiences what may be called a strict historical sense. When, in the Association of Producing Artists' production of "War and Peace," Olivia Cole appears as the wife of the 19th-century Russian prince Andrei Bolkonski, I find my head instantly filled with thoughts that have nothing to do with the meaning or movement of the play. The production is naturalistic or realistic in feeling, but I am aware that members of the Russian ruling class in the 19th century did not marry Negroes; it is doubtful that they even had any opportunity to do so. At the same time that the historical stage picture is being jarred out of focus for me, I am busy explaining away what has startled me. "Oh," I say to myself, "the A.P.A. has at last taken some Negro members into the company." I now struggle between moral approval of this step and historical disbelief in what I am seeing. All the while I am doing this the play is going on without me, or against me. I am temporarily uprooted, taken out of the 19th-century play and into the 20th-century United States. Wires have been crossed. The experience has not been spoiled but it has been in some way fuzzed. In fact, naturalistic form has violated itself.

These distractions lead Kerr to ask:

> What is naturalism worth to the theater? How deeply ingrained, how important to the sustained illusion we seek in the theater, is our habit of looking at the stage with the eyes of photographers? Is the particular kind of historical sensibility which naturalism has engendered in us part and parcel of the theater as such, one of its real roots, or is it perhaps a passing, superficial and irrelevant phenomenon?[1]

Kerr's conclusion is the latter. In the final paragraphs of his extensive and perceptive exploration of the network of questions raised by the integration of theater companies, he writes: "What is good about approaching the matter theatrically rather than sociologically is this: so long as we undertake to increase Negro employment in the theater simply as a social obligation, without in any way altering the over-all stage image we have so recently become accustomed to, we shall be in a position of forcing. We shall be asking naturalism to do what it can't honestly do, not at this time."[2] The solution he advocated was an accelerated revision of the dominant system of dramatic representation—an end to "the reign of commonplace realism"—which was already under way. A return to properly theatrical forms of playwriting, staging, and performing, he argued, would obviate the disorienting effects of multiracial casting:

> When the play is sufficiently formalized, no period of adjustment is required. The very first gestures of the evening say immediately that we are to suspend any lingering, literal historical sense or any interest in photographic duplication. What this sort of theater does require is a shift in the playwright's habit of mind and of eye: he must give over his slavish copying of the surfaces of life and go for the depths. Going for the depths has always required one or another degree of distortion, of deliberate artifice.[3]

Kerr was prescient in understanding that the dominant system of representation would foster continued resistance to cross-racial casting long after social barriers had given way. But time has shown that he was also overly pessimistic in gauging the extent to which the eye and mind could become accustomed to new casting configurations. By injecting an element of artifice that was hard to ignore, in fact, nontraditional casting exposed the concealed formality of even realistic or naturalistic forms of theater. The necessary adjustments followed in the never-ending line of accommodations to convention that stretch back to ancient Greece.

Indeed, it is ironic that a new cause for concern in the twenty-first century has been the success with which "nontraditional" casting has become the new tradition in American theaters.[4] Any continued discomfort or resistance tends to be localized—the reactions of individual spectators in response to particular works.

While the expanded artistic opportunities regularly offered to African American, Asian American, and Latino actors are widely appreciated, there has also been some sense that the full artistic and social benefits to be derived from the diversification of company rosters and the opening of the Euroamerican repertory are not always being realized. In becoming automatic, racially mixed casting has lost much of its original force. Where once, cross-racial casting was a creative method of "exploring to explode," to borrow a phrase from actor and director Shishir Kurup, increasingly it has become a matter of routine.

As is so often the case, the state of affairs is manifested in the language used. As racially and ethnically diverse casting has become a common practice, the term *nontraditional* increasingly has been replaced by the term *multicultural*. This is not a simple substitution. It may be either a capitulation or a declaration. The term *multicultural* represents a capitulation if it is used to avoid the more accurate but more loaded term *multiracial*. When theater companies use the term *multicultural* casting, they are almost always referring to what has become the predominant approach to staging works with racially diverse casts, namely the old "colorblind" approach in which the actor best suited for a particular role receives the part. By not calling attention to the racial identities of the actors, multicultural casting enjoys the benefits of diversification while minimizing artistic and economic risks. In contrast, the term can also be used as a declaration of the permanent and profound effects of racial integration. In a genuinely multicultural working environment, diverse casting is not about surface appearances but about the life experiences that actors bring to a collective process of creation. It is for this reason that director Timothy Bond prefers the term *multicultural* to *multiracial* or *interracial*. The last term, he points out, should be reserved to describe a growing segment of the American population—people of mixed-race ancestry.

The need to complicate both the language of casting and the level of awareness of the ever increasing demographic and cultural complexity of the United States is stressed in a 2003 retrospective assessment of the impact of nontraditional casting published in *Black Masks*. In this essay, director Daniel Banks begins by recognizing the undeniable impact of nontraditional casting as a concept and a set of practices that have changed the American theater industry, noting that "The conversation about 'non-traditional casting' in this country over the past seventeen years, has been essential in opening up the way we think about theater and creating much-needed dialogue."[5] He then turns to the limitations of the concept, focusing on the implied marginalization of actors of color, historically as well as in the present, and the reduction of complex issues of identity to outmoded racial binaries of black and white, brown and white, or yellow and white. Banks calls for a shift in the conversation about representation and diversity in the theater that will begin with language. Thanks in large part to "the work done in the name of non-traditional casting," he suggests the time is ripe for "a more precise and historically accurate verbiage about 'race'" that "does not conflate color and ethnicity, that does not continue to teach the fiction of racial difference, and that, in fact, allows us to understand how class and culture are just as crucial elements in this equation as skin color."[6]

The question then becomes, not what would a theater that translates this language into practice *look* like, but what would it *be* like. Can any of the practices if not the original terminology associated with "nontraditional" casting continue to offer ways for theater to remain an active force in understanding, exploring, and redefining both cultural identities and cultural production? There is no denying that the most nuanced explorations of multifaceted identities must begin with the work of contemporary playwrights, whether they prefer realistic or antirealistic modes of expression and whether they create entirely new plays or produce adaptations. But can dramatic works, including musical drama, written in earlier eras be staged and more specifically be cast in ways that can represent and even introduce finer gradations and more fluid qualities into portrayals of characters, locations, and cultures? I would say that this is already what casting practices introduced since the 1960s have often done and can continue to do effectively. The 1989 Arena Stage production of *The Glass Menagerie* directed by Tazewell Thompson and the many multiracially cast versions of *Our Town* are just a few examples of how casting drew attention to intersections of race, class, and gender; illustrated a period in the long history of migrations and cultural mixing; and updated the microcosm of American society to correspond more closely to its current cultural composition.

There are unquestionably new approaches to racially, ethnically, and culturally aware casting that can afford new insights. It is true that in many ways the situation has not changed significantly since Walter Kerr gave theater absolution for not taking the lead in bringing about critical social changes. As a cultural institution, American theater may not have the mass appeal, political positioning, or social authority to effect widespread changes in isolation from other educational or cultural organizations, even when the desire or mission to do so is present. But theater does have unique semiotic resources and phenomenal properties that derive from the live human embodiment of word and narrative. The national movement toward integration and equal opportunities for racial minorities provided the initial impetus for exploring and exploiting these resources and properties. As the social and cultural formations of the United States have altered significantly, there are new motives for continued exploration, new opportunities for American theaters to take an active role in defining a twenty-first-century U.S. culture that is both local and global, where race, ethnicity, and nationality are more intricately delineated but still matter. Kerr's exhortation to "direct our energies to exploring to the full the actual, mysterious, freely imaginative nature of the stage" in order to better understand, accommodate, and challenge the current ordering of our society is as pertinent now as it was decades ago.

Notes

Epigraphs: First definition of "non-traditional casting" devised by the founders of the Non-Traditional Casting Project (NTCP), now called the Alliance for Inclusion in the Arts; Anna Deavere Smith, "Non-traditional Casting, What Tradition?" in *Beyond Tradition: Transcripts of the First National Symposium on Non-Traditional Casting,* ed. Clinton Turner Davis and Harry Newman (New York: Non-Traditional Casting Project, 1988), 28.

1. There have been numerous studies of forms of drama and performance that use the unique resources of theater as a medium to challenge received notions of identity and demonstrate the flexible and fluid qualities of categories such as gender, sexuality, race, ethnicity, and nationality. Key references that focus on race and ethnicity or else discuss the characteristics of performance most pertinent to the analysis of racial or ethnic identities in performance include the chapter "Performance and Identity" in Marvin Carlson, *Performance: A Critical Introduction* (London: Routledge, 1996); Peggy Phelan, *Unmarked: The Politics of Performance,* particularly the chapter titled "The Ontology of Performance: Representation without Reproduction" (London: Routledge, 1993); Coco Fusco, *English Is Broken Here* (New York: New Press, 1995), notably "The Other History of Intercultural Performance"; José Esteban Muñoz, *Disidentifications: Queers of Color and the Performance of Politics* (Minneapolis: University of Minnesota Press, 1999); Una Chaudhuri, *Staging Place: The Geography of Modern Drama* (Ann Arbor: University of Michigan Press, 1997). While Helen Gilbert and Joanne Tompkins's *Post-colonial Drama: Theory, Practice, Politics* (London: Routledge, 1996) deals with countries that once formed the British Empire of the nineteenth and twentieth centuries, much of the authors' analysis of history, language, and bodies is equally relevant for the former British colony that became the United States of America.

2. The first full-length volume devoted to the topic appeared only in 2006—Ayanna Thompson, ed., *Colorblind Shakespeare: New Perspectives on Race and Performance* (New York: Routledge).

3. Alan Eisenberg, "Artistic Good Sense," in *Beyond Tradition: Transcripts of the*

First National Symposium on Non-Traditional Casting, ed. Clinton Turner Davis and Harry Newman (New York: Non-Traditional Casting Project, 1988), 4.

4. The name change was accompanied by a shift of emphasis in the opening sentence of the statement of purpose. The late-1990s version read: "The Non-Traditional Casting Project (NTCP) is a not-for-profit advocacy organization whose purpose is to address and seek solutions to the problems of racism and exclusion in theatre, film and television" (http://www.arts.gov/re sources/Accessibility/NTCP.html, accessed 29 May 2009). The new statement begins: "The Alliance's mission is to serve as an expert advocate and educational resource for full inclusion in theatre, film, television and related media" (http://www.inclusioninthearts.org/missionframe.htm, accessed 29 May 2009).

5. Harry Newman, "Beyond Limitations," in *Beyond Tradition: Transcripts of the First National Symposium on Non-Traditional Casting,* ed. Clinton Turner Davis and Harry Newman (New York: Non-Traditional Casting Project, 1988), 6.

6. Valdez defended his choice of Laura San Giacomo to play Frida in both artistic and pragmatic terms. According to several sources, the main reason was pressure from New Line Cinema to feature an established actor as Frida. (Her costars were to have been Raul Julia as Diego Rivera and Edward James Olmos in the role of her lover Leon Trotsky.)

7. Robert Stam, "Multiculturalism and the Neoconservatives," in *Dangerous Liaisons: Gender, Nation, and Postcolonial Perspectives,* ed. Anne McClintock, Aamir Mufti, and Ella Shohat (Minneapolis: University of Minnesota Press, 1997), 188–89.

8. Stam, "Multiculturalism and the Neoconservatives," 189.

9. Samuel G. Freedman, "Debate Persists on Minority Casting," *New York Times,* 22 August 1984, C15.

10. Zelda Fichandler, "Casting: Beyond Tradition to a Different Truth; A Proposal for Staging a Revolution," *Washington Post,* 22 November 1987, F1.

11. The mission statement has since been modified to reflect changes in both society and the industry, many of which were facilitated by the NTCP's efforts. The new mission statement may be read at http://www.inclusionint hearts.org/missionframe1.htm (accessed 29 May 2009).

12. "NTCP at a Glance: Mission, Goals, and Activities," *New Traditions—The NTCP Newsletter (New York)* 2, no. 3 (Winter 1994): 6.

13. Joe Brown, "Nontraditional Casting: Not Just a Character Issue," *Washington Post,* 23 November 1987, B1.

14. Dan Sullivan, "Colorblind Casting: It's Not Yet a Tradition when Black Is White, Women Are Men, and the Theater Is Challenging," *Los Angeles Times,* 2 October 1988, 50.

15. "Theater Groups Endorse Diversity," *New Traditions—The NTCP Newsletter (New York)* 3, no. 1 (Winter 1996): 1.

16. This portion of the statement seems to articulate a position on the issues raised by high profile cases such as the *Miss Saigon* controversy: "While we recognize that there can be no interference with the artistic integrity or contractual rights of the author, director, or choreographer, we urge all members of the theater community to challenge traditional stereotypes."

17. This is the definition presented on the unnumbered opening page of Davis and Newman, *Beyond Tradition*.

18. Clinton Turner Davis, "Beyond the Wilson-Brustein Debate: To Whom It May Concern," *Theater* 27, no. 2–3 (1997): 31.

19. Michael Banton, "Modelling Ethnic and National Relations," *Ethnic and Racial Studies* 17, no. 1 (1994): 102, reprinted in *Ethnicity*, ed. John Hutchinson and Anthony D. Smith (Oxford: Oxford University Press, 1996), 98–104.

20. For a discussion of how ethnic and national identity is established through speech, see my "False Accents: Embodied Dialects and the Characterization of Ethnicity and Nationality," *Theatre Topics* 14, no. 1 (March 2004): 353–72.

21. Harry Newman, "Holding Back: The Theatre's Resistance to Non-Traditional Casting," *Drama Review* 33, no. 3 (1989), 26–27. The alliance now maintains an online database—Artists Files Online (AOF)—that allows searches using multiple criteria.

22. These interviews, as well as others with playwrights, directors, theater administrators, and funding organization executives, which first appeared in the Non-Traditional Casting Project's newsletter *New Traditions*, can be found on the Alliance for Inclusion in the Arts website, http://www.inclusioninthearts.org/compendium/compendiumframe.html (accessed 29 May 2009).

23. For example, the repertoire of the East West Players during the 1970s and 1980s was dominated by Japanese American and Chinese American works. When Tim Dang became artistic director in 1993, one of his stated goals was to increase the representation of Vietnamese, Filipinos, Koreans, Thais, and Hawaiians. Also in southern California, there has been some resentment at the perceived dominance of Chicano artists in Latino theaters. In a 1989 interview with the *Los Angeles Times*, José Armand, a Cuban American theater producer who had recently been appointed director of Los Angeles's Festival Latino, described himself as feeling "like an outsider both as a Latino in the white world and as a Cuban among clannish Chicanos" (Douglas Sadownick, "Paving the Way for Festival Latino," *Los Angeles Times*, 9 July 1989, Home, 4).

24. Jose Febus posed this question from the audience (Davis and Newman, *Beyond Tradition*, 99).

25. The notable exception to the pan-Asian model has been immigrant theaters. These groups, however, tend to be composed largely of amateur performers and favor musical rather than dramatic forms. Such theaters have been the subject of recent studies such as those by Josephine Lee ("Between Immigration and Hyphenation: The Problems of Theorizing Asian American Theater," *Journal of Dramatic Theory and Criticism* 13, no. 1 [Fall 1998]: 45–69), Daphne Lei ("The Production and Consumption of Chinese Theatre in Nineteenth-Century California," *Theatre Research International* 28, no. 3 [2003]: 289–302), and Esther Kim Lee (*A History of Asian American Theatre* [Cambridge: Cambridge University Press, 2006]).

26. Among the major works documenting the history of Hispanic theater in the United States are the following: Nicolas Kanellòs, *A History of Hispanic Theatre in the United States: Origins to 1940* (Austin: University of Texas Press, 1990); *Hispanic Theatre in the United States* (Houston: Arte Publico Press, 1984) and *Mexican*

American Theatre: Then and Now (Houston: Arte Publico Press, 1989), both edited by Kanellòs; and Jorge Huerta, *Chicano Theater: Themes and Forms* (Ypsilanti: Bilingual Press, 1982) and *Chicano Drama: Performance, Society, and Myth* (New York: Cambridge University Press, 2000).

27. "Joshua Spafford Biography," http://208.233.94.244/spafford/bio.html (accessed 21 February 2001).

28. http://www.inclusioninthearts.org/missionframe1.htm (accessed 29 May 2009).

29. http://www.inclusioninthearts.org/Deal/ (accessed 29 May 2009).

30. http://www.inclusioninthearts.org/Written_on_the_body/ExecSum mary418CB.htm (accessed 29 May 2009).

31. http://www.inclusioninthearts.org/openEye/openeyeframe.htm (accessed 29 May 2009).

32. http://www.naatco.org/index.html?about.html (accessed 29 May 2009).

33. Thompson, ed., *Colorblind Shakespeare*, 6.

CHAPTER 1

Epigraph: Judith Butler, "Performative Acts and Gender Constitution: An Essay in Phenomenology and Feminist Theory," *Theatre Journal* 40 (1988): 527, reprinted in *Performing Feminisms: Feminist Critical Theory and Theatre*, ed. Sue-Ellen Case (Baltimore: Johns Hopkins University Press, 1990), 270–82.

1. Constantin Stanislavsky, *Creating a Role*, trans. Elizabeth Reynolds Hapgood (New York: Routledge/Theatre Arts Book, 1961), 116.

2. Stanislavsky, *Creating a Role*, 117.

3. "Le comédien est le tout du théâtre. On peut se passer de tout dans la représentation, excepté de lui. Il est la chair du spectacle, le plaisir du spectateur. Il est la présence même, irréfutable. Mais le saisir en fonction des signes qu'il produit n'est pas chose simple. . . . Il est le lieu de tous les paradoxes." Anne Ubersfeld, *L'Ecole du Spectateur* (Paris: Éditions sociales, 1981), 165.

4. Fernando de Toro, *Theatre Semiotics: Text and Staging in Modern Theatre*, ed. Carole Hubbard, trans. John Lewis (1987; Toronto: University of Toronto Press, 1995), 88.

5. "un être humain, dont le rôle, dans sa pratique propre est de *faire signe,* d'être transformé (de se transformer en système de signes)."

6. "mais cette transformation ne saurait être totale, il y a un reste non semantisé" (Ubersfeld, *L'Ecole du Spectateur*, 166).

7. These studies include the work of Marco De Marinis, Fernando de Toro, Keir Elam, Erika Fischer-Lichte, André Helbo, Tadeusz Kowzan, Patrice Pavis, Alessandro Serpieri, and Anne Ubersfeld.

8. Gay McAuley, *Space in Performance: Making Meaning in the Theatre* (Ann Arbor: University of Michigan Press, 2000), 90.

9. Ubersfeld, *L'Ecole du Spectateur*, 322.

10. Photographs of the production can be found at http://www.shake spearetheatre.org/plays/photos.aspx?id=64.

11. Joe Brown, "Nontraditional Casting: Not Just a Character Issue," *Washington Post*, 23 November 1987, B4.

12. Ubersfeld, *L'Ecole du Spectateur*, 39–40.

13. Bert O. States, *Great Reckonings in Little Rooms: On the Phenomenology of Theatre* (Berkeley: University of California Press, 1985), 21, 35, 49.

14. Stanton B. Garner Jr., *Bodied Spaces: Phenomenology and Performance in Contemporary Drama* (Ithaca: Cornell University Press, 1994), 44.

15. Michael D. Bristol, "Race and the Comedy of Abjection in Othello," in *Shakespeare in Performance*, ed. Robert Shaughnessy (New York: St. Martin's Press, 2000), 161.

16. Michael Bristol's research uncovered no accounts of this particular incident in Maryland newspapers of the period, although there was a story about an attack on a black theater company in 1822, the year before the *Othello* story appeared in *L'Almanach des spectacles*. See Bristol, "Race and the Comedy of Abjection in Othello," 161–63.

17. Eric Lott, *Love and Theft: Blackface Minstrelsy and the American Working Class* (Oxford: Oxford University Press, 1993), 112.

18. Errol Hill, *Shakespeare in Sable: A History of Black Shakespearean Actors* (Amherst: University of Massachusetts Press, 1984), 126.

19. St. Clair, Bourne, director, *Paul Robeson: Here I Stand*, American Masters, television documentary, written by Lou Potter, produced by Chiz Schultz (Thirteen/WNET and Menair Media International, WinStar Home Entertainment, 1999).

20. Herbert Blau, *Blooded Thought: Occasions of Theatre* (New York: Performing Arts Journal Publications, 1982), 134.

21. E. D. Hirsch, *Validity in Interpretation* (New Haven: Yale University Press, 1967), 78.

22. Thomas O. Beebee, *The Ideology of Genre: A Comparative Study of Generic Instability* (University Park: Pennsylvania State University Press, 1994), 28.

23. Marco De Marinis, *The Semiotics of Performance*, trans. Aine O'Healy (1982; Bloomington: Indiana University Press, 1993), 177.

24. Hirsch, *Validity in Interpretation*, 76.

25. This term was first used by Roland Barthes to refer to the impressions created by photographic representations.

26. "la manifestation théâtrale ne renvoie jamais à un réel, mais à un discours sur le réel, non pas à l'histoire, mais à une idée sur l'histoire" (Ubersfeld, *L'Ecole du Spectateur,* 259).

27. "*L'effet de réel* dans la référentialisation théâtrale correspond toujours à un fonctionnement idéologique: la scène dit toujours non pas comment est le monde, mais comment est le monde qu'elle montre. Au spectateur de construire—et personne ne le fera pour lui—la relation avec le réel de son expérience à lui" (Ubersfeld, *L'Ecole du Spectateur,* 259).

28. Postmodern directors such as Peter Sellars add multiple frames of reference but in the process explode the reality effect.

29. Alan Armstrong, "Multicultural Casting: Notes from the Oregon Shake-

speare Festival," paper presented at the Annual Meeting of the Shakespeare Association of America, Montreal, 2000.

30. John Simon, "A Clash of Cymbelines," *New York Magazine,* 12 June 1989, 86.

31. Frank Rich, "Fantasy 'Cymbeline' Set Long after Shakespeare," *New York Times,* 1 June 1989, C15.

32. Armstrong, "Multicultural Casting."

33. Richard Hornby, "Interracial Casting at the Public and Other Theatres," *Hudson Review* 42, no. 3 (Autumn 1989): 462.

34. Hornby, "Interracial Casting at the Public and Other Theatres," 462–63.

CHAPTER 2

Epigraph: Ralph Waldo Emerson, *The Conduct of Life* (Boston: Houghton Mifflin, 1898), 142, 143.

1. August Wilson, "The Ground on Which I Stand," *American Theatre* (September 1996): 72.

2. Wilson, "The Ground on Which I Stand," 72.

3. "Inside the Tent—Casting: Colorblind or Conscious," *American Theatre* (September 1996): 20.

4. Wilson, "The Ground on Which I Stand," 72.

5. Robert Brustein, "Subsidized Separatism," *American Theatre* (October 1996): 100.

6. Wilson, "The Ground on Which I Stand," 71.

7. Brustein, "Subsidized Separatism," 27.

8. Michael Omi and Howard Winant, *Racial Formation in the United States from the 1960s to the 1990s,* 2nd ed. (New York: Routledge, 1994), 2–3.

9. Omi and Winant, *Racial Formation in the United States from the 1960s to the 1990s,* 15.

10. Omi and Winant, *Racial Formation in the United States from the 1960s to the 1990s,* 17.

11. Omi and Winant, *Racial Formation in the United States from the 1960s to the 1990s,* 16.

12. John Patterson, "Joe Papp Responds to Charges That a Black-Hispanic Shakespeare Company Doesn't Scan," *Villager (New York),* 9 April 1979, 11.

13. New York Shakespeare Festival, *Semi-Annual Report of the Director of Education* (13 September 1965), 3.

14. Whitney Bolton, review of *The Winter's Tale,* by William Shakespeare, *New York Morning Telegraph,* 16 August 1963.

15. Richard Faust and Charles Kadushin, *Shakespeare in the Neighborhood: Audience Reactions to "A Midsummer Night's Dream" as Produced by Joseph Papp for the Delacorte Mobile Theater* (New York: Bureau of Applied Research of Columbia University and the Twentieth Century Fund, 1965), 28.

16. Faust and Kadushin, *Shakespeare in the Neighborhood,* 37.

17. John Simon, "Mugging the Bard in Central Park," *Commonweal,* 3 September 1965, 635–36.

18. Arthur Gelb, "Integrated Cast Will Act in South," *New York Times,* 11 April 1963, 10.

19. Patterson, "Joe Papp Responds to Charges That a Black-Hispanic Shakespeare Company Doesn't Scan," 9.

20. Eleanor Blau, "Papp Starts a Shakespearean Repertory Troupe Made up Entirely of Black and Hispanic Actors," *New York Times,* 21 January 1979, 55.

21. "Shakespeare for City Students," *Newsday (New York),* 8 October 1986, 21.

22. Omi and Winant, *Racial Formation in the United States from the 1960s to the 1990s,* 18.

23. Omi and Winant, *Racial Formation in the United States from the 1960s to the 1990s,* 17.

24. Omi and Winant, *Racial Formation in the United States from the 1960s to the 1990s,* 1–2.

25. Harry Newman, "Holding Back: The Theatre's Resistance to Non-Traditional Casting," *Drama Review* 33, no. 3 (Fall 1989): 26–27.

26. Newman, "Holding Back," 35.

27. Newman, "Holding Back," 35.

28. Currently, the Alliance for Inclusion in the Arts has expanded the racial and ethnic categories to include African American, Asian American, Caribbean Black, South Asian, Latino, Arab American, Persian American, and Native American.

29. Newman, "Holding Back," 31.

30. Helen Epstein, *Joe Papp: An American Life* (Boston: Little, Brown, 1994), 169.

31. Geoffrey Owens, "Alliance for Inclusion in the Arts," *New Traditions Compendium Forums and Commentaries (1992–1996),* 1992, http://www.inclusionint hearts.org/compendium/compendiumframe.html (accessed 29 May 2009).

32. Benny Sato Ambush, "Inside the Tent—Casting: Colorblind or Conscious," *American Theatre* (September 1996): 20.

33. Omi and Winant, *Racial Formation in the United States from the 1960s to the 1990s,* 37.

34. Omi and Winant, *Racial Formation in the United States from the 1960s to the 1990s,* 38.

35. Omi and Winant, *Racial Formation in the United States from the 1960s to the 1990s,* 40.

36. Omi and Winant, *Racial Formation in the United States from the 1960s to the 1990s,* 45.

37. Wilson, "The Ground on Which I Stand," 16.

38. Wilson, "The Ground on Which I Stand," 16.

39. Wilson, "The Ground on Which I Stand," 16.

40. Wilson, "The Ground on Which I Stand," 72.

41. Josephine Lee, "Bodies, Revolution and Magic: Cultural Nationalism and Racial Fetishism," in *Modern Drama: Defining the Field,* ed. Ric Knowles, Joanne Tompkins, and W. B. Worthen (Toronto: University of Toronto Press, 2003), 148.

42. Josephine Lee, "Racial Actors, Liberal Myths," *XCP: Cross-Cultural Poetics* 13 (2003): 94.

43. For extensive critical analyses of the *Miss Saigon* casting controversy, see also Karen Shimakawa, *National Abjection: The Asian American Body Onstage* (Durham: Duke University Press, 2002) and Esther Kim Lee, *A History of Asian American Theatre* (Cambridge: Cambridge University Press, 2006).

44. Mervyn Rothstein, "Union Bars White in Asian Role: Broadway May Lose 'Miss Saigon,'" *New York Times,* 8 August 1990, A1.

45. Don Shirley, "The Fall of 'Miss Saigon' Casting," *Los Angeles Times,* 9 August 1990, Home, 1.

46. Mervyn Rothstein, "Producer Cancels 'Miss Saigon': 140 Members Challenge Equity," *New York Times,* 9 August 1990, C15.

47. Prominent figures in American theater added their voices to the dispute, many expressing support for Actors' Equity's moral stance but ambivalence regarding the union's interference with artistic decisions. For Joseph Papp (NYSF), Michael Kahn (Washington Shakespeare Theatre), and the Mark Taper Forum's casting director Stanley Soble, the critical point was whether or not genuine efforts had been made to find a suitable Asian actor. Megan Rosenfeld, "No 'Miss Saigon' for Broadway: Casting Choice Cancels Run," *Washington Post,* 9 August 1990, D1; Shirley, "The Fall of 'Miss Saigon' Casting," 1. Diane White, producing director of the Los Angeles Theatre Center, decried the move as censorship; her statement prompted the resignation of Dom Magwili, director of the Asian American Theatre Project at the LATC. Don Shirley, "'Saigon' Spurs Resignation," *Los Angeles Times,* 10 August 1990, 22.

48. Rothstein, "Producer Cancels 'Miss Saigon,'" C15.

49. Frank Rich, "Jonathan Pryce, 'Miss Saigon' and Actors' Equity's Decision," *New York Times,* 10 August 1990, C1.

50. Rothstein, "Union Bars White in Asian Role," A1.

51. Shirley, "'Saigon' Spurs Resignation," 22. Not all Asian Americans involved with the performing arts opposed the casting of Pryce. Many, particularly actors, were dismayed by Actors' Equity's position, which resulted in the cancellation of the Broadway production and the loss of over thirty roles for Asian American performers.

52. Rosenfeld, "No 'Miss Saigon' for Broadway," D1.

53. Jon Lawrence Rivera, "The Fallout over "Miss Saigon"—The Issue Is Nothing Less than Artistic Integrity," *Los Angeles Times,* 13 August 1990, Counterpunch, 3.

54. George F. Will, "The Trendy Racism of Actors' Equity," *Washington Post,* 12 August 1990, C7.

55. Gordon Davidson, "Artistic Freedom," *Los Angeles Times,* 1 October 1990, Counterpunch Letters, 4.

56. Michael Omi, "A Perspective on 'Miss Saigon': The Issue Is about Race and Racism," *Hokubei Mainichi,* 25 September 1990.

57. Omi, "A Perspective on 'Miss Saigon.'"

58. Velina Hasu Houston, "The Fallout over 'Miss Saigon'—It's Time to Overcome the Legacy of Racism in Theater," *Los Angeles Times,* 13 August 1990, Counterpunch, 3.

59. Houston, "The Fallout over 'Miss Saigon,'" 3.

60. David Henry Hwang (playwright) and Francis Jue (actor), interview by Jeff Lunden in which Hwang's new play, *Yellow Face,* is discussed, *Morning Edition,* National Public Radio, 10 December 2007.

61. Omi and Winant, *Racial Formation in the United States from the 1960s to the 1990s,* 55.

62. Omi and Winant, *Racial Formation in the United States from the 1960s to the 1990s,* 55.

63. Omi and Winant, *Racial Formation in the United States from the 1960s to the 1990s,* 60–61.

64. Omi and Winant, *Racial Formation in the United States from the 1960s to the 1990s,* 55.

65. Omi and Winant, *Racial Formation in the United States from the 1960s to the 1990s,* 55.

CHAPTER 3

Epigraph: Toshio Mori, "Japanese Hamlet," in *The Chauvinist and Other Stories* (Los Angeles: Asian American Studies Center, 1979), 39.

1. Laurie Winer, "From Cosby's Father to Colonel Pickering, by Way of Norway," *New York Times,* 24 March 1991, sec. 2, 5.

2. Carl Sandburg, *Smoke and Steel* (New York: Harcourt, Brace and Howe, 1920).

3. The music, lyrics, and sheet music cover image for this song can be viewed online at the Brown University library's special collections website, http://memory.loc.gov/cgi-bin/ampage?collId=rpbaasm&fileName=0100/0127/rpbaasmo127page.db&recNum=0.

4. Paul West and John W. Bratton, *I Want to Play Hamlet* (New York: M. Witmark and Sons, 1903).

5. West and Bratton, *I Want to Play Hamlet.*

6. Mark Knowles, *Tap Roots: The Early History of Tap Dancing* (Jefferson, NC: McFarland, 2002), 123.

7. Ania Loomba, foreword to *Colorblind Shakespeare: New Perspectives on Race and Performance,* ed. Ayanna Thompson (New York: Routledge, 2006), xv.

8. For a full account of African American performances of Shakespeare see Errol Hill, *Shakespeare in Sable: A History of Black Shakespearean Actors* (Amherst: University of Massachusetts Press, 1984).

9. See Hill, *Shakespeare in Sable,* 111–14.

10. Hill, *Shakespeare in Sable,* 130.

11. In the 1968 Washington, DC, Summer Shakespeare Festival production, Juliet's family was black and Romeo's white; Cornerstone Theater's 1989 Port Gibson, Mississippi, production reversed the races—the Capulets were white and the Montagues were black.

12. This was the premise of Baz Luhrmann's 1996 film version of *Romeo and Juliet,* although the Capulets were not all played by Latino actors, John Leguizamo's Tybalt being the notable exception.

13. The production ran from 10 February to 4 March 2000 at the Connelly

Theatre in New York City. Jonathan Bank directed, and the cast included Joshua Spafford (Othello), Joel de la Fuente (Iago), Tina Horii (Desdemona), Tess Lina (Emilia), and Andy Pang (Cassio).

14. Statistics from Kay Atwood, *Minorities of Early Jackson County, Oregon* (Medford, OR: Gandee Printing, 1976), 4–5. Cited in Alan Armstrong, "Multicultural Casting: Notes from the Oregon Shakespeare Festival," paper presented at the Annual Meeting of the Shakespeare Association of America, Montreal, 2000.

15. This information was compiled by Judy Kennedy, a retired company member and an OSF archives volunteer, in 1997.

16. Armstrong, "Multicultural Casting," 1.

17. Armstrong, "Multicultural Casting," 3.

18. Derrick Lee Weeden, interview, *Update* (Oregon Shakespeare Festival) 1, no. 1 (2003): 1.

19. Armstrong, "Multicultural Casting," 4.

20. Carol Beadle, *The [In] Crowd* (Oregon Shakespeare Festival) 1, no. 1 (May 2002): 1.

21. Armstrong, "Multicultural Casting," 7.

22. These and other excerpts from letters to the *Ashland Daily Tidings* from 1995 to 1998 were compiled by Alan Armstrong for his 2000 paper "Multicultural Casting: Notes from the Oregon Shakespeare Festival."

23. "OSF's PC casting," letter to the editor, *Mail Tribune (Medford, OR)*, 12 May 2002.

24. Bill Varble, "Yes, Virginia," *Mail Tribune (Medford, OR)*, 21 April 2002, 4B.

25. Gina Marchetti, *Romance and the "Yellow Peril"* (Berkeley: University of California Press, 1993), 5.

26. Armstrong, "Multicultural Casting," 12.

27. Rick Vanderknyff, "Theater Rejects Interracial 'Romeo and Juliet,'" *Los Angeles Times,* 24 August 1990, 1.

28. Vanderknyff, "Theater Rejects Interracial 'Romeo and Juliet,'" 1.

29. Vanderknyff, "Theater Rejects Interracial 'Romeo and Juliet,'" 1.

30. Vanderknyff, "Theater Rejects Interracial 'Romeo and Juliet,'" 1.

31. Erik Hamilton, "Group Acts Irate at Official Rejection of Black 'Romeo,'" *Los Angeles Times,* 27 October 1990, 7, Orange County edition.

32. Tony Taccone, "Coriolanus: 'From the Director,'" notes from the souvenir program for the 1996 Oregon Shakespeare Festival Volume II, 13.

33. Taccone, "Coriolanus," 13.

34. Armstrong, "Multicultural Casting," 12.

35. Just the previous year, Vanessa Redgrave had played the role of Prospero in Lenka Udovicki's production of *The Tempest* at the Globe Theatre in London (12 May–10 September 2000). Critics were more bothered by her accent than her sex.

36. Penny Metropulos, "Director's Note: Creativity, Spirit and True Power in *The Tempest*," notes from the souvenir program for the 2001 Oregon Shakespeare Festival, 2.

37. "'The Tempest,'" review of *The Tempest,* by William Shakespeare, Oregon Shakespeare Festival, *Ashland Daily Tidings* 16 March–22 March 2001, 7.

38. Ron Cowan, "Production Has Fresh Take on 'The Tempest,'" review of *The Tempest,* by William Shakespeare, Oregon Shakespeare Festival, *Statesman Journal (Salem, OR),* 4 March 2001.

39. Molly Tinsley, "Prospero/Prospera," *Jefferson Monthly,* March 2001.

40. Celia R. Daileader traces a similar phenomenon of race-based typecasting in British theater, using the Royal Shakespeare Company as her example. She argues even more specifically that the relationship between Othello and Desdemona provides a mold for the casting of black male actors in nonblack roles. She writes: "I have focused exclusively on the RSC because it is the world's most prominent theatre company devoted to Shakespeare and his contemporaries: the sheer numbers attending its productions, its high visibility and cultural clout encourage other Shakespeare companies to follow where it leads. Needless to say, the form of stereotyping discussed in this essay is pandemic to Anglo-American culture and not unique to a handful of British directors" ("Casting Black Actors: Beyond Othellophilia," in *Shakespeare and Race,* ed. Stanley Wells and Catherine Alexander [Cambridge: Cambridge University Press, 2000], 179).

41. Lady Macbeth (La Mama, Barbara Montgomery, 1977; New Federal Theatre, Esther Rolle, 1977; Cleveland Playhouse, Yolande Bavan, 1977; New York Shakespeare Festival, Angela Bassett, 1998; Shakespeare Theatre Company, Franchelle Stewart Dorn, 1988), Goneril (New York Shakespeare Festival, Rosalind Cash, 1973; American Shakespeare Festival, Jane White, 1975), Regan (New York Shakespeare Festival, Ellen Holly, 1973), Volumnia (New York Shakespeare Festival, Gladys Vaughan, 1965; 1996, Oregon Shakespeare Festival, Debra Lynne Wicks).

42. Juliet (Washington Shakespeare Theatre, Jennifer Ikeda, 2001–2), Cordelia (Oregon Shakespeare Festival, Miriam A. Laube, 1997; Washington Shakespeare Theatre, Monique Holt, 1999–2000), Agnes (La Jolla Playhouse, Michi Baral, 1997). Black actors have also played all of these roles except Agnes.

43. Ellen Foreman, review of *Macbeth,* by William Shakespeare, La Mama Experimental Theatre, *Black American* (1977).

44. Armstrong, "Multicultural Casting," 13.

45. Images from these performances can be found in the Shakespeare Theatre's online photo gallery, http://www.shakespearetheatre.org/plays/photos .aspx?id=64 and http://www.shakespearetheatre.org/plays/photos.aspx?id=35.

46. Hill, *Shakespeare in Sable,* 133.

47. Vincent Canby, "Pop 'Hamlet' Presented—Will Tour Parks," *New York Times,* 4 July 1968, 15.

48. Mythili Kaul, ed., *Othello: New Essays by Black Writers* (Washington, DC: Howard University Press, 1996), 15, 18.

49. Recent studies that include overviews of scholarship and staging practices relating to the question of Othello's racial and cultural identity are Virginia Mason Vaughan, *Othello: A Contextual History* (Cambridge; Cambridge University Press, 1994); Mythili Kaul, background essay in *Othello: New Essays by Black Writers,* ed. Mythili Kaul (Washington, DC: Howard University Press, 1997); E. A. J. Honigmann, introduction to *Othello* (London: Thomas Nelson and Sons, 1999; reprinted by the Arden Shakespeare, 2001).

50. Lois Potter, *Othello* (Manchester: Manchester University Press, 2002), 16.

51. Potter, *Othello*, 33.

52. At least there has not been any evidence in surviving documents. For as Errol Hill has pointed out, once black actors and audiences were involved in the nineteenth century, it would be hard to imagine that it had not occurred to someone that "Iago's irrational malice typifies for blacks the senseless color prejudice they experience in their daily lives" (*Shakespeare in Sable,* 41).

53. She first sets the figure of Othello against the wars between Christian Europe and the Ottoman Empire during the Renaissance, when there was also a noticeable black African presence in Elizabethan England as a result of the capture of Spanish slave ships. She then traces his evolution into an aristocratic officer and gentleman during the Restoration; his conversion into a romantic, exotic lover beginning in the mid-eighteenth century; and his transformation into a protagonist in a domestic melodrama in the nineteenth century.

54. Vaughan, *Othello: A Contextual History,* 133–34.

55. Edward Pechter, *Othello and Interpretive Traditions* (Iowa City: University of Iowa Press, 1999), 15.

56. See Marvin Rosenberg, *The Masks of Othello: The Search for the Identity of Othello, Iago, and Desdemona by Three Centuries of Actors and Critics* (Berkeley: University of California Press, 1961), 118–19; and Hill, *Shakespeare in Sable,* 19–40.

57. Errol Hill provides the most thorough account of the repression of black classical theater companies and actors in *Shakespeare in Sable.*

58. Lower mentions in particular James H. Dormon Jr., *Theater in the Ante Bellum South 1815–1861* (Chapel Hill: University of North Carolina Press, 1967).

59. Charles B. Lower, "Othello as Black on Southern Stages, Then and Now," in *Shakespeare in the South,* ed. Philip C. Kolin (Jackson: University Press of Mississippi, 1983), 201.

60. Lower, "Othello as Black on Southern Stages," 218.

61. It should be noted that not all African Americans or other members of postcolonial societies are necessarily eager to embrace Othello as their representative in the Shakespearean canon. Many black artists and scholars strongly feel that Othello represents an irredeemably caricatured picture of a black man and so is most appropriately performed by a white actor. For instance, in S. E. Ogude's opinion: "In a sense, every production of *Othello* is a reenactment of racial tensions, and Othello is preeminently a caricature of the black man. There is something grotesque in the presentation of Othello. That explains why it is a travesty of Shakespeare for a 'veritable Negro' to play the role of Othello. A black Othello is an obscenity. The element of the grotesque is best achieved when a white man plays the role. As the play wears on, and under the heat of lights and action the makeup begins to wear off, Othello becomes a monstrosity of colors: the wine-red lips and snow-white eyes against a background of messy blackness" ("Literature and Racism: The Example of *Othello,*" in *Othello: New Essays by Black Writers,* ed. Mythili Kaul [Washington, DC: Howard University Press, 1997], 163).

American director and educator Sheila Rose Bland proposes a production that would foreground the fact that Othello was written by a white writer for white audiences, and Desdemona imagined by a male writer for male actors: "I would direct *Othello* as a comedy, almost as a minstrel show. The entire show would be played for laughs—even the murders and suicides. I would make Othello the butt of the jokes, and Iago the hero—saving the values of white purity. I would make Desdemona a woman who deserves what she gets. . . . I would cast the show entirely with white males, having Othello played by a white male in blackface. White males dressed in female clothing would play Desdemona, Emilia, and Bianca" ("How I Would Direct *Othello*," in *Othello: New Essays by Black Writers,* ed. Mythili Kaul [Washington, DC: Howard University Press, 1997], 29).

62. Harold Scott's production for the Shakespeare Theatre Company ran from 27 November 1990 to 27 January 1991. An earlier version, with the same actors playing the roles of Othello, Iago, and Desdemona, had played the previous summer at the Philip J. Levin Theater of the Rutgers Arts Center. The production was restaged in May 1993 for the Great Lakes Theater Festival in Cleveland.

63. Liza Henderson, "Harold Scott on Color, Cast, Shakespeare, America," *Asides: Quarterly Publication of the Shakespeare Theatre at the Folger* (Winter 1990): 1.

64. Additional photographs of the production can be seen at http://www.shakespearetheatre.org/plays/photos.aspx?id=73.

65. Henderson, "Harold Scott on Color, Cast, Shakespeare, America," 7.

66. Henderson, "Harold Scott on Color, Cast, Shakespeare, America," 7.

67. Henderson, "Harold Scott on Color, Cast, Shakespeare, America," 7.

68. Marianne Evett, "Othello: The Role 'Challenges Everything One Has,'" *Plain Dealer (Cleveland),* 9 May 1993, Final/West, H1. Andre Braugher had just recently completed his training at Stanford and Juilliard when he was chosen by Scott to play Iago. His relationship to Scott and Brooks therefore paralleled the relationship to Othello being envisioned by Scott. Expressing his excitement about the opportunity to work with the two older men whom he respected and admired, Braugher said: "I'm just two years out of school. It's so rare for me to work with *two* mature Black artists . . . two incredibly articulate, intelligent, well-informed scholars who are *also* very talented artists" ("Andre Braugher as Iago," *Asides: Quarterly Publication of the Shakespeare Theatre at the Folger* [Winter 1990]: 6).

69. Miranda Johnson-Haddad, "The Shakespeare Theatre at the Folger, 1990–91," *Shakespeare Quarterly* 42, no. 4 (1991): 477.

70. *Asides: Quarterly Publication of the Shakespeare Theatre at the Folger* (Winter 1990): 3.

71. Chris Westberg, "Avery Brooks as Othello," *Asides: Quarterly Publication of the Shakespeare Theatre at the Folger* (Winter 1990): 7.

72. "Andre Braugher as Iago," 5.

73. Lloyd Rose, "'Othello': The Two Faces of Tragedy," review of *Othello,* by William Shakespeare, Shakespeare Theatre, *Washington Post,* 5 December 1990, C1.

74. Courtland Milloy, "Black-on-Black Lesson from Hawk," *Washington Post,* 11 December 1990, B3.

75. Milloy, "Black-on-Black Lesson from Hawk," B3.

76. "A Cleveland Stage for 'Othello,'" *Plain Dealer (Cleveland),* 20 May 1993, B4.

77. Marianne Evett, "Casting Change Delays Opening of 'Othello,'" *Plain Dealer (Cleveland)*, 1 April 1993, E16.

78. Alvin Klein, "Striking Performances Light up 'Othello,'" *New York Times* 1 July 1990, NJ 15.

79. Marianne Evett, "Mistrusting Happiness until We Destroy It," review of *Othello*, by William Shakespeare, Ohio Theater, Cleveland, *Plain Dealer (Cleveland)*, 17 May 1993, C3. Miranda Johnson-Haddad, with her scholar's perspective and the more extensive format of *Shakespeare Quarterly* reviews, offered more in-depth analyses of how the revised casting. functioned visually, psychologically, and semiotically in specific scenes. See Johnson-Haddad, "The Shakespeare Theatre at the Folger, 1990–91," *Shakespeare Quarterly* 42, no. 4 (1991): 472–84.

80. Rose, "'Othello': The Two Faces of Tragedy," C1.

81. Johnson-Haddad, "The Shakespeare Theatre at the Folger, 1990–91," 478–79.

82. Acting Company, 5 June 2009, http://www.theactingcompany.org/.

83. Clive Barnes, "No Moor Needed," review of *Othello*, by William Shakespeare, Acting Company, *New York Post*, 18 May 1995, 44.

84. Wilborn Hampton, "Two Very Different Women in Distress," *New York Times*, 17 May 1995, C14.

85. Hampton, "Two Very Different Women in Distress," C14.

86. Barnes, "No Moor Needed," 44.

87. Howard Kissel, "Most Unhappy 'Othello,'" review of *Othello*, by William Shakespeare, Tribeca Performing Arts Center, *Daily News (New York)*, 17 May 1995, 35.

88. Henderson, "Harold Scott on Color, Cast, Shakespeare, America," 7.

89. Metropulos, "Director's Note," 7.

90. Marco De Marinis, *The Semiotics of Performance*, trans. Aine O'Healy (1982; Bloomington: Indiana University Press, 1993), 14.

91. De Marinis has proposed a tripartite categorization of theater conventions: the general, the particular, and the unique. A concise definition of the general conventions is given by Fernando de Toro: "General conventions have to do with the *rules* of theatre production in the achievement of fiction. From the moment the spectator enters into the theatre, he/she knows that a series of conventions distinct from social conventions must be accepted, for a stage production does not provide an exact replica of exterior reality and is not the world exactly as the spectator knows it . . . They are general in that there are no unique forms for each theatre production" (*Theatre Semiotics: Text and Staging in Modern Theatre*, ed. Carole Hubbard, trans. John Lewis [1987; Toronto: University of Toronto Press, 1995], 55).

92. Toro, *Theatre Semiotics*, 56.

93. Ray Greene, "Patrick Stewart," *Asides: Quarterly Publication of the Shakespeare Theatre at the Folger,* 1997–98 Season, no. 2 (1997): 1.

94. Greene, "Patrick Stewart," 1, 5.

95. Greene, "Patrick Stewart," 5.

96. David Richards, "Patrick Stewart, Inside a Murderous Mind," *Washington Post*, 12 November 1997, D1.

97. Lyn Gardner, "Jude Kelly," Publication of the Shakespeare Theatre, *Asides: Quarterly Publication of the Shakespeare Theatre at the Folger,* 1997–98 Season, no. 2 (1997): 5.

98. Photographs from this production can be seen at http://www.shake speare theatre.org/plays/photos.aspx?id=44.

99. Pechter, *Othello and Interpretive Traditions,* 133.

100. Pechter, *Othello and Interpretive Traditions,* 132.

101. Edward Washington, "'At the Door of Truth': The Hollowness of Signs in Othello," in *Othello: New Essays by Black Writers,* ed. Mythili Kaul (Washington, DC: Howard University Press, 1997), 171.

102. Gardner, "Jude Kelly," 5.

103. Miranda Johnson-Haddad, "The Shakespeare Theatre Othello," *Shakespeare Bulletin* (Spring 1998): 10.

104. Johnson-Haddad, "The Shakespeare Theatre Othello," 10.

105. Toby Zinman, "Beam Me Up, Patrick Stewart," *American Theatre* (February 1998): 14.

106. Zinman, "Beam Me Up, Patrick Stewart," 14.

107. Gardner, "Jude Kelly," 5.

108. Earle Hyman, "*Othello:* Or Ego in Love, Sex and War," in *Othello: New Essays by Black Writers,* ed. Mythili Kaul (Washington, DC: Howard University Press, 1997), 24.

109. Hyman, "*Othello:* Or Ego in Love, Sex and War," 25.

110. Rosenberg, *The Masks of Othello,* 195.

111. Richards, "Patrick Stewart," D1.

112. Robert L. King, "The Seeing Place," *North American Review* 283, no. 1 (January–February 1998): 2.

113. Zinman, "Beam Me Up, Patrick Stewart," 13.

114. Lloyd Rose, "'Othello': Twist on Timeless Tragedy," review of *Othello,* by William Shakespeare, Shakespeare Theatre, *Washington Post,* 18 November 1997, C1.

115. Rose, "'Othello': Twist on Timeless Tragedy," C1.

116. Peter Marks, "The Green-Eyed Monster Fells Men of Every Color," *New York Times,* 17 November 1997, E5.

117. Marks, "The Green-Eyed Monster Fells Men of Every Color," E5.

118. Johnson-Haddad, "The Shakespeare Theatre *Othello,*" 9.

119. Miranda Johnson-Haddad, "Patrick Stewart on Playing Othello," *Shakespeare Bulletin* (Spring 1998): 11.

120. King, "The Seeing Place," 36.

121. King, "The Seeing Place," 36.

122. King, "The Seeing Place," 36.

123. Stuart Hall, "Minimal Selves," in *Black British Cultural Studies,* ed. Houston A. Baker Jr., Manthia Diawara, and Ruth A. Lindeborg (Chicago: University of Chicago Press, 1996), 116.

124. Colin Counsell, *Signs of Performance: An Introduction to Twentieth-Century Theatre* (London: Routledge, 1996), 44.

125. Johnson-Haddad, "The Shakespeare Theatre at the Folger, 1990–91," 479.

126. Miranda Johnson-Haddad, "'Haply, for I Am Black,'" program notes to *Othello*, Shakespeare Theatre, 1997, 24.

127. Timothy Murray, *Drama Trauma: Specters of Race and Sexuality in Performance, Video, and Art* (London: Routledge, 1997), 155.

128. Richards, "Patrick Stewart," D1.

129. Vaughan, *Othello: A Contextual History*, 7.

CHAPTER 4

Epigraph: Arthur Miller, "The Family in Modern Drama," in *The Theater Essays of Arthur Miller*, ed. Robert A. Martin (1956; New York: Viking Press, 1978), 70.

1. Clarke Taylor, "Non-Traditional Casting Explored at Symposium," *Los Angeles Times*, 29 November 1986, 12.

2. Mark Berman, "An All-White Company," letter to the editor, *Washington Post*, 28 November 1987, A26.

3. Kenneth H. Washington. National Diversity Forum: Opinion Pieces, Alliance for Inclusion in the Arts, 2002, http://www.ntcp.org (accessed 20 September 2008).

4. Hyman's appearances in works by Ibsen have included his Dr. Rank in the Yale Repertory Theater's 1982 production of *A Doll's House* and a 1992 Broadway performance in the title role of *The Master Builder*, directed by Tony Randall for his National Actors Theatre.

5. Jan Breslauer, "Whom Do You Serve First?" *Los Angeles Times*, 16 April 1995, 3.

6. Ray Loynd, "Stage Beat: 'The Lady from the Sea,'" review of *Lady from the Sea*, by Henrik Ibsen, Fountain Theatre, *Los Angeles Times*, 27 January 1989, 8.

7. Kate Taylor, "Multicultural Stages in a Small Oregon Town," *New York Times*, 15 August 2009, C7.

8. Robert Massa, "The Great White Way," *Village Voice (New York)*, 2 December 1986, 126.

9. Barry Moss, panelist, "Session: Realizing the Play or Playing with Reality," in *Beyond Tradition: Transcripts of the First Symposium on Non-Traditional Casting*, ed. Clinton Turner Davis and Harry Newman (New York: Non-Traditional Casting Project, 1988), 45

10. Maria Irene Fornes, panelist, "Session: Realizing the Play or Playing with Reality," in *Beyond Tradition: Transcripts of the First Symposium on Non-Traditional Casting*, ed. Clinton Turner Davis and Harry Newman (New York: Non-Traditional Casting Project, 1988), 47.

11. Don Nelsen, "Not the Type," *Daily News (New York)*, 22 November 1987, City Lights, 5.

12. John Houseman, "On Non-Traditional Casting," in *Beyond Tradition: Transcripts of the First Symposium on Non-Traditional Casting*, ed. Clinton Turner Davis and Harry Newman (New York: Non-Traditional Casting Project, 1988), 15.

13. Margo Jefferson, interview, "Beyond the Wilson-Brustein Debate: War of the Worlds," *Theater* 27, no. 2–3 (1997): 18.

14. *Glass Menagerie,* program notes, Arena Stage Company, 1989, 7.

15. Bob Mondello, "Soapy Glass," review of *The Glass Menagerie,* by Tennessee Williams, Arena Stage Company, *City Paper* (Washington, D.C.), 20 October 1989.

16. Tennessee Williams, *Cat on a Hot Tin Roof* (1954; New York: New Directions, 1975), 129.

17. Williams, *Cat on a Hot Tin Roof,* 135.

18. Williams, *Cat on a Hot Tin Roof,* 79.

19. Howard Shapiro, "A Jumping-Off Point: James Earl Jones and Phylicia Rashad Headline a Victory of a 'Cat on a Hot Tin Roof,' " review of *Cat on a Hot Tin Roof,* by Tennessee Williams, Broadhurst Theatre, New York, *Philadelphia Inquirer Features Magazine,* 8 March 2008, E1.

20. Simi Horwitz, "Ever since 'Saigon': A Non-Traditional Casting Update," *TheaterWeek* 13–19 February 1995, 22–23.

21. Michal Kobialka, ed., *Of Borders and Thresholds: Theatre History, Practice, and Theory* (Minneapolis: University of Minnesota Press, 1999), 4.

22. Richard Hornby, "Interracial Casting at the Public and Other Theatres," *Hudson Review* 42, no. 3 (Autumn 1989): 459.

23. Stanton B. Garner Jr., *Bodied Spaces: Phenomenology and Performance in Contemporary Drama* (Ithaca: Cornell University Press, 1994), 101.

24. Garner, *Bodied Spaces,* 102.

25. Tori Haring-Smith, "A Director's Response to Cultural Pluralism," *Theatre Topics* 3, no. 1 (March 1993): 90.

26. Zelda Fichandler, "Casting for a Different Truth," *American Theatre* 5, no. 2 (May 1988): 23.

27. Photographs of the National Asian American Theatre Company productions can be found in an earlier version of this section: "Changing Faces: Recasting National Identity in All-Asian(-)American Dramas," *Theatre Journal* 53 (2001): 389–409. There is rich visual documentation of the Beijing production in Miller's *Salesman in Beijing.*

28. http://www.columbia.edu/cu/china/AboutCenter.html.

29. The idea for this collaboration grew out of discussions between Arthur Miller; the director of the Center for United States–China Arts Exchange, Chou Wen-chung; Ying Ruocheng; and Chinese playwright Cao Yu, when Ying and Cao were visiting New York as guests of the center in 1980.

30. Miller describes various frictions that arose in connection with television coverage in the 30 April and 1 May entries of his daily journal, which has been published under the title *Salesman in Beijing* (New York: Viking Press, 1984).

31. Among the distinguished members of the delegation were Alex North, the composer of incidental music for *Death of a Salesman;* novelist Louis Auchincloss; British fashion designer Jean Muir; and Geraldine Stutz, president of Henri Bendel, Inc., and a member of the National Council on the Arts.

32. Prior to this, Miller had worked with the directors of two productions on specific problems but had never been fully involved in directing *Salesman* in any language.

33. Miller, *Salesman in Beijing,* 251–52.

34. Liu, Hou-sheng, "Death of a Salesman—a Profound and Bitter Play," review of Beijing production of *Death of a Salesman,* by Arthur Miller (review trans. Pao-yung Pao), *Ren Ming Ri Bao (People's Daily) (Beijing),* 28 June 1983.

35. "Play Leaps Cultural Barriers—'Death of a Salesman' Tear-Jerker in China Too," *Chicago Tribune,* 8 May 1983, sec. 1, 6.

36. Hanna Scolnikov, introduction to *The Play out of Context: Transferring Plays from Culture to Culture,* ed. Hanna Scolnikov and Peter Holland (Cambridge: Cambridge University Press, 1989), 1.

37. Hornby, "Interracial Casting at the Public and Other Theatres," 460.

38. Miller, *Salesman in Beijing,* 5.

39. Alan Nadel, "Beyond the Wilson-Brustein Debate: August Wilson and the (Color-Blind) Whiteness of Public Space," *Theater* 27, no. 2–3 (1997): 39.

40. Mia Katigbak, "National Asian American Theatre Company Positioning Statement," 1996, 2.

41. Katigbak, "National Asian American Theatre Company Positioning Statement," 1.

42. Although other companies such as the East West Players and the Asian American Theater Company of San Francisco have on occasion performed European and Euro American plays without any cultural transposition to an Asian or Asian American setting, NAATCO is the first Asian American company to have this practice at the core of their founding philosophy.

43. "East Meets West," *InTheater,* 31 October 1997, 6.

44. Irene Backalenick, "Long Day's Journey into Night," review of *Long Day's Journey into Night,* by Eugene O'Neill, National Asian American Theatre Company, *Back Stage* 28 November 1997, 56.

45. "East Meets West," 6.

46. This point was explicitly made when the Chinese government announced that it was canceling all cultural and athletic cooperation between the two countries following the United States government's decision in early April 1983 to grant defecting tennis player Hu Na asylum as a political refugee. There was initially some concern that this incident would have consequences for the *Salesman* project, but since it had been sponsored by a private organization, it was not affected by the frictions between the two governments. The production was indirectly involved in the controversy, however, when Chinese authorities denied ABC permission to film a rehearsal of *Death of a Salesman* because of their dissatisfaction over ABC's coverage of the defection. "China Bars ABC from Play Rehearsal," *Japan Times,* 2 May 1983, 4. Miller gives his reaction to these events in the 10 and 12 April entries of *Salesman in Beijing.*

47. John C. Mahoney, "East West Neutral 'Godspell,'" review of *Godspell,* by Stephen Schwartz and John-Michael Tebelak, East West Players, *Los Angeles Times,* 22 May 1981, sec. 4, 4.

48. Yuko Kurahashi, *Asian American Culture on Stage: The History of the East West Players* (New York: Garland, 1999), 124.

49. Michael Portantiere, "Color-Blindness in the Theater: Non-Traditional Casting Is Not a Black-or-White Issue," *TheaterWeek,* 13–19 April 1992, 22.

50. Jefferson, "Beyond the Wilson-Brustein Debate: War of the Worlds," 13.

51. John Tomlinson, *Cultural Imperialism: A Critical Introduction* (Baltimore: Johns Hopkins University Press, 1991), 70.

52. Miller, *Salesman in Beijing*, 79–80. This was Miller's analogy: "It's like the dilemma of the Cultural Revolution: Jiang Qing's leadership was also full of self-deluded demands on you, wasn't it? . . . She also claimed to be acting out of devotion to China, and that may have been what she felt for all we know. Just like Willy, who believes he is trying to help you, not himself. But no matter how you tried to obey her and come up to the regime's expectations, you had to see that objectively China's economy was falling apart, her arts, commerce, the whole civilization going down the drain. And your father, Mao, seemed to be backing her, isn't that right? The point is, you felt a powerful frustration, didn't you, an anger that nobody was able to tear away that complex of half-truths and deceptions to raise up the truth before the people—before Mao himself!—the facts of the destruction going on. And maybe this is why Deng Xiaoping is using the slogan 'Truth from Facts,' rather than from ideology . . . Biff is trying to do something very similar—tear Willy away from his ideology to face himself and you in detail, as a real individual who is at a certain time in his life. You can use the same Cultural Revolution frustration, that feeling of anger and the violence in you, in this role. The same thwarted love."

53. Katigbak, "National Asian American Theatre Company Positioning Statement," 2–3.

54. Stuart Hall, "Cultural Identity and Cinematic Representation," in *Black British Cultural Studies*, ed. Houston A. Baker Jr., Manthia Diawara, and Ruth A. Lindeborg (Chicago: University of Chicago Press, 1996), 213.

55. Anthologies on whiteness that are particularly useful for cultural analyses include *Displacing Whiteness: Essays in Social and Cultural Criticism*, ed. Ruth Frankenberg (Durham: Duke University Press, 1997); and *Whiteness: A Critical Reader*, ed. Mike Hill (New York: New York University Press, 1997). Thomas DiPiero, *White Men Aren't* (Durham: Duke University Press, 2002), focuses on intersections of whiteness and masculinity. *Working through Whiteness: International Perspectives*, ed. Ruth Frankenberg (Albany: State University of New York Press, 2002), offers a comparative overview of the subject.

56. Frankenberg, *Displacing Whiteness*, 15–16.

57. Timothy Bond, interview, 6 May 2003, Ashland, OR.

58. Andrea Frye, interview, *Update* (Oregon Shakespeare Festival) 1, no. 3 (2003), 2.

59. Patricia O'Haire, "David Mamet Opposes All-Female Production of His Plays," *Daily News (New York)*, 19 January 1999, 30.

60. Sylvie Drake, "Stage Watch: Color It Black, Sam," *Los Angeles Times*, 29 August 1985, 2.

61. Gerald Nachman, "Last Gasps from the WASP World," *San Francisco Chronicle*, 30 March 1992, E1.

62. A. R. Gurney, "The Dining Room," in *Collected Plays 1974–1983* (Lyme, NH: Smith and Kraus, 1997), 224.

63. A set of "Do's and Don'ts" preceding the text of the play makes it very clear that this was a right reserved for the author: "Don't mess around with the

text. No embellishments, insertions, cuts, or silent mouthings, please. Trust what I wrote, perform it as written, and all will be well" (A. R. Gurney, "Love Letters," in *Collected Plays 1984–1991* [Lyme, NH: Smith and Kraus, 2000], 223).

64. Gurney, "Love Letters," 230.

65. Gurney, "Love Letters," 244.

66. Don Shirley, "Stage Watch: New Lines in Black 'Love Letters,'" *Los Angeles Times,* 4 October 1990, 6.

67. Shirley, "Stage Watch: New Lines in Black 'Love Letters,'" 6.

68. Shirley, "Stage Watch: New Lines in Black 'Love Letters,'" 6.

CHAPTER 5

Epigraph: Jean Genet, *The Blacks: A Clown Show* (Les Nègres: clownerie), trans. Bernard Frechtman (New York: Grove Press, 1960).

1. Hendricks, "They Said I Was Too Short for the Role," cartoon, *Village Voice (New York),* 1 February 1962, 9.

2. Jim Craven, "Integration of Shakespearean Casts Made a Belated Entrance," *Mail Tribune (Medford, OR),* 21 April 2002, 1B.

3. Bill Varble, "Yes, Virginia," *Mail Tribune (Medford, OR),* 21 April 2002, 4B.

4. Diana Maychick, "Papp Demands Simon's Firing," *New York Post,* 30 March 1989, 35.

5. Frank Aston, "Genet Defined by Producer," *New York World-Telegram and Sun,* 8 June 1961, 14.

6. Aston, "Genet Defined by Producer," 14.

7. Kenneth Tynan, "Act of Vengeance by Genet," review of *The Blacks,* by Jean Genet, Royal Court Theatre, *New York Herald Tribune,* 11 June 1961.

8. Jean Genet, *The Screens* (Les Paravents), trans. Bernard Frechtman (New York: Grove Press, 1962), 10.

9. Samuel G. Freedman, "Who's to Say Whether a Playwright Is Wronged?" *New York Times,* 13 December 1984, sec. 4, 6.

10. Samuel G. Freedman, "Actors Equity Protests Beckett Cast Criticism," *New York Times,* 9 January 1985, C17.

11. Freedman, "Actors Equity Protests Beckett Cast Criticism," C17.

12. Freedman, "Actors Equity Protests Beckett Cast Criticism," C17.

13. Sylviane Gold, "The Beckett Brouhaha," *Wall Street Journal,* 28 December 1984, 1.

14. "Two Women Must Wait Some Time Longer for Godot," *Irish Times,* 27 July 1998, Home News, 3.

15. Sarah-Kate Templeton, "Beckett Estate Rules out Female Version of Godot," *Scotsman,* 27 July 1998, 6.

16. Diana Blamires, "Women Are Still Waiting to Play Godot," *Independent* (London), 27 July 1998, News, 4.

17. "Two Women Must Wait Some Time Longer for Godot," 3.

18. Shoshana Weitz, "Mr. Godot Will Not Come Today," in *The Play out of Context: Transferring Plays from Culture to Culture,* ed. Hanna Scolnicov and Peter Holland (Cambridge: Cambridge University Press, 1989), 186.

19. Weitz, "Mr. Godot Will Not Come Today," 187.

20. Weitz, "Mr. Godot Will Not Come Today," 187.

21. Weitz, "Mr. Godot Will Not Come Today," 187.

22. Brooks Atkinson, "'Godot' Is Back: Beckett Play Staged with Negro Cast," review of *Waiting for Godot,* by Samuel Beckett, *New York Times,* 22 January 1957, 25.

23. Atkinson, "'Godot' Is Back," 25.

24. "300 at 'Godot' Wait: Dispute Halts Play," *New York Times,* 23 January 1957, 24.

25. Mel Gussow, "Critic's Notebook: Didi and Gogo in Middle Age, Unchanging but Fresh," *New York Times,* 3 December 1998, E2.

26. Dan Hulbert, "D.C. Dispenses Raves for 2 Atlanta Actors: Jones, Griffin Team for 'Godot,'" *Atlanta Journal and Constitution,* 15 September 1998, Features, 9F.

27. Lloyd Rose, "Godot Watch Continues, with a Smile," review of *Waiting for Godot,* by Samuel Beckett, Studio Theatre, *Washington Post,* 8 September 1998, B1.

28. Hulbert, "D.C. Dispenses Raves for 2 Atlanta Actors," 9F.

29. Peter Marks, "A Street-Smart 'Godot' in a Cultural Wasteland," review of *Waiting for Godot,* by Samuel Beckett, Studio Theatre, *New York Times,* 24 September 1998, E1.

30. Marks, "A Street-Smart 'Godot' in a Cultural Wasteland," E1.

31. Jane Horwitz, "At Studio, 'Godot's' Woes," *Washington Post,* 10 November 1998, B1.

32. Vivian Mercier, *Beckett/Beckett* (New York: Oxford University Press, 1977), vii.

33. Hugh Kenner, *Samuel Beckett: A Critical Study* (1961; rev. ed., Berkeley: University of California Press, 1968), 10.

34. Lance St. John Butler, "Beckett's Stage of Deconstruction," in *Twentieth-Century European Drama,* ed. Brian Docherty (New York: St. Martin's Press, 1994), 66.

35. Butler, "Beckett's Stage of Deconstruction," 67.

36. While the production did arouse controversy when it was to be performed at the Baltimore International Theater Festival in May 1981, this time the protests did not originate with Beckett's agents. Instead, the opposition came from an American group known as the Coalition in Support of Liberation Struggles of Southern Africa, which was protesting the inclusion of a theater from South Africa and the lack of African American participation in the theater festival. Although the Baxter Company was integrated long before the end of apartheid and their visit was in no way being sponsored by the South African government, the coalition leaders maintained that including any group from South Africa legitimized the government. The matter ended with the Baxter Theater withdrawing from the festival.

37. Mel Gussow, "South Africans in 'Godot' at Long Wharf," review of *Waiting for Godot,* by Samuel Beckett, Long Wharf Theatre, *New York Times,* 5 December 1980, C4.

38. Mel Gussow, "Art and Politics in Bonafede's 'Advice,'" *New York Times*, 27 April 1986, sec. 1, pt. 2, 63.

39. Gussow, "South Africans in 'Godot' at Long Wharf," C4.

40. Hulbert, "D.C. Dispenses Raves for 2 Atlanta Actors," 9F.

41. Hulbert, "D.C. Dispenses Raves for 2 Atlanta Actors," 9F.

42. Images from the New York production can be viewed at http://www.classicaltheatreofharlem.org/waitingforgodot_05-06.html.

43. Images from the New Orleans productions are available at http://www.classicaltheatreofharlem.org/waitingforgodot_07-08.html.

44. Samuel Beckett, *Waiting for Godot: Tragicomedy in 2 Acts* (1954; New York: Grove Weidenfeld, 1982), 51.

45. Imogen Carter, "In Godot We Trust: New Orleans 2007," *Observer* (England), 8 March 2009, Review Features, 9.

46. Mel Gussow, "Will Godot Ever Show? Beckett Waits in Silence," *New York Times*, 10 April 1986, C18.

47. Lloyd Rose, "Stage Guild's 'Mad' Genius: In Morgan Duncan, the Godot-Ful Truth," review of *Waiting for Godot*, by Samuel Beckett, Stage Guild, *Washington Post*, 11 January 1999, C1.

48. John Rouse, "Brecht and the Contradictory Actor," in *Acting Re(Considered)*, ed. Philip Zarrilli (London: Routledge, 2002), 249.

49. Rouse, "Brecht and the Contradictory Actor," 258.

50. Colin Counsell, *Signs of Performance: An Introduction to Twentieth-Century Theatre* (London: Routledge, 1996), 97.

51. Counsell, *Signs of Performance*, 99.

52. David Richards, "Brecht, Darkly: At Arena, 'Good Person' as a Modern Fable," review of *Good Person of Setzuan*, by Bertolt Brecht, Arena Stage Company, *Washington Post*, 11 October 1985, B1.

53. Megan Rosenfeld, "At Arena, a Richley Drawn 'Chalk Circle,'" review of *Caucasian Chalk Circle*, by Bertolt Brecht, Arena Stage Company, *Washington Post*, 28 September 1990, C1.

54. Suzan-Lori Parks, "A Director Seeks Human Truths in a 'Ben Hur' of Haiti," *New York Times*, 2 December 1990, sec. 2, 5.

55. Parks, "A Director Seeks Human Truths in a 'Ben Hur' of Haiti," sec. 2, 5.

56. David Armstrong, "A Complex, Ambitious Brecht by Berkeley Rep," review of *The Good Person of Szechuan*, by Bertolt Brecht, Berkeley Repertory Theatre, *San Francisco Examiner*, 21 May 1987, F3.

57. Bernard Weiner, "A Timely Revival of Brecht's 'Person,'" review of *The Good Person of Szechuan*, by Bertolt Brecht, Berkeley Repertory Theatre, *San Francisco Chronicle*, 22 May 1987, 95.

58. Bernard Weiner, "Another Take on the Rep's Signing," *San Francisco Chronicle*, 30 May 1987, 44.

59. Michael Phillips, "Kushner to Adapt Brecht's 'Good Person,'" *San Diego Union-Tribune*, 26 January 1994, Lifestyle, E6.

60. Anne Marie Welsh, "A New 'Setzuan' Cooking: Playhouse Adaptation

Multicultural to the Max," *San Diego Union-Tribune,* 24 July 1994, Entertainment, E1.

61. Welsh, "A New 'Setzuan' Cooking," E1.

62. Chesley Plemmons, "'Good Person' Sings New Haven's Praises," review of *The Good Person of New Haven,* by Bertolt Brecht (adaptation), Long Wharf Theatre/Cornerstone Theater Company, *News-Times (Danbury, CT),* 21 May 2000.

63. David A. Rosenberg, "'Good Person' Blazes with Life at Long Wharf," review of *Good Person of New Haven,* by Bertolt Brecht (adaptation), Long Wharf Theatre/Cornerstone Theater Company, *Wilton Villager/Norwalk Hour,* 18 May 2000.

64. Laura Collins-Hughes, "Idealism in Action: The City of New Haven Takes Center Stage in Long Wharf Theatre's Grand Experiment," *New Haven Register,* 7 May 2000, F7.

65. Alvin Klein, "Taking Inspiration from Brecht," review of *The Good Person of New Haven,* by Bertolt Brecht (adaptation), Long Wharf Theatre/Cornerstone Theater Company, *New York Times,* 28 May 2000, CT6, Connecticut edition.

66. The actors were Alvin Lum, Sab Shimono, Calvin Jung, Lori Chinn, Katie San, and Irene Sun.

67. George Melloan, "The Theater," review of *Narrow Road to the Deep North,* by Edward Bond, Repertory Theater of Lincoln Center, *Wall Street Journal,* 10 January 1972, 8.

68. Frank Ching, "Asian-American Actors Fight for Jobs and Image," *New York Times,* 3 June 1973, 65.

69. Ching, "Asian-American Actors Fight for Jobs and Image," 65.

70. The first season of the television series *Kung Fu* (October 1972 to May 1973), which rationalized the casting of David Carradine as a Shaolin monk by making the character half Chinese and half Caucasian, was aired almost precisely during the interval between the Human Rights division's initial hearing and the Appeal Board's decision regarding the Repertory Theater of Lincoln Center.

71. Malcolm Goldstein, "*Our Town* and Everytown," program notes, Arena Stage Company production of *Our Town,* by Thornton Wilder, 1990, 15, 16.

72. Megan Rosenfeld, "The Talk of 'Our Town': At Arena, the Connections to Everyone's Lives," *Washington Post,* 23 November 1990, Style, C1.

73. Jonathan Yardley, "At Arena Stage, a Casting Miscue," review of *Our Town,* by Thornton Wilder, Arena Stage Company, *Washington Post,* 3 December 1990, C2.

74. Yardley, "At Arena Stage, a Casting Miscue," C2.

75. Yardley, "At Arena Stage, a Casting Miscue," C2.

76. Yardley, "At Arena Stage, a Casting Miscue," C2.

77. Douglas Wager, "'Our Town' Has No Borders," *Washington Post,* 8 December 1990, A19.

78. Wager, "'Our Town' Has No Borders," A19.

79. Paul Hodgins, "Mark Rucker Is Determined to Make 'Our Town' a Place You'll Recognize," *Orange County Register,* 15 February 1998, F8.

80. Paul Hodgins, "'Our Town' Like Home, Sweet Home," review of *Our Town*, by Thornton Wilder, La Jolla Playhouse, *Orange County Register*, 22 May 2001.

81. Hodgins, "'Our Town' Like Home, Sweet Home."

82. Hodgins, "'Our Town' Like Home, Sweet Home."

83. Thornton Wilder, *Our Town: A Play in Three Acts* (New York: Coward Mc-Cann, 1938), iv.

84. Wilder, *Our Town.*

CHAPTER 6

Epigraph: Nicholas Hytner quoted by Bruce Weber in "Correctness and 'Carousel,'" *New York Times*, 1 April 1994, C2.

1. Stacy Wolf, *A Problem Like Maria: Gender and Sexuality in the American Musical* (Ann Arbor: University of Michigan Press, 2002), 33.

2. Stephen Neale, *Genre* (1980; reprint, London: British Film Institute, 1983), 46.

3. The production had been developed for the Royal National Theatre in London in 1992 and then moved to commercial West End theater before being brought to New York.

4. Robert Osborne, "'Carousel'; Vivian Beaumont Theatre NY; Runs Indefinitely," review of *Carousel*, by Richard Rodgers and Oscar Hammerstein II, Vivian Beaumont Theater, *Hollywood Reporter*, 25 March 1994.

5. John Simon, "No Brass Ring," review of *Carousel*, by Richard Rodgers and Oscar Hammerstein II, Vivian Beaumont Theater, *New York*, 4 April 1994, 73.

6. William A. Henry III, "This Carousel Doesn't Go Anywhere," review of *Carousel*, by Richard Rodgers and Oscar Hammerstein II, Vivian Beaumont Theater, *Time*, 4 April 1994, 85.

7. Bruce Weber, "On Stage, and Off," *New York Times*, 1 April 1994, 2.

8. Weber's article also included the following statistical information: "Since the Nontraditional Casting Project, an advocacy group, was formed in 1986, the percentage of minority performers in Broadway shows has risen and fallen mostly within a range of 16 and 21 percent. Not counting 'Carousel' . . . the current figure is about 15 percent, almost half of which is accounted for by 'Miss Saigon,' which has 33 minority cast members. Of the current musicals on Broadway, 'She Loves Me,' with a cast of 25, has no minority performers; 'My Fair Lady' has 1 out of 32; 'Beauty and the Beast' has 2 out of 38. For nonmusical plays, the numbers are even sparer. According to figures provided by the Actors' Equity Association, minority cast members account for just 2.75 percent of all nonmusical shows on Broadway to date this season."

9. Weber, "On Stage, and Off," 2.

10. Mark N. Grant, *The Rise and Fall of the Broadway Musical* (Boston: Northeastern University Press, 2004), 280–81.

11. John S. Wilson, "Is There a Reason for Pearl Bailey to Record 'Dolly'?" *New York Times*, 17 December 1967, 132.

12. Richard Watts Jr., "Pearl Bailey and the New 'Dolly,'" review of *Hello, Dolly!* by Jerry Herman and Michael Stewart, St. James Theater, *New York Post,* 13 November 1967.

13. Clive Barnes, "Theater: All-Negro 'Hello, Dolly!' Has Its Premiere," review of *Hello, Dolly!* by Michael Stewart and Jerry Herman, St. James Theater, *New York Times,* 13 November 1967, 61.

14. Edwin Bolwell, "Dolly Levi Now Finds Her Match in Pearl Bailey," *New York Times,* 29 July 1967, 12.

15. Ragni Lantz, "Hello, Dolly!" *Ebony,* January 1968, 89.

16. Lantz, "Hello, Dolly!" 89.

17. Bolwell, "Dolly Levi Now Finds Her Match in Pearl Bailey," 12.

18. Bolwell, "Dolly Levi Now Finds Her Match in Pearl Bailey," 12.

19. Barnes, "Theater: All-Negro 'Hello, Dolly!' Has Its Premiere," 61.

20. Alan N. Bunce, "Pearl Bailey Scores in New 'Hello, Dolly!'" review of *Hello, Dolly!* by Michael Stewart and Jerry Herman, St. James Theater, *Christian Science Monitor,* 27 November 1967, 16.

21. See reviews by Clive Barnes (*New York Times*), Michael Feingold (*Village Voice (New York)*), Hobe (*Variety*), George Oppenheirmer (*Newsday*), Allan Wallach (*Courier-Journal & Times (Louisville, KY)*), Douglas Watt (*Daily News (New York)*).

22. Martin Gottfried, "Bailey's 'Hello Dolly!' a Lusterless Pearl," review of *Hello, Dolly!* by Jerry Herman and Michael Stewart, Minskoff Theater, *New York Post,* 7 November 1975, 34.

23. Clive Barnes, "New 'Guys and Dolls' Comes Seven Again," review of *Guys and Dolls,* by Frank Loesser, Jo Swerling, and Abe Burrows, Broadway Theater, *New York Times,* 22 July 1976, 26.

24. Ernest Leogrande, "'Guys and Dolls' in the Black," review of *Guys and Dolls,* by Frank Loesser, Jo Swerling, and Abe Burrows, Broadway Theater, *Daily News (New York),* 22 July 1976, 67.

25. Leogrande, "'Guys and Dolls' in the Black," 67.

26. Brendan Gill, "Noo Yawk," review of *Guys and Dolls,* by Frank Loesser, Jo Swerling, and Abe Burrows, Broadway Theater, *New Yorker,* 2 August 1976, 53.

27. Michael Feingold, "We Can Still Believe the Fable," review of *Guys and Dolls,* by Frank Loesser, Jo Swerling, and Abe Burrows, Broadway Theater, *Village Voice (New York),* 2 August 1976, 90.

28. Martin Gottfried, "Guys and Dolls' Suffers in the Black Version," review of *Guys and Dolls,* by Frank Loesser, Jo Swerling and Abe Burrows, Broadway Theater, *New York Post,* 22 July 1976, 15.

29. John Simon, "Dudes and Chicks," review of *Guys and Dolls,* by Frank Loesser, Jo Swerling, and Abe Burrows, Broadway Theater, *New Leader,* 13 September 1976, 22.

30. Feingold, "We Can Still Believe the Fable," 90.

31. Alan Rich, "Oh, You Beautiful 'Dolls,'" review of *Guys and Dolls,* by Frank Loesser, Jo Swerling, and Abe Burrows, Broadway Theater, *New York,* 9 August 1976, 58.

32. John Beaufort, "All-Black 'Guys and Dolls,'" review of *Guys and Dolls*, by Frank Loesser, Jo Swerling, and Abe Burrows, Broadway Theater, *Christian Science Monitor*, 26 July 1976, 23.

33. Barnes, "New 'Guys and Dolls' Comes Seven Again," 26.

34. Hobe, "Guys and Dolls," review of *Guys and Dolls*, by Frank Loesser, Jo Swerling, and Abe Burrows, Broadway Theater, *Variety*, 28 July 1976, 62.

35. Beatrice da Silva, "Something to Sneeze At," review of *Guys and Dolls*, by Frank Loesser, Jo Swerling, and Abe Burrows, Broadway Theater, *Villager (New York)*, 12 August 1976, 10.

36. Howard Kissel, "Theater," review of *Guys and Dolls*, by Frank Loesser, Jo Swerling and Abe Burrows, Broadway Theater, *Women's Wear Daily*, 23 July 1976, 9.

37. da Silva, "Something to Sneeze At," 10.

38. Charles Michener, "Almost-Nicely," review of *Guys and Dolls*, by Frank Loesser, Jo Swerling, and Abe Burrows, Broadway Theater, *Newsweek*, 2 August 1976, 70.

39. Martin Gottfried, "'Guys and Dolls' Suffers in the Black Version," 15.

40. Nels Nelson, "The Old Original Abe Burrows," *Philadelphia Daily News*, 19 March 1976, reprinted in *Guys and Dolls* program (1976), 16.

41. Judy Klemesrud, "'Guys and Dolls' Comes Back Black," *New York Times*, 18 July 1976, 5.

42. Kissel, "Theater," 9.

43. Klemesrud, "'Guys and Dolls' Comes Back Black," 1.

44. Klemesrud, "'Guys and Dolls' Comes Back Black," 5.

45. Mel Gussow, "Casting by Race Can Be Touchy," *New York Times*, 1 August 1976, D5.

46. Gussow, "Casting by Race Can Be Touchy," D5.

47. Gussow, "Casting by Race Can Be Touchy," D5.

48. Klemesrud, "'Guys and Dolls' Comes Back Black," 5.

49. Beth Fillin Pombeiro, "'Guys and Dolls': Successful Move into Different Culture," *Philadelphia Inquirer*, 21 March 1976, 14, reprinted in *Guys and Dolls* program, 14.

50. Paul Delaney, "From Coast to Coast, the Black Audience Grows," *New York Times*, 10 October 1976, Section 2: 5, 37.

51. Judy Klemesrud, "The Lovable Doll in 'Guys and Dolls,'" *New York Times*, 22 August 1976, 5.

52. Eric L. Goldstein, *The Price of Whiteness: Jews, Race and American Identity* (Princeton: Princeton University Press, 2006), 135.

53. Jesse Green, "Hello, Dollys! (Funny, That One Doesn't Look Jewish)," review of *Hello, Dolly!* by Jerry Herman and Michael Stewart, Paper Mill Playhouse, *New York Times*, 11 June 2006, sec. 2, 9.

54. Wolf, *A Problem Like Maria*, 175.

55. Neil Genzlinger, "A Brogue Helps Keep the Spirits at Bay," review of *Hello, Dolly!* by Jerry Herman and Michael Stewart, Paper Mill Playhouse, *New York Times*, 11 June 2006, 18.

56. The issue of cross-ethnic casting as it relates to Irish roles and actors is ex-

amined by Joseph McBride in his essay "No Non-Irish Need Apply? Ethnic Casting Issues in Movies," which appeared in *Irish America Magazine*, 31 January 2001, 106.

57. Genzlinger, "A Brogue Helps Keep the Spirits at Bay," 18.

58. Judy Wilson, "Funny, Dolly, You Don't Look Irish," *New Jersey Jewish News* (2006) http://www.njjewishnews.com/njjn.com/062906/ltFunnyDollYouDont .html.

59. This distinction is analyzed in my article "False Accents: Embodied Dialects and the Characterization of Ethnicity and Nationality," *Theatre Topics* 14, no. 1 (March 2004): 353–72.

60. Robert Hodge and Gunther Kress, *Social Semiotics* (Ithaca: Cornell University Press, 1988), 30.

61. Harold Stern, "Year's Biggest Smash Hit," review of *Guys and Dolls*, by Frank Loesser, Jo Swerling, and Abe Burrows, 46th Street Theater, *American Jewish Review*, 28 December 1950.

62. Louis Sheaffer, "Runyon Characters Set to Music with 'Guys and Dolls,'" review of *Guys and Dolls*, by Frank Loesser, Jo Swerling, and Abe Burrows, 46th Street Theater, *Brooklyn Eagle*, 25 November 1950, 14.

63. Sheaffer, "Runyon Characters Set to Music with 'Guys and Dolls,'" 14.

64. Sheaffer, "Runyon Characters Set to Music with 'Guys and Dolls,'" 14.

65. Daniel R. Schwarz, *Broadway Boogie Woogie: Damon Runyon and the Making of New York City Culture* (New York: Palgrave Macmillan, 2003), 145.

66. Schwarz, *Broadway Boogie Woogie*, 141.

67. Andrea Most, *Making America: Jews and the Broadway Musical* (Cambridge: Harvard University Press, 2004), is a thorough study of the Broadway musical as a form developed by Jewish Americans, and Mark Steyn, *Broadway Babies Say Goodnight: Musicals Then and Now* (New York: Routledge, 1999), has a chapter unabashedly titled "The Jews."

68. Steyn, *Broadway Babies Say Goodnight*, 79.

69. Farther from New York, however, where ears were less finely attuned to the dialects of the city, the Jewish or Yiddish accents remained undistinguished from a more general New York accent or, more often, were lumped under the heading "American." When *Guys and Dolls* followed shows such as *Oklahoma!, Annie Get Your Gun*, and *South Pacific* onto West End stages in 1953, critics familiar with American speech noted that with very few exceptions English actors had trouble playing Americans because they couldn't successfully reproduce their speech patterns. This shortcoming was especially glaring in musicals where it was the custom to have Americans in the lead roles—often, as in the case of *Guys and Dolls*, with the principals reprising the roles they had created on Broadway and "local talent" in the supporting parts. Stephen Watts, "Accent Problem in West End," *New York Times*, 15 March 1953, X3. W. A. Darlington declared that nothing "more exotically American" had ever been seen in London ("Broadway Argot Echoes in London," *New York Times*, 29 May 1953, 17) and detected "an air of slight bewilderment and, indeed, unhappiness which underlay the applause and the laughter throughout the evening" with some of that bewilderment being attributed to the "Runyonese." W. A. Darlington, "London Report on 'Guys and

Dolls,'" *New York Times,* 7 June 1953, X3. Almost 30 years later, when the musical was performed at the National Theatre in 1982, the situation had improved sufficiently for Russell Davies to comment that "After hard work, the accents throughout are a most honourable near-miss." No longer generically American, Miss Adelaide's "pungent Brooklynese" was singled out for notice. Russell Davies, "The National Theatre Production Reviewed," in *The Guys and Dolls Book* (London: Methuen, 1982), 39.

70. Keith Garebian, *The Making of Guys and Dolls,* The Great Broadway Musicals (Oakville, Ontario: Mosaic Press, 2002), 127.

71. The conflicts, costs, and rewards of the Jewish American pursuit of acceptance as white Americans are examined by Eric L. Goldstein in *The Price of Whiteness.*

72. Neal Gabler, *An Empire of Their Own: How the Jews Invented Hollywood* (New York: Crown Publishers, 1988).

73. Andrea Most, *Making Americans: Jews and the Broadway Musical* (Cambridge: Harvard University Press, 2004), 1–2. With a few exceptions such as *Fiddler on the Roof,* the Jewish or ethnic conarrative would be read through a double process of decoding and encoding that was first identified in relation to African American consciousness. In *Acting Jewish: Negotiating Ethnicity on the American Stage and Screen* (Ann Arbor: University of Michigan Press, 2005), Henry Bial describes this process in a Jewish American context: "The Jewish reading of a performance created by a Jewish American artist is in fact based on selective perception, but the signs that the Jewish American audience perceives are based on a correspondingly selective encoding by the producers. And this coded communication is . . . based not on a preexisting moment of mutual agreement between sender and receiver but on a shared cultural experience that gives both parties the information necessary to understand the sign in a mutually specific way" (70).

74. Bial, *Acting Jewish,* 70.

75. Bial, *Acting Jewish,* 30.

76. Goldstein, *The Price of Whiteness,* 213.

77. William Finn and James Lapine, *The Marvin Songs: Three One-Act Musicals* (Garden City, NY: Fireside Theatre, 1990), 175.

78. Finn and Lapine, *The Marvin Songs,* 244.

79. Alex Witchel, "Find the Ginger! It's Anxiety Time for an Original," *New York Times,* 26 April 1992, Section 2: 8.

80. Finn and Lapine, *The Marvin Songs,* 192–93.

81. Frank Rich, "What Has AIDS Done to Land of 'Falsettos'?" review of *Falsettoland,* by William Finn and James Lapine, Playwrights Horizons, *New York Times,* 29 June 1990, C3.

82. Hap Erstein, "AIDS Plays into Plot of 'Falsetto,'" review of *Falsettoland,* by William Finn and James Lapine, Playwrights Horizons, *Washington Times,* 9 July 1990, E1.

83. As an actor, Muraoka himself has performed in the Broadway productions of *Shogun; The King and I; Pacific Overtures;* and *Miss Saigon,* in which he played the part of the Engineer. He is the cofounder with Christine Toy Johnson

and Bruce Johnson of Asian Americans on Broadway, a company created to give "voice and presence to Broadway's top Asian American actors, directors, and writers" by presenting concerts, workshops, and other theatrical events. See http://www.asianamericansonbroadway.com/home.html (accessed 7 July 2009).

84. Barbara Hoffman, "Amazin' Asian Stagin,'" review of *Falsettoland,* by William Finn and James Lapine, National Asian American Theatre Company, *New York Post,* 11 June 2007, 40.

85. Peter Marks, "It's Family That Matters, No Matter What Family," review of *Falsettoland,* by William Finn and James Lapine, National Asian American Theatre Company, *New York Times,* 17 July 1998, 2.

86. Victor Gluck, review of *Falsettoland,* by William Finn and James Lapine, National Asian American Theatre Company, *Back Stage,* 24–30 July 1998, 33.

87. Les Gutman, review of *Falsettoland,* by William Finn and James Lapine, National Asian American Theatre Company, *CurtainUp,* 17 July 1998. www.curtainup.com/falsetto.html.

88. Adam Feldman, "Falsettoland," review of *Falsettoland,* by William Finn and James Lapine, National Asian American Theatre Company, *Time Out (New York),* 28 June–4 July 2007, www.timeout.com/newyork/articles/off-broadway/8757/falsettoland.

89. National Asian American Theatre Company, 20 September 2008, http://www.naatco.org/index.html.

90. Sallie Han, "Funny, They Don't Look Jewish: An All-Asian Cast Revives a Musical about N.Y. Jews—Who Knew?" review of *Falsettoland,* by William Finn and James Lapine, National Asian American Theatre Company, *Daily News (New York),* 14 July 1998, 21.

91. Marks, "It's Family That Matters, No Matter What Family," E2.

92. Russell Bouthiller, "Broadway Snap-Shot: Fiddler on the Roof," 1 March 2004, http://www.broadwaybeat.com/russell/FiddlerOntheRoof.htm (accessed 29 April 2008).

93. Michael Sommers, "A Fairly Faithful 'Fiddler,'" *Star-Ledger (Newark, NJ),* 27 February 2004, 4.

94. As Zero Mostel acquired celebrity in the role of Tevye, he began ad libbing and throwing in Yiddish expressions to get more laughs from New York audiences (Peter Stone, Jerry Bock, Sheldon Harnick, and Joseph Stein, "Landmark Symposium: Fiddler on the Roof," *Dramatists Guild Quarterly* 20, no. 1 [Spring 1983]: 21); Richard Altman with Mervyn Kaufman, *The Making of a Musical: Fiddler on the Roof* (New York: Crown Publishers, 1971), 39.

95. Altman, *The Making of a Musical,* 34–35.

96. Altman, *The Making of a Musical,* 36.

97. In an essay on the negative reactions to the revival, Ruth Franklin referred to the musical's "Brigadoon-like vision of the prelapsarian shtetl" as she noted that what was really surprising was that "the pseudo-klezmer tunes and schmaltz-laden accents in 'Fiddler' were ever assumed to be the real thing" ("Shtetl Shtick," *New York Times,* 29 February 2004, sec. 2, 4).

98. Seth L. Wolitz, "The Americanization of Tevye or Boarding the Jewish 'Mayflower,'" *American Quarterly* 40, no. 4 (December 1988): 516.

99. Wolitz, "The Americanization of Tevye or Boarding the Jewish 'Mayflower,'" 530.

100. Alisa Solomon, "How 'Fiddler' Became Folklore," *Forward*, 1 September 2006, Arts and Culture, 12.

101. Peter Marks, "A 'Fiddler on the Roof' Hopelessly out of Tune," review of *Fiddler on the Roof*, by Jerry Bock, Sheldon Harnick, and Joseph Stein, *Washington Post*, 27 February 2004, C1.

102. Robert Feldberg, "Director's Challenge Is to Find a New Balance for 'Fiddler,'" *Record (Bergen County, NJ)*, 15 February 2004, Entertainment, E4.

103. Charles Isherwood, "Fiddled Fiddler," *Times* (London), 8 March 2004, Features, 18.

104. Jessica Hillman, "Goyim on the Roof: Embodying Authenticity in Leveaux's *Fiddler on the Roof*," *Studies in Musical Theatre* 1, no. 1 (2007): 28.

105. Marks, "A 'Fiddler on the Roof' Hopelessly out of Tune," C1.

106. Extensive discussions of the controversy arising from Leveaux's staging appear in Henry Bial's chapter on *Fiddler on the Roof* in *Acting Jewish* and Jessica Hillman's article "Goyim on the Roof."

107. Thane Rosenbaum, "A Legacy Cut Loose," *Los Angeles Times*, 15 February 2004, E1.

108. Michael Riedel, "Shtetl Shock," *New York Post*, 18 February 2004, 45.

109. Blake Eskin, *"Fiddler* Crabs," *Nextbook*, 5 March 2004, 6 August 2008, http://nextbook.org/cultural/print.html?id=12 (accessed 6 August 2008).

110. Riedel, "Shtetl Shock," 45.

111. Richard Zoglin, "Getting beyond Zero," *Time*, 1 March 2004, http://www.time.com/time/printout/0,8816,596135,00.html (accessed 9 December 2007).

112. Stone et al., "Landmark Symposium," 19.

113. Robert Altman, the original production's codirector, recalls his experiences working with Jerome Robbins during the casting and rehearsal process in chapters 5 and 6 of Altman, *The Making of a Musical*.

114. Zoglin, "Getting beyond Zero."

115. Mark Kennedy, "Alfred Molina Scales New Heights in 'Fiddler on the Roof,'" Associated Press, Entertainment News, New York, 25 February 2004.

116. Michael Kuchwara, "Harvey Fierstein to Play Tevye in Broadway's 'Fiddler on the Roof,'" Associated Press, Entertainment News, 11 November 2004.

117. Simon Houpt, "Hate to Kvetch, but Is This Casting Entirely Kosher?" *Globe and Mail* (Canada), 10 January 2005, R1.

118. Jesse McKinley, "Fierstein as Tevye: Sounds Crazy, No?" *New York Times*, 2 January 2005, sec. 2, 5.

119. Clive Barnes, "'Roof' Tops," review of *Fiddler on the Roof*, by Jerry Bock, Sheldon Harnick, and Joseph Stein, Minskoff Theater, *New York Post*, 21 January 2005, 40.

120. In fact, Fierstein found parallels between a parent who has a homosexual son and a father whose daughter is marrying outside her faith (Joe Dziemianowicz,"Playing It Straight: Harvey Fierstein Takes on 'Fiddler' Tevye?! Meshuga, It's Not," *Daily News (New York)*, 3 January 2005, Now, 31).

121. Alisa Solomon, "Tevye, Today and Beyond," *Forward.Com,* 8 September 2006, http://www.forward.com/articles/tevye-today-and-beyond (accessed 7 September 2008).

122. Ben Brantley, "A Cozy Little McShtetl," review of *Fiddler on the Roof,* by Jerry Bock, Sheldon Harnick, and Joseph Stein, Minskoff Theater, *New York Times,* 27 February 2004, E1, 4.

123. Marc Miller, "Fiddler on the Roof," review of *Fiddler on the Roof,* by Jerry Bock, Sheldon Harnick, and Joseph Stein, Minskoff Theater, *Theatermania,* 21 January 2005, http://www.theatermania.com/story/5558? (accessed 29 April 2008).

AFTERWORD

Epigraph: Walter Kerr, "The Negro Actor Asks Himself: 'Am I a Negro or Am I an Actor?'" *New York Times Magazine,* 15 October 1967, 35.

1. Kerr, "The Negro Actor Asks Himself," 35.

2. Kerr, "The Negro Actor Asks Himself," 156.

3. Kerr, "The Negro Actor Asks Himself," 156.

4. Although race and casting would be one of the dominant issues in the American theater industry for the last third of the twentieth century, it would not be until 1999 that casting became the subject of a play. Caleen Sinette Jenning's serio-comedy "Casting Othello" deals with the frictions and disagreements that arise in a small theater company as it rehearses for a production of *Othello.* The dialogue dramatized many of the exchanges taking place throughout the 1980s and 1990s as multiracial casting became established as a new tradition.

5. Daniel Banks, "A Director's Work: Re-Thinking Non-Traditional Casting," *Black Masks* 16, no. 2 (August/September 2003): 7.

6. Banks, "A Director's Work," 15.

Bibliography

"300 at 'Godot' Wait: Dispute Halts Play." *New York Times,* 23 January 1957, 24.

Acting Company. http://www.theactingcompany.org/ (accessed 5 June 2009).

"Actors and Non-Traditional Casting: What Do They Think?" *New Traditions—The NTCP Newsletter (New York)* 1, no. 3 (Fall 1992): 3–6.

Aguirre-Sacasa, Roberta. "Ron Canada: An Actor's Homecoming." *Asides: Quarterly Publication of the Shakespeare Theatre at the Folger,* 1997–98 Season, no. 2 (1997): 4–5.

Alba, Richard D. *Ethnic Identity: The Transformation of White America.* New Haven: Yale University Press, 1990.

Alexander, Catherine M. S., and Stanley Wells, eds. *Shakespeare and Race.* Cambridge: Cambridge University Press, 2000.

Alliance for Inclusion in the Arts. http://www.inclusioninthearts.org/. Accessed 27 May 2009.

Altman, Richard, with Mervyn Kaufman. *The Making of a Musical: Fiddler on the Roof.* New York: Crown Publishers, 1971.

Ambush, Benny Sato. "Inside the Tent—Casting: Colorblind or Conscious." *American Theatre* (September 1996): 20.

"Andre Braugher as Iago." *Asides: Quarterly Publication of the Shakespeare Theatre at the Folger* (Winter 1990): 5, 6.

Armstrong, Alan. "Multicultural Casting: Notes from the Oregon Shakespeare Festival." Paper presented at the Annual Meeting of the Shakespeare Association of America, Montreal, 2000.

Armstrong, David. "A Complex, Ambitious Brecht by Berkeley Rep." Review of *The Good Person of Szechuan,* by Bertolt Brecht, Berkeley Repertory Theatre. *San Francisco Examiner,* 21 May 1987, F3.

Asides: Quarterly Publication of the Shakespeare Theatre at the Folger (Winter 1990).

Aston, Elaine, and George Savona. *Theatre as Sign System.* London: Routledge, 1991.

Aston, Frank. "Genet Defined by Producer." *New York World-Telegram and Sun,* 8 June 1961, 14.

Atkinson, Brooks. "'Godot' Is Back: Beckett Play Staged with Negro Cast." Review of *Waiting for Godot,* by Samuel Beckett. *New York Times,* 22 January 1957, 25.

Auden, W. H. *Lectures on Shakespeare.* Edited by Arthur Kirsch. Princeton: Princeton University Press, 2000.

Backalenick, Irene. "Long Day's Journey into Night." Review of *Long Day's Journey into Night,* by Eugene O'Neill, National Asian American Theatre Company. *Back Stage,* 28 November 1997, 56.

Banks, Daniel. "A Director's Work: Re-Thinking Non-Traditional Casting." *Black Masks* 16, no. 2 (August–September 2003): 7–8, 15.

Banton, Michael. "Modelling Ethnic and National Relations." *Ethnic and Racial Studies* 17, no.1 (1994). Reprinted in *Ethnicity,* edited by John Hutchinson and Anthony D. Smith (Oxford: Oxford University Press, 1996), 98–104.

Barnes, Clive. "New 'Guys and Dolls' Comes Seven Again." Review of *Guys and Dolls,* by Frank Loesser, Jo Swerling, and Abe Burrows, Broadway Theater. *New York Times,* 22 July 1976, 26.

Barnes, Clive. "No Moor Needed." Review of *Othello,* by William Shakespeare, Acting Company. *New York Post,* 18 May 1995, 44.

Barnes, Clive. "'Roof' Tops." Review of *Fiddler on the Roof,* by Jerry Bock, Sheldon Harnick, and Joseph Stein, Minskoff Theater. *New York Post,* 21 January 2005, 40.

Barnes, Clive. "Stage: 'Hello, Dolly!' Back where She Belongs—on Broadway." Review of *Hello, Dolly!* by Jerry Herman and Michael Stewart, Minskoff Theater. *New York Times,* 7 November 1975, 24.

Barnes, Clive. "Theater: All-Negro 'Hello, Dolly!' Has Its Premiere." Review of *Hello, Dolly!* by Michael Stewart and Jerry Herman, St. James Theater. *New York Times,* 13 November 1967, 61.

Barthes, Roland. *S/Z.* New York: Hill and Wang, 1974.

Beadle, Carol. *The [In] Crowd* (Oregon Shakespeare Festival) 1, no. 1 (May 2002): 1.

Beaufort, John. "All-Black 'Guys and Dolls.'" Review of *Guys and Dolls,* by Frank Loesser, Jo Swerling, and Abe Burrows, Broadway Theater. *Christian Science Monitor,* 26 July 1976, 23.

Beaufort, John. "Goodbye, Dolly (Pearl)." *Christian Science Monitor,* 21 November 1975, 35.

Beckerman, Jim. "Dolly with a Thick Irish Brogue?" Review of *Hello, Dolly!* by Jerry Herman and Michael Stewart, Paper Mill Playhouse. *Record (Bergen County, NJ),* 14 June 2006, F9.

Beckett, Samuel. *Waiting for Godot: Tragicomedy in 2 Acts.* 1954. New York: Grove Weidenfeld, 1982.

Beebee, Thomas O. *The Ideology of Genre: A Comparative Study of Generic Instability.* University Park: Pennsylvania State University Press, 1994.

Bennett, Susan. *Theatre Audiences: A Theory of Production and Reception.* London: Routledge, 1990.

Berman, Mark. "An All-White Company." Letter to the editor. *Washington Post,* 28 November 1987, A26.

Bial, Henry. *Acting Jewish: Negotiating Ethnicity on the American Stage and Screen.* Ann Arbor: University of Michigan Press, 2005.

Blamires, Diana. "Women Are Still Waiting to Play Godot." *Independent* (London), 27 July 1998, News, 4.

Bland, Sheila Rose. "How I Would Direct *Othello.*" In *Othello: New Essays by Black Writers,* edited by Mythili Kaul, 29–41. Washington, DC: Howard University Press, 1997.

Blau, Eleanor. "Papp Starts a Shakespearean Repertory Troupe Made up Entirely of Black and Hispanic Actors." *New York Times,* 21 January 1979, 55.

Blau, Herbert. *Blooded Thought: Occasions of Theatre.* New York: Performing Arts Journal Publications, 1982.

Bolton, Whitney. "Pearl Bailey Brings down 'Dolly' House." Review of *Hello, Dolly!* by Michael Stewart and Jerry Herman, St. James Theater. *Morning Telegraph,* 14 November 1967.

Bolton, Whitney. Review of *The Winter's Tale,* by William Shakespeare. *New York Morning Telegraph,* 16 August 1963.

Bolwell, Edwin. "Dolly Levi Now Finds Her Match in Pearl Bailey." *New York Times,* 29 July 1967, 12.

Bond, Timothy. Interview. *The [In] Crowd* (Oregon Shakespeare Festival) 1, no. 1 (May 2002): 1–2.

Bordman, Gerald. *American Musical Theatre.* New York: Oxford University Press, 1978.

Bourne, St. Clair, director. *Paul Robeson: Here I Stand.* American Masters. Television documentary. Written by Lou Potter. Produced by Chiz Schultz. Thirteen/WNET and Menair Media International, WinStar Home Entertainment, 1999.

Bouthiller, Russell. "Broadway Snap-Shot: Fiddler on the Roof." 1 March 2004. http://www.broadwaybeat.com/russell/FiddlerOntheRoof.htm. Accessed 29 April 2008.

Bradley, A. C. *Shakespearean Tragedy: Lectures on Hamlet, Othello, King Lear, and Macbeth.* Foreword by John Bayley. 1904. Reprint, London: Penguin Books, Macmillan, 1991.

Brantley, Ben. "A Cozy Little McShtetl." Review of *Fiddler on the Roof,* Minskoff Theater. *New York Times,* 27 February 2004, E1, 4.

Brantley, Ben. "Yet Another Life for Maggie the Cat." *New York Times,* 7 March 2008, E1.

Breslauer, Jan. "Whom Do You Serve First?" *Los Angeles Times,* 16 April 1995, 3.

Bristol, Michael D. "Race and the Comedy of Abjection in Othello." In *Shakespeare in Performance,* edited by Robert Shaughnessy, 142–70. New York: St. Martin's Press, 2000.

"Broadway Argot Echoes in London." *New York Times,* 29 May 1953, 17.

Brown, Joe. "Nontraditional Casting: Not Just a Character Issue." *Washington Post,* 23 November 1987, B1, 4.

Brown, Joe. "The Truth about 'Falsettos': William Finn and His Coming-Out Tragicomedy." *Washington Post,* 10 May 1992, G1.

Brustein, Robert. "Subsidized Separatism." *American Theatre,* October 1996, 26–27, 100–104, 106–7

Bunce, Alan N. "Pearl Bailey Scores in New 'Hello, Dolly!'" Review of *Hello, Dolly!* by Michael Stewart and Jerry Herman, St. James Theater. *Christian Science Monitor,* 27 November 1967, 16.

Butler, Judith. "Performative Acts and Gender Constitution: An Essay in Phenomenology and Feminist Theory." *Theatre Journal* 40 (1988): 519–31. Reprinted in *Performing Feminisms: Feminist Critical Theory and Theatre,* edited by Sue-Ellen Case, 270–82 (Baltimore: Johns Hopkins University Press, 1990).

Butler, Lance St. John. "Beckett's Stage of Deconstruction." In *Twentieth-Century European Drama,* edited by Brian Docherty, 63–77. New York: St. Martin's Press, 1994.

Canby, Vincent. "Pop 'Hamlet' Presented—Will Tour Parks." *New York Times,* 4 July 1968, 15.

Carlson, Marvin. *Performance: A Critical Introduction.* London: Routledge, 1996.

Carter, Imogen. "In Godot We Trust: New Orleans 2007." *Observer* (England), 8 March 2009, Review Features, 9.

Center for U.S.-China Exchange. "Purpose and Organization." http://www.columbia.edu/cu/china.

Chapman, John. "Pearl Bailey, Cab Calloway & Co. Make a Brand-New Hit of 'Dolly!'" Review of *Hello, Dolly!* by Michael Stewart and Jerry Herman, St. James Theater. *Daily News (New York),* 13 November 1967, 56.

Chaudhuri, Una. *Staging Place: The Geography of Modern Drama.* Ann Arbor: University of Michigan Press, 1995.

"China Bars ABC from Play Rehearsal." *Japan Times,* 2 May 1983, 4.

Ching, Frank. "Asian-American Actors Fight for Jobs and Image." *New York Times,* 3 June 1973, 65.

Christon, Lawrence. "Black Theater—Its Decline since 1960." *Los Angeles Times,* 31 January 1988, Home, 41.

"A Cleveland Stage for 'Othello.'" *Plain Dealer (Cleveland),* 20 May 1993, B4.

Clum, John. *Something for the Boys: Musical Theatre and Gay Culture.* New York: Palgrave Macmillan, 1999.

Collins, Glenn. "Men of 'Falsettoland' as Their Old Selves but with New Fears." *New York Times,* 23 July 1990, C11.

Collins-Hughes, Laura. "Idealism in Action: The City of New Haven Takes Center Stage in Long Wharf Theatre's Grand Experiment." *New Haven Register,* 7 May 2000, F1–2, 7.

Cooke, Richard P. "Pearl as Dolly." Review of *Hello, Dolly!* by Michael Stewart and Jerry Herman, St. James Theater. *Wall Street Journal,* 14 November 1967.

Cooper, John S. "Rolling the Dice on Old Broadway." Review of *Guys and Dolls,* by Frank Loesser, Jo Swerling, and Abe Burrows, Broadway Theater. *Wall Street Journal,* 27 July 1976.

Counsell, Colin. *Signs of Performance: An Introduction to Twentieth-Century Theatre.* London: Routledge, 1996.

Cowan, Ron. "Production Has Fresh Take on 'The Tempest.'" Review of *The Tem-*

pest, by William Shakespeare, Oregon Shakespeare Festival. *Statesman Journal (Salem, OR),* 4 March 2001.

Craven, Jim. "Integration of Shakespearean Casts Made a Belated Entrance." *Mail Tribune (Medford, OR),* 21 April 2002, 1B.

Crouch, Stanley. "Beyond the Wilson-Brustein Debate: Who's Zooming Who?" *Theater* 27, no. 2–3 (1997): 20–23.

Curtis, Susan. *The First Black Actors on the Great White Way.* Columbia: University of Missouri Press, 1998.

da Silva, Beatrice. "Something to Sneeze At." Review of *Guys and Dolls,* by Frank Loesser, Jo Swerling, and Abe Burrows, Broadway Theater. *Villager (New York),* 12 August 1976, 10.

Daileader, Celia R. "Casting Black Actors: Beyond Othellophilia." In *Shakespeare and Race,* edited by Stanley Wells and Catherine Alexander, 177–202. Cambridge: Cambridge University Press, 2000.

Darlington, W. A. "London Report on 'Guys and Dolls.'" *New York Times,* 7 June 1953, sec. X, 1, 3.

Davidson, Gordon. "Artistic Freedom." *Los Angeles Times,* 1 October 1990, Counterpunch Letters, 4.

Davies, Russell. "The National Theatre Production Reviewed." In *The Guys and Dolls Book,* 39–40. London: Methuen, 1982.

Davis, Clinton Turner. "Beyond the Wilson-Brustein Debate: To Whom It May Concern." *Theater* 27, no. 2–3 (1997): 30–34.

Davis, Clinton Turner, and Harry Newman, eds. *Beyond Tradition: Transcripts of the First Symposium on Non-Traditional Casting.* New York: Non-Traditional Casting Project, 1988.

De Marinis, Marco. *The Semiotics of Performance.* 1982. Translated by Aine O'Healy. Bloomington: Indiana University Press, 1993.

De Marinis, Marco. "Theatrical Comprehension: A Socio-Semiotic Approach." *Theatre* XV, no. 1 (Winter 1985): 12–17.

Delaney, Paul. "From Coast to Coast, the Black Audience Grows." *New York Times,* 10 October 1976, Section 2: 5, 37.

Drake, Sylvie. "Stage Watch: Color It Black, Sam." *Los Angeles Times,* 29 August 1985, 2.

Dziemianowicz, Joe. "Playing It Straight: Harvey Fierstein Takes on 'Fiddler' Tevye?! Meshuga, It's Not." *Daily News (New York),* 3 January 2005, Now, 31.

"East Meets West." *InTheater,* 31 October 1997, 6.

Eden, Ami. "Fiddling with Tradition: Does Musical Misstep?" *Forward,* 12 March 2004, 1.

Eisenberg, Alan. "Artistic Good Sense." In *Beyond Tradition,* edited by Clinton Turner Davis and Newman Harry, 3–4. New York: Non-Traditional Casting Project, 1988.

Elam, Keir. *The Semiotics of Theatre and Drama.* 2nd ed. London: Routledge, 2002. First ed. published 1980 by Methuen.

Emerson, Ralph Waldo. *The Conduct of Life.* Boston: Houghton Mifflin, 1898.

Epstein, Helen. *Joe Papp: An American Life.* Boston: Little, Brown, 1994.

Erstein, Hap. "AIDS Plays into Plot of 'Falsetto.'" Review of *Falsettoland,* by

William Finn and James Lapine, Playwrights Horizons. *Washington Times,* 9 July 1990, E1.

Eskin, Blake. "*Fiddler* Crabs." *Nextbook* 5 March 2004. http://nextbook.org/cultural/print.html?id=12 (accessed 6 August 2008).

Evans, Everett. "'Falsettoland' Strikes Emotional High Note." Review of *Falsettoland,* by William Finn and James Lapine, Main Street Theater. *Houston Chronicle,* 7 June 1997, 4.

Evett, Marianne. "Casting Change Delays Opening of 'Othello.'" *Plain Dealer (Cleveland),* 1 April 1993, E16.

Evett, Marianne. "Mistrusting Happiness until We Destroy It." Review of *Othello,* by William Shakespeare, Ohio Theater, Cleveland. *Plain Dealer (Cleveland),* 17 May 1993, C3.

Evett, Marianne. "Othello: The Role 'Challenges Everything One Has.'" *Plain Dealer (Cleveland),* 9 May 1993, Final/West, H1.

Faust, Richard, and Charles Kadushin. *Shakespeare in the Neighborhood: Audience Reactions to "A Midsummer Night's Dream" as Produced by Joseph Papp for the Delacorte Mobile Theater.* New York: Bureau of Applied Research of Columbia University and the Twentieth Century Fund, 1965.

Feingold, Michael. "Miss Bailey Builds a Vehicle." Review of *Hello, Dolly!* by Jerry Herman and Michael Stewart, Minskoff Theater. *Village Voice (New York),* 24 November 1975, 127.

Feingold, Michael. "We Can Still Believe the Fable." Review of *Guys and Dolls,* by Frank Loesser, Jo Swerling, and Abe Burrows, Broadway Theater. *Village Voice (New York),* 2 August 1976, 90.

Feldberg, Robert. "Director's Challenge Is to Find a New Balance for 'Fiddler.'" *Record (Bergen County, NJ),* 15 February 2004, Entertainment, E4.

Feldman, Adam. "Falsettoland." Review of *Falsettoland,* by William Finn and James Lapine, National Asian American Theatre Company. *Time Out (New York),* 28 June–4 July 2007. www.timeout.com/newyork/articles/off-broadway/8757/falsettoland.

Fichandler, Zelda. "Casting: Beyond Tradition to a Different Truth; A Proposal for Staging a Revolution." *Washington Post,* 22 November 1987, F1.

Fichandler, Zelda. "Casting for a Different Truth." *American Theatre* 5, no. 2 (May 1988): 18–23.

Finn, William, and James Lapine. *The Marvin Songs: Three One-Act Musicals.* Garden City, NY: Fireside Theatre, 1990.

Fischer-Lichte, Erika. *The Semiotics of Theater.* Translated by Jeremy Gaines and Doris L. Jones. Bloomington: Indiana University Press, 1992.

Foreman, Ellen. Review of *Macbeth,* by William Shakespeare, La Mama Experimental Theatre. *Black American* (1977).

Fornes, Maria Irene, panelist. "Session: Realizing the Play or Playing with Reality." In *Beyond Tradition: Transcripts of the First Symposium on Non-Traditional Casting,* edited by Clinton Turner Davis and Harry Newman, 37–61. New York: Non-Traditional Casting Project, 1988.

Frankenberg, Ruth, ed. *Displacing Whiteness: Essays in Social and Cultural Criticism.* Durham, NC: Duke University Press, 1997.

Franklin, Ruth. "Shtetl Shtick." *New York Times,* 29 February 2004, sec. 2, 4.

Freedman, Samuel G. "Actors Equity Protests Beckett Cast Criticism." *New York Times,* 9 January 1985, C17.

Freedman, Samuel G. "Debate Persists on Minority Casting." *New York Times,* 22 August 1984, C15.

Freedman, Samuel G. "Who's to Say Whether a Playwright Is Wronged?" *New York Times,* 13 December 1984, sec. 4, 6.

Friedman, Jonathan C. *Rainbow Jews: Jewish and Gay Identity in the Performing Arts.* Lanham MD: Lexington Books, 2007.

Frye, Andrea. Interview. *Update* (Oregon Shakespeare Festival) 1, no. 3 (2003): 1–2.

Fusco, Coco. *English Is Broken Here: Notes on Cultural Fusion in the Americas.* New York: New Press, 1995.

Gabler, Neal. *An Empire of Their Own: How the Jews Invented Hollywood.* New York: Crown Publishers, 1988.

Gans, Andrew. "Diva Talk: Chatting with *Dolly's* Tovah Feldshuh." *Playbill,* 9 June 2006. http://www.playbill.com/celebritybuzz/article/print/100180.html.

Gardner, Lyn. "Jude Kelly." *Asides: Quarterly Publication of the Shakespeare Theatre at the Folger,* 1997–98 Season, no. 2 (1997): 4–5.

Garebian, Keith. *The Making of Guys and Dolls.* The Great Broadway Musicals. Oakville, Ontario: Mosaic Press, 2002.

Garner, Stanton B., Jr. *Bodied Spaces: Phenomenology and Performance in Contemporary Drama.* Ithaca: Cornell University Press, 1994.

Gelb, Arthur. "Integrated Cast Will Act in South." *New York Times,* 11 April 1963, 10.

Genet, Jean. *The Blacks: A Clown Show* (Les Nègres: clownerie). Translated by Bernard Frechtman. New York: Grove Press, 1960.

Genet, Jean. *The Screens* (Les Paravents). Translated by Bernard Frechtman. New York: Grove Press, 1962.

Genzlinger, Neil. "A Brogue Helps Keep the Spirits at Bay." Review of *Hello, Dolly!* by Jerry Herman and Michael Stewart, Paper Mill Playhouse. *New York Times,* 11 June 2006, sec. 14NJ, 18.

Gilbert, Helen, and Joanne Tompkins. *Post-colonial Drama: Theory, Practice, Politics.* London: Routledge, 1996.

Gill, Brendan. "Noo Yawk." Review of *Guys and Dolls,* by Frank Loesser, Jo Swerling, and Abe Burrows, Broadway Theater. *New Yorker,* 2 August 1976, 53.

Glass Menagerie. Program notes. Arena Stage Company, 1989.

Gluck, Victor. "'Falsettoland.'" Review of *Falsettoland,* by William Finn and James Lapine, National Asian American Theatre Company. *Back Stage,* 24–30 July 1998, 33.

Gold, Sylviane. "The Beckett Brouhaha." *Wall Street Journal,* 28 December 1984, 1.

Goldstein, Eric L. *The Price of Whiteness: Jews, Race and American Identity.* Princeton: Princton University Press, 2006.

Goldstein, Malcolm. "*Our Town* and Everytown." Program notes, 15–20. Arena Stage Company production of *Our Town* by Thornton Wilder, 1990.

Gottfried, Martin. "Bailey's 'Hello Dolly!' a Lusterless Pearl." Review of *Hello,*

Dolly! by Jerry Herman and Michael Stewart, Minskoff Theater. *New York Post,* 7 November 1975, 34.

Gottfried, Martin. "'Guys and Dolls' Suffers in the Black Version." Review of *Guys and Dolls,* by Frank Loesser, Jo Swerling, and Abe Burrows, Broadway Theater. *New York Post,* 22 July 1976, 15.

Grant, Mark N. *The Rise and Fall of the Broadway Musical.* Boston: Northeastern University Press, 2004.

Green, Jesse. "Hello, Dollys! (Funny, That One Doesn't Look Jewish)." Review of *Hello, Dolly!* by Jerry Herman and Michael Stewart, Paper Mill Playhouse. *New York Times,* 11 June 2006, sec. 2, 9–10.

Greene, Ray. "Patrick Stewart." *Asides: Quarterly Publication of the Shakespeare Theatre at the Folger,* 1997–98 Season, no. 2 (1997): 1, 5.

Gurney, A. R. "The Dining Room." In *Collected Plays 1974–1983,* 223–84. Lyme NH: Smith and Kraus, 1997.

Gurney, A. R. "Love Letters." In *Collected Plays 1984–1991,* 221–60. Lyme, NH: Smith and Kraus, 2000.

Gussow, Mel. "Art and Politics in Bonafede's 'Advice.'" *New York Times,* 27 April 1986, sec. 1, pt. 2. 63.

Gussow, Mel. "Broadway Enjoying Black Talent Boom." *New York Times,* 15 October 1976.

Gussow, Mel. "Casting by Race Can Be Touchy." *New York Times,* 1 August 1976, D5.

Gussow, Mel. "Critic's Notebook: Didi and Gogo in Middle Age, Unchanging but Fresh." *New York Times,* 3 December 1998, E2.

Gussow, Mel. "South Africans in 'Godot' at Long Wharf." Review of *Waiting for Godot,* by Samuel Beckett, Long Wharf Theater. *New York Times,* 5 December 1980, C4.

Gussow, Mel. "Will Godot Ever Show? Beckett Waits in Silence." *New York Times,* 10 April 1986, C18.

Gutman, Les. Review of *Falsettoland,* by William Finn and James Lapine, National Asian American Theatre Company. *CurtainUp,* www.curtainup.com/falsetto.html, 17 July 1998.

The Guys and Dolls Book. London: Methuen, 1982.

Hall, Joan Lord. *Othello: A Guide to the Play.* Westport: Greenwood Press, 1999.

Hall, Stuart. "Cultural Identity and Cinematic Representation." In *Black British Cultural Studies,* edited by Houston A. Baker Jr., Manthia Diawara, and Ruth A. Lindeborg, 210–22. Chicago: University of Chicago Press, 1996.

Hall, Stuart. "Minimal Selves." In *Black British Cultural Studies,* edited by Houston A. Baker Jr., Manthia Diawara, and Ruth A. Lindeborg, 114–19. Chicago: University of Chicago Press, 1996.

Hamilton, Erik. "Group Acts Irate at Official Rejection of Black 'Romeo.'" *Los Angeles Times,* 27 October 1990, 7, Orange County edition.

Hampton, Wilborn. "Two Very Different Women in Distress." *New York Times,* 17 May 1995, C14.

Han, Sallie. "Funny, They Don't Look Jewish: An All-Asian Cast Revives a Musical about N.Y. Jews—Who Knew?" Review of *Falsettoland,* by William and James

Lapine Finn, National Asian American Theatre Company. *Daily News (New York)*, 14 July 1998, 30.

Haring-Smith, Tori. "A Director's Response." *Theatre Topics* 3, no. 1 (March 1993): 89–93.

Harris, Jessica B. "'Guys and Dolls' Most Exciting on B'way." Review of *Guys and Dolls*, by Frank Loesser, Jo Swerling, and Abe Burrows, Broadway Theater. *N.Y. Amsterdam News*, 31 July 1976, D14.

Harrison, Eric E. "Strong Cast Makes 'Falsettos' March." Review of *Falsettos*, by William Finn and James Lapine. *Arkansas Democrat-Gazette*, 27 May 1995, 7B.

Henderson, Liza. "Harold Scott on Color, Cast, Shakespeare, America." *Asides: Quarterly Publication of the Shakespeare Theatre at the Folger* (Winter 1990): 1, 7.

Hendricks. "They Said I Was Too Short for the Role." Cartoon. *Village Voice (New York)*, 1 February 1962, 9.

Henry, William A., III. "This Carousel Doesn't Go Anywhere." Review of *Carousel*, by Richard Rodgers and Oscar Hammerstein II, Vivian Beaumont Theater. *Time*, 4 April 1994, 85.

Hewes, Henry. Review of *Guys and Dolls*, by Frank Loesser, Jo Swerling, and Abe Burrows, Broadway Theater. *Saturday Review*, 16 October 1976, 50.

Hill, Errol. *Shakespeare in Sable: A History of Black Shakespearean Actors*. Amherst: University of Massachusetts Press, 1984.

Hill, Errol G., and James V. Hatch. *A History of African American Theatre*. Cambridge: Cambridge University Press, 2003.

Hill, Mike, ed. *Whiteness: A Critical Reader*. New York: New York University Press, 1997.

Hillman, Jessica. "Goyim on the Roof: Embodying Authenticity in Leveaux's *Fiddler on the Roof*." *Studies in Musical Theatre* 1, no. 1 (2007): 25–39.

Hipp, Edward Sothern. "Pearl Bailey New 'Dolly.'" Review of *Hello, Dolly!* by Michael Stewart and Jerry Herman, St. James Theater. *Newark Evening News*, 13 November 1967, 26.

Hirsch, E. D. *Validity in Interpretation*. New Haven: Yale University Press, 1967.

Hobe. "Guys and Dolls." Review of *Guys and Dolls*, by Frank Loesser, Jo Swerling, and Abe Burrows, Broadway Theater. *Variety*, 28 July 1976, 62.

Hobe. "Hello, Dolly!" Review of *Hello, Dolly!* by Jerry Herman and Michael Stewart, Minskoff Theater. *Variety*, 12 November 1975, 62.

Hodge, Robert, and Gunther Kress. *Social Semiotics*. Ithaca, NY: Cornell University Press, 1988.

Hodgins, Paul. "Mark Rucker Is Determined to Make 'Our Town' a Place You'll Recognize." *Orange County Register*, 15 February 1998, sec. F, 8.

Hodgins, Paul. "'Our Town' Like Home, Sweet Home." Review of *Our Town*, by Thornton Wilder, La Jolla Playhouse. *Orange County Register*, 22 May 2001.

Hoffman, Barbara. "Amazin' Asian Stagin.'" Review of *Falsettoland*, by William Finn and James Lapine, National Asian American Theatre Company. *New York Post*, 11 June 2007, 40.

Holly, Ellen. "Why the Furor over 'Miss Saigon' Won't Fade." *New York Times*, 26 August 1990, H7.

Hornby, Richard. "Interracial Casting at the Public and Other Theatres." *Hudson Review* 42, no. 3 (Autumn 1989): 459–66.

Horwitz, Jane. "At Studio, 'Godot's' Woes." *Washington Post,* 10 November 1998, B1.

Horwitz, Simi. "Ever since 'Saigon': A Non-Traditional Casting Update." *Theater-Week,* 13–19 February 1995, 19–24.

Houpt, Simon. "Hate to Kvetch, but Is This Casting Entirely Kosher?" *Globe and Mail* (Canada), 10 January 2005, R1.

Houseman, John. "On Non-Traditional Casting." In *Beyond Tradition: Transcripts of the First Symposium on Non-Traditional Casting,* edited by Clinton Turner Davis and Harry Newman, 9–16. New York: NTCP, 1986.

Houston, Velina Hasu. "The Fallout over 'Miss Saigon'—It's Time to Overcome the Legacy of Racism in Theater." *Los Angeles Times,* 13 August 1990, Counterpunch, 3.

Huerta, Jorge. *Chicano Drama: Performance, Society, and Myth.* Cambridge: Cambridge University Press, 2000.

Huerta, Jorge. *Chicano Theater: Themes and Forms.* Ypsilanti: Bilingual Press, 1982.

Hulbert, Dan. "D.C. Dispenses Raves for 2 Atlanta Actors: Jones, Griffin Team for 'Godot.'" *Atlanta Journal and Constitution,* 15 September 1998, Features, 9F.

Hutchinson, John, and Anthony D. Smith, eds. *Ethnicity.* Oxford Readers. Oxford: Oxford University Press, 1996.

Hwang, David Henry (playwright), and Francis Jue (actor). Interview by Jeff Lunden in which Hwang's new play, *Yellow Face,* is discussed. *Morning Edition,* National Public Radio, 10 December 2007.

Hyman, Earle. "*Othello:* Or Ego in Love, Sex and War." In *Othello: New Essays by Black Writers,* edited by Mythili Kaul, 23–28. Washington, DC: Howard University Press, 1997.

"Inside the Tent—Casting: Colorblind or Conscious." *American Theatre,* September 1996, 20.

Interview with Sharon Jenson, 20 October 2000, New York, NY.

Interview with Timothy Bond, 6 May 2003, Ashland, OR.

Isherwood, Charles. "Fiddled Fiddler." *Times* (London), 8 March 2004, Features, 18.

Isherwood, Charles. "She's Back with a Brogue from Way Back When." Review of *Hello, Dolly!* by Jerry Herman and Michael Stewart, Paper Mill Playhouse. *New York Times,* 13 June 2006, E1.

Jackson, C. Bernard. "Iago." In *The National Black Drama Anthology,* edited by Woodie King Jr. New York: Applause, 1995.

Jacobson, Matthew Frye. *Whiteness of a Different Color: European Immigrants and the Alchemy of Race.* Cambridge: Harvard University Press, 1998.

Jefferson, Margo. Interview. "Beyond the Wilson-Brustein Debate: War of the Worlds." *Theater* 27, no. 2–3 (1997): 13–20.

Jennings, Caleen Sinnette. *Playing Juliet/Casting Othello.* Woodstock, IL: Dramatic Publishing, 1999.

Jensen, Sharon. *Non-Traditional Casting Project.* . http://www.arts.gov/resources/Accessibility/NTCP.html. Accessed 27 May 2009.

Johnson-Haddad, Miranda. "'Haply, for I Am Black.'" Program notes to *Othello,* Shakespeare Theatre, 1997.

Johnson-Haddad, Miranda. "Patrick Stewart on Playing Othello." *Shakespeare Bulletin* (Spring 1998): 11–12.

Johnson-Haddad, Miranda. "The Shakespeare Theatre at the Folger, 1990–91." *Shakespeare Quarterly* 42, no. 4 (1991): 472–84.

Johnson-Haddad, Miranda. "The Shakespeare Theatre Othello." *Shakespeare Bulletin* (Spring 1998): 9–11.

Kanellòs, Nicolas, ed. *Hispanic Theatre in the United States.* Houston: Arte Publico Press, 1984.

Kanellòs, Nicolas. *A History of Hispanic Theatre in the United States: Origins to 1940.* Austin: University of Texas Press, 1990.

Kanellòs, Nicolas, ed. *Mexican American Theatre: Then and Now.* Houston: Arte Publico Press, 1989.

Katigbak, Mia. "National Asian American Theatre Company Positioning Statement," 1996.

Kaufman, Glenn. "A Thoroughly Retro Millie?" Review of *Thoroughly Modern Millie,* by Richard Scanlan and Dick Morris. *Herald-Times,* 10 February 2006, C2.

Kaul, Mythili, ed. *Othello: New Essays by Black Writers.* Washington, DC: Howard University Press, 1996.

Kennedy, Mark. "Alfred Molina Scales New Heights in 'Fiddler on the Roof.'" Associated Press. Entertainment News, New York, 25 February 2004.

Kenner, Hugh. *Samuel Beckett: A Critical Study.* 1961. New ed. Berkeley: University of California Press, 1968.

Kerr, Walter. "Kerr: Life with 'Dolly' Is Delovely." Review of *Hello, Dolly!* by Michael Stewart and Jerry Herman, St. James Theater. *New York Times,* 26 November 1967, D3.

Kerr, Walter. "The Negro Actor Asks Himself: 'Am I a Negro or Am I an Actor?'" *New York Times Magazine,* 15 October 1967, 35, 142ff.

Kershaw, Baz. *The Radical in Performance: Between Brecht and Baudrillard.* London: Routledge, 1999.

King, Robert L. "The Seeing Place." *North American Review* 283, no. 1 (January–February 1998): 36–39.

Kirle, Bruce. *Unfinished Business: Broadway Musicals as Works-in-Process.* Carbondale: Southern Illinois University Press, 2005.

Kissel, Howard. "'Hello, Dolly.'" Review of *Hello, Dolly!* by Jerry Herman and Michael Stewart, Minskoff Theater. *Women's Wear Daily,* 7 November 1975, 18.

Kissel, Howard. "Most Unhappy 'Othello.'" Review of *Othello,* by William Shakespeare. Tribeca Performing Arts Center. *Daily News (New York),* 17 May 1995, 35.

Kissel, Howard. "Theater." Review of *Guys and Dolls,* by Frank Loesser, Jo Swerling, and Abe Burrows, Broadway Theater. *Women's Wear Daily,* 23 July 1976, 9.

Klein, Alvin. "Striking Performances Light up 'Othello.'" *New York Times,* 1 July 1990, sec. 12NJ, 15.

Klein, Alvin. "Taking Inspiration from Brecht." Review of *The Good Person of New Haven,* by Bertolt Brecht (adaptation), Long Wharf Theatre/Cornerstone Theater Company. *New York Times,* 28 May 2000, CT6, Connecticut edition.

Klemesrud, Judy. "'Guys and Dolls' Comes Back Black." *New York Times,* 18 July 1976, 1, 5.

Klemesrud, Judy. "The Lovable Doll in 'Guys and Dolls.'" *New York Times,* 22 August 1976, 5, 30.

Knapp, Raymond. *The American Musical and the Formation of National Identity.* Princeton: Princeton University Press, 2005.

Knowles, Mark. *Tap Roots: The Early History of Tap Dancing.* Jefferson, NC: McFarland, 2002.

Kobialka, Michal, ed. *Of Borders and Thresholds: Theatre History, Practice, and Theory.* Minneapolis: University of Minnesota Press, 1999.

Kuchwara, Michael. "'Cat' Finds a New Life on Stage with Its All-Black Cast." Associated Press, Entertainment News, 6 March 2008.

Kuchwara, Michael. "Harvey Fierstein to Play Tevye in Broadway's 'Fiddler on the Roof.'" Associated Press, Entertainment News, 11 November 2004.

Kurahashi, Yuko. *Asian American Culture on Stage: The History of the East West Players.* New York: Garland, 1999.

Lantz, Ragni. "Hello, Dolly!" *Ebony,* January 1968, 83–89.

Laskin, Stacey. "Enthralling Acting, Long Legs Make 'Millie' a Success." Review of *Thoroughly Modern Millie,* by Richard Scanlan and Dick Morris. *Indiana Daily Student (Bloomington),* 10 February 2006, 12.

Laskin, Stacey. "'Millie' Comes to Auditorium." *Indiana Daily Student (Bloomington),* 8 February 2006, 13.

Launer, Pat. "Thoroughly Modern Millie." Review of *Thoroughly Modern Millie,* by Richard Morris and Dick Scanlan, La Jolla Playhouse. KPBS-FM, 3 November, 2000. http://www.kpbs.org/events/plays/plays_thoroughlymodernmillie .htm.

Lee, Esther Kim. *A History of Asian American Theatre.* Cambridge: Cambridge University Press, 2006.

Lee, Josephine. "Between Immigration and Hyphenation: The Problems of Theorizing Asian American Theater." *Journal of Dramatic Theory and Criticism* 13, no. 1 (Fall 1998): 45–69.

Lee, Josephine. "Bodies, Revolution and Magic: Cultural Nationalism and Racial Fetishism." In *Modern Drama: Defining the Field,* edited by Ric Knowles, Joanne Tompkins, and W. B. Worthen, 144–61. Toronto: University of Toronto Press, 2003.

Lee, Josephine. "Racial Actors, Liberal Myths." *XCP: Cross-Cultural Poetics* 13 (2003): 88–110.

Lei, Daphne. "The Production and Consumption of Chinese Theatre in Nineteenth-Century California." *Theatre Research International* 28, no. 3 (October 2003): 289–302.

Leogrande, Ernest. "'Guys and Dolls' in the Black." Review of *Guys and Dolls,* by Frank Loesser, Jo Swerling, and Abe Burrows, Broadway Theater. *Daily News (New York),* 22 July 1976, 67.

Levine-Rasky, Cynthia, ed. *Working through Whiteness: International Perspectives.* Albany: State University of New York Press, 2002.

Liu, Hou-sheng. "Death of a Salesman—a Profound and Bitter Play." Review of Beijing production of *Death of a Salesman,* by Arthur Miller (review translated by Pao-yung Pao). *Ren Ming Ri Bao (People's Daily) (Beijing),* 28 June 1983.

Loomba, Ania. "Foreword." In *Colorblind Shakespeare: New Perspectives on Race and Performance,* edited by Ayanna Thompson, xiii–vii. New York: Routledge, 2006.

Lott, Eric. *Love and Theft: Blackface Minstrelsy and the American Working Class.* Oxford: Oxford University Press, 1993.

Lower, Charles B. "Othello as Black on Southern Stages, Then and Now." In *Shakespeare in the South,* edited by Philip C. Kolin, 199–228. Jackson: University Press of Mississippi, 1983.

Loynd, Ray. "Stage Beat: 'The Lady from the Sea.'" Review of *Lady from the Sea,* by Henrik Ibsen, Fountain Theatre. *Los Angeles Times,* 27 January 1989, 8.

Magwili, Dom. "The Fallout over 'Miss Saigon'—Makibaka! Asian-American Artists Should Struggle—and Not Be Afraid." *Los Angeles Times,* 13 August 1990, Counterpunch, 3.

Mahoney, John C. "East West Neutral 'Godspell.'" Review of *Godspell,* by Stephen Schwartz and John-Michael Tebelak, East West Players. *Los Angeles Times,* 22 May 1981, Sec. 4, 4.

Marchetti, Gina. *Romance and the "Yellow Peril."* Berkeley: University of California Press, 1993.

Marks, Peter. "It's Family That Matters, No Matter What Family." Review of *Falsettoland,* by William Finn and James Lapine, National Asian American Theatre Company. *New York Times,* 17 July 1998, sec. E, 1, 2.

Marks, Peter. "A 'Fiddler on the Roof' Hopelessly out of Tune." Review of *Fiddler on the Roof,* by Jerry Bock, Sheldon Harnick, and Joseph Stein. *Washington Post,* 27 February 2004, C1.

Marks, Peter. "The Green-Eyed Monster Fells Men of Every Color." *New York Times,* 17 November 1997, E5, Washington, DC, edition.

Marks, Peter. "A Street-Smart 'Godot' in a Cultural Wasteland." Review of *Waiting for Godot,* by Samuel Beckett, Studio Theatre. *New York Times,* 24 September 1998, E1.

Marowitz, Charles. "An Othello." In *Open Space Plays,* edited by Charles Marowitz. Hammondsworth, England: Penguin Books, 1974.

Massa, Robert. "The Great White Way." *Village Voice (New York),* 2 December 1986, 128.

Maychick, Diana. "Papp Demands Simon's Firing." *New York Post,* 30 March 1989, 35.

McAuley, Gay. *Space in Performance: Making Meaning in the Theatre.* Ann Arbor: University of Michigan Press, 2000.

McBride, Joseph. "No Non-Irish Need Apply? Ethnic Casting Issues in Movies." *Irish America Magazine,* 31 January 2001, 106.

McCauley, Robbie. "Beyond the Wilson-Brustein Debate: Working around Power." *Theater* 27, no. 2–3 (1997): 34–38.

McGehee, Scott, and David Siegel. "Identity Politics at Face Value: An Interview with Scott McGehee and David Siegel." By Roy Grundmann. *Cinéaste* 20, no. 3 (1994): 24–26.

McKinley, Jesse. "Fierstein as Tevye: Sounds Crazy, No?" *New York Times*, 2 January 2005, sec. 2, 5.

Melloan, George. "The Theater." Review of *Narrow Road to the Deep North*, by Edward Bond, Repertory Theater of Lincoln Center. *Wall Street Journal*, 10 January 1972, 8.

Mercier, Vivian. *Beckett/Beckett*. New York: Oxford University Press, 1977.

Merwin, Ted. "Sunset on a Jewish 'Fiddler.'" *New York Jewish Week*, 27 February 2004.

Metropulos, Penny. "Director's Note: Creativity, Spirit and True Power in *The Tempest*." Notes from the souvenir program for the 2001 Oregon Shakespeare Festival, 2.

Metz, Christian. *Film Language: A Semiotics of the Cinema*. Oxford: Oxford University Press, 1974.

Michener, Charles. "Almost-Nicely." Review of *Guys and Dolls*, by Frank Loesser, Jo Swerling, and Abe Burrows, Broadway Theater. *Newsweek*, 2 August 1976, 70.

Miller, Arthur. "The Family in Modern Drama." 1956. In *The Theater Essays of Arthur Miller*, edited by Robert A. Martin, 69–85. New York: Viking Press, 1978.

Miller, Arthur. *Salesman in Beijing*. New York: Viking Press, 1984.

Miller, Marc. "Fiddler on the Roof." Review of *Fiddler on the Roof*, by Jerry Bock, Sheldon Harnick, and Joseph Stein, Minskoff Theater. *Theatermania*, 21 January 2005. http://www.theatermania.com/story/5558?.

Milloy, Courtland. "Black-on-Black Lesson from Hawk." *Washington Post*, 11 December 1990, B3.

Mondello, Bob. "Soapy Glass." Review of *The Glass Menagerie*, by Tennessee Williams, Arena Stage Company. *City Paper* (Washington DC), 20 October 1989.

Mori, Toshio. "Japanese Hamlet." In *The Chauvinist and Other Stories*, 39–41. Los Angeles: Asian American Studies Center, 1979.

Moss, Barry, panelist. "Session: Realizing the Play or Playing with Reality." In *Beyond Tradition: Transcripts of the First Symposium on Non-Traditional Casting*, edited by Clinton Turner Davis and Harry Newman, 36–61. New York: Non-Traditional Casting Project, 1988.

Most, Andrea. *Making Americans: Jews and the Broadway Musical*. Cambridge: Harvard University Press, 2004.

Munk, Erika. "Up Front." *Theater* 27, no. 2–3 (1997): 5–8.

Muñoz, José Esteban. *Disidentifications: Queers of Color and the Performance of Politics*. Minneapolis: University of Minnesota Press, 1999.

Murray, Timothy. *Drama Trauma: Specters of Race and Sexuality in Performance, Video, and Art*. London: Routledge, 1997.

Nachman, Gerald. "Last Gasps from the WASP World." Review of *The Cocktail*

Party, by A. R. Gurney, American Conservatory Theatre. *San Francisco Chronicle,* 30 March 1992, E1.

Nadel, Alan. "Beyond the Wilson-Brustein Debate: August Wilson and the (Color-Blind) Whiteness of Public Space." *Theater* 27, no. 2–3 (1997): 38–41.

National Asian American Theatre Company. http://www.naatco.org/index.html (accessed 20 September 2008).

Neale, Stephen. *Genre.* 1980. Reprint, London: British Film Institute, 1983.

Nelsen, Don. "Not the Type." *Daily News (New York),* 22 November 1987, City Lights, 5.

Nelson, Nels. "The Old Original Abe Burrows." *Philadelphia Daily News,* 19 March 1976. Reprinted in *Guys and Dolls* program (1976), 16.

Nesmith, Eugene. "Beyond the Wilson-Brustein Debate: Present, Past, Future." *Theater* 27, no. 2–3 (1997): 23–29.

New York Shakespeare Festival. *Semi-Annual Report of the Director of Education,* 13 September 1965.

Newman, Harry. "Beyond Limitations." In *Beyond Tradition: Transcripts of the First National Symposium on Non-Traditional Casting,* edited by Clinton Turner Davis and Harry Newman, 5–7. New York: Non-Traditional Casting Project, 1988.

Newman, Harry. "Holding Back: The Theatre's Resistance to Non-Traditional Casting." *Drama Review* 33, no. 3 (Fall 1989): 22–36.

Nichols, Bill. *Representing Reality: Issues and Concepts in Documentary.* Bloomington: Indiana University Press, 1991.

"NTCP at a Glance: Mission, Goals, and Activities." *New Traditions—The NTCP Newsletter (New York)* 2, no. 3 (1994): 6–8.

Ogude, S. E. "Literature and Racism: The Example of *Othello.*" In *Othello: New Essays by Black Writers,* edited by Mythili Kaul, 151–66. Washington, DC: Howard University Press, 1997.

O'Haire, Patricia. "David Mamet Opposes All-Female Production of His Plays." *Daily News (New York),* 19 January 1999, 30.

Omi, Michael. "A Perspective on 'Miss Saigon': The Issue Is about Race and Racism." *Hokubei Mainichi,* 25 September 1990.

Omi, Michael, and Howard Winant. *Racial Formation in the United States from the 1960s to the 1990s.* 2nd ed. New York: Routledge, 1994.

Oppenheimer, George. Review of *Hello, Dolly!* by Jerry Herman and Michael Stewart, Minskoff Theater. *Newsday,* 24 November 1975.

Osborne, Robert. " 'Carousel': Vivian Beaumont Theatre NY; Runs Indefinitely." Review of *Carousel,* by Richard Rodgers and Oscar Hammerstein II, Vivian Beaumont Theater. *Hollywood Reporter,* 25 March 1994.

Owens, Geoffrey. "Alliance for Inclusion in the Arts." In *New Traditions Compendium Forums and Commentaries (1992–1996).* 1992. http://www.inclusion inthearts.org/compendium/compendiumframe.html.

Parks, Suzan-Lori. "A Director Seeks Human Truths in a 'Ben Hur' of Haiti." *New York Times,* 2 December 1990, sec. 2, 5.

Patterson, John. "Joe Papp Responds to Charges That a Black-Hispanic Shakespeare Company Doesn't Scan." *Villager (New York),* 9 April 1979, 9, 11.

Pavis, Patrice. *Problèmes de Sémiologie Théâtrale.* Montreal: Presses de l'Université du Québec, 1976.

Pechter, Edward. *Othello and Interpretive Traditions.* Iowa City: University of Iowa Press, 1999.

Phelan, Peggy. *Unmarked: The Politics of Performance.* London: Routledge, 1993.

Phillips, Michael. "Kushner to Adapt Brecht's 'Good Person.'" *San Diego Union-Tribune,* 26 January 1994, Lifestyle, E6.

"Play Leaps Cultural Barriers—'Death of a Salesman' Tear-Jerker in China Too." *Chicago Tribune,* 8 May 1983, sec. 1, 6.

Plemmons, Chesley. "'Good Person' Sings New Haven's Praises." Review of *The Good Person of New Haven,* by Bertolt Brecht (adaptation), Long Wharf Theatre/Cornerstone Theater Company. *News-Times (Danbury, CT),* 21 May 2000.

Pombeiro, Beth Fillin. "'Guys and Dolls': Successful Move into Different Culture." *Philadelphia Inquirer,* 21 March 1976. Reprinted in *Guys and Dolls* program, 14.

Portantiere, Michael. "Color-Blindness in the Theater: Non-Traditional Casting Is Not a Black-or-White Issue." *TheaterWeek,* 13–19 April 1992, 19–22.

Portantiere, Michael. "Tovah Feldshuh Gets Her Irish up to Play Dolly Gallagher Levi." *TheaterMania.Com* 17 May 2006. http://www.theatermania.com/content/news.cfm/story/8252.

Potter, Lois. *Othello.* Manchester: Manchester University Press, 2002.

Reed, Rex. Review of *Guys and Dolls,* by Frank Loesser, Jo Swerling, and Abe Burrows. *Daily News (New York),* 23 July 1976, 56.

Rendell, Bob. "Tovah Feldshuh's Quixotic Quest for Dolly Gallagher." *Talkin' Broadway,* 13 June 2006. Review. www.talkinbroadway.com/regional/nj/nj159.html. Review of *Hello, Dolly!* by Michael Stewart and Jerry Herman, Paper Mill Playhouse.

Rich, Alan. "Oh, You Beautiful 'Dolls.'" Review of *Guys and Dolls,* by Frank Loesser, Jo Swerling, and Abe Burrows, Broadway Theater. *New York,* 9 August 1976, 58.

Rich, Frank. "The 'Falsetto' Musicals United at Hartford Stage." Review of *March of the Falsettos* and *Falsettoland,* by William Finn and James Lapine. *New York Times,* 15 October 1991, C13.

Rich, Frank. "Fantasy 'Cymbeline' Set Long after Shakespeare." *New York Times,* 1 June 1989, C15.

Rich, Frank. "Jonathan Pryce, 'Miss Saigon' and Actors' Equity's Decision." *New York Times,* 10 August 1990, C1.

Rich, Frank. "What Has AIDS Done to Land of 'Falsettos'?" Review of *Falsettoland,* by William Finn and James Lapine, Playwrights Horizons. *New York Times,* 29 June 1990, C3.

Richards, David. "Brecht, Darkly: At Arena, 'Good Person' as a Modern Fable." Review of *Good Person of Setzuan,* by Bertolt Brecht, Arena Stage Company. *Washington Post,* 11 October 1985, B1.

Richards, David. "Patrick Stewart: Inside a Murderous Mind." *Washington Post,* 12 November 1997, D1.

Riedel, Michael. "Shtetl Shock." *New York Post,* 18 February 2004, 45.

Rivera, Jon Lawrence. "The Fallout over 'Miss Saigon'—The Issue Is Nothing Less than Artistic Integrity." *Los Angeles Times,* 13 August 1990, Counterpunch, 3.

Rose, Lloyd. "'Falsettos': Low-Key Three-Part Harmony." Review of *Falsettos,* by William Finn and James Lapine, Church Street Theater. *Washington Post,* 24 June 1997, B1.

Rose, Lloyd. "Godot Watch Continues, with a Smile." Review of *Waiting for Godot,* by Samuel Beckett, Studio Theatre. *Washington Post,* 8 September 1998, B1.

Rose, Lloyd. "'Othello': The Two Faces of Tragedy." Review of *Othello,* by William Shakespeare, Shakespeare Theatre. *Washington Post,* 5 December 1990, C1.

Rose, Lloyd. "'Othello': Twist on Timeless Tragedy." Review of *Othello,* by William Shakespeare, Shakespeare Theatre. *Washington Post,* 18 November 1997, C1.

Rose, Lloyd. "Stage Guild's 'Mad' Genius: In Morgan Duncan, the Godot-Ful Truth." Review of *Waiting for Godot,* by Samuel Beckett, Stage Guild. *Washington Post,* 11 January 1999, C1.

Rosenbaum, Thane. "A Legacy Cut Loose." *Los Angeles Times,* 15 February 2004, E1.

Rosenberg, David A. "'Good Person' Blazes with Life at Long Wharf." Review of *Good Person of New Haven,* by Bertolt Brecht (adaptation), Long Wharf Theatre/Cornerstone Theater Company. *Wilton Villager/Norwalk Hour,* 18 May 2000.

Rosenberg, Marvin. *The Masks of Othello: The Search for the Identity of Othello, Iago. and Desdemona by Three Centuries of Actors and Criticis.* Berkeley: University of California Press, 1961.

Rosenfeld, Megan. "At Arena, a Richley Drawn 'Chalk Circle.'" Review of *Caucasian Chalk Circle,* by Bertolt Brecht, Arena Stage Company. *Washington Post,* 28 September 1990, C1.

Rosenfeld, Megan. "No 'Miss Saigon' for Broadway: Casting Choice Cancels Run." *Washington Post,* 9 August 1990, D1.

Rosenfeld, Megan. "The Talk of 'Our Town': At Arena, the Connections to Everyone's Lives." *Washington Post,* 23 November 1990, Style, C1.

Rothstein, Mervyn. "Producer Cancels 'Miss Saigon': 140 Members Challenge Equity." *New York Times,* 9 August 1990, C15, 17.

Rothstein, Mervyn. "Union Bars White in Asian Role: Broadway May Lose 'Miss Saigon.'" *New York Times,* 8 August 1990, A1.

Rouse, John. "Brecht and the Contradictory Actor." In *Acting Re(Considered),* edited by Philip Zarrilli, 248–59. London: Routledge, 2002.

Runyon, Damon. *Guys and Dolls: The Stories of Damon Runyon.* New York: Penguin, 1992.

Sacks, Marcy S. *Before Harlem: The Black Experience in New York City before World War I.* Philadelphia: University of Pennsylvania, 2006.

Sadownick, Douglas. "Paving the Way for Festival Latino." *Los Angeles Times,* 9 July 1989, Home, 4.

Sandburg, Carl. *Smoke and Steel.* New York: Harcourt, Brace and Howe, 1920.

Scanlan, Richard. "Thoroughly Modern Millie: Red, White and Blues." *Stagebill (Southern California)*, November 2000, 22–22A.

Schwarz, Daniel R. *Broadway Boogie Woogie: Damon Runyon and the Making of New York City Culture*. New York: Palgrave Macmillan, 2003.

Scolnikov, Hanna. Introduction to *The Play out of Context: Transferring Plays from Culture to Culture*, edited by Hanna Scolnikov and Peter Holland, 1–6. Cambridge: Cambridge University Press, 1989.

Shakespeare, William. *Othello*. Edited by London Oval Projects Limited. New York: Workman Publishing, 1983. Illustrated by Oscar Zarate in comic book format.

"Shakespeare for City Students." *Newday (New York)*, 8 October 1986, 21.

Shapiro, Howard. "A Jumping-Off Point: James Earl Jones and Phylicia Rashad Headline a Victory of a 'Cat on a Hot Tin Roof.'" Review of *Cat on a Hot Tin Roof*, by Tennessee Williams, Broadhurst Theatre. *Philadelphia Inquirer Features Magazine*, 8 March 2008, E1.

Shay, Michele, panelist. "Session: Next Tradition." In *Beyond Tradition: Transcripts of the First Symposium on Non-Traditional Casting*, edited by Clinton Turner Davis and Harry Newman, 89–107. New York: Non-Traditional Casting Project, 1988.

Sheaffer, Louis. "Runyon Characters Set to Music with 'Guys and Dolls.'" Review of *Guys and Dolls*, by Frank Loesser, Jo Swerling, and Abe Burrows, 46th Street Theater. *Brooklyn Eagle*, 25 November 1950, 14.

Shimakawa, Karen. *National Abjection: The Asian American Body Onstage*. Durham: Duke University Press, 2002.

Shirley, Don. "The Fall of 'Miss Saigon' Casting." *Los Angeles Times*, 9 August 1990, Home, 1.

Shirley, Don. "'Saigon' Spurs Resignation." *Los Angeles Times*, 10 August 1990, 22.

Shirley, Don. "Stage Watch: New Lines in Black 'Love Letters.'" *Los Angeles Times*, 4 October 1990, 6.

Simon, John. "A Clash of Cymbelines." *New York Magazine*, 12 June 1989.

Simon, John. "Dudes and Chicks." Review of *Guys and Dolls*, by Frank Loesser, Jo Swerling, and Abe Burrows, Broadway Theater. *New Leader*, 13 September 1976, 21–22.

Simon, John. "Mugging the Bard in Central Park." *Commonweal*, 3 September 1965, 635–36.

Simon, John. "No Brass Ring." Review of *Carousel*, by Richard Rodgers and Oscar Hammerstein II, Vivian Beaumont Theater. *New York*, 4 April 1994, 73.

Solomon, Alisa. "Fiddling with Fiddler: Can the Broadway Revival of Everyone's Favorite Jewish Musical Ignore Today's Radically Different Cultural Context?" *Village Voice (New York)*, 13 January 2004. http://www.villagevoice.com/2004-01-13/news/fiddling-with-fiddler/ (accessed 29 April 2008).

Solomon, Alisa. "How 'Fiddler' Became Folklore." *Forward*, 1 September 2006, Arts and Culture, 12.

Solomon, Alisa. "Tevye, Today and Beyond." *Forward.Com*, 8 September 2006.

http://www.forward.com/articles/tevye-today-and-beyond (accessed 7 September 2008).

Sommers, Michael. "Black 'Cat' Prowling." *Star-Ledger (Newark, NJ),* 7 March 2008, Ticket, 4.

Sommers, Michael. "A Fairly Faithful 'Fiddler.'" *Star-Ledger (Newark, NJ),* 27 February 2004, Ticket, 4.

Stam, Robert. "Multiculturalism and the Neoconservatives." In *Dangerous Liaisons: Gender, Nation, and Postcolonial Perspectives,* edited by Anne McClintock, Aamir Mufti, and Ella Shohat, 188–203. Minneapolis: University of Minnesota Press, 1997.

Stanislavsky, Constantin. *Creating a Role.* Translated by Elizabeth Reynolds Hapgood. New York: Routledge/Theatre Arts Book, 1961.

Stanislavsky, Constantin. *Stanislavsky Produces Othello.* Translated by Helen Nowack. London: Geoffrey Bles, 1948.

Stasio, Marilyn. "Whisper 'So Long Dearie,' Dolly Doesn't Live Here Any More." Review of *Hello, Dolly!* by Jerry Herman and Michael Stewart, Minskoff Theater. *Cue,* 22 November 1975.

States, Bert O. *Great Reckonings in Little Rooms: On the Phenomenology of Theatre.* Berkeley: University of California Press, 1985.

Stendhal. *Racine et Shakespeare.* Paris: Garnier-Flammarion, 1970.

Stern, Harold. "Year's Biggest Smash Hit." Review of *Guys and Dolls,* by Frank Loesser, Jo Swerling, and Abe Burrows, 46th Street Theater. *American Jewish Review,* 28 December 1950.

Steyn, Mark. *Broadway Babies Say Goodnight: Musicals Then and Now.* New York: Routledge, 1999.

Stone, Peter, Jerry Bock, Sheldon Harnick, and Joseph Stein. "Landmark Symposium: Fiddler on the Roof." *Dramatists Guild Quarterly* 20, no. 1 (Spring 1983): 10–29.

Sullivan, Dan. "Colorblind Casting: It's Not Yet a Tradition when Black Is White, Women Are Men, and the Theater Is Challenging." *Los Angeles Times,* 2 October 1988, 50.

Swander, Homer. "Musings on the Stewart/Kelly Othello." *Shakespeare Bulletin* (Spring 1998): 13.

Taccone, Tony. "Coriolanus: 'From the Director.'" Notes from the souvenir program for the 1996 Oregon Shakespeare Festival Volume II, 13–17.

Taylor, Clarke. "Non-Traditional Casting Explored at Symposium." *Los Angeles Times,* 29 November 1986, 12.

Taylor, Kate. "Multicultural Stages in a Small Oregon Town," *New York Times,* 15 August 2009, C1, 7.

Taylor, William R. "Broadway: The Place That Words Built." In *Inventing Times Square: Commerce and Culture at the Crossroads of the World,* edited by William R. Taylor, 212–31. New York: Russell Sage Foundation, 1991.

"'The Tempest.'" Review of *The Tempest,* by William Shakespeare, Oregon Shakespeare Festival. *Ashland Daily Tidings,* 16–22 March 2001, 7.

Templeton, Sarah-Kate. "Beckett Estate Rules out Female Version of Godot." *Scotsman,* 27 July 1998, 6.

"Theater Groups Endorse Diversity." *New Traditions—The NTCP Newsletter* 3, no. 1 (Winter 1996): 1.

Thompson, Ayanna, ed. *Colorblind Shakespeare: New Perspectives on Race and Performance.* New York: Routledge, 2006.

Tinsley, Molly. "Prospero/Prospera." *Jefferson Monthly,* March 2001.

Tomlinson, John. *Cultural Imperialism: A Critical Introduction.* Baltimore: Johns Hopkins University Press, 1991.

Toro, Fernando de. *Theatre Semiotics: Text and Staging in Modern Theatre.* 1987. Translated by John Lewis. Edited by Carole Hubbard. Toronto: University of Toronto Press, 1995.

Torrens, J. S. "Conversations, Falsettos." Review of *Falsettos,* by William Finn and James Lapine, John Golden Theater. *America* 166, no. 20 (6–13 June 1992): 516.

"Two Women Must Wait Some Time Longer for Godot." *Irish Times,* 27 July 1998, Home News, 3.

Tynan, Kenneth. "Act of Vengeance by Genet." Review of *The Blacks,* by Jean Genet, Royal Court Theatre. *New York Herald Tribune,* 11 June 1961.

Ubersfeld, Anne. *L'Ecole Du Spectateur.* Paris: Éditions sociales, 1981.

Ubersfeld, Anne. *Lire le Théâtre.* Paris: Éditions sociales, 1977.

Ubersfeld, Anne. *Reading Theatre.* 1977. Translated by Frank Collins. Toronto: University of Toronto Press, 1999.

Vanderknyff, Rick. "Theater Rejects Interracial 'Romeo and Juliet.'" *Los Angeles Times,* 24 August 1990, 1.

Varble, Bill. "Yes, Virginia." *Mail Tribune (Medford, OR),* 21 April 2002, 1B, 4B.

Vaughan, Virginia Mason. *Othello: A Contextual History.* Cambridge: Cambridge University Press, 1994.

Wager, Douglas. "'Our Town' Has No Borders." *Washington Post,* 8 December 1990, A19.

Wallach, Allan. "Pearl Is 'Languid Ease.'" Review of *Hello, Dolly!* by Jerry Herman and Michael Stewart, Minskoff Theater. *Courier-Journal & Times (Louisville, KY),* 30 November 1975, H5.

Washington, Edward. "'At the Door of Truth': The Hollowness of Signs in Othello." In *Othello: New Essays by Black Writers,* edited by Mythili Kaul, 167–87. Washington, DC: Howard University Press, 1997.

Washington, Kenneth H. 2002. National Diversity Forum: Opinion Pieces. Alliance for Inclusion in the Arts. http://www.ntcp.org (accessed 20 September 2008).

Watt, Douglas. "'Hello, Dolly!' Marks Pearl's Swan Song." Review of *Hello, Dolly!* by Jerry Herman and Michael Stewart, Minskoff Theater. *Daily News (New York),* 7 November 1975, 64.

Watts, Richard, Jr. "Pearl Bailey and the New 'Dolly.'" Review of *Hello, Dolly!* by Jerry Herman and Michael Stewart, St. James Theater. *New York Post,* 13 November 1967.

Watts, Stephen. "Accent Problem in West End." *New York Times,* 15 March 1953, X3.

Weber, Bruce. "On Stage, and Off." *New York Times,* 1 April 1994, C2.

Weeden, Derrick Lee. Interview. *Update* (Oregon Shakespeare Festival) 1, no. 1 (2003): 1–2.

Weiner, Bernard. "Another Take on the Rep's Signing." *San Francisco Chronicle,* 30 May 1987, 44.

Weiner, Bernard. "A Timely Revival of Brecht's 'Person.'" Review of *The Good Person of Szechuan,* by Bertolt Brecht, Berkeley Repertory Theatre. *San Francisco Chronicle,* 22 May 1987, 84, 95.

Weiner, Bob. Review of *Guys and Dolls,* by Frank Loesser, Jo Swerling, and Abe Burrows. *Soho Weekly News,* 22 July 1976, 32.

Weitz, Shoshana. "Mr. Godot Will Not Come Today." In *The Play out of Context: Transferring Plays from Culture to Culture,* edited by Hanna Scolnicov and Peter Holland, 186–98. Cambridge: Cambridge University Press, 1989.

Welsh, Anne Marie. "A New 'Setzuan' Cooking: Playhouse Adaptation Multicultural to the Max." *San Diego Union-Tribune,* 24 July 1994, Entertainment, E1.

West, Paul, and John W. Bratton. *I Want to Play Hamlet.* New York: M. Witmark and Sons, 1903.

Westberg, Chris. "Avery Brooks as Othello." *Asides: Quarterly Publication of the Shakespeare Theatre at the Folger* (Winter 1990): 1, 7.

Wilder, Thornton. *Our Town: A Play in Three Acts.* New York: Coward McCann, 1965.

Will, George F. "The Trendy Racism of Actors' Equity." *Washington Post,* 12 August 1990, C7.

Williams, Tennessee. *Cat on a Hot Tin Roof.* 1954. New York: New Directions, 1975.

Wilshire, Bruce. *Role Playing and Identity.* Bloomington: Indiana University Press, 1982.

Wilson, August. "The Ground on Which I Stand." *American Theatre* (September 1996): 14–16, 71–74.

Wilson, Cynthia. "Guys and Dolls." Review of *Guys and Dolls,* by Frank Loesser, Jo Swerling, and Abe Burrows, Schubert Theater. *Soho Weekly News,* 29 July 1976, 24.

Wilson, John S. "Is There a Reason for Pearl Bailey to Record 'Dolly'?" *New York Times,* 17 December 1967, 132.

Wilson, Judy. "Funny, Dolly, You Don't Look Irish." *New Jersey Jewish News* (2006). http://www.njjewishnews.com/njjn/com/062906/ltFunnyDollYouDont.html.

Winer, Laurie. "From Cosby's Father to Colonel Pickering, by Way of Norway." *New York Times,* 24 March 1991, sec. 2, 5.

Winn, Steven. "'Falsettos' Puts Family Values to Test." Review of *Falsettos,* by William Finn and James Lapine, Curran Theatre. *San Francisco Chronicle,* 30 April 1993, C1.

Witchel, Alex. "Find the Ginger! It's Anxiety Time for an Original." *New York Times,* 26 April 1992, sec. 2, 8.

Wolf, Stacy. *A Problem Like Maria: Gender and Sexuality in the American Musical.* Ann Arbor: University of Michigan Press, 2002.

Wolitz, Seth L. "The Americanization of Tevye or Boarding the Jewish 'Mayflower.'" *American Quarterly* 40, no. 4 (December 1988): 514–36.

Woll, Allen. *Black Musical Theatre: From Coontown to Dreamgirls.* Baton Rouge: Louisiana State University Press, 1989.

Worthen, W. B. *Modern Drama and the Rhetoric of Theater.* Berkeley: University of California Press, 1992.

Worthen, W. B. *Shakespeare and the Authority of Performance.* Cambridge: Cambridge University Press, 1997.

Yardley, Jonathan. "At Arena Stage, a Casting Miscue." Review of *Our Town,* by Thornton Wilder, Arena Stage Company. *Washington Post,* 3 December 1990, C2.

Zeisler, Ernest Bloomfield. *Othello: Time Enigma and Color Problem.* Chicago: Alexander J. Isaacs, 1954.

Zinman, Toby. "Beam Me Up, Patrick Stewart." *American Theatre* (February 1998): 12–15, 68–70.

Zoglin, Richard. "Getting beyond Zero." *Time,* 1 March 2004. http://www.time .com/time/printout/0,8816,596135,00.html.

Zolotow, Sam. "All-Negro Troupe to Offer 'Dolly!'" *New York Times,* 25 July 1967, 31.

Index

Page numbers in italics refer to illustrations.